CAUGHT BY THE BILLIONAIRE

ERIN SWANN

SWANN PUBLICATIONS

Cover image licensed from Shutterstock.com

Cover design by Swann Publications

ISBN-13: 978-1091820203

Edited by Jessica Royer Ocken

Proofreaders: Donna Hokanson, Tamara Mataya, Rosa Sharon

Typo Hunter Extraordinaire: Renee Williams

The following story is intended for mature readers. It contains mature themes, strong language, and sexual situations. All characters are 18+ years of age, and all sexual acts are consensual.

If you would like to hear about Erin's new releases and sales, join the newsletter at http://ERINSWANN.COM/SUBSCRIBE. We only email about sales or new releases, and we never share your information.

If you enjoy this book, please leave a review.

Find out more about the author and upcoming books online at:

WWW.ERINSWANN.COM

❀ Created with Vellum

ALSO BY ERIN SWANN

The Billionaire's Trust - Available on Amazon, also in AUDIOBOOK

(Bill and Lauren's story) He needed to save the company. He needed her. He couldn't have both. The wedding proposal in front of hundreds was like a fairy tale come true—Until she uncovered his darkest secret.

The Youngest Billionaire - Available on Amazon

(Steven and Emma's story) The youngest of the Covington clan, he avoided the family business to become a rarity, an honest lawyer. He didn't suspect that pursuing her could destroy his career. She didn't know what trusting him could cost her.

The Secret Billionaire – Available on Amazon, also in AUDIOBOOK

(Patrick and Elizabeth's story) Women naturally circled the flame of wealth and power, and his is brighter than most. Does she love him? Does she not? There's no way to know. When he stopped to help her, Liz mistook him for a carpenter. Maybe this time he'd know. Everything was perfect. Until the day she left.

The Billionaire's Hope - Available on Amazon, also in AUDIOBOOK

(Nick and Katie's story) They came from different worlds. She hadn't seen him since the day he broke her brother's nose. Her family retaliated by destroying his life. She never suspected where accepting a ride from him today would take her. They said they could do casual. They lied.

Previously titled: Protecting the Billionaire

Picked by the Billionaire – Available on Amazon, also in AUDIOBOOK

(Liam and Amy's story) A night she wouldn't forget. An offer she couldn't refuse. He alone could save her, and she held the key to his survival. If only they could pass the test together.

Saved by the Billionaire – Available on Amazon

(Ryan and Natalie's story) The FBI and the cartel were both after her for the same thing: information she didn't have. First, the FBI took everything, and then the cartel came for her. She trusted Ryan with her safety, but could she trust him with her heart?

Caught by the Billionaire – Available on Amazon

(Vincent and Ashley's story) Her undercover assignment was simple enough: nail the crooked billionaire. The surprise came when she opened the folder, and the target was her one-time high school sweetheart. What will happen when an unknown foe makes a move to checkmate?

The Driven Billionaire – Available on Amazon

(Zachary and Brittney's story) Rule number one: hands off your best friend's sister. With nowhere to turn when she returns from upstate, she accepts his offer of a room. Mutual attraction quickly blurs the rules. When she comes under attack, pulling her closer is the only way to keep her safe. But, the truth of why she left town in the first place will threaten to destroy them both.

Nailing the Billionaire – Available on Amazon

(Dennis and Jennifer's story) She knew he destroyed her family. Now she is close to finding the records that will bring him down. When a corporate shakeup forces her to work with him, anger and desire collide. Vengeance was supposed to be simple, swift, and sweet. It was none of those things.

Undercover Billionaire – Available on Amazon

(Adam and Kelly's story) Their wealthy families have been at war forever. When Kelly receives a chilling note, the FBI assigns Adam to protect her. Family histories and desire soon collide, causing old truths to be questioned. Keeping ahead of the threat won't be their only challenge.

Trapped with the Billionaire – Available on Amazon

(Josh and Nicole's story) When Nicole returns from vacation to find her company has been sold, and she has been assigned to work for the new CEO. Competing visions of how to run things and mutual passion collide in a volatile mix. When an old family secret is unearthed, it threatens everything.

CHAPTER 1

Vincent

THE MAN IN THE SUIT HAD FOLLOWED ME ALL THE WAY HERE FROM WORK this evening. It was the third time I'd noticed him in the last two weeks.

I stepped inside Holmby's Grill and peeked out the tinted window after the door closed. After a few seconds of not seeing the suited man, I found my way to my usual table in the corner. I mentally kicked myself for not getting a picture of him for our security team to check out.

Less than a minute later, *she* walked in atop her tall black heels with the self assurance of the runway model she'd once been. Her tits jiggled under the thin fabric of her low-cut dress—a dress that flaunted her ample braless cleavage and threatened to open just a bit too far.

Unfortunately for me, it never quite did.

Holmby's had been her choice tonight, and fine by me. Steak would be a welcome change, and the meat here was arguably Boston's finest.

Half the men in the restaurant stared as she greeted me with a warm, tight hug—and not the lean-forward-to-avoid-touching-your-

1

tits-to-the-guy type, but a real hug. As we parted I breathed in the faint hint of jasmine perfume she'd applied to her neck.

No doubt the male onlookers wished they were me, and rightly so. Staci Baxter and I would be getting hot and heavy between the sheets before the night ended. She had a body to die for, and knew how to work it. A night with Staci never disappointed.

Her makeup was subtle and nicely done, accentuating the high cheekbones she was proud of.

"Vince," she purred as I pulled out her chair.

A quick peek down her dress before I rounded the table to my seat jolted my cock. Staci had no doubt gotten a million teenage boys off via her body-paint pictures in the *Sports Illustrated* swimsuit issue.

As I sat, I noticed her jaw showed an uncommon tenseness this evening.

"You okay? I asked.

She glanced down. "I'm a little nervous is all. I could use some wine."

I waved our waiter over. "That I can help with."

He arrived quickly.

"A bottle of Opus One Proprietary Red, please," I told him.

She managed a pasted-on smile after the waiter left and sipped her water—this was a definite off night for her.

I inquired about her sister, and that seemed to calm her while we waited for the wine.

When the bottle arrived, I approved it, and Staci guzzled down most of a glass.

She fiddled with her silverware. "I'm not sure I'm ready."

Since retiring from modeling, she had devoted all her time to her new clothing line. It was understandable that she felt apprehensive about tomorrow's meeting.

"Don't worry. The meeting with the bank will go just fine with the presentation you've got."

"Vince, you've been such a help. But I just don't know if it's good enough."

Asking for a two-million-dollar bank loan to expand her business would stress most anybody. But for a woman with the confidence to walk a runway nearly naked with cameras flashing, this should be a piece of cake.

"You've got this," I assured her.

Our waiter returned, and I ordered the gorgonzola truffle-crusted New York strip steak, while Staci chose the lamb chops.

"Would you like to go over it one last time?" I asked.

She smiled. "Please." She pulled the presentation folder from her oversized purse.

She placed it on the table and smiled. "Gentlemen…" She began the spiel I'd worked out with her.

The food arrived just as she finished her mock presentation.

I topped off our wine glasses and raised mine to hers. "Sounded damn good to me. You don't have anything to worry about."

An enticing blush rose in her cleavage.

I cut my first piece of steak. "Now, tell me more about how your little sister is getting on in New York."

She perked up and started in about how hard it had been for her sister to find a place to live in the city.

An hour later, we had finished dinner and decided against dessert.

We had long since left the topic of Staci's presentation tomorrow, but the undercurrent of nervousness in her demeanor hadn't dissipated. This was more than an off night for her.

"Staci, do you want to talk about what's really bothering you?"

She hesitated before retrieving her purse. After a moment of rummaging, she pulled out a piece of folded paper and extended it across the table with a shaky hand.

I opened it.

Stay away from Vincent Benson unless you want to become collateral damage, the note read.

My stomach turned over.

"What's going on, Vince?"

I sighed. Someone was messing with me and using her to do it.

"It's probably nothing… I can arrange some security for you, though."

"I live on the safest street in town. The chief of police lives next door. It looks like *you* should be the one watching out."

I took a picture of the note before grasping it with my napkin and folding it up. "Mind if I take this?"

She shook her head.

There might be nothing worthwhile on it, but I folded it inside the napkin and stuffed it in my pocket nonetheless.

I turned the conversation back to her clothing business while I mulled over who would be messing with me. No faces came to mind, except the nameless suit who'd followed me.

When we'd finished the last of the wine, I offered a very nice bottle of port I had at my place, just a few blocks away.

She wiped her lips with her napkin, but her eyes telegraphed the answer before the words arrived. "Not tonight, Vince. I've been stressing over this presentation all day, and I'm bushed. How 'bout a rain check?"

Begging off from our after-dinner gymnastics *was* unusual. This was a standing date we had pretty much every Monday night—no strings attached, just a good time.

Neither of us did commitments, so neither of us expected anything more than companionship and physical pleasure. "Casual intimacy with friendship on the side," she had once called it. She seemed to be the only woman in town who didn't want or expect anything more from me—except Barb, of course.

I had a more commercial situation with Barbara. Gifts changed hands, but never cash. She made attractive arm candy when I needed it and an enthusiastic bed partner when I wanted some variety, but the side of friendship I had with Staci wasn't there with Barb.

"I'll call you," Staci said when we made it to the door.

"Don't forget the LA trip is coming up," I reminded her.

I was counting on her for that, and it wasn't a trip I could make alone.

"Sure," she said in a less-than-enthusiastic tone.

I opened the door for her and waited while she hailed a cab. I checked up and down the street for the suited man. All clear, for now.

After Staci entered the cab, I checked again in the direction of my condo on Tremont Street. Its safety was not far away.

Before starting out, I felt in my pocket for the coin I always carried.

4

CHAPTER 2

*A*SHLEY

"I'M GOING TO BEAT YOU OUT FOR THAT LA PROMOTION," MY OPPONENT, Elizabeth Parsons, said as she stepped sideways on the mat, looking for an opening to attack me.

I slid to my left and dodged her first attempt. "Try all you want, Liz. But you know they only take blondes in California."

She sneered and lunged at me again, grabbing my hair.

It hurt like fuck, and I ended up on the mat.

I patted out ten seconds later. "That's against the rules. That one doesn't count."

She got off me. "Get over your rule hang-up; winning is what counts."

I got up, massaged my sore scalp, and tucked my ponytail down the back of my T-shirt.

She came for me again, ever the aggressor.

We tumbled to the ground, and she initially had the upper hand, but I had the leverage and weight advantage and pinned her fifteen seconds later.

She patted out.

"That makes three," I said.

"Best of seven?" she asked.

As the only women in our section of the FBI's Boston field office, we usually sparred against each other—and Liz hated losing.

I checked the wall clock in the gym. "Out of time today."

We had gone through Quantico together. At the Academy and every day since, she had made up for her lack of stature with competitiveness and pure determination. She was shorter than me, and more buxom, which meant men often underestimated her. More than one bad guy had taken her for a pushover and ended up with a cracked skull thanks to her baton skills.

We grabbed our towels and headed to the locker room. We didn't have a lot of time before our eight am bullpen meeting.

FORTY MINUTES LATER, WE ENTERED THE BULLPEN UPSTAIRS ON OUR FLOOR of the Boston field office precisely at eight. Special Agent in Charge Randy White checked his watch. "You're late."

Liz started to complain. "But—"

"New rule: no less than three minutes early, understood?"

Anybody else would have accepted our arrival or told us five minutes early. Only SAC White would come up with something asinine like three minutes. He invented another stupid rule every few weeks—something my partner, John McNally, called Caesar moments. And I suppose he should know. John and Randy—excuse me, SAC White—had been partners previously.

"Yes, sir," Liz and I said in unison.

From across the room, John rolled his eyes just enough for me to see.

White had been promoted six months ago to the SAC position. Before that he'd been one of us in the bullpen, and only a little difficult to get along with. Now he was the boss, and beyond difficult. *Randy* was no longer allowed. *Sir* had replaced it. The running joke was that the next budget would have to have a remodeling line item for new doors his ego could fit through.

The special agents had started betting on how long this phase would last. My bet had been six months—that's how long it had taken SAC Sinella, the previous occupant of that office, to settle down. Sinella's transfer to Nashville had triggered White's promotion to Asshole Behind the Glass.

Liz and I both had to kiss up to him, because he would ultimately recommend one of us for the Los Angeles opening that was coming up.

White motioned for Liz to join him in his office. "Parsons, new assignment."

She followed him and closed the door.

I moved over next to John. "What the fuck's with the stupid three-minute rule?"

He shrugged. "He told us just before you two got here." He shook his head. "I'm changing my bet to nine months. The guy should be over his stupid Caesar routine by now, but he's definitely not."

I shrugged and settled at my desk, opening the first folder at the top of my stack.

"I'll call the agency," Liz said as she left White's office a few minutes later. "Sweet undercover assignment," she mumbled as she passed my desk, trying to get a rise out of me.

I didn't take the bait. I wasn't letting her get to me today. My last undercover had netted me a month in a cockroach- and bedbug-infested cover apartment that still gave me the shivers when I thought about it. When your cover persona was down and out, the bureau went out of its way to make the entire experience realistic, and the latest budget cut had us going even further down-market in arranging cover locations.

Recently, Liz had been snagging the easier undercover assignments.

The men in the office seemed oblivious, but it was clear to me: White had gotten balls-deep into Liz during that ski weekend in New Hampshire last year before he'd been promoted.

She'd denied it when I confronted her about it, but the shift had been easy enough to see. Back when we were all in the bullpen together, she would walk in front of Randy's desk on her way to the coffee room, and although he tried to hide it, his eyes would follow her.

And now, although his eyes didn't follow like they used to, White had given Liz another plum assignment. It was mean of me, but I couldn't help hoping that when his wife found out, she had a sharp implement handy to fix him for good.

I closed my eyes and silently counted to ten. I had to let it slide—again. The Bureau didn't reward people who rocked the boat. If Liz was still seeing him on the side, it would be wrong on so many levels. But in this tight-knit family, back-stabbing wasn't allowed. An agent that snitched on another was a bigger problem than the one who'd committed the original error. The Bureau's antibodies would work to expel the offending snitch and keep the organization pure. I'd worked too hard at my career to let a little thing like the SAC's favoritism derail me.

Liz opened the folder on her desk. "Which cover should I use?" she mumbled rhetorically. She shook her head and kept reading.

I didn't answer.

She didn't expect one.

After a moment she picked up her purse. "I'm going out for a smoke."

"Those things are going to kill you," John said wearily, for the hundredth time at least, echoing my feelings.

"Not for a long time," she shot back over her shoulder. "And they keep the weight off."

Arguing with her wasn't worth the effort.

CHAPTER 3

Vincent

My Tuesday morning started with fireworks.

This one had a temper. "Fired? You can't fire me. I quit," Marcy
yelled.

The stapler she threw missed me and hit the wall with a bang.
Security grabbed her arms and escorted her out.

It took Mason Parker, my number two, all of a minute to enter my
office and close the door. "What the hell did you do this time?"

"Nothing," I insisted.

Nothing more than I ever did. I insisted on accuracy with my PAs,
and that didn't suit Marcy very well. I needed diligent office help, not
a personal assistant who thought the emphasis should be on *personal*.

He plopped down in the red chair he always chose. "At this rate, in
a year there won't be anybody left in Boston willing to apply."

"Fuck you."

"What's got you in such a piss-poor mood this morning?"

I pulled up the picture of the note Staci had received and handed
my phone to Mason. "Staci found that on her car yesterday."

He scanned it. "Somebody's messing with you."

"No shit, Sherlock. Now you tell me who."

He handed the phone back. "Fuck anybody's wife lately?"

"Fuck no, and you know that."

I had played the field, but married women were never my style. And after Marilyn went full-house psycho on me last year when I wouldn't call her back, I'd limited myself to Barbara and Staci: the only two certified commitment-phobes I knew.

As long as they were provided with lavish dinners, shopping trips, and the occasional extravagant gift, those ladies were happy and supplied me with enjoyable interludes in the bedroom. The gifts were most often jewelry, but never ever would they expect a ring.

"Just checking," Mason responded. "You ought to give it to security."

"Already did."

He pointed a finger at me. "At least you have the advantage now."

"How so?"

"They've given up the element of surprise. You know somebody's coming at you."

I let Mason badger me for a few more minutes before I changed the subject. "We need to get back on the Semaphore deal right away."

"No, we don't. Let them stew a few days. We don't have to be so reactive."

"We need this. I don't want it to get away."

"If you really want it, get your dad's help."

I resisted reaching for my coin. My mission here in Boston was simple and clear: grow the eastern division of Covington to a billion in revenue. That's the target my father had set. Reach ten figures, he'd said, and I'd be ready to come back to LA, my hometown, and take over Benson Corp., our family business.

That was my ultimate career choice, but so far he wasn't ready to give me control. He'd said I wasn't seasoned enough, or experienced enough, nor did I have the right instincts—his list was a long one. But after I closed the Semaphore deal, that impression would change.

Mason shifted in his chair. "We can't seem too eager."

"I want this one. I'm not letting Gainsboro win."

"If you want it that bad, ask your dad for help," he said again.

"Not necessary."

We both knew the Semaphore deal was big enough to put us on the map and for me to reach my personal goal. But asking for Dad's help was out of the question.

"It's your show," Mason responded. "But it's like dating. Sometimes hard-to-get is the right approach. So put me down as wanting to wait."

Noted. But it was my show, and I wasn't waiting. "Meet back here at ten."

Mason left, shaking his head. He usually had balls, but for some reason, not with this deal.

Wait, my ass.

I called down to Nina in HR.

She had been expecting my call. "I'll have another candidate here tomorrow morning, Mr. Benson."

"Not soon enough. After lunch," I said.

Her response came quickly. "Yes, sir."

I returned to my spreadsheet on the Semaphore acquisition. I took out my coin and turned it over in my hand while reading.

An hour later, the numbers were swimming on the screen in front of me. I needed a break to clear my head.

Once I was on the treadmill downstairs, the hum of the machine and the pounding of my feet relaxed me. Exercise always cleared my slate mentally and allowed me to return to a problem with renewed focus.

When I dismounted, I pulled up the picture of the note on my phone again. The question remained: who was coming after me and why?

The *why* could only be answered by knowing the *who*, and only knowing the *who* would tell me how dangerous this foe would be, not to mention enabling me to counterattack. Sometimes the best defense was a counterpunch.

~

*A*SHLEY

. . .

11

JOHN AND I HAD SPENT THE MORNING INTERVIEWING NEIGHBORS OF JOHN Spinetti, a suspect we were investigating in connection with a pair of bank robberies. He hadn't been back here to his home in two weeks, the same span of time as the robberies.

We didn't learn much from the group. This neighborhood in Brighton contained a lot of Russian émigrés, and although they interacted with one another, they didn't seem to have had much to do with Spinetti. It wasn't clear who had been avoiding whom, but not speaking Russian had made Spinetti a minority in this part of town.

My partner spoke just enough Russian that we'd landed the case as soon as White realized the suspect was from this area. Too bad his interviews in Russian hadn't offered anything better than mine in English.

We were now at the second to last house.

"What do we know about these people?" I asked.

John consulted his notes. "Oh, this should be fun. The Zubeks: Petra and Vanda both have petty theft priors for pickpocketing, so check your pockets on the way out; and Dorek, assault and burglary. Arrests, no convictions."

Petra answered the door and let us in when we said we were investigating Spinetti. The way her face wrinkled when she said his name made it clear she didn't like him.

Dorek descended the stairs and got in John's face. "Get out. No cops in heres." He was as tall as John, but much heavier.

John stood his ground and pointed to the three televisions on the floor against the wall. "We're not here about those. We just want to ask about your neighbor, John Spinetti."

"I makes it quick. We don't knows nothing," Dorek replied, taking a step back.

John stared at him for a moment. "Not good enough. Give us a few minutes, or we can start checking serial numbers. Your choice."

Dorek shrugged.

John took him back to the kitchen to start the interview.

From what I could hear, Dorek wouldn't even admit he knew the name of the cross-street.

John interviewed Petra second, with similar outcome, and finally went into the kitchen with the younger sister, Vanda.

After a minute, I could tell Vanda had started to open up.

I was in the front room keeping an eye on Petra and Dorek, who didn't look pleased with what his little sister was saying.

He stood and started for the back.

I moved to the doorway.

"Gets out of the way, little lady."

I moved one hand to my gun and pushed him back with the other. "Stand back."

"Or what? You gonna shoots me?"

I pushed him again. "Sit down."

He glared at me and instead of sitting, motioned for his sister to get up, which Petra did.

The big man grabbed for me.

I shifted back and gave him a swift kick in the balls.

He groaned and fell to the floor in a fetal position, moaning.

Still with a hand on my weapon, I pointed at Petra. "Sit down now."

Her face was red with anger, but after a quick glance at my gun, she sat.

"You okay out there?" John called.

"Yeah," I yelled.

"You too. Sit on the couch," I told Dorek.

He crawled over and climbed onto the sofa, cradling his groin.

A few minutes later, John finished with Vanda and returned to the front room. He eyed Dorek, who was still bent over, holding his crotch.

"What's his problem?"

I didn't answer until we had closed the front door behind us. "He wanted to check out my footwear."

"Ouch," John replied. We walked down the steps. "You know, with two of them you could have called me."

"Would you be saying that if I was a man?"

"It's not your gender; it's your size."

I dropped it. He was just looking out for me, as a partner should.

CHAPTER 4

VINCENT

AFTER LUNCH, A KNOCK CAME AT MY OFFICE DOOR.

I checked my watch: half-past one. "Yes?"

Nina from HR popped in. "Sir, I've got your new PA candidate outside, if you're ready to meet her."

I closed the spreadsheet and rose.

The girl walked in with plenty of hip swivel and offered a firm handshake. Tall red heels, a short blue skirt, and an only partially buttoned pink top were meant to distract—and were having the desired effect.

She extended her resume. "Jacinda Wilder, sir."

Nina excused herself.

I accepted the resume and caught myself drawn to the well of her cleavage as she sat—definitely deep enough to get lost in. I glanced down at the resume and asked her about her experience.

She had an impressive list of prior jobs, but none had lasted very long.

"The nature of temporary work," she explained. "I often get called to fill in for maternity leaves or unexpected vacancies."

The way she smirked when she said *unexpected vacancies* made me guess she'd played the part of the revenge the boss brought in when his wife decided the old assistant had been too good looking.

"This position can be quite demanding," I told her.

She smiled. "Sir, I'm available any time of the day or night, as much time as you need, and whatever services you require."

The implication was naughty, but I wasn't interested.

I liked this girl. Her answers were all couched cautiously, not divulging very much information—exactly the kind of discretion we needed here. And, with a stint as a copy editor at the *Globe*, she'd likely be up to the task of my need for perfection as well.

*A*SHLEY

THAT AFTERNOON, JOHN AND I WERE SETTLED BACK IN AT THE OFFICE after our Brighton interviews when Liz came back early from her first day undercover. She didn't look happy from what I could see through the glass of the boss's office.

I couldn't make out any of his words, but White was gesticulating in a menacing manner.

Abruptly, he stood and opened the door. "Newton, get in here."

I hustled over.

"You fucked up the top case on my desk," White said, pointing at Liz. "Getting blown in less than a day? What were you thinking, Parsons?"

Liz wisely didn't answer.

"This is way too important a case for you to screw up."

"It's not screwed, not yet," Liz argued. "They threw me out, but we can still get Ashley in, and I don't think they made me."

"What do you call getting caught in the subject's office on the first day and being walked out?"

"I got them thinking I worked freelance for a tabloid. The guy is a gossip magnet. They think I was looking for dirt to publish—nothing to connect me to here. That tabloid identity just has to be fully back-stopped, and they'll stop looking. We're not blown yet."

Liz had thought ahead if she'd already worked that out. It sounded plausible enough to me.

White scratched his chin. "Tabloid could work. Get Frank to help you backstop that front."

"In the meantime," Liz continued, "we should send Ashley in right away. They have no way to connect the two of us."

White closed his eyes momentarily. "Newton, you're up, then." His eyes bored into mine. "And you better do a better job than Parsons here."

"Yes, sir," I answered.

White's reputation would suffer for a long time if he messed up a big case. Translation: I was cannon fodder, and if anything went wrong now, I'd take the blame. I'd fall on the boss's sword for him, or suffer the consequences—in Alaska.

"Newton, a word," he said, indicating Liz should leave, which she did.

The door closed.

I took a seat.

"Parsons has better evals than you," he said. "We should have dinner and discuss how you could improve." The slight hint of a lech-erous grin appeared.

I schooled my face to not show the anger I felt. In terms of my eval-uations under Sinella, our previous boss, I knew the statement to be a lie. Liz and I had shared once, and our evals had been identical. This could only mean Liz's recent evals had been helped by her hide-the-salami sessions with our new SAC, and that wasn't fair. I wouldn't travel that road. I ignored the roiling in my stomach.

He took my silence as a no and continued. "This is DOJ's top prior-ity, so I really want to get this guy. If you close this case quickly and solidly, I'll make sure you beat Parsons for the LA slot. But the loser heads to the parka store."

He'd hinted before that one of us was heading to LA and the other to Alaska, but never this directly.

"Thank you, sir" was all I said. We both knew he could swing the promotion whichever way he wanted it to go.

He tapped the closed folder in front of him. "DOJ has information that this guy is conspiring with organized crime on something related to gambling. The objective here is to cut off the head of the snake, not just a low-level minion. We want the top guy, the guy who can give us the mob side of the equation. Wiretap warrants have been turned down, so you're going undercover inside this guy's business so we can get him."

"In what capacity?" That connection took this case to the next level for me.

White opened the folder on his desk. "His secretary."

I nodded. This certainly beat out my last assignment; an executive assistant wouldn't require the crap cover motel with bed bugs.

"This won't be an easy undercover," he added. "Parsons isn't the first secretary he's fired this month, so you have to figure out how to last longer than the others did."

"Not a problem, sir."

"Good. I'm counting on you." He slid the folder across the desk.

"Our contact at the personnel agency is listed on the first page, and she'll be expecting your call. She'll see that you get sent over. It's up to you to get hired. Develop a cover and use John for whatever backup you need."

"Got it."

"We'll do dinner after this is over."

I ignored the dinner statement. "Is that all, sir?"

He went back to his screen and flicked his hand toward the door, shooing me away as if I were a fly. I didn't rate a verbal response.

After I closed the door behind me, I gritted my teeth and realized the faint odor in his office wasn't the new carpet. It was the stench of the swine inhabiting it.

My new boss was a much bigger pig than I'd thought possible yesterday, but I could only deal with the situation presented to me. Escape was imperative, and for that I had to nail this assignment and get the hell out of Dodge—away from him, and not by way of Anchorage. Taking down someone connected to organized crime would be the icing on the cake.

Back at my desk, I opened the file. The problem appeared on the second page: Our target was Vincent Benson.

Turning this assignment down wasn't an option. A few months ago, Ralph Turnbull had refused an assignment White gave him and was now in the Minot office chasing moose rustlers or something. Half the agents sent to North Dakota didn't make it to their second winter.

However…

Vincent Benson had taken me to our high school prom. I'd thought we had a future at one point, and I had just been assigned to nail his hide to the wall.

I am so fucked.

And I couldn't avoid it.

CHAPTER 5

VINCENT

I walked back toward my office after a second gym session. I'd needed it to work off steam after finding that Jacinda girl on my computer.

Why was good help so hard to find? All I wanted was someone who took the job seriously, did accurate work, was willing to work as hard as I did—and yeah, didn't poke her nose where it didn't belong. I paid ridiculously well, but I still wasn't getting what I wanted.

Mason had suggested I split the job in two—and it might come to that, but it shouldn't have to. Plus, that would mean finding two competent people, and so far I couldn't even find one.

Opening the door, I found Mason in my chair with his feet up on the desk.

He quickly pulled them down and stood.

"Checking it out?" I asked.

"Yeah, for the day Daddy pulls you back to LA."

I'd never hidden my longer-term goal, and he knew it better than anybody.

"You know who gets the job isn't up to me."

"I have confidence," he replied.

That was marketing bluster. I knew better. After a few beers, he was incapable of keeping anything from me, and he'd admitted one evening that he didn't expect Bill Covington to promote him to my office.

He changed the subject. "Where's that hottie Jacinda? She go home early?"

"I *sent* her home."

His brow creased. "Huh. If you didn't like her, you should've sent her my way. I could use a distraction like her sitting outside my office. If you don't need her tomorrow, I'll take her."

She had been distracting, for sure, and intentionally.

"You've got Anita," I reminded him.

"We could switch for a while," he offered.

He always joked about wanting a younger assistant, but if I called his bluff, he'd fold in a second. Anita provided him the organization he knew he needed, and all the talk aside, he was too smart to give her up.

"She's not coming back."

"Why the hell are you pissing everybody off? Is it that fucking note?"

I stood to look out the window behind me. "I fired her."

"Already? That has to be a record for you. Two in two days. Keep this up, and you know Nina is going to be right. Nobody's gonna take your job."

I turned to face him again. "I caught her at my computer."

That got Mason's attention. "And you think she was looking for something?"

"I don't know." I rubbed my temples. "After that note, I don't know what to think. But she had no business being on my computer."

"And you think this is related?" Mason asked.

"No idea, but let's have security check her out. If she's working for somebody, I want to know who it is. If they're sending people in to infiltrate us, this is a lot more serious than some prank note on a windshield. And, we're gonna have to take some precautions."

Mason got up to leave. "I'll get her particulars from HR and have security chase her down."

I leaned back in my chair and took a deep breath. "Tell them, what-ever it takes. Budget is not an issue."

"You got it," he said as he departed.

After the door closed, I was alone with my worries. This had to be what paranoia felt like. Twice this morning I had noticed a car behind me, convinced it had been following me, only to have it turn off on a side street.

As they said, even the paranoid have enemies, and I had no doubt that was true. These coincidences couldn't be written off as random. Somebody had been following me, Staci had gotten the note, and this latest girl had been somewhere she had no right to be.

This unknown adversary was clearly dangerous. Jacinda could have been a random, clueless hire who didn't know any better than to poke around my computer, but if not, whoever it was wasn't wasting any time.

I turned in my chair and stared out the window again. Somewhere out there was my opponent, and his chief advantage was that he knew me, but I didn't know him. Yet. That needed to change.

I picked up the phone and dialed security.

Benjamin Murdoch, our director of security, picked up. "Hey, boss-man, your idiot Mason is down here trying to give me orders."

"I'm just doing what he told me," I heard Mason complain in the background.

Ben knew how to press Mason's buttons and enjoyed doing it.

The team Murdoch had built was top notch, including several with government alphabet-soup backgrounds.

"Ben, do we know anything about that note yet?"

"The note's a dead end. No fingerprints but the girl's, and the paper is common. It won't get us anywhere."

I'd hoped for more, but expected this result. "Thanks, Ben. Now help Mason and me by tracking down what you can on that Jacinda Wilder girl. I want to know who she's working for and what their game is."

"Yes, sir."

"And Ben…"

"Yes, sir?" he asked.

"Be nice to Mason for a change."

"Sure thing, boss. We hadn't thought of using him for Taser practice, but that's a good suggestion."

"I heard that," Mason grumbled in the background.

"Call me when we have something on her. And one other thing—I'm going to have Nina run any more candidates by you if she deems them worthy to come upstairs. We won't hire anyone you haven't checked out thoroughly."

"Yes, sir. When will that start?"

"Right now." I hung up to let Mason and Ben sort out their differences.

One of these days I might get Mason back with some electric burn marks on him, but if anybody could track down Jacinda Wilder's pedigree, it was Ben and his team.

THE TEXT ARRIVED LATER THAT AFTERNOON.

STACI: Thank you so much 4 the help - I got the loan

I smiled as I composed my reply.

ME: It was all you - great news

She deserved to get the loan; her proposal had been solid.

STACI: Monday?

I didn't answer right away. I was in no mood to be pushed around by the anonymous note-writer, but Staci had been freaked out by the message and probably still was.

ME: Let you know later

CHAPTER 6

*A*SHLEY

"WHAT'S THE PROBLEM?" JOHN ASKED.

I flicked my head toward the conference room. "We have a new assignment."

I stood and wended my way between desks to the smaller of our two conference rooms.

My partner grabbed a notepad and followed. He closed the door behind him, twisted the blinds closed, and took the seat across from me.

"The pressure's on because Liz was out in less than a day."

John didn't respond. He was smart enough to not voice his opinion of Liz.

"She broke procedure," I continued. "And now I'm in the crosshairs because she didn't follow the rules. If it goes south, White's gonna blame me."

"It's not always so black and white. Sometimes you have to operate in the gray and it's a matter of judgment."

"You defending her?" I shot back.

He raised his hands. "Hold on, I didn't say that."

I let it go, opened the folder, and slid it toward him. "I'm going in as a personal assistant," I said with confidence that didn't match the way I felt.

He perused it for a moment and slid it back. "Randy and I talked about this one a few days ago."

I suppressed an eye roll. Naturally they'd talked. They'd been partners before White's promotion. John still called him Randy and got away with it. His opinion would always carry more weight with White than any of the rest of ours. That was just the way it went with ex-partners. Those two had been involved in more than one shoot-out together—the kind of experiences that created a lasting bond.

"Any thoughts?" I asked.

"I've never seen him so wound up about a case. This is a big deal for him for some reason. Closing this is your best chance to get on his Christmas list."

I bit my lower lip. That last part I already knew.

"I've met this Benson guy," John said. "Had lunch with him at his fancy country club last year. With what's in this folder, he must be one slippery mother. You're going to need to build a careful cover. Companies like this have the resources to dig deep."

I took a breath before laying out our biggest problem, and maybe my one advantage. "He knows me."

John jerked back. "Fuck. Why didn't you tell Randy?"

I shook my head. "We haven't seen each other since high school. I left to go to Tufts, and he went to USC. Never saw each other after that. It's been a lot of years."

He settled into his chair. "And we're talking because you want to go in anyway?"

I didn't see any choice. "Yup. He'll trust me more than somebody new." Hell, he'd canned Liz in an afternoon. "I'll have an advantage we can't get with anybody else. I think it'll work."

My words made sense, but was I trying to convince him or myself? Vincent Benson had been my Kryptonite back then, but like I'd said, a lot of time had passed.

"He doesn't know you joined the Bureau?"

That was the sixty-four-thousand-dollar question. But I was pretty certain of the answer.

"Nope. We never had any contact after he left." I'd dredged through my memory and was confident I hadn't run into any of his friends or family since I left LA.

"You sure he doesn't know?" he asked.

It was John's responsibility to be sure I wasn't compromising the operation, but knowing that didn't make the accusation sting any less.

"Hundred percent. Outside of my family, only my roommate Hannah knew I was applying to the CIA. Everybody else thought I moved to Virginia to take a marketing job."

My original desire had been to work at the CIA, but my language skills hadn't cut it. The recruiter there had recommended me to the FBI, which turned out to be the best thing that ever happened to me. Here at the Bureau I'd developed skills, found a home, and made a difference taking bad guys off the street. At the CIA I would have been behind a desk analyzing intelligence and eating my way through bag after bag of Cheetos.

John scratched his chin. "You'll still have to clear this with the SAC." He was the responsible one, pointing out the obvious. "And no time like the present."

I gathered up the case folder and followed John back to the boss's office.

It was empty.

Frank informed us White had left for the courthouse and said he wouldn't be back this afternoon.

"Looks like you get the night to think it over," John told me. "But first thing in the morning, you better be sure you can handle it, or else pull the plug before going in. Once you're inside, it would be a career-ender to cry uncle because it's too hard."

I nodded. I had to do this. For so many reasons.

"Personally, I think you're stupid to try," John added. "I haven't done it myself, but the last guy who went under against somebody he knew said it was the hardest assignment he'd ever pulled."

I grabbed my laptop and turned for the conference room. "Let's get started on the prep."

I'd have this evening to think about it, but none of it would matter if we weren't ready.

John closed the door and put his laptop on the table. "What we need is something to make sure your resume floats to the top and gets you hired. You said he knows you. How well?"

I couldn't hide this from my partner; we trusted each other with our lives and our secrets. "He was my boyfriend for a while."

John sat back in his chair with his super-curious look, the one that meant at least a dozen questions were likely coming my way. He could pull a loose string until he'd unwound the entire ball.

"Go on."

"He took me to the prom."

"And now he's ex-boyfriend, right?"

I nodded. "We broke up in high school before leaving for college."

I could sense the next questions would be *who* and *why*.

John didn't disappoint. "And he broke up with you, or you broke up with him?"

"He broke it off."

"What caused that?" His question had been longer than *why*, but no less intrusive.

"A disagreement."

"Over what?" he asked.

"It doesn't matter."

"Hey, I'm not the enemy here. I understand it's sensitive, but your previous relationship affects the case. You know that."

"Look, he wanted to have sex, and I wasn't ready. Okay?"

That backed him off. "Sorry. I had to ask."

"You may not get it, but it was a big deal to me at the time."

"I get it, Ashley. Just one more thing—what do you think his reaction to seeing you again will be?"

I didn't have a good answer to that one. I'd thought about him a million times my freshman year at college. I'd fantasized about us meeting again, and how we would get back together. I'd wanted him to be my first. It hadn't worked out that way, but the memory of our time together had never left me, and never would.

"I don't know. It's been a long time, so I'm sure he's over it." Without so much as a call since then, he'd clearly been over me the day he left.

I'd seen pictures of him with a lot of different women. He might not even remember the girl who'd turned him down.

John and I spent hours devising my cover story. Liz had burned the cover we'd prepared months ago for any kind of office work, and we didn't have a second. Anyway, this one had to dovetail with my actual history to some extent.

It was late when we finally felt comfortable with what we had and left the field office.

Before opening his car door, John said, "Just be sure before you take this on. The time to back out is before you go in, not after."

OPENING THE DOOR TO MY SMALL APARTMENT THAT NIGHT, I TURNED ON the light and removed my weapon. I locked it away in my gun safe. If I was going in as an executive assistant tomorrow, I wouldn't be armed. My creds went in the drawer. Opening my wallet, I purged business cards from the last case and my ammo discount card from Minuteman Arms. My wallet couldn't contain anything that linked me to law enforcement or guns.

Was I really doing this?

Was I ready to straight-up lie to Vincent Benson, and then turn around and slap the cuffs on him when I found the evidence?

I slid my work phone into the drawer with my credentials and gun safe, and removed the undercover phone for this op from my purse. John and I had loaded it with all the right history and contacts to match my story.

Pulling down a contact from the list, my fingers hovered over the call button before I eventually pressed it.

Australia was literally the other side of the world, and that meant it would be mid-afternoon there. Hopefully my sister would answer. She was spending a few months there working with a medical non-profit.

"Hello?" Rosemary said hesitantly when she answered.

"Rose, it's me."

She laughed. "Ashley, you know it's polite to tell people your name instead of just saying *it's me*."

"Sorry, maybe I'll get that right next time."

"Doubtful. But it's still good to hear your voice. It must be about midnight in Boston. Is everything okay?"

"I just needed to talk to my big sister."

"So that's a no. It's good you called today, because tomorrow we head into the bush for a while. No cell coverage where I'm going."

That was my sister, always volunteering to help in the most remote places on Earth, God bless her.

I sat on the couch and pulled my knees up. "It's an assignment."

"Normally you can't talk about those. What's different this time?"

"It's somebody you know."

"I'm listening," she said.

"My next assignment is undercover, and the target is…Vincent Benson."

"From high school? That Benson?"

"The same," I admitted.

"That's fucked up. Can't you get out of it?"

"Maybe, but I don't really get to choose my assignments."

I didn't bother to tell her the alternative was probably a transfer to Alaska—she wouldn't have believed me anyway. She'd never worked for a guy like White. I also didn't mention my boss's dinner invitation, which was clearly an invitation to more than dinner.

"Are you sure you're not doing this to get even?"

"You mean for our breakup?" I asked, knowing full well what she meant.

"Breakup makes it sound mutual. He dumped you because you wouldn't put out, and it messed you up for a whole year."

"I'm over it," I replied, although my words were more certain than I felt.

That was the part I couldn't sort out.

"So now you're telling me it didn't make you mad?"

I knew a lie wouldn't get past her. "I was mad; I admit that, but that's not why I'm taking the assignment."

"That's the reason you should seriously consider *not* doing it. Can you be unbiased when it comes to him?"

"I'm not biased," I objected.

"But can you stay that way?"

"You know I'm all about the rules. I'll follow the rules no matter what." I caught myself feeling the thin silver ring I wore on my right hand.

"You sound like you've already made up your mind to do this."

"I don't know," I told her, and that was the truth.

I didn't know how I felt about Vince. There was the period before he left and the period after. The period before was the happiest I'd ever been, and the period after had been the worst. I didn't know how to weigh the two against each other. And besides, I could have tried to contact him later, but I hadn't.

"So you called me so I could play devil's advocate?"

"I guess," I said.

This was our way of talking through problems. She seemed to know I needed her to explore the other side of the argument, and for the next fifteen minutes, she did.

"Did it help?" she asked when the grilling was done.

"A little."

But I was still confused. Tomorrow I would need to walk into the office in pants, carrying my weapon like any other day, and tell White I couldn't do an adequate job because the target knew me. Or I would go in without my gun, dressed for an office environment, and ready to tell White I was the perfect candidate for the assignment because I could easily get the target to trust me.

After hearing about Rose's next few weeks planned in the bush, I was happy my apartment had running water, a toilet, and a shower.

In that respect, Rosemary was tougher than I was.

I went to bed determined to fall asleep with nice dreams instead of nightmares, so I filled my head with memories of the night of the prom.

It worked.

CHAPTER 7

ASHLEY

FIRST THING WEDNESDAY MORNING, JOHN AND I WERE OUTSIDE THE SAC's office.

I was in a skirt.

"Is there a problem?" White asked after we closed the door.

We both took seats. I let John take the lead, as White's ex-partner.

"The target knows Ashley," John said, laying it out.

"Why the fuck didn't you say so?" White half yelled at me.

It didn't matter that he hadn't told me the target's name. I hadn't even opened the folder while I was in his office.

"It can still work," I said. "We haven't seen each other in years. He has no idea I work for the Bureau."

White rose up in his chair. "What's the first rule of undercover? The first fucking rule is that you're not you; you're somebody else, goddamn it."

"Randy," John said calmly. "This could be good. Ashley doesn't have to gain his confidence; she already has it. He has no reason to be suspicious of her, and gaining the target's confidence is what it's all about. This could shave weeks or months off the time frame."

White steepled his hands. "Well, we are under a real time crunch here. You're sure he never knew you wanted to work for the Bureau?" he asked me.

I relaxed; it looked like John had convinced him. "Last he knew, I wanted to teach high school."

White chuckled. To him, high school teacher was the perfect occupation for a woman.

He fixed me with a stare. "Newton, you better be right about that. We are damned well taking Covington Industries and this Benson guy down. There's no room to fuck this one up. Do we understand each other?"

"Yes, sir. I'm positive."

"Okay then, keep me up to date," the boss said, returning to his computer.

After the door closed behind us, John whispered to me. "I don't get why he has such a hair up his ass, but your butt really is on the line. We need a clean bust that holds up."

"Yeah, that was loud and clear."

I had no idea why this was such a big deal either. But Vincent Benson was no longer the football jock I'd dated in high school. The folder made it clear that he and his company were conspiring with organized crime, and it was up to me to put an end to it.

By nine forty-five I was walking toward the Covington building downtown, going over the details of my cover background in my head. I had contacted the personnel agency shortly after five last evening. The Covington people had already called, requesting the replacement for Jacinda Wilder, Liz's cover identity. I was expected to report for an interview at ten this morning.

I shook my head thinking about her—out in less than half a day. Beating that wasn't a very high bar.

I checked my reflection in the glass before entering. I'd chosen conservative, professional: black pumps, a knee-length, gray skirt-and-jacket business suit with a white, long sleeve, collared blouse buttoned up demurely. Liz had chosen to dress provocatively, which could sometimes work but evidently had backfired on her yesterday.

Satisfied, I freshened my lipstick and pushed through the swinging glass doors into the lobby. I presented myself to the security desk at five minutes before ten. A call upstairs and I was quickly escorted to the third floor and the office of Nina Zaleski.

She perused my resume for a moment. "Assistant to the VP of marketing and then the CEO at Tenerife. That's quite impressive. I see that you have been out of work for the last year, though."

I nodded. "It was my aunt. She got sick, and I took time off to take care of her."

She smiled. "That's quite kind. How is she doing?"

I looked down and managed the beginning of a tear. "She passed two months ago."

This part of the cover was a pretty standard explanation for not having a recent reference to check. But I had no problem putting on a sad face. The facts of my aunt Michelle's death were even worse than the fiction we had concocted and backed up with a few changes to the records of the Middlesex County Medical Examiner's Office. I knew this part of my cover would stand up to scrutiny.

Her face fell as my answer had the desired effect. Now she would feel guilty asking much more about my background.

"I'm sorry. That was insensitive of me."

"It was cancer," I added.

The big C always threw a significant damper over the conversation as the questioner considered their own mortality and the randomness with which cancer took its victims.

"Breast cancer," I added.

If she had been a smoker, I would have chosen lung cancer, but her fingers and teeth were stain free.

Ms. Zaleski fidgeted and put down the paper. "I'm sorry to hear that."

I reached down and lifted my purse, pulling a tissue from the side pocket. I dabbed at the corner of my eye.

Ms. Zaleski folded her hands. "The position you're here to interview for is the personal assistant to the executive vice president of Covington Industries' east coast operations. The hours will be long. After your recent loss, are you sure you feel up to such a demanding position?"

I didn't hesitate. "Yes. That's exactly what I need right now, to throw myself back into work. The less time sitting at home thinking about my aunt the better."

"The man can be difficult and very demanding, and also quite gruff. You'll need to understand that going in."

Her description didn't sound anything like the Vincent Benson I'd known, but hell, people changed—or sometimes the job changed the person—and we'd only been teenagers before.

Anyway, I'd expected a warning along this line. We knew Vincent Benson had chewed through numerous assistants recently, so perhaps he *had* changed.

"After Mr. Honeycutt, anybody else would be a pussycat," I told her.

Honeycutt had been the CEO of Tenerife Inc. before he and his head marketing guy had been killed in a plane crash six months ago. The HR person at Tenerife was ready to field a reference call if they made one, and it was unlikely anybody would question my comment about Honeycutt. Dead men tell no tales.

She steepled her hands. "And you feel prepared for the pressure?"

"I have a friend who worked for the executive VP at Federated," I told her. "And she had pretty much the same experiences I did. It seems to go with the territory. High-stress jobs don't always bring out the best in people."

She nodded and seemed ready to agree on principle. She stood. "Very well. I'll take you up to interview with Mr. Benson while security runs your background check. You won't start, however, until after security has completed their investigation."

I felt a slight chill. A background check had not been part of the plan. This morning all John and I had prepared for was a possible reference call to Tenerife, or a search about my aunt. We wouldn't be prepared for anything deeper for at least another day or two. It took time to assemble the necessary backstop information with people that only worked business hours.

If they got started quickly, my cover might be blown even faster than Liz's. *Poof*—everything would be up in smoke, including my career.

CHAPTER 8

Vincent

Sitting in my office, I rubbed my tired eyes. Sleep hadn't come quickly last night. That fucking note, and then the girl messing with my computer had me worried—and I never worried. Dad had taught me to be the master of my destiny, not a victim of it, but today was different. An enemy I'd identified was easy to combat, but an unseen one? How did you counterpunch a shadow?

I pushed the intercom before I realized I didn't have an assistant outside my office to freshen my coffee this morning. Lifting the cup, I rounded my desk and started for the dining room. The lower floors had break rooms and a cafeteria. My floor had a small dining room for the executive staff when we wanted to eat in.

The two people in there left when I entered.

The touch screen on the expensive coffee machine took me a minute to figure out. Indecipherable icons instead of words didn't help. The first cup didn't come out right. I gave up when the second was worse.

I returned to my office, coffee-less, to find two women waiting: Nina Zaleski and another who had her back to me.

She turned. It was Ashley Newton, from high school.

"Ash?"

She was a vision from my past, and even more lovely than my memory.

Her emerald green eyes lit up as she recognized me. "Vince?"

Ashley had once been my very special Kitten, but that was a long time ago.

"You two know each other?" Nina asked.

"It's been a long time," Ashley said.

"Miss Newton is here about the PA opening," Nina informed me, as she handed me Ashley's resume.

"Is that so? Thank you, Nina. I'll take it from here."

Nina nodded as she turned to go.

I motioned to the office door. "Please."

Ashley entered, and I followed, trying hard to not stare at her ass.

"You look great," I told her.

Not my best line, but an understatement if anything. She filled out her gray business suit well, curves not hidden, but not shouting out. She'd been beautiful before, and she'd only grown more so. Her hair was up, which wasn't my favorite, but was suited to an office. She presented as the complete opposite of yesterday's girl.

"You don't look so bad yourself," she said. "But here? Boston?" She looked around the office. "I thought you were destined to run your family's company, not Covington."

That hit a sore spot. "Let's just say Dad didn't see it that way."

She pulled back. "Oh, I'm sorry."

I tried not to stare at the beautiful woman she had become. "No. This is better. Really. Out here away from headquarters, I get to call my own shots, and maybe someday…"

I didn't finish the sentence. Explaining what went on between Dad and me was not my favorite subject.

I felt for Dad's coin. I willed myself to not stare again, and failed.

～

ASHLEY

. . .

My HEART HAD ALMOST STOPPED. THE SIGHT OF HIM TOOK MY BREATH away. He had certainly grown since high school. He had been the star tight-end on the football team, but now he was even taller. Judging by the way he filled out his suit, he'd grown more buff as well. His chiseled jawline seemed more pronounced.

"How many years has it been?" Vince asked with a smile that broadened by the second, accentuating his dimples.

I smiled, remembering prom night. He was a solid ten on anybody's scale. I mentally slapped myself for losing my concentration.

"Nine," I responded. *Hold it together, girl. This is an assignment, not a date. And you know nothing about who he is now.*

In 1934, Clyde Barrow had been a handsome rake, and where had falling for him gotten Bonnie? Shot full of holes. In the real world you couldn't tell the good guys from the bad by the color of their hats—or their looks.

Vince's eyes slowly traveled the length of me. "You look great, Ash," he said again with a hint of a twinkle in his eye—the same dangerous twinkle that had pulled me in nearly a decade ago.

I bit my lip. "Thank you."

John had warned me this would be hard, and it turned out he was right.

It was a large office, with a couch along one wall, a small conference table and a whiteboard at the close end, and Vince's desk on the far end with a pair of visitor chairs. Before I realized how inappropriate it was, I wondered how many women had shed their clothes on that couch. A dozen, maybe more?

He closed the door behind us.

I could see the harbor from here through the full-length windows. "Nice view." I took one of the chairs facing the desk.

"Thanks," he said as he took his seat. "I guess I don't take the time to appreciate it enough."

Zaleski had warned me he would be gruff, but so far his demeanor was anything but.

He took a slow breath. "Ashley, you look great."

"You already said that," I reminded him.

I felt the heat of a blush rise in my cheeks, signaling my unconscious reaction to his presence—the part of me my rational brain couldn't control.

I reminded myself I had a job to do, my career to secure. I touched my silver ring for just a second.

His eyes narrowed. "So what have you been doing with yourself? Last time I saw you, you planned on going pre-med."

That wasn't the whole story. The last time we'd seen each other, he'd left because I wasn't ready for sex yet. He'd decided to move on.

Before that decision, being Vincent Benson's girlfriend had been the high point of my life. But I'd promised my aunt I wouldn't take that step in high school, and I'd kept my promise, even when it meant losing Vince.

My aunt felt high school girls weren't old enough to make that choice. Most of my classmates disagreed and were eagerly sucking dick and spreading their legs in the backs of cars or wherever privacy was available.

When I'd made my limits known, I'd been the oddity—not quite the freak, but not one of the cool girls, that's for sure.

I'd seen the sideways glances and the conversations cut short as I approached. It was almost as if they had to be careful I didn't talk them out of a good time, not that I ever tried. Their choices were just that, *their* choices. I was comfortable with mine.

"Did you?" he asked.

I'd missed the question while playing my private way-back machine in my head. "Pardon?"

He glanced at the resume and put it down. "Did you like studying psychology at Tufts?"

This was where I had to be sure to stick to the script. "I did. After that, I got into this: executive assistant work."

"And you like it?"

The question had an undercurrent of disdain. He didn't think much of the position he was hiring me for. We had come from different worlds. Him the son of a powerful family with unimaginable wealth, and me, the girl who went on to become—at least in this cover—a secretary.

"Sure, and you know what they say about a psych degree: it qualifies you to work at Starbucks, and this beats that."

Too bad I couldn't tell him I was actually doing much more important work, work I could be proud of every day at a job he wouldn't dare look down on. I proudly carried the badge and gun of the premier law enforcement agency in the world, and I spent my days putting crooks away.

I took this moment to remind myself he was one of them.

His brow creased slightly. His degree had been in marketing, I'd learned, and it would have helped us bond if I could have claimed the same background. But undercover, it was best to make up as few lies as possible. Remembering the truth was always easiest.

"I like the interaction with people," I continued. "And in my last job, I worked for the CEO, which gave me a good overview of how the company operated. I look at this as future job training, for when I run my own operation."

A smile tugged at the corners of his mouth. That answer seemed to satisfy him more than the prior one. "That's quite perceptive."

"Thanks." Just that tiny compliment was better than anything I'd gotten from White in weeks, and it felt good.

"Where was that last job?" he asked. He didn't bother with the resume.

"Tenerife."

"So you worked for old man Honeycutt?"

"If he heard you call him *old man*, he'd hand you your ass in a sling and your balls in a cup."

I hadn't expected Vince to know anybody at Tenerife, but either way, we hadn't found a better choice when figuring out my cover resume last night.

He laughed. "I heard that about him."

He watched me with a slowly widening smile. His eyes bored into me, asking an indecipherable silent question. For a moment I was afraid he might have actually met Honeycutt's assistant, which would end this charade quickly.

I broke the silence. "Ms. Zaleski said you would want to interview me and another candidate as well."

"We'll see. At the moment I want to learn more about Ashley Newton." He checked his watch. "But first I have gym time. "We'll continue the interview after that."

If his time at the gym interrupted his work schedule in the middle of the morning, this guy had a serious issue.

"I can come back tomorrow, if that works better," I offered.

"Nonsense. Just make yourself at home here until I return. Won't be long." He winked and rose from his chair. In a few seconds he was gone, and I was alone in his office with the door closed.

I froze in place. Was this what had tripped up Liz? Had they left her alone in the office, and the temptation to begin a search had done her in?

He seemed sincere, but that could be my submerged feelings for the man talking.

I stood and walked to the window. The view was magnificent. The Covington building was one of the tallest in town, and nothing obstructed the view of the harbor or the old center of town. The lofty height of the office was a testament to the powerful position Vince commanded here.

But when it came to the law, position was immaterial. The mighty fell harder than the weak, but they ended up in the same place, behind the same bars. They had to eat the same food and obey the same rules in prison.

It was going to be quite a fall for Mr. Spit-and-Polish to trade his expensive business suit for prison garb. But that was the penalty for getting involved with the mob.

I returned to my seat. Liz hadn't explained exactly how she'd fucked up, just that she'd gotten caught in his office. I wouldn't chance it by making any move this early.

An executive assistant would probably be passing the time by checking her phone. I pulled out mine and looked up the weather. I pretended to check my email and send responses. The emails went to a dormant dummy address. As the time ticked by, I controlled the urge to follow in Liz's footsteps and possibly get caught.

At the Academy, it had been drilled into us that successful penetration of a criminal enterprise took time, and rushing things beyond their natural pace attracted unwanted attention. Blending in and seeming innocuous was the goal. I took a breath and slowly let it out.

CHAPTER 9

VINCENT

AFTER TWENTY QUICK MINUTES ON THE WEIGHTS, I RETURNED FROM THE gym and opened my office to find Ashley exactly as I had left her. "I'm back. We're going for a walk."

She stood. "What?"

"We'll continue the interview over lunch," I responded. "I told you we weren't done."

"Could I use the restroom first?" she asked.

I pointed down the hallway when she arrived at the door. "Down the hall, on the left."

I waited for her outside my office door. "Let's go," I said as she returned.

"Where to?" she asked.

I didn't respond. Downstairs I made a left turn at the street, and we started down the sidewalk.

"Where are we going?" she asked again.

"Is Italian okay?" She deserved better than just any old restaurant.

"Sure," she replied. After a moment she asked, "Why the gym in the middle of the day?"

"I'm training for a triathlon."

"That's heavy duty," she said.

"It's a goal of mine."

Three blocks later, without another word passing between us, I stopped and opened the door to Vitaliano's, where I ushered her inside. The crowd waiting to be seated was dense, befitting the restaurant's reputation as the best Italian dining in all of Boston.

We threaded our way between waiting guests up to the hostess station. Angelica was behind the desk, explaining over the phone that no, they didn't take reservations. She was dressed in her normal short, tight skirt and even tighter top.

I waited for her to get off the phone. "Hi, Angelica." That was all I needed to say.

She grabbed two menus. "This way, Mr. Benson." She escorted us through the packed dining room to a booth at the back.

I nodded as we passed a few guests I recognized. The lunch crowd was full of the usual movers and shakers.

I pressed a Benjamin to Angelica's palm before she left.

As Ashley slid into the booth, she said in a low voice, "I thought I heard her say they didn't take reservations."

I leaned forward to match her hushed tones. "They don't."

My normal waiter, Tony, arrived.

I knew the menu well enough to not need to open it. "Tony, would you choose us a nice Chianti, and we'll start with the calamari and the olive plate."

Tony nodded. "My pleasure, Mr. Benson."

Ashley's brow crinkled slightly. "So what's the story?" she asked, pointing a finger at the retreating waiter.

"Come again?"

She leaned forward slightly. "We waltzed right past the crowd out front to an open table, and the waiter wasn't wearing a nametag, but you know his name."

"I've been here a few times," I answered.

She lifted her water glass and pursed her lips. "And?"

As her lips parted and the word came out, I was tempted to reach a finger out to touch them, to feel the softness I knew they'd hold if I pulled her head all the way to mine.

I banished the thought. "And I loaned Carlo some money to get this place started."

That bought me priority seating whenever I came.

She smiled. "I guess, like they say, it's not what you know, but who you know."

"Something like that," I answered.

Ashley put her water down. "I thought this was an interview."

Evidently she wasn't interested in a social lunch. I took a cleansing breath. Getting her to relax was going to take some effort. "Yes, that's right."

She fiddled with her knife, as if it were a sword to keep me at bay, before finally putting it down.

Tony broke the awkward silence between us when he returned with the wine. He retreated after it had been tasted and poured.

"If you're going to work for me, I need to know all about you," I began.

But I wanted to know all about what had happened in her life, even if she didn't work for me. So much time had gone by since that fateful day I'd said goodbye, and I'd regretted being too proud to get in touch with her. Today I needed to fix what had happened between us.

Her eyes narrowed. "What do you need to know?"

I noted her use of the word *need* instead of *want*.

"I'd like to know what's happened since we last saw each other."

Her countenance darkened. "You mean since you broke up with me."

It wasn't a question, but a statement.

I nodded, avoiding words that might make the situation worse.

"Why does it matter?"

"It matters because…" I started. "Because I need somebody I can trust under me."

A second too late, I realized *under me* had not been the right choice of words.

"That's the problem right there," she countered. "Because I wasn't ready to be under you, you up and left. And without another word to me," she spat. "You treated me like shit."

"Can we call a truce on that subject?"

"Sure," she sneered, though she didn't convince me she meant it. She looked down and fidgeted with her napkin.

I broke the awkward silence. "I'm sorry for the way I acted. It was immature and selfish of me."

Those were the words I should have said back then. But years ago in school, I'd been too headstrong, too hurt, too...too a lot of things, and not man enough to admit my mistake.

Her eyes softened to the beautiful green I'd longed for back then.

"I'm sorry," I said again.

"You mean that?" she asked.

I offered a hand across the table. "I do."

She took my hand and squeezed. "Thank you. Truce accepted."

The electric feel of her touch brought me back to the nights we'd made out in my Mustang on secluded Poplar Avenue. Before I'd screwed it all up.

~

ASHLEY

I PULLED BACK MY HAND. THE FEELINGS HIS TOUCH BROUGHT TO THE surface were not compatible with my mission. On a rational level, I understood he was the target, and I couldn't get involved emotionally. But keeping my rational brain in charge was going to be incredibly difficult if I allowed myself the luxury of his touch.

Just that short bit of hand-holding had reawakened feelings I thought I'd outgrown, urges I'd moved past, impulses I'd learned to control.

I'd made him think I was angry, and I had been, but anger didn't properly describe my current state of mind. I'd been hurt, but that touch told me how wrong I'd been to assume I was completely over him. John had been right that this would be hard.

Years ago, I would have died to hear that apology, to take Vince back and explore our future, but now I didn't have that option. Last night, I wasn't sure if I was going to be happy to nail his hide to the wall for payback, or sorry I had to be the one to bring him to justice.

Today it was clear the end of this wouldn't be a happy day for either of us.

Sometimes in undercover work you had to challenge the target, put him on the defensive, and I'd accomplished that with my reaction. Now it was time to calm the discussion.

"Tufts was good. The weather here took some getting used to." This wasn't hard. The truth was always easier to remember than lies and made-up backstories.

His eyes were on the tablecloth and his mind seemed somewhere else as I spoke.

"My freshman-year roommate was from Hawaii, and it was her first time away from home. She got so homesick, she didn't last past Thanksgiving, and I ended up with the room to myself for the rest of the year."

He twisted his spoon and looked ready to bend it in two.

"Classes were easy enough. But after AP English Lit with Mr. Peterson, anything would seem easy."

When I looked back at his spoon, he had bent it. Hearing about college wasn't why we were here. That was clear enough.

He put it down and sipped his wine with pained eyes.

"Vince, what's bothering you?" I feared I'd pushed too hard.

He put the wine down. "What?"

I motioned to the contorted spoon. "Do you always destroy your utensils?"

"No, no." He shook his head. "Just got carried away is all. Go ahead, I'm listening." His words were warm, but his eyes held something different. I couldn't tell whether it was anger or disgust, and I didn't know what I'd done to earn it.

With him wound so tight, I was loath to continue.

Our waiter returned, saving me for the moment. He brought calamari that smelled scrumptious and a plate of assorted olives.

I speared an olive and held it up. "Your turn. How was USC? That's where you went, right?"

Although I feigned uncertainty, I knew exactly where he'd gone to school. And thanks to his sister, I knew which of the eighteen fraternities he had pledged. I'd even driven the length of West 28th, checking out the frat houses to locate his, although I would never in a million years admit that. We might have broken up, but for the better part of the next year, I'd regretted it, and I'd almost called him at least a dozen times.

"Your resume said you got a psychology degree," he stated, ignoring my question. "I thought you were planning to go pre-med?"

Becoming a doctor had been an aspiration, but I'd only mentioned pre-med once with him that I could recall. The fact that he remembered took me by surprise. With a memory for detail like that, I wasn't going to get by with any mistakes in this undercover.

I nodded. "Yup, that was the plan. I was a bio-chem major for the first year, but that only lasted two semesters."

"What happened?"

I speared a dark Kalamata olive. "I joined the Tufts Premedical Society, and in the spring we went on a field trip downtown to the med school."

He waited while I swallowed the olive.

"They were giving us a treat, letting us watch an actual surgery." I rolled my eyes. "I ended up passed out on the floor."

He chuckled. "The blood, huh?"

"That and the idea of dissecting dead people—I mean, real people? I barely managed the frogs in high school. Between the blood and cutting into somebody's dead grandmother, med school lost its appeal."

I didn't add that I'd had to learn to deal with blood from gunshot and stab wounds at my current job, so I could have tackled medical school now if I'd cared to.

"Why psychology, then?"

"After messing up the differences between sulfates, sulfites, and sulfamates a few times, I gave up on chemistry."

I forked a calamari ring, and just as it reached my mouth, Tony returned to take our orders. I flipped open the menu I'd ignored.

Vince chose the parmesan-crusted halibut for himself, and I decided on the spinach and ricotta ravioli.

As we waited for the main course to arrive, we talked more about college. Every time I shifted to asking Vince about his experiences, he turned the conversation back to my history.

Tony eventually brought our plates.

"How's your ravioli?" Vince asked after a bit.

I nodded. "Perfect."

I could bet this place charged exorbitant prices. This was the best ravioli I'd had yet, and Boston was the town to get good Italian food. "I always thought the hole-in-the-wall places had the best food, but this..." I circled my fork over the plate. "...is proving me wrong."

The corners of his mouth turned up. "I hoped you'd like it."

I asked the obvious question. "You take all your PAs here?"

He tilted his head as he finished chewing and pointed his fork. "You're the first."

I didn't need a mirror to tell me a four-alarm blush had risen in my cheeks.

"I brought you here because you're special to me still, and I wanted to apologize for my behavior."

I put up a hand. "Truce, remember? You don't need to say any more."

He shook his head. "No, I do. Apologies are not something I do well, so let me finish. I wanted to tell you I was sorry a hundred times, but I wasn't grown up enough to do it. I should have been man enough to accept your decision, but at the time I wasn't. I've been ashamed of that for a long time. The way I acted was childish, and what I put you through was mean. For that I'm sorry."

His words flowed over me in warm waves. I'd never had anyone give me such a sincere apology. "Apology accepted. And now you owe me one."

His dimples erupted with a smile that melted me. "One what? Never mind. Whatever it is, I owe you two at least."

I raised my wine glass. "Two will be fine. Two favors."

"Shoot. What can I do for you?"

"Later. I'll save them until I need them."

He raised his glass to me and sipped. "Like I should have said long ago, when you're ready."

I liked the sound of that. "Now will you tell me about USC?"

Now that he'd said his piece, the utensil torturing stopped, and I thought I understood this lunch.

We talked through the rest of our meal, dessert, and an hour beyond. It was the most relaxing time I'd had with a man in years.

I stopped him. "Vince, we need to do the interview. It's important. I need this job."

I hoped I'd built up enough goodwill that my desire for the position would carry weight.

"Can you type?" he asked.

"Naturally."

"Can I trust you?"

"Absolutely," I lied.

I'd practiced my innocent face in the mirror this morning before coming in, and it seemed to be working.

He pointed a finger at me. "Ash, you're hired."

"Just like that?" I'd expected a more rigorous interview.

The teenage me had been smitten with him. Hell, the whole class had been. When he'd asked me to the prom, I'd thought it was a prank. But the next day he brought me flowers, and I moved up a million notches in the social standing of our school. The star tight-end of the football team was asking me to the senior prom. It was a day out of Cinderella. Just remembering that feeling brought a smile to my face.

"Just like that," he said. "I need somebody I can trust, more than anything."

In the end, when justice was served and he was behind bars, he'd no doubt regret trusting me, or ever even meeting me. That would be a hard day, but the job wasn't meant to be easy. I'd taken an oath, and dirty guys like him had to be caught. Once I found the evidence we needed, I'd do the right thing, no matter my feelings. What happened to Vince after that was up to the system.

Even bank robbers could be good looking and pleasant dinner conversationalists. I had to remind myself that justice needed to remain blind. I couldn't apply one set of standards to friends and another to strangers.

The file on him was clear: he was conspiring with the head of the Alfonso crime family that was breaking the law on a large scale, hurting a lot of innocent citizens. Those citizens paid my salary so I could keep them safe from the likes of him—the sharks who preyed on the weak. In my book there was a special place in hell reserved for the mob and their enablers.

He picked up his phone and dialed. "Nina, please put Ashley on the payroll and forget the other interview… Yes, that's right. And tell Ben to scratch the background check. I know everything I need to about Ashley." He hung up.

I cocked my head. "No more questions about my work experience?" His instructions to call off the background check relieved me.

"We can finish your interview later."

He'd told me I was hired, and now he wanted to interview me more later? This guy had a seriously backward process, which might explain why he went through so many assistants. Hire first, interview second, fire third, and repeat.

He put up a finger. "Nina wouldn't have brought you up if she was concerned. Just one thing—you understand this isn't a nine-to-five job, right?"

I nodded. "I'm your beck-and-call girl. Whenever you need me, and for whatever." The words escaped before I realized how flirty they sounded. I had to control my inner Bonnie.

His mouth opened for a split second, followed by a fleeting hungry look that he quickly controlled. He'd caught the same unfortunate connotation of my comment, but decided against pursuing it.

I smiled. I was *in* now, and I couldn't let feelings of yesteryear interfere with the performance of my duties. If I wasn't careful, we might get pushed in an uncomfortable direction, given our history.

You are going down, Mr. Bigshot. Working with the mob was a one-way ticket to the slammer.

CHAPTER 10

VINCENT

WHAT LUCK! JUST WHEN I NEEDED IT, I'D BUMPED INTO SOMEBODY FROM my past who I could trust. Now things were going my way.

The walk back from lunch in the sunshine was a perfect cap to the day so far.

Upstairs, I asked Anita to get her set up.

"We can catch up later," I said, backing away. "After Anita gets you situated."

Anita didn't look amused.

I went back to my office and dialed the phone for the call I'd been avoiding since this morning.

"Vincent," my mother said as she answered. "Thanks for calling back."

"What's up?" I asked, although I already knew thanks to a heads-up from my brother Josh.

"It's about the barbecue. I just wanted to be sure you're still coming."

"Sure, Mom. I'll be there."

These barbecues were mandatory family events, even though I was now three thousand miles away. But that was only half the question.

"And will you be bringing anyone with you?" She dropped the rest of the inquiry.

"Mom, don't worry. She'll…she'll be coming along this time."

Mom sighed loudly. "Good, I'm looking forward to meeting this mystery woman."

I hadn't given Mom or Dad her name. I'd just told them I was seeing someone.

I had been expected to bring along a plus one and disappointed my mother too many times. Staci had agreed to do me this favor, and she would make a good impression. She knew how to play the part, even though we weren't really boyfriend and girlfriend.

"You promise now?"

"Promise, Mom. You're gonna love her."

"No excuses."

My visit to LA was my semiannual responsibility check with Dad. I had to come home to be grilled, quizzed, and inspected to see that I was being responsible. And arriving without a woman in tow would be unacceptable. At my age—second eldest in the family—I was expected to be married already. However, bringing a girl like Staci and pretending to be in a serious relationship would buy me some time. Not right, but close.

I would never be good enough for Dad without that final step, but fuck it. Today I didn't care. My older brother, Dennis, had given in to the emotional blackmail. He'd gotten married too early after giving in to Dad's view of morality. It had ended in a divorce. His ex-wife had seemed okay before the wedding bells and the altar, but after the ceremony she'd morphed pretty quickly into the bitch she was underneath. It had cost Dennis a sizable settlement, but the resulting pain was the worse price to pay.

His example had taught me pretty clearly the downside to getting married, especially to the wrong woman. I certainly had not met the right one yet—not that I was looking. Marriage was an institution that made sense once you were ready to have kids, but before then, what use was it?

Dad's seriousness about this whole thing became clear when he essentially forced my boss, Bill Covington, to get married—or at least commit to it—before he followed through on a promise to invest in Covington Industries. It had nothing to do with the economics of the situation; Bill's character was just a litmus test of sorts. A test like that didn't make any sense to me.

There was a knock at the door. "Great talking to ya, Mom. Gotta go."

She hung up only after complaining I was just like Dad, rushing her off the phone.

"Come in," I called.

Mason opened the door and checked the room before entering.

"Who you expecting?" I asked.

He closed the door behind him. "Nobody. I just heard you were busy."

I played dumb. "That never stopped you before."

"Anita introduced me to your new PA."

"Yeah, Ashley." I nodded.

"What happened to waiting on background checks after the last one?"

"No need on Ashley. I know her from way back. We went to the same high school."

"You're sure?"

"Like I said. I know her."

"Okay. If you say so. I reworked some of the Semaphore numbers. Want to go over them?"

I did, but suddenly I didn't feel like it just yet. "Later. I'm going to hit the treadmill first."

"Worried about the note?"

Mason had a knack for cutting through the bullshit, and he knew I ran when I needed to clear my mind.

"Yeah, a little."

He turned to go. "Fine. You go ruin your knees while I do some real work."

"In forty years when you can't get it up, you're going to wish you'd been exercising," I told him. "It's all about blood flow, you know."

He turned at the door and laughed. "In forty years, I'll have the little blue pill, and you, you're going to be on crutches and unable to catch even the slowest old lady."

"Get outta here."

I followed him out the door. The treadmill awaited.

~

AFTER A HALF HOUR OF POUNDING THE MOVING STRIP OF RUBBER, I'D banished the note from my brain, and it had been replaced by memories from years ago—memories of a wonderful dance and a not-so-wonderful aftermath.

The incline increased as the machine simulated a run through Central Park.

I'd asked Ashley to the senior prom, half because I'd been taken with her infectious laugh and always-present smile, and half to piss off Cynthia. Cynthia Powell had been after me forever, and we'd dated on and off senior year.

Cynthia had been easy on the eyes, and still was. In high school, she'd been easy in another way, and she'd been my first. When she assumed that meant I'd take her to the prom, I rebelled.

It had been my younger brother, Josh, who had the bright idea for me to invite Ashley instead, and it had worked.

Cynthia had blown a gasket, and I was rid of her, at least for a while.

Then I remembered the way I'd ruined everything with Ashley. After listening to all the guys in the locker room recount how they'd closed the deal with their dates at some point after the prom, I couldn't take it, and I'd pushed too hard.

She hadn't been ready, and I hadn't been patient enough. I'd said things I didn't mean. It hadn't gone well, and in my anger I'd hooked up with Cynthia again. As I'd admitted to Ashley, I hadn't been mature enough.

Only later, after I started at USC, did I realize how big a jerk I'd been. And then it had been too late. With me at college and Ashley still a senior in high school, I hadn't seen her again. Until today.

Until I'd taken the job out here in Boston with Covington, Cynthia had periodically reappeared in my life. All through college I'd been foolish enough to believe it was me she wanted. Only later did it become clear that if my last name had been Smith or Black—or almost anything else but Benson—she wouldn't have had the slightest interest in me. She hadn't gone to college for a BA or BS; she was just biding time until she could get her MRS degree, and only if it was attached to the right last name. In Cynthia's world, right depended on the number of zeros attached to your bank balance.

The treadmill took pity on me and leveled out for a flat virtual stretch through the park.

My lunch with Ashley had dredged up memories of good times and shameful ones. I'd treated her badly back then. Today, she needed a job, and I needed someone I could trust. It was a perfect fit.

∾

ASHLEY

BEFORE HE DISAPPEARED INTO HIS OFFICE, VINCENT INTRODUCED ME TO Anita Santos, the PA to his VP of Strategic Marketing, Mason Parker, and also to the marketing guy, Will Marston, who Anita explained handled divisional marketing.

I nodded, making a mental note to look up the terms later.

Anita was older than the other assistants here on executive row and clearly the alpha of the pack, based on the looks the others gave her as I was introduced around.

I would be joining Anita, Sophia, and Daphne in this area outside the executives' offices. Daphne and Sophia handled the other four executives. I was the only one on the floor assigned to just one person, Vince.

Anita caught me eyeing the romance novel in her drawer as she pulled it open to get her keys.

"I'm done with this one, if you haven't read it." She offered me the book.

I'd noticed a paperback on Daphne's desk with a bare-chested hunk on the cover, but hadn't caught the title before she covered it up.

I accepted the book. "Thanks, I haven't yet."

The title was *Secretary to the Bazillionaire*, and the cover featured a guy in a suit—more office-appropriate than Daphne's book.

"I think you'll like it," Anita said with a grin I couldn't decipher.

I deposited it in my purse to look at later. Fitting in to the environment was a key to successful undercover work. At Quantico, we'd been warned: if the subject drank wine, we didn't order a beer. I'd never had the time or inclination to read anything beyond the occasional detective mystery before—maybe three books a year. But this book would be my study material tonight. If this is what executive assistants read, it was going on my list.

After getting me through the process to get a badge, keycard for access, and keys to my boss's office as well as my desk, Anita sat me down at the computer to run me through the login procedures.

She quickly explained the file structure they used on the computer system before walking me to the end of the office area. She took me through a locked door on the end.

"This is the common file storage area we use for executive row," she explained. "The key to Mr. Benson's office will get you in here as well."

I nodded.

She tapped a row of tan file cabinets. "These four here are for Mr. Benson."

The rest of the room consisted of file storage for the other executives.

The final stop was back inside Vince's office at two locked file cabinets that held the most confidential materials.

"How do I file things in these?"

"You don't," she answered. "Mr. Benson is the only one with a key to these. He may unlock them and have you locate something for him or file it away, or he may not, depending on his mood. Remember, you don't touch them without his permission."

I nodded. "Got it."

Along the wall sat an old IBM Selectric typewriter. "What's the typewriter for?" I asked. "Does he collect antiques?"

These had gone out of use decades ago.

"On occasion, Mr. Benson or one of the others will need something confidential prepared and sent. If it is ultrasensitive, it will be typed. That way nobody can see a copy of it in a computer file."

This was an unforeseen complication.

"Interesting" was my only reply.

It was a security measure I hadn't seen implemented before, and a sensible one. It was also just the kind of subterfuge a criminal might think up—no electronic copies to be subpoenaed.

The logging and storage of email and text messages had made the bureau's job easier over the years. Electronic messages lived forever and were instantly searchable. If Vince was communicating with hard copies, the message had to be intercepted en route or risk being destroyed by the receiver and lost forever.

We had numerous tools to intercept electronic communication, and we could even surveil and record audio, but a written note passed between parties was the toughest thing to catch.

So far these two cabinets in Vince's office interested me most.

We passed a room with tables covered in white tablecloths. I stopped to look in.

"This is the executive dining room," Anita explained.

"Pretty posh."

"For those that get to eat in there," she added dryly.

Apparently, that didn't include us.

The room had space for about twenty, by my estimation, and a view of downtown that any restaurant owner would kill for. Whoever used this room had a treat in front of them. Even the place settings looked elegant.

An hour and more introductions than I could keep straight later, I was at my desk when Anita's boss, Mason, stopped by.

"How about dinner tonight?" His question immediately indicated where he was coming from. He probably came on to all the new assistants, and I was fresh meat.

"Sorry, I can't."

He didn't skip a beat. "Maybe tomorrow then?"

I paused thoughtfully. "That might work. I think my boyfriend is busy with SWAT training tomorrow. You know, kicking down doors and shooting people. I'll have to double-check and get back to you."

His face indicated that my boyfriend comment had gotten the point across.

"Let me get back to you instead," he said, retreating to his office.

I'd gotten the line from a TV show, and it had never failed me.

CHAPTER 11

Ashley

For the rest of the afternoon, I handled the phones and tried to manage the crowd outside Vince's office, as new people constantly arrived, demanding access to him. The job was apparently going to be part personal assistant and part traffic cop.

Vince had given me the task of pulling data out of some old annual and quarterly reports for a company to generate spreadsheets. The work was tedious, and after a while, the numbers started to run together. I took a break to get a cup of coffee to aid my concentration. Screwing this up wasn't part of the plan.

Just as I returned with my java, Vince buzzed me to get him another cup as well.

I did as requested and knocked at the door before walking it into his office.

The look in his eyes as I approached sent a tingle through me and heated my cheeks. I'd seen that look before, more than once. It was a look that undressed me as I walked, and the smile that went with it indicated he liked what he saw—as well as what he imagined.

I gave him a playful wink as I deposited the coffee on his desk.

He thanked me, and I left the room with an exaggerated hip motion. It was my turn to imagine what he looked like as he watched my ass from behind. As I closed the door, I snuck a peek in his direction. His grin was as full as I'd hoped it would be. As I took my seat, I realized that excited me more than it should have.

In a while, things would settle down and I would blend in enough at this job to start poking around. I wasn't eager to repeat Liz's mistake by being overanxious.

As I opened the next quarterly report, I realized how unprofessional that thought had been. I was personalizing my relationship with the target, *who was being investigated as a criminal*. That would only lead to problems down the road, making what should be clear-cut decisions seem fuzzy and open to interpretation. I recalled John's admonition that this would be harder than I thought. I shook my head free of the concerns and started back on the spreadsheet.

An hour later, another meeting in Vince's office broke up and the participants filed out.

"Getting settled in?" Mason asked, stopping in front of my desk.

I looked up. "Sure. Anita has been a big help."

He came around behind me to look at what I was working on. "We'll need annual rates of change for each of the quarters," he offered, pointing to the left-hand column on my screen.

I flipped to the next tab. "Already done. I moved all the rate comparisons to one sheet, where they would be easier to analyze."

I showed him where I'd moved the calculations he was asking about, careful to not appear as insulted as I felt. All these executive types thought they were smarter than the rest of us. Big paychecks led to big egos. Little did he know I could punch him in the throat and have him hog-tied in less than a minute, if I wanted.

"Good idea. I like it," he said.

Apparently I'd passed his test.

He turned to leave. "Good work."

I caught my new boss eyeing the exchange from his doorway with a smirk.

Vince approached. "He trying to give you instructions?"

I kept my irritation in check. "More like suggestions."

He looked at his watch. "I need that spreadsheet finished tonight."

I had more than a dozen more quarters to finish. "I can't get it all done this afternoon."

He put up his hand to stop me. "Remember, this isn't a nine-to-five job, right?"

"Yes, but…"

I couldn't tell him I'd scheduled a debriefing meeting with John after my first day. Keeping my partner up to date was imperative early in an undercover.

"Tonight," was all he said before walking off down the hallway.

Anything you say, Mr. Bigshot.

I grabbed my purse and headed to the ladies room. This was going to mess up my schedule big time.

Once safely in the end stall, I pulled out my white undercover phone and typed a message to John.

ME: Can't make tonight - working late

I turned off the phone, not waiting for a reply. I would have to be off the grid for the evening. My plan to go shopping this evening for skirts and dresses that fit this assignment was also going to be a lost cause.

Before I put my phone away, I heard two others enter from the hallway.

"She seems nice enough." It was Anita's voice.

"I guess," said Sophia, another of the assistants in the executive area. She worked for Mike, the sales VP, and the manufacturing guy whose name I'd already forgotten.

I stayed still and quiet.

"He knows her. She'll get the benefit of the doubt," Anita said.

"Knows her from where?"

From the sounds at the sink, they were rinsing out their coffee mugs.

"Back in LA before college, I think," Anita answered.

"I'm glad I didn't get sucked back into that job. The hours and the trips—I couldn't take it again."

Anita laughed. "He wouldn't do that to you."

"I guess," Sophia answered

"Bet she doesn't last the week," Sophia said as they walked toward the door. "Did you see how slow she types?"

"I'll give her two or three," Anita answered.

The door closed, and I stayed silent in the stall.

They had mentioned bad hours, and I'd expected that, but trips? That hadn't come up in the briefing materials, or with Ms. Zaleski.

And they were clearly betting I wouldn't last long enough in the job to complete my assignment. Nothing like a vote of confidence to give me a boost. I rolled my eyes.

I waited another few minutes before making my way back to my desk.

～

VINCENT

ASHLEY HAD STAYED LATE WITHOUT COMPLAINT—A TEST MANY A NEW HIRE had failed.

I checked the time: seven thirty.

I opened the door to my office. "What kind of pizza do you like?" I asked her.

She looked up. "Anything, but no anchovies."

"Veggie, pepperoni, combo, all meat?"

"Combo sounds good," she replied.

"Me too," Mason called from his office.

I hadn't looked to see if he was still in, a mistake I didn't normally make. I had Ashley on the brain.

Retreating to my desk, I placed the order, and forty minutes later, the guard called from the lobby saying it was here.

"I'll go down and get it," Ashley offered.

I handed her cash, and she was off to the elevator.

Mason emerged from his office and sighed as we heard the elevator door close. "Just my luck."

"What?"

"She has a boyfriend, and he's a cop. He's on the SWAT team no less."

I walked back into my office and looked away to hide my reaction. "I don't hire them for you to date," I called.

I closed the door behind me and tried to breathe. I hadn't asked her; I'd merely assumed from the way she'd acted at lunch that there might still be a spark between us. I'd certainly felt it.

What Mason just said had knocked the wind out of me for no reason. I was tougher than this.

I didn't let women get to me this way. Letting one go to move onto the next had always been easy. Attachments were dangerous: it was the lesson I'd first learned from Ashley those many years ago. The pain of giving her up had been one I didn't care to repeat, and not caring was the one and only way to assure it.

I straightened my spine. This didn't change the fact that I'd hired her to do a job, and she was the one I could trust, the one I knew to be honest. And that was a damned sight better than a random girl off the street.

She returned with the pizza, and the three of us ate around the table in the small conference room. I was careful not to stare at her, but I had to face the feelings I'd had when Mason said she had a boyfriend. It had been a gut punch to think someone else had her heart, and that realization scared me. What did it say about me that this bothered me?

I was just being protective of an old friend, that's all. That made sense. Friends deserved protection.

At nine o'clock, when Ashley sent over the completed spreadsheet, I chased her and Mason out of the office for the evening.

I said goodnight to Ashley as if it were just another day and slunk back to my condo for a drink—or maybe three.

≈

ASHLEY

. . .

WHEN I GOT HOME, MY HEELS DIDN'T MAKE IT PAST THE ENTRY TO MY apartment. I padded barefoot to the fridge for a bottle of hard apple cider. After taking off my clothes and hanging them neatly, I changed into sweats and a Tufts rugby shirt. The couch beckoned, and I plopped down with my bottle of cider and the book from my purse.

The book had several dog-eared pages. I turned to the first one.

Holy shit.

The heroine, Juliet, had gotten herself banged over the boss's desk —his name was Dalton—and this was only page sixty-eight. It went on for pages, with moaning, dirty talk, and orgasms in the office. By the end of the section, I was hot and bothered myself. I reread it again, substituting my name for Juliet, and Vince's for Dalton.

I was damp down below, with heat in my core as I closed my eyes and imagined the scene playing out between Vince and me—a dirty, passionate encounter with animal desires taking over. I found myself breathing heavily as I opened my eyes.

If only, girl—get real.

He's a real billionaire. And in bed with the mob.

Besides, I'm the one who turned him down and pushed him away, never to see him again.

We'd both moved on with our lives: him the rich kid with every-thing he wanted, and me. What was I? The FBI agent, make that special agent, trying to put him behind bars so I could get promoted out of Boston and away from my pig of a boss.

We fit together like a tuxedo and a baseball cap—or a special agent and a crook.

I went to the next dog-eared page. They had sex against the door, and the next was against the window—so far no in-the-bed scenes. Either that or Anita hadn't bothered to mark them.

Now I understood Anita's grin when she'd handed me the book.

Finally I got to a scene in bed, not to mention outdoors on the patio, in the shower, and on the kitchen table. These two were like bunnies— the very definition of fantasy.

If only life could be like this.

Instead of going to the next folded page, I started at the beginning to read the entire story.

At two thirty in the morning, I read the final words with a smile on my face and warmth in my heart. It had ended well for Juliet and Dalton.

They were on their well-deserved honeymoon, the bad guy was in the hospital after the gun he'd intended to shoot the heroine with exploded in his hands, and he was destined for jail when he recovered. The hero had even saved the bad guy's life by controlling the bleeding, because he was just that nice.

I would have rewritten that part. I wanted the villain dead for attacking poor Juliet, but that's just me.

I went to bed content, understanding for the first time what women saw in these books, and wanting to eventually have the time for another. But that wouldn't be for a while if they kept me up until three every night.

I closed my eyes and imagined myself as Juliet, saved by Vince, but only after I replayed the office scene over the desk in my head—page sixty-eight.

My God, that would be hot.

CHAPTER 12

ASHLEY

IT WAS TEN O'CLOCK THURSDAY MORNING. I'D MADE IT TO THE OFFICE early, but I still needed to set up the debriefing with John I'd had to skip last night.

I dialed the phone. "Hey, Donnie, is your mother home?" I asked the voicemail box.

I continued the fake conversation for another half minute before hanging up. Anita looked over briefly, but neither Sophia nor Daphne paid me any heed.

We'd agreed on several scripts I could leave on the voicemail to communicate different messages back to the office. The phone number couldn't be traced to the Bureau, and the conversations would all sound innocuous to bystanders.

This particular script told John to meet me at the back of a small Chinese restaurant about ten blocks from here at lunchtime.

At eleven forty-five, I told Anita I was heading to lunch. I gathered my bag and made my way to the elevator. The door closed just as Vince emerged from his office.

I'd told Anita I would be out for an hour, but I'd avoided checking with Vince for fear of being overruled. Downstairs, I turned right for the walk to the meeting spot.

A block later I heard him.

"Ash, hold up a sec," Vince called from behind me.

I turned to find him jogging my direction.

Shit.

I hadn't escaped after all. I turned and smiled.

"Glad I caught you," he said reaching me. "I wanted to have lunch with you today."

I started walking again down the street. "Oh, I'm sorry. I made other plans. I'm meeting Maggie from school."

"Great, she can join us."

The guy was unreal. Was it not clear that my plans didn't include him?

"That won't work today. Maybe another time."

He stepped in front of me and forced me to stop. His smile was ear to ear. "Call her and suggest it. Or better yet, give me the phone and I'll convince her."

He seemed to have the billionaire disease. He was so used to people altering their schedules to accommodate him that he didn't understand the meaning of the word *no*.

I smiled up at him. "We can't join you, but maybe you'd like to join us. Maggie's been having heavy periods, and I mean really heavy— like, double-maxi-pad heavy." I sighed. "You can't imagine what that's like."

He backed up a few inches. It was starting to work. He wasn't turning green yet, but I was getting to him.

"Anyway, she has a gyno appointment scheduled, and I'm going in with her. The doctor's concerned she might have a uterine fibroid. You know how scary that can be—I mean the cramping and the bleeding. So she needs some serious hand holding. Actually, an extra pair of hands like yours could really help." I smiled innocently. "We shouldn't be there more than an hour."

The talk of periods and an hour in a gynecologist's waiting room had done the trick. It always did. Even asking most guys to go buy a box of tampons was like verbal kryptonite.

"Maybe we can have lunch tomorrow?" he offered.

"Tomorrow works for me, but I'll have to check with Maggie. She might still be cramping too much, ya know?"

He turned toward the Covington building. "Tomorrow then, but make it dinner instead of lunch." He waved as I continued my march down the sidewalk.

After a few more blocks, I looked back to be certain he hadn't changed his mind.

I breathed easier; it was all clear.

Once inside the restaurant, I wended my way through the tables to the back and down the restroom hallway. After checking behind me, I double-knocked on the storeroom door, and it opened.

Liz ushered me inside and quickly closed and locked the door.

Seeing her confused me. "Where's John?"

"He got sent to the New Haven office on some joint terrorism task force. Randy decided you get me instead."

I sighed. It was the SAC's call on replacing John, and I wasn't in any position to complain. I noticed she used the SAC's first name. She was getting careless, but it wasn't my place to tell her to hide her relationship better.

I eyed the two takeout bags sitting on the shelf. They smelled scrumptious. "Which one's mine?"

She pointed to the one on the left. "Got you the usual."

I nodded.

"Okay. You up to speed on the cover?" I asked.

"I looked at the folder. It seems pretty straightforward." She brought out her voice recorder and turned it on. "So what's the status so far?"

I gave several detailed minutes of dialog on the situation as it had developed over the last day. I left out any mention of my feelings, as they didn't pertain to the case, and I was sure I could keep things under control. My background reading last night was also not relevant.

She asked a few routine follow-up questions.

"The security is pretty tight, and I doubt it would be a good idea to try any interior surveillance," I said.

"We don't have a warrant for any of that yet," Liz said.

I continued speaking into the recorder. "It might blow the op. They

do routine bug sweeps, and IT also runs virus checks on the computers. They're not haphazard in any way." Anita had made a point of
explaining the routine virus checks IT ran.

Distress clouded Liz's face. She turned off the recorder. "What kind
of software are they using?"

"I don't know, but everything about their security operation is top
notch."

Her eyes widened. "We may have a problem."

"What?" I asked.

She stashed the recorder away. "We have to get the software off his
computer."

"What software?"

"The keylogger we installed," she said in an almost hushed tone.

"When did we get a warrant for that?" I asked.

I could see panic in her eyes. "We didn't. That's the problem."

She was scared, and the reason was obvious now. The SAC
wouldn't have authorized this—not ever.

I fixed her eyes with mine. "Who exactly is the *we* who installed the
software?"

Her shame was apparent. "I put DarkGecko7 on his machine."

"Liz, that was stupid," I spat. "And illegal."

That could get her fired.

"Stop being so black and white. I thought I could get a lead that
way and get it off before anybody noticed. It could've wrapped up the
case in no time."

"It *is* black and white. It's illegal surveillance, and it torpedoes the
case," I shot back.

"Not if nobody knows."

I tried in vain to calm myself. "That's not the point."

Her eyes pleaded with me. "If we take it off, nobody will ever
know. Ashley, you gotta help."

"How could you be so dumb?" I grabbed my lunch, turned, and
unlocked the door. I sighed and left without another word.

She followed me out to the street.

Her voice turned pleading. "Ashley, please."

She had just deposited a giant, stinking turd in my lap.

I turned back to her before walking off. "You're an idiot."

I left her there to contemplate her stupidity. This operation officially sucked now.

At a Starbucks on the way back, I snagged a coffee and sat outside, slowly picking at my Chinese lunch. I had to kill an hour, based on the story I'd given Vince.

Almost every bite tasted worse than the last as I contemplated my options. I had a terrible one, and even worse ones. I could go in and delete the software Liz had placed on Vince's computer and become complicit in her crime. That sucked.

I could tell the SAC how Liz had screwed up and let him deal with what to do, or even worse, I could clean up Liz's mess for White and then go tell him what she'd done. Crooks hated snitches, but cops might hate them even more.

If I finked on Liz, I'd pay the price. My career would be effectively over. I'd forever have *rat* tattooed on my forehead. Rats didn't have your back, and that was the kiss of death.

I forked some more rice into my mouth. It wouldn't be illegal for me to clean my boss's computer of the malware. But Liz had made me an accomplice after the fact the moment she told me, and that couldn't be undone. The conversation hadn't been recorded, but if asked, I wouldn't perjure myself by denying it. I couldn't leave it either. If it was discovered, Liz would have given any competent defense attorney grounds to sink the entire investigation.

The law was supposed to be clear: Black, white, right, wrong—not dark gray and darker gray. I needed a benchmark of right and wrong to measure against, but there wasn't one for this situation. There was no happily-ever-after solution available to me.

After clearing the table, I started back for the office, intent on treading the least-gray path available to me. Liz wasn't a close friend, but she was a fellow agent, and a female agent at that. I had to have her back and clean up her mess. If we didn't stick together, it would be harder for both of us in the future.

As I walked back to work, I went over past cases in my head, and it made sense now. Twice recently, she'd had a hunch about where the bad guy would be for his next meeting. Both times she'd been right. It could have been luck, but now it reeked of illicit knowledge she'd gathered without a warrant. This was a pattern with her, but that was a conversation for another day.

She is such an ass.

CHAPTER 13

Vincent

After failing to convince Ashley to join me for lunch, I'd ordered a meal from Vitaliano's so I could work at my desk. I craved something that didn't come from Subway.

Over a chicken parmigiana sandwich, I contemplated the photo of that fucking note on my phone until a text arrived.

MURDOCH: Need to talk right away

I dialed Ben Murdoch, my security director, and told him now was as good a time as any.

I left the office to deposit my trash in the dining room. The smell would be distracting if I left it in my wastebasket.

Ashley was back from lunch. She instantly put a book down and busied herself on the computer.

"How'd it go with Maggie?" I asked.

She hesitated. "She'll be okay. She has a fibroid, but the doctor said it was minor, and she has a follow-up scheduled to deal with it. The good news is the doctor said it shouldn't cause any long-term problems."

"That is good." I continued to the dining room to dispose of my trash.

On the return trip, Ashley was away from her desk, so I stopped to check out the book she'd been reading. *Secretary to the Bazillionaire.* With dog-eared pages no less.

Interesting.

Back at my desk, I logged into Amazon and ordered a rush copy just before Ben Murdoch arrived at my door.

He'd brought along a skinny blond kid.

"Boss, I'd like you to meet Johan Tervo." He closed the door behind him.

We shook, and they took seats opposite my desk and waited for me to sit.

"Johan works with Gemini Insight Forensics. We brought him in to examine some malware we found on your computer."

I waited for the punchline.

Tervo fidgeted in his seat.

"Tell him what you found, Johan," Ben urged.

"The malware we identified is called DarkGecko7."

If it weren't so serious, I would have laughed at the names they gave these things. "And what's the risk from that? How much of my information has been compromised? Can you tell?"

"It's a keylogger only, which means it hasn't sent any of the data on your disk off site. But it has been transmitting your keystrokes, so passwords, email, memos, and the like would be at risk."

"It's not that bad, then?" I asked.

Ben urged Tervo to continue.

"Yes and no. If your passwords have been compromised, that can be quite dangerous. Our major concern, though, is the sophistication of the attack."

Ben decided to fill me in on this part. "This particular malware is very hard to detect and remove. It is state-level spycraft."

That chilled me to the bone. "International spying?"

"Possibly, but not necessarily," Tervo continued. "It was developed by the Russians, but it's now used by the CIA and several top corporate players."

"The tabloids?" I asked.

Ben shrugged and looked to Tervo for guidance.

"Not that we know of," he answered. "But it is possible. In the meantime, it has been disabled. As far as the other party knows, you've been off your computer. We can re-enable it, and you can use it for disinformation, if you want."

I contemplated the suggestion. "That might be useful if I knew who was spying on us. Is there any way to track this to the other end?"

Tervo shook his head. "No, sir. That might work in the movies, but in real life we can't do that."

I still didn't have any idea who the fuck was after me, except that his description made clear it was no Mickey Mouse outfit. "Any idea how it got on my computer?"

"No, sir. Any of the normal channels—email trojans, things like that —are possible."

"Mason and I have been working on the Semaphore transaction. Could our proposals have been compromised by this?"

"If you worked on it on your computer, absolutely," he responded. "But only what you typed, nothing more."

"And what about Mason's computer?"

"We've started daily automated sweeps," Ben said. "So far yours is the only one we've found compromised. And this wasn't picked up last month, so the infection is recent."

"It happened within the last couple of weeks?" I asked.

"Yes, sir," Ben answered.

I walked to the window and looked out over the city. Somewhere out there, somebody was stalking me. No names or faces came to mind as I scanned the cityscape.

"Come out in the open, you fucking coward," I mumbled to the window.

"Sir?" Ben asked.

"Sorry, just talking to myself. Thanks for the update. Any other steps you'd recommend?"

He hesitated.

"Out with it. What else?"

"Johan, could you excuse us, please?" Ben asked.

The kid left and closed the door behind him with only a slightly hurt look.

"Video, sir," Ben said.

"Explain."

"I understand it could be sensitive. But we could set up video surveillance of the executive offices. Because it's possible the software was installed by someone with physical access."

"One of our own?"

He nodded wordlessly.

The thought was chilling. A Covington employee? An inside job. I closed my eyes, breathed in through my nose and out slowly. There was only one possible answer to his suggestion. The fucking enemy had to be defeated, and if that meant finding a co-conspirator, no means were out of bounds.

"How soon can you set it up?"

"It's best that nobody else here know."

His suggestion was wise. I couldn't even let Mason in on it. We had to start without any preconceived notions of who it could be, and we couldn't risk a leak by widening the circle.

"Understood. Just you and me."

"I can do it over the weekend, when the offices are empty."

"Another thing, Ben. Video only, no audio. I don't want to be listening in on people's conversations." The undisclosed video was creepy enough.

"I was going to propose that."

I stood. "It's authorized then."

"One more thing. This office?"

I couldn't see excluding my space if we were going to be spying on everybody else. "Including this office, yes. Only, nobody reviews the footage of this office without my approval, and that includes you."

"Understood, sir."

CHAPTER 14

ASHLEY

IT WAS FRIDAY MORNING, AND IT HAD NOW BEEN ALMOST TWENTY-FOUR hours since Liz told me of her idiot move to put software on Vince's computer. I hadn't gotten an opening to go in and remove it yesterday afternoon, and Anita had said the IT guys checked the computers every few days. I didn't have long—if they hadn't found it already.

Vince had ordered in for lunch today, and it looked like I still might not get an opportunity to clean up Liz's mess.

A few minutes later, his meeting with the sales VP and the controller broke up. He stopped by my desk after seeing them off.

"I didn't get my morning run in. I'll be down in the gym if you need me."

"Sure," I replied.

"And dinner tonight at seven," he added.

I didn't object. "Oh, and where are the other quarterly reports when I need them?"

"Already?"

I nodded. I was now on to part two of my spreadsheet assignment, and I wasn't really ready for them yet, but I needed the excuse to enter his office while he was out.

"On the credenza," he said, backing toward the elevator.

I waved. "Have a nice run."

He smiled, waved, and turned for the elevator bank.

Ten minutes later, when I was certain he wouldn't return because he'd forgotten something, I waited for my opening. It came while Anita was in the copy room and Sophia and Daphne were also away from their desks. I slipped into Vince's office.

I closed the door behind me and quickly located the quarterlies I'd told him I needed. Then I took a seat at his desk. The computer's monitor was off. A tap of the power button brought the screen to life, and it showed he hadn't logged out.

My throat constricted, and I froze as I heard voices outside the door. I stood and waited silently.

Whoever it was walked away.

I sat back down and pulled up a window. The search for the innocuous file name DarkGecko7 hid under started slowly. I could feel my heart beating as the seconds ticked by. Staring at the window didn't speed it up. The search came back after half a minute, and seconds later I'd deleted it.

I closed the window and powered off the monitor. Placing the chair back where I'd found it, I grabbed the quarterly reports and returned to my desk.

Anita looked my way momentarily as I left Vince's office. "Ashley." She motioned for me to come over.

Shit.

A lump formed in my stomach, and my mouth dried. I forced a smile.

"Did you see where Mason went?" she asked as I approached.

I could breathe again. "No, isn't he in there?"

"That man is always forgetting to tell me where he's going," she complained.

I leaned forward to whisper, "They have these little tracking pendants for cats. You should get one for him."

She laughed. "I like the way you think."

I returned to my desk and sat down, taking a deep, relieved breath. I pulled a tissue from my purse and dabbed at my sweaty brow.

My heartbeat slowly returned to normal as I busied myself at my computer.

Success.

∼

VINCENT

ON THE TREADMILL, I WONDERED IF I HAD DONE THE RIGHT THING IN authorizing the video surveillance yesterday. Eventually I decided it was the best countermove, given the severity of the situation. By compromising my computer, whoever my fucking opponent was had taken off the gloves, and I needed to do the same.

I finished my run, and in the late afternoon Mason and I began working on the Semaphore acquisition again—with the door closed and locked. Ashley had instructions to keep the hordes at bay for the next two hours. Weird muffled versions of the occasional altercation outside came through the barricaded door. So far she had been more than a match for all the would-be visitors.

Semaphore had just informed us of another competing offer. The situation was getting completely out of hand. Every time we planned a move, Gainsboro seemed to see what we were going to do and made a countermove.

My cell dinged with a text. I ignored it, and we kept working.

Two minutes later it dinged again, and I checked the messages.

MURDOCH: I have something we need to talk about

MURDOCH: It's important

Security guys could get pretty alarmed about the simplest things, but that wasn't Ben Murdoch's style. If he said it was important, it generally was.

After his report yesterday, I wasn't about to put him off. I pulled up his number on my cell.

"Give me a second to check this, Mason," I said before I hit dial.

Ben picked up instantly. "Boss, I need to see you right away."

"Were pretty tied up right now..."

"I wouldn't bother you if it wasn't critical," he said in his *I'm serious* tone.

"Come on up, and tell Ashley I'm expecting you."

Mason and I tried to deal with the next line item before he arrived. We weren't successful.

It took less than two minutes before the insistent knock came.

Mason got up to let him in and locked the door after him.

"What's so important it can't wait?" I asked.

Ben looked warily at Mason. "It's about your last secretary."

"Mason is fine," I told him. "So what's the story, Ben?"

Ben sat and opened the folder he'd brought with him on my desk. Mason shimmied his chair closer.

"You wanted us to dig into that Wilder girl."

I nodded. "Yeah, and?"

"Here are some surveillance photos you might find interesting," Ben said, pulling a picture out. "Look who she talked with yesterday."

My heart almost stopped. The picture showed Ashley on the sidewalk with that Jacinda Wilder bitch we had fired. Things were suddenly cloudy.

"That looks like the girl we caught in here messing with your computer," Mason said. "What's Ashley doing meeting with her?"

It was certainly a question I wanted to ask. I picked up my phone to buzz Ashley in to explain this.

"You might want to wait on that, boss. There's more," Ben said.

"Go ahead." I put the phone back in its cradle. *More* didn't sound good.

He pulled another photo from the folder. "We still don't know much about this Wilder lady, but we followed her." He placed the picture on the desk. "We followed her to Cambridge, and this is where she went." The picture showed her entering a red brick building I didn't recognize.

"Pat, you're killing us. Who owns the building?" Mason asked.

"The *Daily Inquisitor*," Ben said.

"So now we know which tabloid," Mason chimed in.

I put a hand up to silence him. "Is it confirmed, then, that she works for them?"

Ben nodded. "We called in to personnel and got it confirmed."

"Good thing you got rid of the bitch quickly," Mason said.

Ben picked up his pictures. "The note you got said collateral damage. What do we think they have planned?"

I could answer that easily enough. "Gossip and lies to boost circulation. Their whole business plan is lies—three-headed cows, visits by Martians, and the like."

"Do you want us to continue to follow her? Or perhaps talk to her, to find out what the plan was?" Ben asked.

I didn't know for sure what *talk to her* meant in Ben's lexicon, but it probably involved threats, which would be counterproductive. She'd hide behind the First Amendment and make us out to be the bad guys.

"No, let her go. She wasn't here long enough to get anything. With some luck, they'll get tired and move on to an easier target."

Mason spoke up. "If your new PA is friends with her, you can't keep her. She might even work with her. You know that, right?"

"I'll be the judge of that, thank you." If it were someone else, I might have agreed with him, but I knew Ashley.

He grimaced but said nothing further.

CHAPTER 15

*A*SHLEY

AFTER TWENTY FOUR HOURS ON HIGH ALERT AFTER FINDING OUT ABOUT THE keylogger from Liz and then almost getting caught bailing her out of that jam, I needed to relax. It was just past seven in the evening. I located the sign halfway down the block and hurried. I was already late.

I pushed past the door into the darkened interior. I'd never been in Holmby's Grill, the kind of place the movers and shakers frequented. Sizzler was a better fit for my budget if I was looking for a steak. It took my eyes a moment to acclimate enough to spy Vince in a back booth, and I made my way over.

He checked his watch and rose as I took a seat across from him, but he smiled rather than berating me for being tardy. "You look lovely tonight."

"Thank you." I welcomed the compliment, but I was not sure what to make of it as I was wearing exactly what I'd had on earlier at work. "What's good here?"

He opened his menu. "I come here for the steak, but I understand the lamb chops and swordfish are both quite delicious."

I opened my menu as well. "Is that what your dates usually order?"

Our DOJ background folder on Vince contained tabloid stories about him and various women from about a year ago, plus a few more recent surveillance photos of him with two other women.

His glare had me regretting my words. "Are we really going there?"

"Sorry, I didn't mean—"

"I invited *you* to dine with me tonight. Nobody else."

I'd come across as a total bitch. "I'm sorry."

It had been too long since I'd spent time in polite company. My manners clearly needed refreshing.

Our waiter arrived.

"Any wine preference?" Vince asked me.

I pasted on my apologetic smile. "I'll defer to you."

"Stu, surprise me with your choice of a pinot. And we'll start with the garlic shrimp."

Once again, Vince was on a first name basis with the wait staff.

Stu vanished as quietly as he had arrived.

I could see why Boston's elite chose this place. The high-backed booths lent themselves to private conversations not meant to be overheard. The occasional yuppie had snagged a table to impress his date, but they were outnumbered by Boston's business leaders. Many of the men in expensive suits sat across from dates decked out in even more expensive jewelry, and the other half were accompanied by other businesspeople.

The wine and appetizer arrived, and we indulged in the shrimp and light conversation, reminiscing about high school.

Vince's dimples were in full bloom as he smiled and laughed and we traded our recollections of that time. The gravitational pull of his smile and the intensity of his eyes pushed all thoughts of him being a mob conspirator to the back of my mind. He became once again the prince charming that had chosen me for the prom.

That night had been magical, far and away the highlight of my years on the west coast— and actually since then as well.

As he spoke, the words floated past me. I imagined myself dancing in his arms again—a slow dance, swaying to the music, pressed up against him, lost in time and space with no cares, only hopes.

"Your thoughts?" he said, breaking me out of my reverie.

"Pardon?" I'd completely missed the question.

"You look so happy. I asked what you were thinking about."

The heat of a blush rose quickly. "Nothing," I lied.

"I can tell it's not nothing."

I looked down at the tablecloth. "It's silly."

"I want to know, Ash."

I decided on a quick lie. "It's just nice to have a boss take me to dinner. Mr. Honeycutt never did."

"Then he wasn't as smart as people said."

I gave myself a mental slap. Vince was the target of our investigation, and I had to keep my guard up and pay attention.

Our waiter, Stu, broke the conversation as he arrived carrying the steak Vince had ordered and the swordfish I'd chosen.

"Stu, can we please add a side of those wonderful parmesan truffle fries?"

He nodded. "Certainly, Mr. Benson. It will be only a few minutes."

"What's a truffle fry?" I asked after Stu left us.

Vince sipped his water. "French fries, but drizzled with truffle oil and parmesan cheese."

I cut a piece of swordfish and slipped it into my mouth. The mustard vinaigrette sauce on the succulent fish set a new standard for seafood in my book.

He finished chewing his bite of steak and put down his fork. "Did you know the girl that had the job right before you only lasted an afternoon?"

He was referring to Liz, of course.

I looked up. "I heard that." I picked up my wine glass and sipped.

"So, how do you know her?"

This innocent dinner had suddenly taken a serious turn.

I put down my wine, wondering what the question really was. "Know who?"

He cut another piece of meat before answering. He glanced up at me. "Jacinda."

My heart almost stopped, but I kept my cool. "Jacinda who?"

He put down his fork, and his stare froze me. "Ash, are we going to play this game?"

A shiver went through me, but I kept my game face on. We'd been taught to not give in to simple bluffs like this.

I giggled. "What game are we playing?"

He slid his hand inside his jacket and pulled out a photograph. "It's time for the truth." He laid the picture on the table for me to see.

My heart skipped a beat. It was a picture of Liz and me on the sidewalk after our meeting yesterday. "Oh… Yeah, I know her. But her name is Elizabeth, not Jacinda. I bumped into her after Maggie's appointment."

I put on my best innocently confused face. There was a possibility I could still get out of this without blowing my cover, but the options were narrowing.

He took another sip of his wine, staring at me.

I couldn't tell if my innocent face was working or not.

He looked down to cut another piece of steak. "We suspect she might work for one of those muckraking tabloids."

It seemed Liz's backup identity had worked.

"Really? She told me she was a freelance journalist."

He looked up at me as his fork stopped midway to his mouth. "Journalist, huh? Is that what they call themselves now?"

The fork completed its journey, and he held my eyes as he chewed slowly, a slight smile on his face.

I sensed I'd made a mistake offering those words. I remembered our dance together, and like magic, my best smile appeared again. I didn't know if it would be sufficient, but it was the best I had to offer my interrogator.

He put his fork down and pulled another picture from his coat. "I guess she had us both fooled then, huh?" He put the second photo down.

"And where is that?" I could feel the blood draining from my face, a reaction I couldn't control. The picture was Liz entering a brick building I didn't recognize.

He took a sip of his wine, silently daring me to say more, watching me struggle in my quicksand of lies.

There was nothing more for me to say, nothing to explain, nothing to ask. The next move was his.

"She actually works in that building," he said, "at the *Daily Inquisitor*."

I looked away and cut another bite of my fish. "Really?" When I looked back at him, he was staring again.

"You should know; she's your friend."

"Acquaintance," I shot back. "And if her name is Jacinda, she's messing with both of us. She and I met at yoga." I inserted the yoga reference, guessing that's what executive assistants did in their time off. "We had coffee once or twice back when I worked for Tenerife. Then I saw her on the sidewalk…" I pointed to the picture. "And she asked where I was working now."

His eyes narrowed as he considered my response.

Would he believe Liz's cover or not? And mine as well?

He resumed attacking his steak with knife and fork. "You can't have any more contact with her. Is that clear?"

I was careful not to show my relief. "Why not?"

He pointed at me with his fork. "Because I don't want to end up in one of their hit pieces, that's why."

The covers were going to stick.

He nodded his head toward the front door. "You might recognize Nancy at the table near the front. She works in the Channel 8 newsroom—the television station Covington owns, by the way. And her dinner partner tonight is her cameraman, Tony."

I glanced toward the door and noticed the striking blonde who had looked oddly familiar as I walked in. This was dangerous. Rule number one for undercover work: never ever, under any circumstances, end up in the news.

"I didn't know if you worked with that Jacinda character, but in case you did, I had them come here to document the underhanded way that tabloid operates."

I froze in place.

"It would have been on the news for at least a week, maybe longer —catching the tabloids at their own game. A real ratings booster, not to mention a counterpunch that would keep them at bay for a while."

My throat was too dry to swallow. I grabbed for the water. "I barely know her. I certainly don't work with her."

~

VINCENT

SITTING ACROSS THE TABLE, ASHLEY WAS INDIGNANT IN A PRETTY WAY.

"And I didn't tell her anything," she added. "I swear. What's with the paranoia?"

I finished chewing and pulled out my phone. After a few clicks, I slid it over to her. "This is what."

She looked at the screen and read the note. "When did you get this?"

She seemed even more shocked than Staci had been.

"A friend of mine found this on her windshield Monday."

"A friend?" she asked.

"A friend," I repeated.

The glint in her eye said she'd caught that Staci was more than an acquaintance. She studied my face. "Who would do something like this?"

She cut a bite of her fish, seeming calmer than she'd been a second ago.

"Somebody who has a beef with me, and I have no idea who."

"No jealous boyfriends...or husbands?"

"Why does everybody ask that? I haven't ever dated a married woman. And no, no jealous boyfriends either."

"That's not what the *Daily Inquisitor* said last year."

"That is exactly the problem," I hissed. I took a calming breath before continuing. "Those assholes print lies."

She reached a hand across to mine. "Sorry. It was a joke. You really have no idea who wrote it?"

I took another deep breath. Every time this note came up, it angered me. "I've wracked my brain, and I don't have a candidate."

She checked her watch. "I need to go soon."

"You can't leave yet. How's the swordfish?" I asked.

Her jaw relaxed slightly. "Very nice, thank you." She forced a semi-smile. "I'm your prisoner, is that it?"

I waited to finish chewing. "You're my dinner guest, and I have a proposal I hope you'll like."

"I'm here because I'm your employee," she stated.

I ignored her move back to argumentative. "I invited Ashley Newton to dinner, not my PA."

Her cheeks reddened.

I nodded toward the news crew. "I'm going to give you your fifteen seconds of fame—"

"No. You can't—"

"Let me finish," I said, cutting her off.

She bit her lip and quelled her tongue.

"You'll like it…"

She almost interrupted me again, but controlled herself. The tenseness in her jaw was apparent.

"I really can't," she said.

I scooted out of my side of the booth and moved to her side, trapping her. I wasn't taking no for an answer.

I waved over the news team, Nancy and Tony. "It won't take long."

CHAPTER 16

ASHLEY

VINCE MOVED TO MY SIDE OF THE TABLE AND SLID OVER.

I needed to figure a way out of this, but I was drawing a blank. I couldn't tell him being on camera would ruin my undercover career.

He waved over Nancy Newslady, whose last name escaped me at the moment.

I panicked. "You can't."

His eyes narrowed. "Watch me."

I was trapped in the booth without any way to escape. No gun, no taser, no badge, no baton, no pepper spray, nothing.

Nancy patted her lips with her napkin and rose. Tony followed her with his camera in hand, but at least not on his shoulder yet.

I couldn't control my breathing, and my heart was speeding past its redline. "Vince, please don't do this."

He smiled toward the approaching newspeople and mumbled quietly, "Just calm down."

I pasted on a smile for the approaching duo and begged him. "Please, no."

As Nancy Newslady arrived at our table, Vince rose to greet them.

"Nancy, Tony, how is the dinner?" He stood right by the edge of the bench, still blocking my exit.

Nancy took the lead. She was the anchor and certainly outranked Tony Cameraman in the television hierarchy. "Wonderful food. Thank you, Mr. Benson."

Tony nodded his agreement. "Yeah, great. Thanks."

Vince introduced me. "I wanted to introduce my dinner guest this evening. This is Ashley Newton, my new assistant."

I exchanged seated greetings with the pair.

Nancy's handshake was firm and confident, Tony's less so.

"Ashley and I knew each other growing up in California." Vince told them. "Nancy, I thought you could interview Ashley in a month or two and do a short character piece for some filler when you need it later."

Nancy nodded politely. She didn't seem thrilled to be assigned a fluff piece on the boss's assistant.

Vince continued. "Something along the lines of a woman coming up the ranks, learning from the bosses she's worked for, and finally being promoted into management training—a women's empowerment piece of sorts. Ashley here is about to get a big promotion."

I had no idea where Vince was going with this, but I smiled and nodded, playing along. Inside I was almost ready to upchuck my dinner.

Nancy looked at me, and her smile turned from forced to genuine. Vince's "women's empowerment" comment seemed to have done the trick.

"We'd love to."

As a woman working in a male-dominated field, I could see her relishing a piece about women succeeding in the workplace.

"Maybe you could get a five-second shot of us now?" Vince suggested. "You know, a mentoring session. Nothing much."

A few guests at a neighboring table were staring, probably having recognized Nancy.

Tony hefted the camera to his shoulder.

Vince was really going to do this.

"I'll have to check with the manager," Nancy said.

Vince shook his head. "Already cleared it."

"Yes, ma'am," our waiter, Stu, said. He had come up behind them and waited. "If we could just keep it brief, that would be appreciated."

Vince returned to his seat across from me.

This was my chance to escape, but before I could, the light from Tony's camera came on.

I kicked Vince under the table.

He winced, but recovered quickly.

"I'm not sure this is a good idea right now," I told him.

Vince had painted me into an inescapable corner.

He winked at me. "Sure it is. It will just take a second."

I couldn't stay, but I also couldn't run. I took a breath and tried to calm my racing heart.

"It will just be one question," Vince told Nancy.

"In, three, two, one, go," Nancy counted down.

Vince looked straight into my eyes, and those dimples reappeared as he smiled. "Ashley, will you accept the promotion?"

At least he hadn't ambushed me about Jacinda. I had no play here except the one he had maneuvered me into. "Thank you, Mr. Benson. I'd love to. But what if it doesn't turn out the way you expect?" He wouldn't understand my question until later.

He extended his hand across the table to shake. "Welcome to the team. I have every confidence in you. Things will work out just fine."

I took his hand, and we shook.

"Wrap," Nancy said.

Tony's camera light went off.

Nancy handed her card to me: *Nancy Sanchez.* "In a few months, then."

I lifted my wine glass. "Look forward to it." At least now I knew her last name.

Tony lowered the camera, and I took a big slug of wine. I needed it to calm my nerves. Actually, I needed something much stronger, and more than a single swallow.

"Enjoy the rest of your dinner," Vince told the news pair, who retreated to their table.

After they were out of earshot, I had to ask. "Promotion?"

He smirked. "We're buying a footwear division, and I need help. You'd be a natural."

"I've got no experience with anything like that."

He reached across to touch my hand.

The same electric shock hit me as at our previous dinner. A dangerous feeling of warmth crept up my arm.

"I have faith in you, Ashley."

I couldn't tell him his faith was misplaced, and that I'd be gone as soon as he was cuffed.

"That makes one of us."

He lifted a piece of steak. "The deal doesn't close for another three months. Plenty of time to get comfortable with the idea. Now, how much do you know about outdoor footwear?" He licked his lips before taking the meat into his mouth.

For just a second, I allowed myself to wonder if those lips tasted as good as they had those many years ago.

We talked through the rest of dinner about the shoe and boot business he was buying, as if nothing had happened tonight.

Before dessert arrived, I looked over. The news duo had left. This whole episode had illuminated another side to Vince. As puppetmaster he enjoyed pulling his various strings to get people to do what he wanted: Nancy Newslady to run a story he dreamed up, and me to take on a role I hadn't been hired for, just on a whim. He probably didn't see how his assistant getting promoted to run a division would be perceived. Come on, how common was that? Not that I would be around that long anyway...

Vince acted as if I were a prize employee, grooming me for greatness and completely unaware that I was instead the federal agent sent to investigate him and put him in jail.

And he still couldn't take no for an answer. Nonetheless, I found myself liking the charming man who explained my new job to me. Playing the part of happy employee at dinner with the boss was easier by the minute.

This reminded me of the Bond film *Casino Royale*. I had now bet all-in, and everything I had hoped to accomplish at the Bureau was riding on this: the bet that I could catch him, seal the case, and exit undetected.

But if I did win, what did I also lose? I could still hope the intel on him was false, and he really was the same Vince I'd known so long ago. That could be a win too.

Now the stakes felt ten times higher, but I was committed. It was all or nothing—game on.

"You're not listening," Vince said, catching me contemplating my fate.

"I'm sorry. It's late."

"What were you thinking about?"

"I was wishing I wasn't in this predicament."

He finished the wine in his glass. "Not me. For nine years I've wished I hadn't been a jerk. And now I have you back again. It's a miracle."

"You don't *have* me," I spat. I was *not* a plaything, or anybody's possession.

He put his hands up. "Sorry. Not what I meant. I just... Let me put it this way: seeing you come through my door on Wednesday made me happy."

His words mirrored my feelings, but I wouldn't admit that to him. "So we're clear?" I asked.

His shame gave me the upper hand for the moment.

"Crystal," he replied.

His guilt could be my one piece of leverage over him, if I used it wisely. And now wasn't the time. "Thanks. I was glad to see you too."

We went back to discussing shoes and boots.

I wasn't going to fail like Liz had.

～

VINCENT

AFTER DINNER I WAS GREETED BY OUR DOORMAN, CARL, AS I WALKED through the glass doors into the lobby of my building on Tremont Street.

Originally I'd chosen a house in a secluded section of Brookline past Boston University, but I hadn't liked the extra time it cost me getting to the offices downtown.

Liam Quigley, my boss's brother, had encouraged me to look at an opening here when it came available, and now he and I had the two penthouse suites atop the building.

I entered the elevator and punched the button for the twenty-sixth floor.

Upstairs, I opened the condo door and was greeted by Rufus. There'd been a backyard at the house in Brookline, and maybe that was better for a dog his size, but here I had the services of a dog walker to take Rufus out, and the Common, our city's version of a downtown park, was just across the street. He had the black color and brains of his Labrador father, the size of his Great Dane mother, and the appetite of both combined.

I couldn't let him loose to run, but at least it had grass instead of concrete.

I shucked off my jacket and poured a tumbler of scotch before settling into the couch. Rufus put his head on my knee, and I gladly gave in to his demands to be petted. My dog loved me and didn't care if I was rich or poor, so long as I could afford to feed him.

The scotch slowly warmed my stomach as I drank. I pulled up the photo of that note again.

"Who the hell are you?" I asked the empty room. "You're a coward, ya know that?"

I was only half finished with my drink when I composed my message to Staci.

ME: I can't make it Monday - sorry

Staci would be glad to get the text and not have to make the decision herself. If the writer of the note was to be believed, even meeting me for dinner posed a risk.

I got up to refresh my tumbler with more of the amber liquid. I also threw a chew across the room for Rufus, who quickly located it and lay down, grasping it between his front paws, to start gnawing.

I put the phone back in my pocket. The note writer would reveal his identity sooner or later.

"Who do you think it is?" I asked Rufus.

My question didn't merit diverting his attention from the chew.

I leaned back into the couch and closed my eyes. The memory of tonight played against my eyelids. I'd fucked up my choice of words.

"You don't have me," Ashley had snapped, and the defiance in her eyes had been unmistakable. She didn't feel the attraction anymore.

And she had a boyfriend. A boyfriend with a gun.

I'd lost Ashley once—been stupid enough to walk away. I was richer than sin, but the one thing I couldn't buy was a time machine to go back and make it right with her. I had learned from my mistake, but that had been a costly lesson. Discovering the woman she had grown up to be made me realize just *how* costly.

Whenever Ashley walked into my office, or I walked by her desk, the electricity in the air was palpable—at least to me. I could feel the pull.

But I had to face the fact that wishing for something didn't make it real.

I pulled my wallet out of my pocket and retrieved the photo hidden inside. I gazed at it for a minute.

Wishing can't make it come true.

Rufus interrupted my musing, nuzzling my hand to get a scratch behind his ears. No matter how much I screwed up, at least he was always glad to see me.

After scratching him for a minute, I sent him on his way. I replaced the picture safely behind my license, where I'd kept it all these years.

CHAPTER 17

ASHLEY

It was seven o'clock Saturday morning, and I'd taken the MBTA train to Central Square and walked the few blocks to Waffle Castle. I'd chosen this as one of the alternative meeting sites because it was close to John's place—not that it mattered anymore with him sent to New Haven. This morning's debriefing had to be early because Vince expected me at work today. Again.

I pushed open the door and headed for the back.

Liz was waiting with a cup of coffee and scrolling through her phone. She put the phone away as I walked up.

"So?" she asked as soon as I sat.

Her question was obviously about her problem: the software she'd installed on Vince's computer. With Liz, everything was always about her.

I didn't have a chance to respond before the waitress arrived to take our order.

I chose the Belgian waffle, butter on the side.

Liz chose the strawberry-stuffed French toast. The picture of it in the menu looked absolutely scrumptious, like a thousand-calorie bomb even without the extra whipped cream Liz asked for.

After the waitress retreated, I gave my report. "I deleted the copy of DarkGecko7 on his computer."

Liz let out an audible breath and relaxed into her seat. "No problems?"

Of course there had been problems, but not ones I was going to tell her about. My ongoing problem was that everything now relied on me keeping the Bureau in the dark about what Liz had forced me to do.

I took a breath. I was successfully ensconced undercover in the executive offices at Covington and was going to have access to everything we needed. That's all that was important.

"It wasn't easy, but I got it done," I told her. "You owe me." I fixed her with a grimace. "And I collect with interest." I had no intention of letting her forget this.

"Sure," she responded. "Anything, anytime." She sipped her water. "Why do we have to meet this early anyway?"

"And there's more. They already tracked you back to the *Daily Inquisitor*, so you better have that backstopped well. Their security department isn't full of mall cops."

She nodded. "No problem. It'll stand up."

"It better, because if it doesn't, I'm blown too. They got a picture of us meeting Thursday. I had to admit I'd met you before and say you were pumping me for information."

Liz looked nervously out the window. "You shouldn't have let them follow you."

I barely kept from shouting. "You shouldn't have gotten caught on the first day."

"If this blows up, it'll be because they followed you to the meet."

"If this blows up it'll be because you planted the keylogger, not because of me," I spat.

I wasn't taking the fall for her.

She pulled back. "I'll admit that wasn't my best moment."

I didn't comment again on how stupid she'd been. "I'm due at work this morning."

Her eyebrows went up. "Saturday?"

"He works weekends, and therefore so do I."

She shook her head. "Glad you got this assignment then, instead of me."

She'd already changed the history in her mind to omit the part where I was filling in because she blew the assignment and almost the whole case.

She set her voice recorder on the table and started it.

I gave a very quick description of the events of the last day and a half before our food arrived and I reached over to turn off the recorder.

Her breakfast looked even bigger than the photo in the menu had.

"I also had dinner with him last night," I added. I hadn't put that on the recorder.

She raised an eyebrow. "Anything to report there?"

I cut into my waffle. "Nothing of substance. We reminisced about old times, and I made solid progress gaining his trust."

It wasn't complete, but it was good enough for the Bureau.

"I didn't get invited to dinner."

"That's because you were stupid enough to get caught and thrown out in less than a day," I told her.

She wisely decided not to take up the argument.

One day, after this was all over and there was no danger of blow-back, I'd let her know how badly she'd fucked up, and exactly how I felt about it. Today was not that day.

While we ate, Liz prattled on about another case she and her partner, Frank, had been assigned. She didn't like the paperwork involved.

Tough shit.

She devoured her massive plate in record time.

I needed to get to the Covington building, and she mentioned a yoga class. She picked up the bill, per protocol for these meetings. I couldn't have a receipt on my person linking me back to this location for someone to accidentally find.

Liz left first, and I followed a few minutes later.

I reached the Covington building after a quick ride on the MBTA Red Line back into town. I swiped in and found Vince's door open when I reached the top floor, but he wasn't in his office.

Even though I'd had coffee with Liz, I followed my usual routine of stopping by the coffee machine to make myself a cup before starting work. I had no idea who outside of Vince might be around, so I had to follow best practices. That included sticking to a routine, which for me meant coffee first thing in the morning.

Back at my desk, I was a half hour into the same massive spreadsheet as yesterday when footfalls approached.

"Ashley?"

I turned to find Mason, the strategic marketing VP, walking in with surprise written across his face.

"Uh, is Vince here?" he asked before poking his head in the office to check for himself.

"Door was open, but I haven't seen him yet."

A minute later, Vince's office line rang, and I answered it.

"Vincent Benson's office, may I help you?"

An exasperated breath came across the line. "Where is he? He's not answering his cell," the woman demanded.

"Sorry, he's not in the office at the moment. Can I give him a message?"

After a pause she said, "Just tell him Staci can't make the trip to LA to meet his family, and I'll talk to him later."

A knot formed in my stomach. "Certainly, Staci. Should I have him call you?"

Her tone calmed somewhat. "No. I'll call him later."

I wrote out the message and put it on Vince's desk.

Staci was obviously the girlfriend. Who else would he be taking to meet the family?

VINCENT

MY PHONE RANG TWICE ON THE SHELF BY THE WINDOW.

I ignored it and kept running. The treadmill screen registered eleven miles, only one more to go in my simulated two laps of the Central Park running loop.

I saw his reflection in the window before I heard him.

"Hey," Mason shouted over the noise of the treadmill in the otherwise empty gym. He stomped up to the front of my machine. "I saw Ashley upstairs."

I nodded. "Yeah." I kept my pace steady. I wasn't letting him cut my time short this morning.

"I thought you were going to get rid of her." His statement had an accusatory tone, like I hadn't carried out a duty I owed him.

"I said I'd *handle* it."

His eyes went wide. "Have you lost your mind?"

I kept running and ignored the insult.

"What are you thinking? We can't have her hanging around now that we know she has a connection to the *Inquisitor*."

"I'm keeping her." The distance remaining on my display slowly ticked down.

"But we agreed yesterday—"

I raised my hand to stop him and pulled the safety key out of the treadmill, stopping it. "We didn't agree on anything."

"But it's insanity to give her access to the top floor."

I stepped down. "I trust her."

The comment set him back. "I dunno... It doesn't matter. It's still stupid."

"I know her. She won't be a problem."

He laughed. "That's your dick talking."

I took two quick paces toward him. "I know what I'm doing, and it's my decision."

He stepped back. "I still think it's stupid."

The man didn't know when to quit.

I'd made it clear we weren't discussing this further, but his fatal flaw popped right out again. He always wanted to have the last word, and usually I didn't mind, but today was different.

"She stays, and that's not up for debate." I stepped into his space. "Is that clear, Mason?"

He swallowed. "Sure, crystal clear." He opened his mouth to continue the argument, but controlled himself and stayed silent for once.

I got back on the machine and started it up again.

He left, and I returned to running.

After the treadmill's display ticked over to twelve point two miles,

I decided on another mile to make it half-marathon distance this morning. The extra time to cool off after Mason's attack would be good.

My phone chimed with a text, but I kept going. At the end of my run, I discovered two missed calls from Staci and a text.

Staci: I can't make the trip

I stepped off the machine and dialed her number.

She picked up after one ring, no doubt expecting my call. "Vince, I'm sorry. I can't—I can't go. I just can't."

"What's the problem?" I asked.

She hesitated. "I met someone."

Her statement surprised the hell out of me. "You know that doesn't bother me."

"But it would bother him," she said.

There was something off about the tone of her voice.

"I won't be doing any more Mondays either," she added.

So this is what it felt like, being dumped? I wasn't used to being the one told there wasn't going to be another meeting. I'd always been the one to end a relationship. Not that this was a relationship—clearly it wasn't—but it still stung.

"I hope he's a good guy. Staci, you deserve the best. You know that."

"He is. Thanks for understanding. He's flying me to Rome."

I wished her well again, and we hung up.

It didn't do any good to pry, but I didn't believe her. Staci had always been as anti-relationship as me. This was most likely due to that goddamned fucking note. The note writer was fucking up my life again.

I hadn't been looking forward to this trip back home, but it was necessary.

Now, with Staci backing out, I was stuck.

Barb, my other occasional companion, was a nonstarter. She wouldn't and couldn't act the part the way Staci could.

Coming without a girl on my arm was also not a viable plan.

Everything about getting Dad's approval to come back to the company revolved around him judging me to be more mature.

In his antiquated view, being single was a mark of immaturity.

Now I was fucked.

What was I going to do?

On the way to the shower, my phone rang again. The screen showed my father's face.

Answering his call could wait until after lunch. It was never good to talk to him unprepared.

~

ASHLEY

A LITTLE WHILE LATER, MASON RETURNED FROM HIS VINCE HUNT. "HE'S in the gym wearing out his knees. He'll be up in a while." His tone was curt, and he disappeared into his office without lingering.

My fake SWAT-team boyfriend had worked his magic a little too well. Mason had gone from flirtatious to downright cold.

Vince arrived before long, his hair wet from a shower.

"You run every morning?" I asked, already knowing the answer from Anita.

"Pretty much. Except when a customer meeting gets in the way. Bring your stuff tomorrow."

"Stuff?" I asked, leaving out the more obvious question about Sunday work.

"You ran cross country at Tufts. You must still have something you can run in. You can join me."

"Maybe."

He vanished into his office. He poked his head back out. "Please."

"Okay." It wasn't like it was a date or anything; it was just running together.

Sports hadn't come up in our dinner conversation. He had done some background research, or his security guy had told him.

Just before lunchtime, I entered the final set of numbers on the spreadsheet task he'd assigned and emailed the file to him.

"Ash, come in here," he called from his office.

I grabbed pen and paper and entered.

"This isn't right," he said. "I need all the quarterly detail."

"It's all there."

He took a breath. "This summary sheet is fine, but it's not enough."

I huffed and rounded the desk. "Let me show you."

He rolled his chair to the side.

When I grabbed the mouse to click on one of the detail tabs, my arm brushed his, and the sparks shot through me again. Proximity to him fogged my brain, and it took a second to focus on what I meant to say.

"The tabs down here each contain quarterly data that backs into the annual summaries on the front page."

"That's smart," he said, his delectable tone enveloping me like a warm breeze.

I stood and increased my distance from him. "They carry to hidden columns on the front sheet."

"Show me."

Leaning over again, I felt his eyes on me, heating me to the core. I flipped back to the front sheet and expanded the hidden columns. "Here."

He moved toward me, and I could feel his body heat.

"Where?" he asked.

I blinked a few times to clear my head. I moved the mouse to the columns and highlighted them.

He leaned in, and his shoulder met mine. The heat scorched my skin beneath the fabric and welded me to him, unable to move away. I could only wonder if he felt it too.

"I see," he said slowly before leaning back.

Instantly I missed the heat of his touch.

"That's really smart."

"You said that already." I let go of the mouse and stood.

His eyes held mine briefly with a flash of something feral. He pointed to the entrance. "Close the door."

I walked over and did as he asked. I waited by the door, unsure what was coming next.

"Come back over here."

As I walked back toward his desk, his eyes traveled the length of me, appraising me.

From the look in his eyes, I half expected, half hoped his next words would tell me to sit in his lap, or unbutton something, or bend over—anything that would show he felt this too.

Instead he said, "Take a seat," his tone businesslike, impersonal.

I sat and waited.

"This project..." He motioned to his computer. "The last one Sophia did took her twice as long."

Getting on the wrong side of the other assistants would be a bad move. "I'm sure the one she did was harder."

"Right," he said dismissively. "Good job, Ash."

I had to admit, his praise felt good. "What's next?"

He pointed to another two stacks on the credenza. "The left-hand one first."

I gathered up the top several inches of the stack, opened the door, and carried the papers to my desk. I was going to die of boredom if this was all he had me doing.

The moment between us had passed, and I still couldn't decipher if he'd felt it too.

CHAPTER 18

Vincent

When I returned to the condo at the end of the day on Saturday, Rufus greeted me at the door.

"Want a go for a walk?" I asked.

His tail wagging accelerated. That was a yes, as always.

I put the Amazon box I'd picked up downstairs and my briefcase down on the table as I went to change and gather up his retractable leash.

Stopping at the door before we left, I changed my mind and opened the box, slipping the book that had arrived under my arm as we went out.

Across the street, it didn't take Rufus long to fill up my blue doggie bag, which I deposited in the trash.

I'd been watching, and today, as for the last several days now, there had been no sign of the suited man who'd followed me last week—a good omen.

Rufus and I walked on the grass so I could let out his leash for him to roam without tripping anybody. It was still light enough, so I began to read the book Ashley had been reading as Rufus sniffed here and there. I was soon caught up in Juliet and Dalton's story. Dalton was arrogant and sort of a jerk. It seemed that's how all of America saw rich people—so unfair.

Rufus and I made it back across Tremont to the building without him scaring anybody to death, which had happened before.

"Mr. Benson," Carl greeted me as we walked up. "Was he a good boy?"

"Always," I responded.

"Jimmy has been walking him regularly."

"Thanks, Carl."

I'd asked him to keep an eye out to see that Rufus was getting all the walks he was supposed to.

Upstairs, I locked the door, let Rufus off the leash, and prepared his dinner.

Checking the fridge and freezer, things were pretty sparse, and I hadn't stopped to pick up *my* dinner. "It looks like you're eating better than me tonight."

Rufus didn't stop eating to respond.

I moved on to the pantry and decided a can of baked beans and a can of Vienna sausages was the best I could do for tonight, unless I was going to subsist on only ice cream.

While the contents of the cans were warming, I opened the book again on page sixty-seven.

One page later, things got super interesting, and I took a seat at the table. If this is what Ashley was reading all the time, her boyfriend was in for a treat—she wasn't the demure wallflower I took her for.

I kept turning the addictive pages, until I noticed the smell.

"Fuck."

I raced to the stove and pulled the pan off the heat. Some of the beans had burned on the bottom. I spooned the edible top portion onto a plate and, with spoon and napkin in hand, returned to the table to read.

By the end of the evening, I'd gotten through the book. Dalton had saved Juliet, and they were on their happy honeymoon.

After taking Rufus downstairs to take care of business, I retreated to bed with my new book, and some tissue to clean up with.

I went to sleep after jerking off to the desk sex scene, envisioning myself pounding into Ashley again and again. I had page sixty-eight burned into my brain.

~

ASHLEY

TONIGHT I WAS HOME BEFORE DARK. AT LEAST SATURDAY WASN'T AS LATE a day as during the week. Though I did have to go in tomorrow too, it seemed.

I gathered up my running things and shoes and put the packed gym bag by the door so I didn't forget it in the morning.

I decided to make a homemade dinner in my own kitchen for a change, and a glass of wine would be my reward.

As I began to cook, I thought back over my Saturday in the office. I'd managed to get a few minutes to access some of the file cabinet records after Mason had left. But so far nothing of interest had popped up.

The investigation of Vince's records was going to be slow-going, but being upstairs around him was anything but. The man was a dynamo, constantly active, and he had a team that worked well together. He engendered respect the old fashioned way—not through the occasional Caesar moments SAC White was always trying.

I hadn't had much direct interaction with Ben Murdoch in security, but he struck me as extremely competent, which was worrisome, especially if he dug harder into Liz's cover story, or mine.

My phone rang, startling me. The hot pouch of rice I'd pulled out of the microwave started sliding off the plate. I grabbed for it.

"Fucking shit." I pulled my hand back from the steaming bag before getting a serious burn.

A minute under the cold water of the sink and the burn subsided. *I should know better.*

The phone had stopped ringing and sent the caller to voicemail.

Before I could get back to the phone, the oven timer went off, calling me to pull the filet of sole out. Once the oven was off and dinner was on a plate, I took the food and my phone to the table.

Dinner smelled fantastic, and I savored a bite of the fish with lemon-dill sauce before turning my attention to the phone.

My sister Rosemary had called, so I dialed her back and put the phone on speaker so I could continue to eat. I smiled. Talking to Rose was a treat.

"You back from the bush yet?" I asked when she picked up.

"One day back to civilization for a shower and some real food, then back where we belong."

It was odd to hear her say the bush was where she belonged. It had always seemed more her boyfriend's calling than hers.

"So what's up?"

"Just calling to see how my baby sister is doing. Haven't talked to you in almost a week. Shoot any bad guys lately?"

I finished chewing. "You know discharging my weapon is a bad thing, right?" The Bureau viewed *avoiding* a gun battle as an accomplishment.

"So have you caught your boyfriend yet?"

"One, he's an ex-boyfriend, and two, no, not yet. But I will."

She gasped. "I knew you were mad at him, but isn't this taking it a little far? I thought you were going to turn it down."

"I didn't start this. It came down from the DOJ."

"That's twisted. Can't you get out of it?"

I wasn't admitting the whole situation with White to anybody, not even Rose. "No, the other girl blew her chance, and I'm stuck with it."

"How are you coping? It's got to be fucked up trying to put away somebody you know, especially with your history."

She had that part right. The history made everything upside down.

I sighed. "It's okay so far. And they might even be wrong about Vince."

"Why investigate him if you're not sure he's a criminal?"

"We investigate to find out; that's why. Like I said, this came down from the DOJ. They're calling the shots."

"How will you handle it if he's dirty?"

I had an easy answer to that one. "I follow my oath and do my job."

It was the only possible answer. That choice was black and white—no possibility for gray.

"Maybe it won't come to that."

I took a sip of the wine I'd poured. "I hope not."

"You're still hot for the guy, aren't you? I can hear it in your voice."

"It's been nine years," I complained.

"My God, you are."

"Am not."

It wasn't a total lie. I felt an attraction, but I couldn't have the hots for a guy who didn't care about me, and who I might be destined to cuff.

"Are too. I don't have to see your face to know. Now you're really in a fucked-up situation."

"Yeah," I admitted.

She was right. This was going to be a battle of my hormones against my gray matter.

"If he's not dirty, do you have another chance with him?"

"Not a clue. He apologized for before—"

"Well, he should."

My sister had my back on that one.

"But," I continued, "he has a girlfriend, I think."

"Think or know?"

"I can't exactly ask him."

"Well, somebody there has to know," she said.

Asking around was the obvious answer, but wouldn't it seem odd with me working for him?

CHAPTER 19

ASHLEY

SUNDAY MORNING I SLAPPED MY ALARM CLOCK SO HARD IT LANDED ON THE floor, but at least it shut up. Rolling out of bed, I padded to the bathroom for a shower. The first time I'd showered here, the water had turned cold before I'd finished. I'd complained, and the manager had promised to upgrade the water heater when the budget allowed, but that hadn't happened yet. Now I managed by turning off the water while I shampooed and conditioned.

I hadn't slept well last night—Vince had dominated my thoughts. I couldn't get his face or his smile out of my head. Those dimples tormented me. But worst of all, my reaction to his touch scared me. Being unable to control my feelings could be dangerous. My oath required me to put my feelings aside and deal with the facts. In the end, the facts had to rule. I was all about rules. I could hold out hope that the DOJ source was wrong about Vince, but so far that's all it was: hope.

There had been dozens of virile young studs after me at Quantico, and none of them had engendered this kind of reaction. No boy in college ever had either. And there was the problem: they had all been *boys,* and Vince was the very definition of a man. It was as if he used aftershave of pure testosterone, or one of those poorly understood pheromones the magazines wrote about. That had to be it—a chemical that explained this and made it not my fault.

When I finished my shower, I dressed quickly, slung my gym bag over my shoulder, and left. On the way I picked up a breakfast sandwich and coffee at Starbucks.

Vince was already upstairs when I arrived. *Workaholic* was way too mild a description for him. The rest of the executive area was quiet and dark, as it should be on a Sunday morning.

It was lunchtime before Vince came out and ordered me to join him running. His wording didn't leave room for disagreement—not that I wanted to offer any.

We both got changed, and I followed him to the elevator.

When we arrived at the gym, it was immediately clear that, like everything else at Covington, this was a spare-no-expense facility.

He mounted a treadmill, clipped the safety key to his shorts, pressed a few buttons on the display, and the machine started whirring away.

I stopped watching his muscled legs and climbed up on the one next to him, but I was unable to figure out the controls. There were too many choices. I needed go and stop, nothing more complicated.

Vince paused his machine. "Let me help you get started. First you select the course here." He scrolled through some selections and ended on one that said *Boston Common Loop.* "Then we set the starting speed here."

A moment later the thing whirred to life, and I almost lost my footing, but I got caught up as Vince returned to his run. Just when I thought I had the hang of it, the machine changed angle. I stepped on the front cover, lost my balance, and it spit me out onto the floor behind it.

Vince jumped off his machine again. "You okay?" He rushed over. "Are you hurt?"

My ass was sore, but that seemed to be all. "Just my pride. This isn't running. I've done a lot of it, and this isn't it."

"You'll get the hang of it," he said, watching me get up.

I brushed off my butt. "No way. That thing doesn't like me, and the feeling's mutual."

This was obviously a killer robot masquerading as a piece of exercise equipment.

"What's wrong with running outside on solid ground anyway? At least outside you don't have a machine tripping you."

He gestured toward the door. "Okay. Outside then."

I followed him out of the gym and away from the malevolent robots.

Once on the street, he turned toward the Common, and I followed. The route required several stops at intersections, as well as dodging pedestrians who were looking down at their phones and not paying attention.

In short order we crossed Tremont at Park Street and got on the perimeter trail in the Common, where it was wide enough to run side by side.

"Done much running since school?" he asked.

I caught him looking over, checking out my boobs. I straightened up. "A short run in the morning on occasion is all I've had time for. And I chicken out when there's snow on the ground."

"That's the advantage of using an indoor treadmill."

"But then you have to breathe all that stale building air instead of being out here in the open," I replied. Outside was always better.

"You may have a point there," he said, looking over with a sly grin.

I made a show of watching a jogger going the other way, but really I was checking out Vince's powerful legs, and that nice ass. Thank God for short running shorts. There was no harm in looking, was there? If men could do it, why couldn't women?

A kid on a skateboard coming the other way decided he owned the middle of the path.

Vince dodged to the right, and the skateboarder went between us. "It's dangerous out here," he said.

"Sometimes you give way; sometimes they do. That's life."

We ran halfway around the Common.

He stopped at the hot dog vendor by the Charles Street gate. "How 'bout lunch?"

"I didn't bring any money," I countered.

"I'm buying."

He could certainly afford it, and I wasn't too proud to accept. "Sure, boss."

He ordered a polish dog, and I chose a simple hot dog.

A whiff of eucalyptus from his hair wafted my way as he leaned in front of me to pick out his water.

After adding condiments, he chose a nearby bench.

Sitting next to him, though not too close, reminded me of the time we'd spent down by Venice Beach a lifetime ago in LA.

"Has Mason hit on you yet?" he asked.

The question came out of the blue.

I couldn't stifle my giggle. "He tried, but I shut him down with my SWAT team boyfriend story."

His face lit up. "Story?"

I licked a bit of mustard that threatened to drip off the end of my hot dog. "I told him my boyfriend had SWAT training, kicking down doors and shooting people." I turned to give my shit-eating grin. "Dynamite couldn't have gotten him to leave faster."

He almost spit out his food laughing. "Not true?"

I shook my head. "No, but it works every time."

The smile that grew on his face brought out the dimples.

"Mustard," he said, wiping his finger on the corner of my mouth.

His touch was electric. "Thanks," I mumbled with my mouth full. Once I swallowed, I continued. "Once they hear about a boyfriend who carries a gun, they don't stick around long."

"That just means they lack self-confidence."

It had always seemed like more than a lack of confidence to me. "I guess."

I took a breath. "What about you?" I asked.

"Nothing serious," he said before sipping his water. "You shouldn't believe any of what you read in the tabloids."

My heart sped up. Perhaps I had a chance, if I dared. But there had been public pictures of him with a host of other women, all of them drop-dead gorgeous. And there was also the girl he'd mentioned who'd gotten the note.

After a moment I asked the question I really wanted to: "And the girlfriend who got the note? What about her?"

He didn't look at me. "I don't expect to be seeing her again."

"Scared, huh?"

"Seems that way. Staci Baxter is a friend. I was helping her prepare a presentation for a bank loan application when she got that note."

"Staci Baxter the model?" I asked with more than a hint of surprise.

He adjusted his grip on his polish dog. "Ex model. Now she's got a clothing line, and I was helping her line up financing to expand."

Her name landed on me like a stack of bricks. The Staci who had left the message yesterday was world famous. She'd been on the cover of *Sports Illustrated*. She was a twelve on every man's ten-point scale. How could any woman compare to her? Tall, perfect body, perfect teeth, perfect hair, perfect skin—perfect everything. I gulped a slug of water and caught another whiff of his eucalyptus scent as I put the bottle down.

My heart raced. "So you're unattached?" I asked outright.

"Relationships aren't my thing," he responded.

That deflated my balloon.

～

VINCENT

I'D BEEN ENJOYING HER PERKY SMILE WHILE WE ATE, UNTIL HER SHOULDERS slumped at my answer.

"Oh. Me neither," she said.

My spirit soared. I could sense the bullshit in her reply. I had a chance with her after all. *She doesn't have a boyfriend.*

She looked down at the pavement.

The run with Ashley had been half nirvana—even better than I'd imagined—and half torture as I'd tried to keep from staring at her tits while they bounced with every stride under that tight tank top. Now her legs drew my imagination. I wondered how they would feel wrapped around me.

I couldn't take back what I'd said about relationships, but I could try to fix it. "How about dinner tonight, say seven?" I asked.

Her face brightened, but confusion clouded it. "I thought you said—"

I stopped her. "Dinner? It's a simple question."

Her evil smirk appeared. "Is that an order?"

"No. I'm asking Ashley Newton, not my PA."

Her feistiness was one of her more endearing traits.

Her face gave away the answer before her mouth delivered the words. "I'd love to." She took the last of her hot dog in a big bite. And wiped her lips.

I followed suit, devouring my polish dog and trying to hide the smile I felt growing across my face. I leaned back and placed my arm along the bench behind her.

She relaxed, making contact with my arm—contact that sent sparks through my veins.

She slid just slightly toward me. "Have you ever wondered?"

She didn't finish the sentence. She didn't need to.

Knowing she'd had those same questions was a gift from heaven.

I slid my hand to her shoulder. "Hundreds of times," I said.

Would I finally get another chance with Ashley?

The look in her eyes as she turned to me answered my question and sent a jolt to my cock.

She cares.

I pulled my arm back and stood. "Ready?" I needed to get going before my condition got out of control and became obvious to everyone. I dumped my trash and carried the half-full water bottle.

Ashley made her trip to the trash and followed.

We resumed our run around the Common's outer path.

"You up for two laps?" I asked as we made the turn at the southern corner.

She pulled ahead. "If you can keep up."

I stayed back for a minute, enjoying the view and looking forward to having my hands on that ass. When I caught back up to her, I limited myself to the occasional glance to my side. Her tits called to me with each bounce.

When we made it back to the building, I considered it for a moment, but I controlled my tongue and didn't suggest a shower together.

She deserved to have me behave myself—at least for the moment.

The smile she sent my way as she entered the women's locker room convinced me she would have said yes.

Once in the shower, the thought of her in here with me had my cock at attention, begging to show her how I'd missed her. I turned the shower cold to deflate my erection. Going upstairs with an obvious hard-on wouldn't do.

CHAPTER 20

ASHLEY

VINCE WAS ALREADY LOCKED BACK IN HIS OFFICE WHEN I GOT UPSTAIRS after my shower.

I spent the afternoon running through the spreadsheet work on autopilot while replaying our conversation in my head. No, he didn't have a serious girlfriend, and he'd asked about Mason hitting on me. That hadn't seemed to be coming from a protective-boss place.

That was all positive, but then he'd let slip that he didn't do relationships. He hadn't added the word *ever*, but he'd implied it.

If he didn't want a relationship, was dinner just a prelude to getting in my pants?

And what was wrong with that anyway?

I was all mixed up. It was my job to get as close to him as possible. The Bureau couldn't and wouldn't order me to sleep with a target. It was all wink-wink *whatever you're comfortable with*, and we won't ask, wink-wink.

Had I agreed to dinner as an FBI Special Agent, or as his ex-girlfriend? How could I separate the two?

My hormones were battling my brain cells, as I'd known they

would. Did he ask me to get close to me to influence my investigation? It couldn't be that, because he didn't know. Right?

That wasn't my first question, but my training said it should have been.

His door opened.

"I'm going for another run," he said.

"Again?"

"I need more miles to be ready." He meant the triathlon.

"Have fun," I called as he headed to the elevator.

A few minutes after I heard the door close, I slid through his office door and closed it. With nobody else on the floor, I'd finally get a chance to check this space. He worked so many hours that these opportunities were going to be rare.

The file cabinet was locked, and I didn't have a pick set with me.

I checked his center desk drawer; some idiots left the keys in their desks. A check of the center and top side drawers proved Vince was no idiot. But it did yield one interesting item: a copy of *Secretary to the Bazillionaire*, and from the splaying of the pages, it seemed he'd read it.

Anita?

The question didn't merit my time.

I pulled a stack of papers from the bottom of the brass multi-level organizer on the corner of the desk. I leafed through them one by one, turning them face down into a new pile after scanning them, to keep the same order.

That pile was a bust, so I repeated the procedure with the stack on the middle shelf. Once again the papers were routine, nothing of investigatory value, except a few handwritten pages about a meeting. I snapped shots of those with my phone. The top level held only a few papers and nothing of interest.

The desk blotter had a smooth, green leather surface, and I recalled an instructor recalling how he'd raised the impression of something written from a surface like this.

I couldn't see anything from this angle, so I moved around to the other side so I wouldn't be between the window's light and the blotter. I leaned over the desk, and started to make something out. I leaned farther, resting my chest on the wide, wooden desk to glance along the blotter's surface toward the window. I could see an area of writing in the corner.

"What are you doing?" It was Vince from behind me.

I froze. I hadn't heard him open the door. "I was just..."

An explanation escaped me. I stood and turned. Just like Liz, I'd fucked up. The pounding of my runaway heart in my ears was like a freight train.

"This wood feels so good. I was just..." I had turned into a babbling mess.

A wicked grin replaced the surprise on his face. "Page sixty-eight?" he asked.

My jaw dropped at his mention of the book. I saw my one chance to get out of this and took it.

I smiled and nodded.

He closed the door behind him. "Do you want me, Juliet?"

It was Dalton's line from the book.

In the book, Juliet was speechless, so I acted the same.

"Do you?" he asked again.

"Yes. I have since the day I started here." I copied Juliet's line, and it was no lie.

"Will you obey me?"

So far he had all of Dalton's dialog down pat.

I nodded, and I didn't have to act the part to add the smile that came to my face.

"Tell me."

"Yes."

He moved toward me. The bulge in his jeans was obvious. He pulled me to him, and his mouth claimed mine.

My lips parted, and our tongues danced with lustful abandon. I laced my fingers through his hair, pulling myself up and closer. I needed more of this. It was better than high school. As we continued, I realized this is what I'd dreamed of last night.

One hand grasped my ass and pulled me against his hardness, and the other moved to my breast, tracing the underside, then moving over my hardened nipple.

He smelled like the woods, with a hint of eucalyptus, and he tasted like sex and pure lust. Moist heat pooled between my thighs. I clawed at his back to pull us closer, the closeness I'd missed all these years.

His hand found its way under my shirt to my bra strap and undid it with a flick. He moved his hand inside the loose bra cup to cradle my breast, his thumb circling the hardened pebble of my nipple. His pinch sent a shiver through me.

I broke the kiss. "I've wanted this since the first day." Juliet's line matched my feelings.

"And you're going to get it."

He undid my pants and pulled them down, turning me to face the desk. So far he was following the script.

I spread my legs as far as the pants around my ankles would allow and leaned over the desk.

He went around the side and retrieved a condom—from his brief-case of all places. The bulge in his pants was huge, and I was about to find out why.

In school, I'd gone so far as to rub Vince through his jeans, but that was all. I stayed in position while he moved behind me. I heard the tear of the packet and turned to see his pants off. I gasped at the size of the monster he was sheathing—the grande burrito.

He pulled my shirt and bra up to my shoulders and pushed me forward onto the desk. The wood was cool against my hot breasts.

He pulled one of my legs up, wrestled the shoe off, and pulled my foot free of my pants.

I spread my legs farther to give him better access and lowered my hips to the desk. I was about to find out if the words of ecstasy on the pages matched the experience.

He positioned his tip at my wet entrance and pushed in a little.

I winced. He was bigger than anyone I'd had before. "Fuck me, Dalton. Fuck me hard," I said as Juliet.

With that, he started easing into my soaked heat, just a little farther each time, pulling more lubrication onto his length.

Every movement sent heated sparks through me.

With a final push, he was fully in me, his hips flush with mine.

I yelped when he slapped my butt. The spot burned for a second.

His thrusting grew more rapid, and the added force built waves of pleasure that crashed over me.

"Fuck me harder. Harder. Yeah, harder." I'd never understood the line in the book, but now I did, as he granted my wish. My nerve endings were on fire as I climbed toward the peak of my climax.

My moaning matched Vince's grunting as the animal in him took over. The slapping of flesh against flesh grew louder. The rushing of the blood in my ears joined the cacophony of our moans.

He pulled my hips back from the edge of the desk, and his fingers found my clit.

That wasn't in the book.

The sudden pressure on my sensitive nub took me to a level I'd never experienced before as his fingers stroked me to match his thrusts.

He pounded into me again, filling me beyond full, and a tweak of my clit sent fire through my veins and pushed me over into a sea of bliss. Fireworks played against my clenched eyelids, my walls contracted around him, and the spasms shook me. I cried out his name —Vince this time, not Dalton.

My legs shook as he continued, and with a groan he pounded out his release within me.

I was a limp, boneless heap on the desk, perspiration sticking my skin to the wood.

He leaned over me, but spared me his entire weight. "You deserve better," he said.

That wasn't a Dalton line either.

"That was fantastic," I told him. "I mean it. It's what I wanted." I wanted to be certain he knew I wasn't reciting from the book. He needed to know.

The pulsing of his cock within me slowly ebbed. "I missed you, too."

His words sounded heartfelt and warmed me.

Before I could respond, the sound of a vacuum cleaner starting up outside the door filled the office.

He jerked up and pulled out, hurrying to dispose of the condom in tissues from the box on his desk.

I stood and hooked my bra again. "Do they vacuum in here?" I asked softly.

He was trying to fit his still-engorged cock in his underwear. "Yup."

I finished adjusting my bra and shimmied into my pants.

He pulled his shoes on while I located the one of mine that had hidden under the desk.

I got it back on and was fully clothed when he opened the door for me. "Dinner. Don't forget dinner."

"Right. Dinner," I echoed, still trying to get my brain back in gear.

He followed me out of the office. "I need to get more running in."

"I think I'll head home, if that's okay."

"Sure. Pick you up at seven."

The janitor and his vacuum moved from the open space between my desk and Anita's into Vince's office.

I MADE IT BACK TO MY APARTMENT WITH MY BRAIN STILL TRYING TO process the afternoon's events. He'd caught me in his office, and I could have been on my way to Alaska, but somehow it had turned into an afternoon like none other—all due to Anita's book. I wasn't turning my nose up at romance novels ever again. This one had saved me.

The fire he'd ignited in me answered one question: I wanted Vincent Benson, even if only for a short time. I'd pushed him away before, but that wasn't happening again. No fucking way.

I set an alarm on my phone and slumped into the couch. When I closed my eyes, the prom played behind my eyelids. I hadn't dwelled on the event in years, and now I couldn't stop it from hijacking my brain.

What if he was taking advantage of me?

What if he wasn't?

What if I was taking advantage of him?

It didn't fucking matter.

CHAPTER 21

*A*SHLEY

THE ALARM ON MY PHONE QUACKED THAT IT WAS TIME TO GET READY FOR dinner—not just dinner, a dinner *date*, and a special one at that.

Just like with Juliet and Dalton in the book, the sex had preceded the date, all backwards, but it had kept me from botching the assignment. I don't know what I would have done if Vince hadn't decided I was leaning on his desk fantasizing about that book.

I would have to find a way to thank Anita.

Vince hadn't mentioned where we were going, but based on the last two establishments we'd visited, I knew it wouldn't be Sizzler.

I chose my best little black dress. I had curves that could rock a nice, tight LBD, and this one had a neckline to get Vince salivating— low enough to show I was braless for the evening. If he was taking me someplace nice, I was going to make the most of it.

I'd worn this dress exactly once, and what a waste that had been. Monty what's-his-name had been a dud of a blind date, but at least he'd only spilled his wine on himself, not me or my dress.

I added my favorite necklace: a small sapphire pendant. The chain was too short, so I switched it out for one that hung the stone nice and low, drawing the eye toward my assets. I didn't own matching earrings, so I settled for simple hoops instead of the small studs I always wore for field work.

I was so out of practice it took forever to do a decent job on my makeup, and the buzzer rang as I was finishing my mascara. I touched up the right eye before rushing to the door.

When I opened it, Vince took my breath away.

The man could wear the hell out of a nice suit, but at the office he always took his jacket off and avoided a tie. The only time I'd seen a tie on him was the afternoon a customer had come in to meet, and the tie had disappeared as soon as the customer left the floor. But tonight, he had a tie in full effect.

I could tell my dress was working, and my necklace placement had also done the trick. He looked me up and down with ravenous eyes, and his gaze paused perceptibly at my chest.

"Wow," he said. The hunger on his face said even more. "You look gorgeous this evening."

"And you look pretty good yourself. I see I even rate a tie." I reached up to straighten it and received a gratifying smile in return.

"Only the best for you, Kitten."

His use of my nickname melted me. Back in high school, for a brief time I'd been his soft and cuddly kitten, and I'd purred in his embrace. The memories washed over me like a warm Hawaiian wave.

"Ready?" he asked.

I gathered my clutch, locked the door, and followed him downstairs.

The purse was a present from Rosemary that I hadn't been able to use until tonight. It wouldn't accommodate my Glock, which my job required me to carry at all times. But tonight was the exception since I was undercover with an identity that wouldn't be armed.

In high school, Vince had driven a pretty standard car for a teenager, a Mustang. Tonight, when he pressed the key fob, the sleek red Ferrari at the curb flashed its lights and unlocked.

"Nice wheels."

He held the door open for me. "I wanted to impress you, Kitten."

"It's working." I slid in, holding the hem of my short dress down. When he started the engine, the sound was unlike anything I'd ever heard. Not only were the rich different, their cars weren't of this world either. The smell of leather upholstery and the surge of sudden acceleration as he punched the throttle completed the experience. I was not in Kansas anymore. Whether we were off to Oz or down the rabbit hole was yet to be seen, but tonight was destined to be unique.

"Where are we going?" I asked as he turned toward downtown.

"I know the owner at a nice Italian place," he said with a smirk.

The food at Vitaliano's had been superb; it would take a lot more than two dinners there to get bored with the place.

Driving through town, I could see necks crane to get a glimpse of our chariot. This was not your everyday conveyance, and eyeballs tracked us as we flew by. If only Rose could see me now.

When we arrived, the valet knew Vince's name.

Naturally.

Vince hustled around the car to open my door—a more gentlemanly act than I'd ever been afforded in this town. He guided me through the door with a light hand at the small of my back. The heat from that touch threatened to ignite my dress.

Once inside, we bypassed a crowd even bigger than the previous one at lunch to reach Angelica at the hostess desk.

She quickly showed us to a table.

I noticed something I hadn't paid attention to last time we were here: Vince's status in the community was evident by the several well-dressed businessmen who nodded their greeting to him as we passed. I was being escorted by a power player in this town.

After we ordered, all I could do was drink in the experience. This was all way above my GS-11 pay grade: exquisite food, expensive wine, and a ride in a car that cost more than many people's houses.

"How's the soup?"

Vince's simple question woke me. "Great. Even better than my aunt made." Aunt Michelle had made minestrone from scratch for us.

"How is your aunt, by the way?" It was an innocuous question. He couldn't have known about her death or the details.

I took a breath to calm myself. "She passed."

"Sorry to hear that. I liked her." He offered his hand across the table, and I took it. After this afternoon, the warmth of his touch threatened to fuse our hands together permanently. His eyes conveyed his sincerity.

"Thanks. She liked you too."

Aunt Michelle had not been happy to hear Vince and I had broken up, and it had been hard to lie to her about the particulars, but it wasn't anybody's business but mine.

He retrieved his hand to eat another bite of salad.

My brain didn't engage fast enough to stop the question that had haunted me since high school. "What happened with you and Cynthia?"

How can I be such a jerk?

His brow furrowed.

I regretted the words, but couldn't pull them back now. Maybe my subconscious was trying to screw things up with him.

Cynthia Powell had latched onto Vince after our breakup. Her reputation preceded her, and Vince probably got his fill from her of what I'd withheld.

"She tired of me after a while."

Thankfully he didn't elaborate. Knowing they hadn't lasted was all I needed, but it had been rude of me to ask. On reflection, I wished he'd said he'd tired of her instead.

Our waiter, Tony, interrupted the awkward silence to clear my soup and Vince's salad.

"Sorry," I said after the waiter left.

"No need. I don't have any secrets from you."

His words resonated in my heart. I certainly hoped that was true. With the way I felt this evening, it was going to be beyond hard to cuff him, if it came to that. I swatted that thought away. He was a good man; I'd always known that. I just had to fulfill my duty to investigate so I could return a clean report with a clear conscience. The Benson family was a solid one, and I had every reason to believe Vince was still the straight arrow he'd been when I knew him before.

Tony was back quickly with our main course: pollo al peperoncino for me and scallopine toscano for my date. The words rattled around my head for a moment, *my date*.

Just thinking of Vince as my date brightened my outlook. How many women in town, or in the state for that matter, could boast of being out with a man half as dashing, half as considerate, half as rich, and yes, half as virile as Vince looked tonight? Not many, for sure.

And tonight *I* was his date, not his employee.

I sat up straight with the confidence that thought brought me—a date I could honestly brag to my sister about. I was his *Kitten*.

"How is Rosemary?" he asked, shifting the conversation.

"She's doing well. She went into nursing."

"That's noble—a good calling."

I cut a piece of my chicken. "But long hours and worse conditions. She's working down in Australia right now with her boyfriend, helping Doctors Without Borders."

He finished chewing. "Like I said, noble. Nothing wrong with that."

"If you do it for the right reasons. I just want her to be happy."

"Maybe that's what makes her happy."

I nodded, not because I agreed, but because I couldn't tell where her drive ended and her boyfriend's expectations began.

We continued dinner, and I shifted the conversation to the Semaphore company he and Mason had been discussing.

Every time I looked at Vince, those dimples drew me in, and I saw something in his eyes, something from long ago that I'd missed terribly—a warmth that couldn't be faked. I was falling for him all over again, and in record time.

If I was honest with myself, he'd never left my heart. My feelings had merely been concealed by hurt and anger for a time, and then by distance and lack of contact.

When he laughed, I laughed. When he got serious, I listened intently. The man's magnetism was off the charts.

I'd spent a few minutes online earlier reading *Cosmo* articles on how to give head, something I'd never attempted. *Cosmo* said men really liked it. In college, I'd been asked, almost forced, but I always got out of it with some vigorous sex instead. But tonight I was going to try on Vince, and I wouldn't allow myself to fail. I smiled at the thought.

"What's so funny?" he asked.

"Oh, nothing."

Vince went on. Between mouthfuls he explained how much of a

feather in his cap it would be to get Semaphore under the Covington umbrella. It was clearly a top priority.

We finished our dinners, and Vince ordered key lime pie for us to split as a dessert. He'd remembered my favorite. So far his memory was infallible.

While we were waiting, an older man—slightly portly with thinning white hair and a matching mustache-and-goatee combination—walked up beside me and gave me an odd wink through his horn-rimmed glasses.

"Vincent. I knew I'd find you here," he boomed.

Vince's eyes went wide, and his face dropped momentarily before he jumped with a start and turned.

"Dad," he said, standing.

I stood as well.

I hadn't recognized his father, probably because I'd only been to Vince's house during the day back in high school, and his father had always been at work. A picture on the mantle had been as close as I'd come to this man.

CHAPTER 22

VINCENT

DAD'S VOICE GAVE ME A HEART ATTACK.

I stood, and we shook hands vigorously.

"Well, aren't you going to introduce me?" he asked, turning to Ashley.

Ashley extended her hand. "Ashley Newton, Mr. Benson."

Dad took her hand gently, as he always did with women. "Pleasure, Ashley. Please call me Lloyd. Everybody does." He released her hand and pulled out a chair. "I'll just join you for a bit."

It was just like my father to invite himself. Tonight was going downhill quickly.

We retook our seats.

"Dad, I thought you were in London this week," I said.

Mom kept me abreast of his movements, and last I'd heard he wasn't due to leave London for a few more days.

"I was, but we wrapped up early, and I decided to come back home to see your mother. The pilot said the winds were too strong to make LA nonstop. So here I am. Thought I'd make it a surprise visit."

He'd succeeded in the surprise department. Dad was good at that —too good.

If I'd known he planned to stop by tonight, I would have arranged a late customer meeting, or something, anything to avoid a meeting with him. He and Mom were still expecting me at the barbecue with Staci on my arm, and with her unavailable, I'd planned to go alone with a story I hadn't yet concocted to explain.

"And I couldn't wait to meet your lady friend here," Dad said, smiling at Ashley.

"She..." My blood froze. Now I was caught. "She—"

Ashley cut me off. "Has been looking forward to meeting you too, Lloyd."

Dad beamed. "Well, that's very gracious of you."

The Ashley charm had overcome him as well.

"Would you like to order something?" Ashley offered.

My chest constricted when Dad looked ready to accept. A long conversation risked undoing everything.

"Thank you, but no," he finally said. "I need to be going in a minute, and I don't want to interrupt the intimate evening you two are sharing. The missus and I know how special those can be. I just wanted to stop by and say hi while the jet is being refueled."

He and I both knew it was more than that. It only took twenty minutes to top off the company jet, and it took a lot longer to get from Logan to here and back.

I'd dodged a bullet.

Dad cocked his head. "Ashley, have we met before?"

She shook her head. "No."

"Ashley and I dated for a bit in high school," I interjected.

Dad raised a finger in her direction. "That's it. Vincent showed me a picture of you two once. You were a beautiful couple then, and that hasn't changed one bit."

Ashley's face lit up.

Dad patted the table. "Well, I can't keep the pilot waiting forever. Very nice meeting you Ashley, and I look forward to seeing you at the barbecue."

Just a hint of confusion crossed her face. "It would be my pleasure, and it was very nice meeting you, Lloyd."

With that, Dad and I rose and shook hands, and he was off.

I felt a rush of gratitude toward Ashley as I returned to my seat. She had pulled my bacon out of the fire. She could have torpedoed this meeting with Dad, and I would've really been up a creek.

Now I owed her more than the favors I'd already promised.

"I take it the barbecue is the trip Staci was going to take with you?" Ashley asked.

I took a gulp of wine to calm myself. "Yes, but I hadn't told them who I was bringing."

She giggled. "And now he thinks it's me."

"You don't have to come. I'll make excuses for you."

She glared back at me. "Don't you dare. I told him I'd come, and I don't renege on commitments like that."

Somehow I'd dug myself a hole, and it wasn't getting any shallower. "These events can be pretty intimidating. I'm just saying you don't have to."

She put her glass down abruptly. "If you don't want me there, just say so."

I reached for her hand, and the warmth of it settled me. "Kitten, would you please come with me to California to attend my family's barbecue?"

"It would be my pleasure."

I let out a relieved breath.

The dessert arrived, and we split it by feeding each other a spoonful at a time—just as we'd done back in high school.

"Your father's very nice," she said between bites.

"In a social setting."

Her brow furrowed at my response, but she didn't pry. We could discuss my issues with him another time.

I dabbed some of the pie on her nose with my spoon, and her playful smile returned.

~

ASHLEY

. . .

VINCE DROVE ME BACK TO MY PLACE IN HIS RED ROCKET SHIP AND PULLED to the curb out front.

I'd been hoping he would take me back to his place, but I didn't push it.

"Would you like to come up?" I'd been thinking about what was to come the whole ride back, as evidenced by the dampness in my panties.

He turned off the engine. "Sure, for a bit."

The heat of his touch as he guided me to the stairs almost singed my skin. I licked my lips, wondering how he would taste.

I fumbled nervously with my keys at the door, but got it open and flicked on the lights.

He followed me into the kitchen.

"Would you like some wine?" I asked.

"Sure, whatever you're having." He went to the couch, sat, and turned on the DVR.

"White okay?"

"Sure." He was keying in a movie selection. He pulled off his tie and put it on the coffee table.

I brought over the glasses and sat next to him, the warmth of his thigh against mine had my motor revving as the movie started.

He accepted his glass and raised it. "To a do-over."

I clinked my glass against his and repeated, "A do-over." I wasn't sure which do-over he meant, but I didn't ask.

I hadn't seen the movie he chose, *Music and Lyrics*, although it had Drew Barrymore and Hugh Grant, so I was sure it would be good.

He slid his arm around me, and we snuggled.

He declined a second glass of wine.

As the movie progressed, I grew nervous that I would forget what I'd learned from those *Cosmo* articles and screw up my first blowjob. I snuggled closer, but his hand still hadn't left my shoulder.

What was I doing wrong? He hadn't made a move.

I slid my hand over to his thigh.

He removed it, and playfully, I went right back to his thigh. Was this some sort of game?

He took my hand off again. "Stop it."

I tried one more time.

"You said you'd obey. Now stop it." His tone wasn't playful.

I pulled my hand back. "That was this afternoon, and it was from the book."

"I didn't mean just this afternoon. Do you want to change your answer?"

"No, but what did I do wrong?"

He took my face in his hands and brought me in for the lightest of kisses.

I wanted more, but the look in his eyes told me to not complain.

"I told you, you deserve better. This afternoon we started things wrong. You deserve to be dated, to be courted, to be treated better."

So it had felt backwards to him too...

"I didn't complain."

"I know, Kitten. But we're starting again the *right* way. Tonight is just a date: dinner and a movie. I don't expect anything more from you."

I pulled his head to mine for another brief kiss. "Dinner and a movie."

I snuggled into this man who would deny himself what I had once denied him—and offered freely tonight—all because he wanted it to be *right*.

Before the movie finished, I got up to get a bowl of chocolate ice cream, his favorite. I handed him the bowl and spoon and lay down with my head in his lap.

He spooned bits for each of us as I lay there. I alternated between watching the screen and accepting small bites of ice cream.

He put the empty bowl down, and his hand moved to my ribs. His thumb traced the underside of my breast, challenging my self-control.

I could feel his erection under my head. The occasional twitches tormented me.

This had to be difficult for him as well.

I cried when the end of the movie came and Hugh and the singer sang the final song, "Way Back Into Love." I understood then why Vince had chosen this movie, and the song was going onto my phone tomorrow so I could listen to it again. It fit as our new song.

"Got to go," he said, lifting my head off his lap and standing.

The goodnight kiss I received wasn't chaste, but it also wasn't like this afternoon's.

Before he could leave, I pulled him back to me, pressing the heat of my breasts against his chest, my arms around his neck. I went up on my toes.

"Page one-twenty-seven," I whispered.

He squeezed me tight and whispered, "Another time, Kitten."

The gentleman left, and I was alone in my empty apartment with my damp panties.

I leaned against the door after it closed.

The man was impossible. We'd gone from the dirtiest, sexiest escapade of my life this afternoon to him leaving while I still had all my clothes on, even though I'd been ready to offer him something I'd never given anyone else.

CHAPTER 23

VINCENT

LEAVING WAS WHAT SHE DESERVED. FOR HER, I COULD BE A GENTLEMAN for once.

The door to her apartment closed behind me, and I walked down the hall. My cock ached. I could still smell the coconut scent of her hair.

"Page one-twenty-seven," she'd whispered. She was offering to blow me.

Fuck.

My cock tried to rip through my zipper as the pages came to mind.

I paced back to her door and knocked.

The door opened instantly, and my irresistible Kitten was just as she had been, except with surprised, misty eyes.

I strode in and closed and locked the door behind me. I backed her against the wall, one arm on either side of her head, my lips inches from hers.

"Are you ready for our second date?"

She nodded, and a slow smile replaced the surprise on her face.

I moved my lips closer to hers.

She closed the distance, lifting up on her toes.

As our lips met, my need overrode my control, and I pressed her against the wall.

Her tongue sought mine.

She tasted like chocolate and desire. I knotted a hand in her hair as we traded breath and moans. One of her hands pulled at my hair and the other clawed my back.

I broke this kiss to nibble her earlobe and whisper, "Page one-forty-six." I was dying to have her lips on me, but tonight she was going to come for me—twice.

I moved to the side and slid my hand up the inside of her thigh, to a gasp of anticipation and a groan of pleasure. My fingers traced the damp fabric of her panties.

Her breathing hitched when I forced the panties down a few inches and my finger parted her slippery folds. She spread her legs to give me access.

I slid a finger inside and brought her slick wetness to her clit, circling.

She yanked my hair to get my lips back to hers and moaned into my mouth.

I continued pressing, releasing, stroking.

She broke the kiss and pushed at me to give her room to undo my shirt.

I pinned her to the wall with my thigh while my finger worked her little love button to increasing sighs and moans. I slid my finger back into her, and then a second.

Her trembling hands fumbled with my buttons. Exasperated, she yanked and the last one popped off and fell to the floor.

Her nails scratched my chest as I brought my fingers up and sucked her sweet juices off one and then the other.

Her eyes went wide. This was something new to her.

I slid my fingers down through her curls again to the sensitive flesh of her swollen clit.

She gasped as I pressed and circled.

I covered her mouth with mine.

She closed her lips to me, but relented after a moment and my tongue gave her a taste of herself, that sweetness I wanted to lap up. Next time.

Her hand slid down to stroke me through the fabric of my suit.

The sweet torture was too much. I let go of her hair and pulled that hand to my shoulder. If I let her continue, I was sure to burst and shoot my load in my pants.

Her legs trembled as I stroked and circled her tiny bundle of nerves. She was close, oh so close.

Her breathing became erratic, and her words came in staccato bursts.

"Oh God…Right there…More."

She arched up. "Oh shit…Don't stop…Oh my God…Yeah."

I kept it up.

She gasped. "Oh fuck."

I moved my other hand to pinch her nipple through her dress, and she tensed, unable to breathe. Finally she came to the end of her rope.

"Oh my God, Vince." She shook, and her hands clawed at me. "Holy fuck."

I pressed her clit one final time and slid my fingers inside her heat to feel her contract around me.

Her legs wobbled as she panted her way down from her high and rested her head against me.

My cock was about to explode. This holding-off shit was killing me.

Her hands went to my waist, and I pulled back to give her room.

I pulled my wallet out and fumbled for a condom.

She undid my belt and then the button and zipper of my trousers.

My pants dropped to the floor.

I tore the packet open with my teeth and pulled it on in record time as she leaned back against the wall, her face shifting from contentment to excitement at the sight of me rolling the latex down.

I pulled her panties to her ankles, and she stepped out of them. I hiked up her dress and lifted her.

She wrapped her legs around me as I pinned her back against the wall.

She pulled my head to hers, and her lips found mine.

I lowered her down and pressed my tip to her hot, wet entrance.

She gasped as I lowered her farther and started the thrusting—I couldn't hold off.

"Harder. Give me more."

I pounded her against the wall as I went in deeper—deeper and harder. I couldn't last like this. The anticipation had been too much.

Holy shit.

Her tightness was nirvana as electricity shot through my veins with every plunge into her pussy. I ground my pelvis against her clit as I pinned her to the wall each time.

She rocked her hips into the pressure and with a scream, she came undone again, shaking.

The pressure built behind my balls, and I lost it with one last push deep into her tight heat as her contractions milked me.

Panting, I held her against the wall. The pulses of my cock slowed, and she went limp in my arms. I lifted her up off me and shuffled— with my pants around my ankles—to her bedroom. I laid her on her bed.

Her fingers traced my hand as I shuffle-walked to take care of the condom.

On my return, a pout emerged as she noticed I'd pulled my pants back on. She patted the bed beside her. "Won't you stay?"

I shook my head and said the difficult words. "Can't. I have to let my dog out." I leaned over, kissed her, and left. It's what Dalton would have done.

Halfway down the hall, I pulled out my phone to review the message I'd gotten from Ben during dinner.

MURDOCH: The system we discussed is in place

I hoped he meant he'd just finished, but in any event, I'd given him explicit directions not to allow anyone besides me to view the footage of my office.

CHAPTER 24

ASHLEY(FOUR DAYS LATER)

VINCE HAD BEEN IN WALL-TO-WALL MEETINGS ALL WEEK SINCE OUR incredible Sunday. We'd barely had time to exchange pleasantries. I didn't want people at work to know about us, so I'd told him I'd have to wait until the weekend to see him again.

It was torture, but I'd set the rule.

Now it was Thursday, and I was starting the day with another early-morning update with Liz. Unfortunately John was still stuck in New Haven.

"A trip to see the family?" Liz asked across the table.

I nodded over my Waffle Castle breakfast.

"The file said he was dating some model chick."

"Staci Baxter," I answered.

"You mean *Sports Illustrated* Staci Baxter? That one?"

"The same, but that's old news."

Her eyes squinted. "You little slut. You're shagging him, aren't you?"

I brought another forkful of waffle to my mouth without answering.

"Fuck. If I hadn't gotten caught, I could be the one shacked up with the billionaire."

The thought of Liz with Vince made me lose my appetite. I returned my fork to my plate.

Liz started the recorder, and I made my report on the meetings and comings and goings I'd witnessed since my last report.

"And how far along are you on checking his files? Randy wants to know," she asked. Once again she'd slipped up, calling him Randy.

"Not halfway through yet."

She had to finish her French toast mouthful before commenting. "You should be going faster," she said, as if she was my boss and entitled to grade my performance.

I'd had enough. I reached for the recorder and clicked it off. "Look, the office is full of people almost all the time. They work crazy-long hours, and I don't often get an opportunity to poke around. If you hadn't fucked it up so quickly—"

"It was just dumb luck that they caught me."

I calmed myself before continuing. "If this is a level-one op, we both know accuracy is more important than speed. I'm being careful not to blow my cover, and that means it will take time."

"You probably want more time in the sack with the guy."

"Says the girl who almost screwed the whole op on the first day." I was tempted—mightily tempted—to throw her hookup with White in her face, but I decided against it.

My comeback had shut her up.

I turned the recorder back on and finished my report.

"Are you going to finish that waffle?" Liz asked.

I pushed the plate to the center of the table. "Be my guest."

A little while later, as I walked away from the Waffle Castle toward the MBTA station, I couldn't shake the sense that I was leaving something foreign with Liz and the Bureau, and moving back toward something normal in my undercover life with Vince.

It should have been the other way around. Undercover at Covington should be the unfamiliar world I had to be careful in—not the Bureau.

Turning the corner, I squinted into the early morning sun and walked past a vendor selling giant soft pretzels from a cart. The flavorful aroma drew me back. An exchange of cash and I had a warm, chewy one with cinnamon for my walk back to the train. The sun on my face and the sweet taste of the pretzel improved my mood with every step.

Or perhaps my mood was improving with every yard I came closer to Vince, or farther from Liz. Hard to tell—and immaterial this morning.

I was determined to not let her shit on my outlook.

WHEN I CHECKED MY PHONE AFTER ARRIVING AT THE OFFICE, I FOUND THE annual reminder on it that still hurt. Today was the anniversary of my cousin Louise's death. I took a moment to silently ask her a question. My question was always the same: *Why?*

Why had she taken her own life?

Mid morning, Vince emerged from his office in his running clothes.

"Joining me?" he asked.

"Not today. Thanks."

In my mind, the head of the company running with his assistant wouldn't look right to the rest of the employees. I appreciated that he wanted to spend the time with me, but I'd said we needed to wait until the weekend to see each other, and that included running, as far as I was concerned.

Vince, on the other hand, seemed clueless about the appearance problem running together might present.

"Lightweight," he chided as he headed to the elevator.

And I had a second reason for not participating: I hadn't yet gotten access to some of the files in his office.

Vince had left his office door closed.

I continued working on the document he'd assigned me this morning while keeping an eye on the rest of the group on executive row.

The clock on the lower right-hand corner of my monitor eventually clicked over to ten fifteen.

Like clockwork, Anita rose from her desk. The rest of the assistants took their cues from her and also put aside what they were doing.

"Joining us?" Anita asked me.

"Thanks, but I've got to get this done," I said.

I'd joined them on occasion for their ritual coffee break downstairs, but not routinely. It seemed to be Anita's form of a staff meeting. Attending had been useful the first few times, to learn the general gossip running around the office, but otherwise they bored me.

I gave the assistants a minute after the elevator closed behind them. Then I lifted my phone from my purse, unlocked it, and opened the camera app, hoping I wouldn't need it to record anything damaging.

I slid inside Vince's office, closing the door silently behind me.

Taking a seat behind his desk, I surveyed the surface and noted the placement of everything with two clicks of the camera—one to the left and one to the right.

I started with the pile of folders on the left and opened them one by one, leafing through the papers. Everything in these looked quite innocuous. Many of them were things I'd prepared or had crossed my desk on their way into Vincent's: routine company business.

I moved on to the pile on the right. This dealt with the Semaphore acquisition. The spreadsheet printouts were familiar, but then I came across some discrepancies. There were three separate offer letters in the bottom folder. Each of them had been typed by an actual typewriter, not computer-generated and run on the laser printer.

These were obviously in the sensitive category Anita had mentioned my first day, typed rather than put on the computer so there were no records anybody could steal. It really was the perfect way to keep things confidential: never have a copy.

Vince had evidently typed them himself on the old IBM that sat off to the side.

I read each of them carefully. The terms changed slightly from one to the next, but other than that, the wording all appeared to be quite standard. I placed the offer letters back in the folder in the order I'd found them.

I opened my phone to review the pictures I'd taken of the desk before moving things. I repositioned the folders exactly where they'd been before my snooping.

Time was running short as I opened the drawers one by one. Only the lower left contained any papers worth checking.

As I pulled out the folder and opened it, a chill ran through me. I felt dirty looking at these. The folder contained correspondence with Vince's father, none of it recent. I skimmed the letters as quickly as I could, trying not to take in any more of the content than I needed to assure myself these weren't what I was looking for. And they weren't.

I closed the folder quickly and replaced it. Suddenly I felt like I needed a shower. I'd peeked into something private. It was my job to go through everything, but these made me feel dirty.

I shuddered and pushed back from the desk. I knelt on the floor and looked underneath, something they'd taught us at Quantico. I didn't find anything.

I reviewed my pictures once again to make sure the desk was at as it had been. It was, but I noticed one place I hadn't checked.

Rule number one: sometimes the best hiding place is right in front of you. I lifted the edge of the blotter from the desk.

A single-page memo laid underneath.

I took two paper clips from the drawer and used them like tweezers to slide it out. I shivered as I read it. It too had been typed on the old IBM.

I laid it on the blotter and positioned my phone over it, taking several pictures and checking them for clarity before replacing the agreement and putting the paperclips back.

I checked the time on my phone and hurriedly placed the chair back where it had been. The girls were due back upstairs from their coffee klatch any moment now. I had seconds to get out of the office. I sped to the door and listened for a moment.

Silence.

Heart racing, I exited the office, closed the door behind me, and hurried to my seat. I slid the mouse and reawakened my computer just as the door opened and the giggling coffee group returned. I typed gibberish into the next cell on the spreadsheet and hit return to look active.

After the chatter stopped and the others had settled in behind their desks again, I pulled my phone out to review the pictures of the evidence I'd found.

I felt nauseous as I reread the contract, dated two weeks ago. It confirmed that Vince had agreed to relinquish majority control of

Semaphore to a Sonny Alfonso after he bought it, for two hundred million dollars. The DOJ's informant had been eerily accurate.

The one thing I hadn't wanted to happen had come about. I'd just found evidence that Vince was guilty as sin. With this, I would secure the LA promotion and Liz would be the one shopping for parkas.

The old me would've been ecstatic, but my feeling was the opposite.

I rushed to the bathroom and almost didn't make it in time. I knelt, but not fast enough. My breakfast came up. Some hit the toilet seat and splashed on my blouse.

Three more heaves followed.

I stumbled to the sink and turned on the water.

The door opened and Anita came in. "You all right?" she asked, surveying the mess I'd made. "You poor thing."

I splashed water into my mouth, rinsing the taste of bile away. It didn't wash away my feeling of dread.

Anita laid a gentle hand on my shoulder as I spit into the sink again. "You should go home and rest, dear."

I nodded, took another mouthful of water, and spit again. "I need to clean up first."

"Sure. I'll call you a taxi."

I wet a paper towel and wiped at my blouse. "Thank you."

She left, and I continued cleaning myself. Nothing special about this agent today.

Another heave overcame me without warning, but there was nothing left to come up. I hunched over the sink, and my stomach lining tried to make its way up my throat.

I dabbed and wiped, but the stain wouldn't come off my top. It was like rubbing at the guilt I felt. I couldn't make it go away. This was going to ruin everything.

CHAPTER 25

ASHLEY

ANITA HAD PAID THE DRIVER IN ADVANCE, AND THE RIDE WAS QUICK, BUT uncomfortable. I dreaded vomiting again in the taxi.

We made it to my apartment building, and the driver offered to walk me up, but I declined.

How humiliating. A seasoned FBI special agent, and I'd puked after cracking a career-making case. As I unlocked the deadbolt, I decided the bathroom incident would not make it into my report.

Maybe I could stay in bed for two days and claim a stomach bug, but that wouldn't be honest. This needed to be reported. Omitting the inconsequential was allowed; sitting on the consequential was not.

I turned off my phone, locked the door behind me, and shucked off my clothes. I didn't have a super sensitive nose, but the lingering smell of my vomit threatened to make me heave again, so I stuffed every-thing except my shoes into a garbage bag and tied it closed before depositing the mess in the laundry hamper.

I shut myself in the shower and started the water. The hot spray washed over me, but didn't carry away the stink of failure. By succeeding at finding the evidence against Vince, I had once again failed somehow.

But that didn't make sense. My feelings had gotten intertwined with my duty, and it was screwing with my mind. My duty had to be clear. White was right, and black was wrong. The rules were the rules and had to be obeyed. Vince was dirty, and he had to pay the price for his choices. I twisted the silver ring on my finger.

My duty was to provide evidence for the courts to make the determination of guilt. That's how the system worked. I didn't have to like it; I just had to do it.

And, anyway, if Vince was guilty of this, he was definitely not the person he seemed to be.

I closed my eyes, braced my hands against the wall, and put my head under the spray. The water enveloped my head, running into my mouth and ears and down my body. I wished the sound of the water in my ears would drown out the self-doubt racing through my mind.

What have I done?

Wasn't our system predicated on being innocent until proven guilty? I couldn't be the judge and the jury, too. Vince was due the benefit of the presumption of innocence.

I lingered in the water until it started to cool.

After drying off, I slipped into sweats and wrapped a towel around my wet head. A bottle of rum in the cupboard called to me.

I poured half a glass of Coke from a can and added rum. Then I added more. This was no time for half measures. The glass only lasted a few minutes before I poured another.

I needed to forget today—the day my heart broke all over again. I grabbed a straw and slumped on the couch. Memory could be debilitating. My memories of the night of the breakup with Vince in high school had haunted me for a long time. I felt I'd made the right decision at the time, but I could never shake the doubts. What if I'd chosen differently?

The Robert Frost poem came to mind. What if I had chosen the other path? How would my life have turned out? Would I now be Mrs. Vincent Benson?

Wish again, girl. Fairy tales are for fools. You'd be married to the mob.

I took a long sip through the straw.

Had I done the right thing by accepting this case?

Wasn't the system I was part of interested in justice? The FBI was part of the Justice Department, after all.

Didn't the very name of the department mean guilt had to be proven beyond any shadow of a doubt?

In that moment, I realized Vince wasn't yet guilty.

I didn't have the logic or evidence to back it up, but in my bones, I could feel doubt about his guilt. If I felt doubt, didn't that constitute a shadow of a doubt?

I took another sip. I was talking myself in circles. I wasn't the jury, but I knew doubt abounded in this case.

Was I wishing for it because of my feelings for the man? Not just any man, I realized, but the man I wanted to call my own—provided he was the man I felt him to be. And who I so wanted to believe he was. I sipped long and hard, draining the rest of the glass.

I poured another and laid back into the couch. I closed my eyes and brought one of my favorite memories to mind.

The warm, gentle trade winds rustled the fronds of the palm trees. I was back in Hawaii, on Waikiki Beach. I'd been able to get there from LA only one time, but it had defined paradise for me. Sure, California had palm trees in some places and sunshine a lot of the year, yet the water didn't compare. Something about Hawaii's warm saltwater was soothing to the soul.

It was a place without cares. It was my mental escape pod. I shut my eyes, remembered swimming in the ocean, sitting by the pool, and lying on the beach watching tourists try to surf and kids splashed and played in the ocean.

The vision always brought me peace, transporting me to a carefree paradise for a short while. The refuge of sleep came quickly.

～

POUNDING ON THE DOOR WOKE ME.

I pried my eyes open, and the room came slowly into focus. The half-empty rum bottle told its own story—it had started out almost full.

"Ash? Open up." Vince's voice came from the hallway.

I staggered to the door, and it came back to me. I'd been drinking to forget, but that had failed, and now I remembered it all: the memo, the puking. Oh my God, the puking. And now Vince was here. I was so totally fucked. I needed to sort this out, and not with him around.

"I'm worried about you," he called through the door.

"I'm fine," I lied.

"Anita said you got sick and she sent you home."

"I'll be okay," I responded, leaning my head against the door.

"Let me in to see for myself."

I let out a sigh. "I'm fine. Go away...please." I couldn't face him right now, not with what I'd found.

"I'm taking you to the emergency room to get checked out."

I couldn't allow that. "Not necessary. I'll be fine."

After a pause he said, "Last chance, Ash. Open up or I'm calling 9-1-1. Your choice."

What kind of choice was that? I gave in and unlocked the door.

He strode in past me.

I continued to hold the door open. "Why would you call 9-1-1? I'm fine. It's just some sort of bug. You can leave now."

He held his fingers to my forehead, taking my temperature, but then he spied the rum bottle. "Drinking our way to health this afternoon?" He put down his briefcase.

"I needed it to settle my stomach is all."

He closed the door and led me to the couch. "Sit and tell me what's bothering you."

I settled into the couch without arguing. "You should go."

He closed the door and sat as well. "After you tell me what the problem is." He put an arm around me and pulled me to his side.

I pulled away.

Obvious alarm wrote itself across his face. "What's the matter, Kitten? What did I do?"

I couldn't bear to confront him with what I'd found.

He put his arm around me. "I'm so sorry. Dancing might help your mood. Want to go dancing?"

"I need a drink."

"Drinking to forget, huh?" He rose and walked to the kitchen. "What's your poison today? Straight rum?"

I shook my head weakly. "And Coke."

He chuckled. "Really?" He checked the cabinets and found my meager liquor stash. "I still think dancing is a better idea, but if you're really intent on torturing yourself we could switch to Fireball."

I'd kept the remainder of a bottle Liz had brought over once and never touched it again. "No, thanks." That stuff had made me sicker than a skunk.

He opened the fridge and brought the remainder of my six-pack of Cokes over with a glass for himself. He split a can between our glasses and added rum to both. "If you really want to get wasted, I'm here to help." He handed me my glass.

I sipped.

He guzzled half his glass and shook his head. "That's not how you do it. Bottoms up. Time's a wasting if you want to get properly smashed."

I sipped again. "I don't want to get smashed."

"Bullcrap, Kitten."

His calling me Kitten made it that much harder.

"Drinking alone in the middle of the afternoon is the definition of wanting to get wasted," he continued. "Trust me, I know. Now drink up."

"You should go. I'll be fine tomorrow."

I couldn't face him until I'd processed this and figured out a plan. It should've been simple. I turned in the evidence, and the DOJ pieced it together to figure out what to do.

"No way. I'm here as your drinking buddy tonight."

"I don't need a drinking buddy."

"You sure as shit do, and I'm not leaving."

Short of pulling my gun, I didn't see a way to get rid of him—and pulling your gun after drinking was a no-no that had been drilled into us at the Academy. A drunk agent shooting somebody, even if they deserved it, was publicity the Bureau couldn't and wouldn't tolerate. There was probably a secret place in Gitmo they spirited you off to and kept you forever, so the press could never get a hold of you.

Vince's phone dinged with a text. He checked it and put his phone away.

~

VINCENT

THE TEXT WAS FROM BARB.

BARB: How about dinner tonight?

I turned off my phone, put it away, and poured Ashley and me each another. A search of the fridge and freezer revealed a stash of frozen pizzas.

I held them up. "Pepperoni or four-cheese?" I turned on the oven.

"I'm not hungry," she said, predictably.

I shook my head. "Gotta eat. If you won't choose, I'm doing pepperoni."

She was guaranteed to feel even worse in the morning if she didn't eat something.

She sipped her rum and Coke without responding.

I put the four-cheese back in the freezer and located a baking sheet. "Pepperoni it is."

Pouring her another glass, I waited for the pizza to cook.

She sat silently on the couch, shoulders hunched.

I cut the pizza when it finished and brought it to the coffee table in front of her.

I turned on the DVR and located one of her favorite shows.

She had told me she liked *Castle*, even though they weren't putting out new episodes anymore. The female homicide detective was a character she felt she could relate to—a strong woman making her way in a man's world.

She tried unsuccessfully to hide her smile when the show started, a definite improvement.

Slowly, she relaxed as we ate and drank and watched her show.

I started another episode and poured another glass of her chosen poison when she returned from the bathroom.

Her eyelids were getting heavy, and she leaned into me. "Why won't you leave me alone?" she asked quietly.

"Drinking buddies can't leave, and you still haven't talked to me."

She giggled and sipped on the straw, draining the last of the glass. I poured another.

"Yes, you can," she complained.

"You're the one who chose to get smashed instead of going dancing with me."

She sipped daintily on the straw as her eyes threatened to close. "Why do you have to be so nice?"

I put my arm around her and this time didn't get resistance. "Because you're my Kitten. And I'm here to listen," I added after a moment.

Half an hour and another glass later, I learned I'd failed.

She fell asleep leaning against me, and wasn't roused by me asking her again to talk to me.

CHAPTER 26

ASHLEY

THE LIGHT WAS COMING IN AROUND THE SHADES WHEN I WOKE UP WITH MY bladder ready to burst. The pounding in my head as I got up told me the obvious: I'd had way, way too much to drink last night. Something was off as I waddled into the bathroom, and it wasn't just the vicious little woodpeckers trying to peck their way out of my skull.

I pried an eye open wide enough to see myself in the mirror.

I was wearing panties and a bra instead of my nightshirt.

As I sat down, I tried to remember, but couldn't. I must have been too wasted to get completely undressed.

After washing my hands, I flicked on the light and reached for the mouthwash. My tongue felt like it had grown fur. I ditched the bra and rubbed where the underwire had left its nasty mark.

I was getting too old for this crap.

When had getting drunk become so bad the morning after?

I desperately needed the Tylenol in my purse. I needed the whole damned bottle and then some, or I needed another drink. My stomach lurched at the thought.

Veto that.

I reached for the bathrobe I hung on the back of the door, but it was missing. Opening the bedroom door, I discovered why. The aromas of coffee and bacon flooded the doorway.

Vince was in my robe, at the stove, cooking. He turned. "Morning, Kitten. How do you feel? I like the outfit."

I retreated into my room and slipped a T-shirt over my head before venturing out again on my Tylenol quest.

"Morning," I said.

The woodpeckers were getting madder by the minute, now trying to escape through my eyeballs. There was nothing good about this morning. I searched my purse and found the bottle. When I removed the cap, only one tablet fell out.

"Shit," I yelled loud enough for the sound to punish me. I winced.

"That bad, huh?"

"Worse," I told him.

I'd forgotten I'd let Sophia use my Tylenol twice this week, and I hadn't checked the bottle.

"I've got Advil, if you'd like." He handed me a glass of orange juice.

"I'll take a dozen." I accepted the glass and washed down my lone pill while he fished an Advil bottle out of the briefcase he'd brought with him last night.

He handed me only two.

I gobbled down the pills and sat at the table, resting my head in my hands. I closed my eyes. The blaring noise of the blender startled me and infuriated the woodpeckers inside my skull.

"Hey, cut that out."

He slid a glass of something green in front of me and removed the orange juice. "Drink. It'll make you feel better."

"What's in it?"

"Celery and cockroaches. Now drink," he commanded.

I stared at it, cradling my aching head in my hands.

He glared at me. "Stop being obstinate. It tastes like shit, but it's good for hangovers. I should know."

I gave in and swallowed some of the green glop. He was right, it tasted like crap—or worse, like crap and wet sawdust.

He slid a steaming cup of coffee in front of me and a plate with strips of bacon. "Finish the drink, then eat."

"Stop being so bossy."

"Stop being obstinate."

"It's my apartment. I get to do what I want." I reached for the bacon.

He pulled the plate away. "After you drink your medicine."

I stuck my tongue out at him. It didn't do any good.

"Behave yourself, or I'll have to put you over my knee." His face echoed the threat.

Bacon was probably the only food that could overcome my nausea right now. I forced down the last of the green drain cleaner he'd handed me.

He rewarded me with a strip of bacon, and then the whole plate. It had been way too long since I'd had bacon. Like French fries, bacon was one of my vices, and I couldn't stop once I started.

I held up the second bacon strip. "Where did this come from?"

"I went out to get it while you slept it off. Your fridge needed a serious restocking."

I was slowly putting it together. "What do you mean went out?" I chewed another piece of bacon. Why couldn't he have put bacon in the green glop? It would have made it taste better.

"You heard me. I got up and went to the store. You were out like a light."

I didn't remember a thing after drinking and starting *Castle* on the DVR, with pizza and more drinking, but he'd obviously slept over. "Oh."

"Hardest thing I ever did," he added, not making any sense.

The woodpeckers were crowding out any functioning neurons.

I finished another piece of greasy bacon and slurped my coffee. "What?"

"Lying next to you and not being able to touch you."

His words washed over me. He'd stayed, he'd put me to bed, and he'd watched over me, which explained my underwear this morning.

"You didn't need to stay," I chastised.

The way I felt right now was in complete opposition to my words.

"I told you I wasn't leaving until you talked to me, and I meant it."

How could he be so stubborn?

That brought me back to the source of my drinking.

Vince offered me the orange juice again. "I'm listening."

I couldn't tell him what I'd found, so I substituted a half-truth. "Yesterday was the anniversary of my cousin Louise's death. It always puts me in a funk."

He offered me his hand. "I'm sorry. I didn't know. Do you want to talk about it?"

"Maybe later. Right now I want to lie down and make this headache go away." The nausea was fading, but the headache continued. The fog of last night began lifting. I got up and went to lie on the couch.

He brought the rest of my orange juice to me. "It will help if you take a shower, but first finish this."

I took the juice with me to the shower and finished it before turning on the water. He was going to be arrested. There was no avoiding it.

The pain relievers slowly began to help, and a few of the woodpeckers stopped trying to crack my head open from the inside. The pain had diminished to a dull ache by the time I toweled off.

Vince was picking up his briefcase when I came out of the bathroom.

"I have to head in," he told me. He walked over and gave me a gentle kiss. "Come in when you feel better."

I nodded.

Despite everything, as soon as the door closed behind him, I missed him, and I wished we'd shared more than a simple kiss.

I turned on my phone, and it chimed with a text.

LIZ: Where are you? U R Late

Fuck me. I'd forgotten about our scheduled meeting this morning. I typed out a reply.

ME: Can't make it - explain later

CHAPTER 27

ASHLEY

BY LATE MORNING, I FELT HUMAN AGAIN—NOT ONE HUNDRED PERCENT, but well enough to be out in public.

I got dressed to go into the Chelsea field office. It was time to turn in the evidence I'd uncovered.

I reminded myself I'd likely at least secured the California promotion.

Traffic was light, and I reached the FBI building quickly.

Upstairs, Liz's face showed her displeasure. "We were supposed to meet at Waffle Castle at seven. Do you have any idea how early I had to get up?"

As always, the world revolved around Princess Elizabeth.

"I couldn't make it."

"Is that why you look like shit?"

I collapsed into my chair. "Thanks for the compliment."

She pasted on a shit-eating grin. "Just calling it like it is."

She could be mean.

"I drank too much last night," I admitted.

"That's hardly an excuse to blow off an update."

"I couldn't make it."

"Regardless, maybe today you'll get a chance to find it and get back to real work." Her statement was nonsensical.

I cocked my head. "Find what?"

She laughed. "Oh yeah, this morning I was going to give you the intel we got from the DOJ contact about a memo."

What?

I sat down. "What intel, and what contact?"

"I don't know. Randy, I mean the SAC, told me to relay to you that the DOJ contact had gotten information. He said to tell you Benson had signed a contract with Sonny Alfonso and to check his office for it."

"What DOJ contact?"

"How would I know? You know they don't share squat with us."

The Department of Justice guys had always viewed themselves as superior to us simply because the director of the Bureau reported to the attorney general. While it was true they got to make the prosecutorial decisions, we did all the heavy lifting in the cases. If one went south, it was always because they fucked it up in the courts, not because we'd given them bad or insufficient evidence.

"Newton, my office," the SAC called as he strode into the far end of the bullpen, coffee cup in hand.

My phone chimed as a text arrived.

VINCE: When are you coming in - miss you want you need you

I stopped to re-read the text.

"Now, Newton," White repeated from his office door.

"Later," I told Liz as I left.

I pocketed the phone and shut White's door behind me.

"Parsons said you blew off your meeting this morning. What's up?"

I took a seat. "I couldn't make it," I said without elaborating.

His eyes narrowed. "And what are you doing in here instead of being on the assignment?"

"I'm due back in there later today."

"The DOJ tells us Benson signed a contract with Sonny Alfonso himself. You need to find it."

I noticed the hint of that same foul odor as before. His instructions to find the memo were off somehow.

"Liz only just told me. How do we know there's a contract, and what does it look like? How will I know I've found the right one?"

He rolled his eyes, obviously not happy with my questions. "DOJ's asset says it's a single page, Benson and Alfonso. It's in his office."

"Just one page—that may not be easy."

"I don't care if it's easy, just go find it, quickly, and check back in when you have it."

I pulled out my phone. The regs and my duty demanded I show him, so I woke up the device to show him I'd already found it. "I have…"

I paused, wincing at the thought of what my next action would cost Vince.

"You have what? I don't want to hear about cramps or some bull-shit. Just get the job done."

Pig.

I clicked the screen off, pocketed the device, and closed the door behind me as I left.

The foul odor in the office was definitely the swine inhabiting it.

I returned to my desk, put my phone down, and went to get a cup of coffee to figure this out.

I RETURNED TO MY DESK WITH A MUG FULL OF COFFEE AND POWERED UP MY computer.

"If you want, you can dictate, and I'll enter it," Liz offered.

"No thanks. I've got time, and I want to go slow and get this right." This was one report I intended to type myself. I wasn't sure exactly what I was going to put in it yet, though.

SAC Randy D. White's parting words rang in my ears. Cramps, my ass. He was such a pig. How he had ever risen to his current position was beyond me. The process had to include a lot of ass kissing, ass licking, or something equally disgusting. His middle initial clearly stood for disgusting, or dick, or dipshit, or dickhead, or douchebag. Better yet, all of the above.

Since I wasn't traveling Liz's path into his good graces, the promotion out of this office took on even greater importance. Getting three thousand miles away from the douchebag was hardly far enough.

I logged into the computer and pulled up the software to log my report. The first few lines were easy. Then I got to the hard part. I had to explain my actions and observations since the last report.

Minimizing the window and pulling up the last report Liz had entered provided a respite as I got up to speed with where I'd left off. I reread the report several times before returning to the current one.

The first few days I needed to account for were easy. I found myself typing slowly though, not wanting to reach yesterday morning. I gulped down the last of my coffee. This was hard. I opened my phone again.

Liz walked by, and I closed it. Having it out in the open in the bullpen didn't seem like a good idea.

I grabbed the phone and headed for the restroom. I parked myself in a stall and opened the phone again. The pictures were in front of me in full color, the evidence of Vince's wrongdoing—or at least poor decision-making. It was up to the DOJ to figure out what it amounted to.

The regulations were clear: I was to make a full report—clear, concise, and without omissions. I closed the photo viewer and returned to reread my text message.

VINCE: When are you coming in - miss you want you need you

The message haunted me as I recalled the conversation where he'd told me somebody was out to get him and showed me the ominous note Staci had received.

White's words replayed in my head, *"DOJ's asset says it's a single page, Benson and Sonny Alfonso. It's in his office."* Since when did we get information that detailed, that specific, and with timing as convenient? The answer was never. And why was this so fucking high up on the priority list?

I went back to the pictures and expanded them. I flipped from one to the next, studying the text. The clue was in here somewhere, I knew.

I finally found it on the third line from the bottom.

In these days of computer printers, people forgot that sometimes typewriters could be traced the same way firearms could. Some of the letters might have slight imperfections that would be specific to a single typewriter.

I expanded the picture even further. The lowercase Z had a slight imperfection to it. This would tell me if Vince had typed the memo on his typewriter.

I had always logged my evidence and let the lab monkeys figure it out. Those were the rules, and I always followed the rules.

Until today.

I wasn't logging this. I'd found a piece of paper with some writing on it—just a piece of paper and nothing more. I closed my phone, left the restroom, and returned to my desk.

"Last night's bender still getting to you?" Liz asked as I sat.

I put my hand on my stomach. "Yeah, I'm still not a hundred percent."

I finished my report without mentioning my search of Vince's office. It would be consistent with my not having heard yet from either Liz or White to go look for the memo.

I finished the report and saved it. Packing up to leave, I told Liz, "I'll be in touch about the next meeting."

"Just don't make it early in the morning if you're not gonna show," she shot back.

"Sorry about that," I called as I left.

I'd broken a serious rule, and I'd officially gone over to the dark side. Down was now up, and everything was backwards. But I had to get a plan together, and fast.

I was one inch from getting fired, or arrested, or both.

CHAPTER 28

Vincent

When I powered up my phone on the way in to work, the text I'd received last night popped up—along with another from this morning and two missed calls from her.

BARB: How about dinner tonight?

BARB: Call me

I ignored them and continued on. When I arrived upstairs at Covington, I closed the door to my office and dialed the florist.

"A dozen red roses," I told the lady. "No, make them white and two dozen, please." I gave them Ashley's name and our address here at the office.

"What would you like the card to say?"

It took me a second to come up with "Hope you feel better today."

"And how would you like it signed?"

"Uncle Benny," I told her.

Ashley didn't have an Uncle Benny, but I couldn't very well put my name on it.

I typed out the text I'd been mulling over, a text to Ashley.

ME: When are you coming in - miss you want you need you

I sent it and waited.

Nothing.

I walked to the couch and laid down, closing my eyes. I hadn't drunk as much as she had last night, but I would still need some more Advil eventually.

The message arriving on my phone woke me. I sat up too quickly and felt faint for a moment.

ASHLEY: After lunch

I turned toward the window and smiled. My Kitten was out there somewhere, and she was headed my way. Checking my watch, I decided on an early lunch at Vitaliano's. A walk in the fresh air and good food was what I needed to get rid of this headache. That, and another few Advil.

I'D HAD AN EXCELLENT MEAL AND SETTLED MYSELF BACK IN MY OFFICE when Ashley arrived after lunch, just as she'd said she would.

A wide smile lit up her face when she saw the flowers. She read the card and her smiley face turned questioning.

I looked away.

"Those came while you were out," Anita announced, walking up. "Who are they from?" She could barely contain herself.

Daphne and Sophia joined her, crowding around to hear who had sent Ashley flowers.

Ashley looked down at the card. "My uncle...Benny."

Daphne sniffed the roses. "Man, I wish my uncle was that thoughtful. I don't even get a birthday card."

Sophia and Anita agreed.

I looked up and caught Ashley throwing a wicked stare my direction.

I smiled and cast a wave none of the others saw.

The gaggle dispersed after a few more *oohs* and *aahs*, and then Ashley marched into my office.

"You can't..." she said softly.

"I thought it was nice of Uncle Benny to try to cheer you up."

"But..." She stood there with her hands on her hips. "But..."

"I think your uncle Benny is a nice guy," I told her.

I ached to erase the distance between us and take her beautiful face in my hands—kiss the indignant attitude right out of her, lock the door, and introduce her naked skin to the leather of my couch.

But her rules forbade it, and I'd stupidly agreed to follow them.

"You can't." She huffed once more before turning on her heels and marching her cute ass out of reach.

Five minutes later, Ashley had located additional vases in the storage closet and split the flowers among the four assistants, which—based on the comments I heard—earned her points like crazy.

She walked back into my office and shut the door. "Thank you. But please don't do that again."

She'd calmed, but only marginally.

"Why not? It put a smile on your face, and that was kind of the idea."

"I can't have them knowing, that's why. I mean...Uncle Benny? Couldn't you have been more creative, *Mr. Benson*?"

"You're welcome, and how are you feeling?" I asked. "You really tied one on last night."

"Better... Now, at least. That green gunk helped. What was in that anyway?"

"Like I told you, celery and cockroaches." I smirked.

"Tasted like crap."

"The cost of overdrinking. You should have chosen dancing."

She took a seat. "We need to talk."

"Sure, but first, I'm sorry about your cousin, and I really am glad you're feeling better today."

Her eyes turned watery.

I got up and rounded the desk. She surprised me by standing and wrapping her arms around me, resting her head against my chest.

I rubbed her back. "It'll be okay. I'm here for you."

Yesterday had hit her harder than I'd realized—much harder.

"Just hold me," she mumbled into my shirt.

"I can do better than that. Wanna try the couch?"

"Stop that."

"I was being serious."

"That's the problem." She pushed away and tear-stained eyes looked into mine. "Can I trust you?"

Trust wasn't a question I'd anticipated.

I kissed her on the forehead. "You know you can, Kitten."

"You won't hurt me?"

I chuckled. "I could never do that." I pulled her back into a tight hug, and we rocked for a while as I soothed my hurting girl. I wished for the embrace to soak up all her pain, to slay her demons and give her peace. She deserved happiness.

"I got a call yesterday."

It was my turn to break the closeness so I could look into her eyes. "Go ahead."

"It was Jacinda. She said the paper had a tip that you did a deal with the mob."

I huffed. "They've got to be kidding."

She pulled away. "She wanted confirmation. I told her it wasn't true."

"Of course not."

"She said you met with Sonny Alfonso two weeks ago yesterday to ink a deal."

I urged her to sit, and I took the other chair. "You don't actually believe that shit, do you?"

"No, no, no." She shook her head. "But maybe I can help by telling her how wrong her source is. We can document where you were that day."

I thought for a moment and decided I could see how that might work.

She put a hand on my knee. "I think it would be easier to head it off at the pass than sue them after the fact."

I thought back for a moment to make sure I had the right day. "Two weeks ago yesterday, I got a call to meet my brother in Springfield. I drove there, but he didn't show."

"Which brother?" she asked.

"Dennis."

She cocked her head. "Does he do that often?"

I hadn't explained the whole situation. "I said I got a call to meet my brother. I didn't say I talked to him. There was a message left on my desk. It said to meet him at a restaurant by the interstate in Spring-field. I drove over, but he wasn't there."

She nodded and waited for me to continue.

"When I called him, he claimed he hadn't called or left me a message. And I believe him. He may be a practical joker, but that's not his style."

"If he didn't do it, who left the message?" she asked.

"I have no idea. The message was taken by a girl who didn't last long: Marcy. At the time, I thought it was just another screw-up. But she claimed she'd gotten it right."

Ashley cocked her head. "Marcy?"

"Not the sharpest tool in the shed—the girl before that Jacinda bitch."

"I think that's enough for me to get her to back off for now."

"Fuck," I said. Now I could see the connection. "You said a deal with the mob, right?"

She nodded "Yeah."

"Now it's starting to make sense. It has to be Gainsboro behind all this."

"Why him?" she asked.

"Gainsboro is a company—the competition for the Semaphore acquisition."

She sat forward. "Why would they be out to smear you?"

"So far we've outbid them for Semaphore, and with more resources than they have, that isn't going to change. Among other things, Semaphore makes electronic gaming equipment for casinos. Mob involvement is a no-no for all of the gaming commissions, and making it look like I'm in bed with organized crime screws the deal for us and lets them get it."

"Casino machines is a big enough business for somebody to do this?"

"Several hundred million a year."

The number seemed to get her attention.

ASHLEY

HE STOOD. "I DIDN'T GET MY RUN IN THIS MORNING."

"Why not?"

"I was worried about a certain assistant who wasn't feeling well," he said, giving me a light kiss.

"I'll bet you were a little hungover too."

He grinned. "Maybe."

I giggled. "Price of being a drinking buddy."

"It was worth it. I'll be down in the gym for an hour."

"Is it okay if I clean your office while you're gone?" I asked.

"It's all yours," he said as he left.

I followed him out, grabbed my purse, and then shut myself back in the massive room.

I pulled on latex gloves, removed the evidence bag from my purse, moved around behind his desk, and lifted the blotter. The memo was still there. Using paperclips, I shifted it into the evidence bag and sealed it up.

I'd called John on the way over, and he'd agreed to run this for me out of the New Haven office. It would take a few days, given the mail processing time, but I couldn't afford to drive it, and I certainly couldn't risk putting it through the Boston lab.

The fingerprint kit came next out of my purse, and I started on the desk, not expecting anything but hoping nonetheless. The results were as I'd feared: nothing but smudges.

Moving to the typewriter, I carefully dusted all the keys and other surfaces that were smooth enough to take a print. Using tape, I lifted the few possible partials that appeared.

Done with fingerprinting the typewriter, I inserted a page and typed the alphabet and numbers. Checking the paper, I was disappointed to find the same misshapen Z. The memo had been typed on this IBM.

That didn't mean for sure that Vince had typed it, and the fact that he'd been called out of town on exactly the day of the contract gave me hope that I could still exonerate him. *Innocent until proven guilty,* I told myself.

The chances of finding the culprit this way were probably low, but I had to pursue all the avenues. I glanced around the room for other surfaces to check. What came to mind was the edge of his door. People would sometimes pull the edge to close the door rather than the handle. Unfortunately, that area didn't yield anything.

I took a seat on the couch and looked around the room. Closing my eyes, I put myself in place of the culprit planting the memo. What would I do? How would I move around the room and what would I possibly touch?

The blotter.

Standing behind the desk, I carefully pulled the blotter toward me, hanging the first several inches of it off the edge of the wooden desk. Getting down on my knees and looking underneath, I found what I'd hoped I would—a smooth surface, one that could hold a print.

It was uncomfortable to work upside down, but I finally found what looked like a usable print on the right side of the back of the blotter.

After pulling the tape on that print, I scanned the room again. Nothing else seemed likely to help, so I went about cleaning the print dust off of the surfaces I'd checked.

A knock came at the door as I was finishing my cleanup.

I opened the door to find Anita.

"Oh, there you are," she said. "I have to go out to run an errand for Mason. Can you handle his phone? He's expecting some kind of important call."

"Sure. I'm just doing some cleaning in here. I'll be out in just a sec."

She closed the door behind her.

Confident I hadn't missed anything after scanning the room one more time, I went to my desk, pulled out an express mail envelope,

CAUGHT BY THE BILLIONAIRE

and filled it out to get these things to John in the New Haven office tomorrow.

If ever there was a case that needed to be handled with flexibility, this was it.

This seemed like a well-done frame up. Vince had been called out for a few hours, so he was unable to prove he wasn't meeting Alfonso at the time. The memo had likely been planted on his desk, and the DOJ source had fed the Bureau detailed information to send me in to find that specific piece of paper. The Gainsboro guys were playing this well, but there was one hole in their plan. They had to have a person inside Covington. Who else could have gotten into Vince's office?

I had to find that person, and fast.

As I sealed the envelope, I felt as I might have sealed my career as well by going so far off the reservation. But what was done was done. I'd been forced to choose a side, and I'd chosen to believe Vince over SAC White's anonymous source. My gut told me this was the right call.

Vince promised I could trust him.

∼

VINCENT

ANOTHER TEXT ARRIVED FROM BARB JUST AFTER I STARTED MY VIRTUAL run.

BARB: Call me

As my feet pounded out miles on the rubber strip, I thought back to last night. Why had I stayed? Why hadn't I left Ashley to her pity party and joined Barb for an enjoyable evening?

Who am I?

The old me would definitely have taken Barb's invitation. Staying in with Ashley to get drunk watching TV reruns and *not* getting my rocks off was completely out of character—my old character.

I hadn't responded to Barb precisely because she represented the old me.

The new me wanted one thing: Ashley. And I needed her to want me, warts and all. I wasn't going to let her get away again.

By mile seven on the treadmill, I'd decided on a plan of action. She was going to be mine—all mine.

After showering, I returned upstairs.

Ashley was at her desk, working on her computer.

I waved for her to follow me into my office.

Once she closed the door, I moved in close enough to smell the coconut of her shampoo. "Did you make that call to your acquaintance?"

"Sure did, and I think it will help."

That was a relief. If she could get the tabloid dogs off me for a bit, I could figure out how to combat Gainsboro.

I held out my hand. "Give me your apartment key."

She looked at me, stunned.

"I trust you," I told her. "Now, do you trust me?"

"Yes, but…"

I kept my hand out.

She relented and went to retrieve the key from her purse. "Are you making a copy?" she asked.

"Trust," I said.

She turned over the key, which I pocketed.

"We're going to dinner tonight," I told her firmly.

"I'm not sure—"

"Trust me," I repeated. I walked out of the office, leaving her behind.

I left the building, and when I reached her apartment, I let myself in.

I began my search.

When I was done, I dialed Anita.

CHAPTER 29

Vincent

Later that afternoon, I checked my watch and packed up my briefcase.

"Time to leave," I told Ashley after locking my office.

"But I'm not done."

"Yes, you are."

"But it's only four."

"It's a long trip to the restaurant."

She cocked her head at that, but held her tongue.

When we reached the street, the town car was waiting for us at the curb.

I slid in after her.

"Just how far away is this restaurant?" she asked.

"You'll see."

She didn't appear happy with that non-answer, but she leaned back and watched the downtown scenery go by. It wasn't until we entered the Callahan Tunnel that she started up again.

"How much farther?"

I took her hand in mine. "It'll be a very special dinner, I promise."

My phone rang. It was Steven Covington.

"Any problems?" I asked, mentally crossing my fingers that he had come through with what I needed.

"None at all. Your contact will be a Mr. Cromartie. Just have them call him from the desk at the entrance. He has everything arranged for you."

"Thanks, Steven. I owe you."

"Just remember that when I call and need a favor."

I laughed, and we hung up. No doubt that call would come one day.

"Who was that?" Ashley asked.

"An old friend from California."

When we took the exit for the airport, her eyes widened. "I hate to break it to you, but airport food doesn't ring the special bell."

"Just wait. You won't be disappointed."

A few minutes later, we were buzzed through the gate at the private jet terminal and rolled up to my plane.

"You've got to be kidding," she said.

I opened the door and offered her a hand out. "Not in the least. It's faster than driving."

"How far?"

I went to the trunk and accepted our luggage from the driver. "New York, for the weekend."

"But I didn't pack anything," she complained.

"I went to your apartment and picked out a few things, and anything else you need, we can get there."

"Just like that? Pick up and go to New York?"

I carried the luggage to the back of the plane. "Yes, just like that. And you're going to love the dinner location, absolutely love it."

I handed our two bags to the crew member. The three gold stripes on his epaulets marked him as the copilot. He hefted the bags into the cargo compartment at the rear of the plane.

The sun reflected off the white of the jet's fuselage as we made our way to the forward door with the additional garment bag.

"Is this plane yours?" Ashley asked.

"Nope."

"Your father's?"

"After you." I motioned for her to start up the steps. "No, his is bigger. This is just a rental, sort of like a time share. I have partial use of it when I need it. Fractional ownership, it's called." I followed her inside. "My boss was against the idea of a jet, and a quarter share is all I could get him to agree to."

"I can take that," the flight attendant offered as I cleared the door. I handed her the garment bag and followed Ashley.

"Wow," Ashley exclaimed, running her hand over the seats before selecting the forward-facing one on the right. "This is classy."

I took the seat opposite hers. "Buckle up; that rule is still the same." I secured my belt, and she did as well.

The flight attendant returned with champagne, which Ashley accepted and I declined.

"This is what I call first class," Ashley commented. "And in real glass instead of plastic. You sure are spoiled."

It had been ages since I'd flown commercial, and her comment struck a chord with me. I'd become oblivious to the differences.

The copilot climbed in after us. "Mr. Benson, are we expecting any more passengers?"

"No. This is it."

He closed and secured the door. Moments later, an engine started, whirring to life.

"Flight time will be just over an hour, sir," he said before sliding into the cockpit.

I waved an acknowledgment. "Thanks."

The second engine started, and soon we were taxiing for takeoff.

Ashley quickly finished her glass of champagne and held it up for a refill.

Our flight attendant brought over the bottle, but I waved her off. "Maybe later."

The attendant didn't need to be told twice; she understood who the paying passenger was. She retreated to the rear, capping the bottle and placing it back in the refrigerator.

"But I need another," Ashley complained with a hurt look.

"Later."

"I need it to get through the flight."

"What you need is to realize that this is safer than driving."

She bit her lip. "Thirty thousand people a year die in traffic accidents, so that's not saying much." She fixed me with an angry stare. "It's not like if the engine light comes on they can just pull over to the side of the road."

"You don't need to worry. The engines are quite reliable."

She shook her head. "Yeah, until lightning strikes."

"The weather is fine today. No lightning."

"Or birds fly into the engine," she added.

I didn't respond. It was clear that logic was not going to prevail on this subject.

We turned onto the runway, and the engines spooled up to a mild roar. The jet swiftly accelerated.

Ashley's knuckles were white from her death grip on the armrests. I could see fear in her eyes.

"Close your eyes and take slow, deep breaths," I told her.

She didn't.

"Trust me," I insisted.

She finally did as I asked.

Seated facing backwards, I was pitched forward as the nose rose and we climbed away from terra firma. Whirring and clanks came from below us in the belly of the plane.

Her eyes popped open. "What was that?"

"Just the landing gear being retracted. It's perfectly normal."

She closed her eyes again.

"Slow, deep breaths," I repeated.

She kept her eyes closed, and slowly the color returned to her skin, her breathing steadied, and her grip on the armrests loosened.

I waved to our flight attendant, tipping my hand up to my mouth and pointing at Ashley.

The attendant smiled, understanding my signals, and brought over another glass of champagne.

"Now you're ready for the second glass," I told Ashley, tapping her on the knee.

Her eyes opened, and she accepted the champagne. "Thank you."

"Feel better?" I asked.

She sipped rather than guzzled the bubbly liquid as the attendant returned to her seat in the back.

"A little."

"Dad taught me that."

"You used to be scared of flying?"

"Deathly. My first trip in a plane didn't go well. There was lightning, thunder, and thousand-foot drops. I lost my lunch and refused to fly again."

"But you seem so calm now."

"Dad challenged me, as he often does. He said if I couldn't conquer my fear, I would never amount to anything. Anyway, he took me up every weekend for a while, taught me that exercise, and I got over it. Now it's no big deal."

"He sounds like a wise man."

"More like a bully. I was perfectly happy driving between LA and Vegas, but I couldn't let him get away with challenging me like that."

She took another sip and offered me the glass. "Want to share?"

I reached out to accept the champagne. "Thanks."

Encouraged by the increasing altitude of the plane, the bubbles tickled my nose as I sipped. I handed her back the remainder of the golden drink.

CHAPTER 30

ASHLEY

I COULD HAVE DONE WITHOUT THE PLANE RIDE, BUT IF I HAD TO LEAVE THE ground, Vince's jet was certainly the way to do it.

His breathing technique had worked, at least somewhat, but I felt sort of stupid. I knew the statistics said flying was safe, but there was something about giving up control to the pilot and knowing we had miles to drop if something went wrong that paralyzed me in a plane.

The champagne helped, too, but Vince's understanding helped the most.

Sitting across from his entrancing gaze, I found his melodious voice soothing. Listening to him tell me about his childhood fear of flying and the way he'd overcome it brought a smile to my face—and I never smiled when I flew; I was always too worried.

Before I knew it, the plane pitched down and we were descending to land in New York. Once my feet reached solid ground, I felt better.

I didn't see skyscrapers anywhere. "This is New York?"

"No, silly. This is Teterboro Airport in New Jersey. Now we take another ride."

"Are you going to tell me which restaurant we're going to?"

"No. Surprise means surprise. But you will find it quite unique."

I would have been happy with a simple meal anywhere in Boston, but *simple* was not on Vince's radar this evening. I needed to sit back and enjoy the ride.

Instead of walking toward the terminal, however, the crew member was taking our bags to a helicopter—a fucking helicopter.

Vince waved me to come with him in that direction.

"Can't we just take a cab?" I asked.

"This is quicker."

I'd left my gun in my apartment in Boston, so I didn't see any way to dissuade him. "If I die in this, I'm going to come back and haunt you."

"You'll love it."

"Not a chance in hell," I shot back.

The helicopter shook, and it was so loud that we wore headphones to talk to one another, but the view as we crossed the Hudson and skimmed the skyline of Manhattan was breathtaking. That almost made up for it.

In what seemed like a matter of minutes, we were in the second town car of the evening on our way through Manhattan traffic, which seemed lighter than some of the congestion we'd had growing up in Los Angeles.

In short order, the car pulled to a stop in front of a hotel across from Central Park. The sign above the door read *Park Lane Hotel*. It was the tallest building on this end of Central Park.

At the registration desk, they summoned the manager as soon as they heard Vince's name.

The balding man and a bellboy escorted us up in the elevator to the forty-sixth floor, the highest button there was. With a flourish, he stepped out and opened the door that read *Park Lane Suite*.

The space was gargantuan, a hundred times more spacious than any hotel room I'd ever stayed in.

I walked to the window, overcome by the view of Central Park laid out in front of me.

"Isn't this a little overboard?" I asked Vince after they left us.

"Nothing but the best for my Kitten," he said, coming up behind me. He wrapped his arms around me and rested his chin on my head. "How do you like the view?"

The air was clear, and the green of the park magnificent. "Love it. Now tell me, do you book rooms like this every time you travel?"

"Every time I travel with you I will."

"How many women have you brought here?" I instantly regretted being so rude, so insecure.

His grip on me tightened as he lowered his mouth to my ear and whispered. "You're the first."

His words fogged my brain. I really was his Kitten, and I couldn't think of any better title I could aspire to. I snuggled back against his warmth and purred.

He cut the moment short by releasing me. "You have to get changed. We don't have a lot of time."

"Changed?"

He walked to the closet. "I got you something to wear tonight."

"What's wrong with this?" I had on a sophisticated outfit that would've gotten me in the door of any restaurant in town.

He unzipped the garment bag and pulled out a dress. "Tonight you need something more."

My jaw dropped. It wasn't just a dress, it was a Ferrari red dress that looked like it belonged on an actress at a movie premier—it definitely qualified as *more*.

He held the hanger up. "I had Anita pick it out." He laid that one on the bed and retrieved another from the bag. "If you don't like that one, maybe this will do."

I started to object, but he stopped me with a finger to my lips.

"Don't worry. I gave her your sizes, but she doesn't know who these are for."

I breathed a deep sigh of relief. But I didn't see how we were going to keep things under wraps if he continued like this.

The second dress was black, and equally stunning. It was almost floor length, with a dangerously deep V in front, a sheer back panel, and a hip-high slit on one side.

"My God, Vince. Why?" was all I could manage.

"Good, the black it is," he said. Naturally he chose the more provocative one.

"But I can't wear something like that without doing my face."

"Anita packed you some makeup. It's in the red suitcase."

I unzipped the bag and found a Lancôme makeup kit, as promised, along with an assortment of lipsticks. He'd thought of everything.

Underneath those I found a sheer teddy and held it up. "And this?"

"That's for breakfast."

I laughed and retreated to the bathroom to fix my face.

After blush, eye shadow, eye liner, and mascara, I considered a deep cherry lipstick, but chose a more muted peach in the end. I retrieved the dress and examined it.

It really wasn't a dress; this deserved the title of *gown*. The sheer back panel wouldn't allow a bra. I chose the highest-waisted of the undies he had packed and was relieved to find the slit didn't quite expose them. At least I wouldn't be going commando tonight.

I held up the hem as I came out. "Shoes?"

He'd changed into a tux, and the sight halted my breath for a moment. The man looked like he was straight out of a Bond movie.

"Check the bottom of the garment bag."

I shuffled over and discovered three choices of heels. I chose the bright red pair, and God bless Anita, they fit. With the heels on, the hem stopped comfortably off the floor.

"Ready?" Vince asked, checking his watch.

"Just need my lipstick."

When I returned from the bathroom, lipstick in hand, he held out a black leather clutch. It might have been small and simple, but the Gucci logo on it put it in the thousand-dollar price range. "You're spoiling me."

"That's the plan, Kitten."

We went downstairs to a waiting limo, which was soon going north on Madison Avenue—at least that's what the street signs said. Two dozen blocks and a few turns later, we stopped in front of the eight stone columns I would have recognized anywhere: the New York Metropolitan Museum, The Met.

"You remembered," I whispered to my handsome date.

I'd told him once in high school that it was my dream to visit the Met and the Empire State Building someday.

He smiled and squeezed my hand. "When it comes to you, I remember every moment."

He opened the door before I could tell him how romantically mushy he sounded.

He held my hand as we ascended the steps to the entrance.

With every step I took up the stairs, the slit opened wide, threatening to show everything and drawing a fair number of oglers.

Chin up and smile, girl. They're just jealous.

At the desk inside, Vince asked for a Mr. Cromartie, and either the James Bond outfit or the name got an immediate reaction, as the two employees at once started phoning to find the man.

Minutes later, a gray-haired man with an oddly askew bow tie rushed up and introduced himself. He turned out to be the director of the entire museum.

"Mr. Benson, Miss Newton, we have been expecting you," Cromartie said. "If you will please follow me, I hope you will find our arrangements acceptable."

We followed as he rattled off details about the exhibits we passed like a tour guide. Eventually he took us behind velvet ropes and held open a curtain as we passed into a room without any visitors. An elegantly set dinner table for two graced the middle of the room. The heavy curtain did a good job of muffling the sounds of the people shuffling through the museum beyond the velvet rope. Another curtain closed off the opposite opening.

"I thought the Vermeer room would be most appropriate for your dinner."

"Thank you," Vince replied.

Cromartie went back into tour guide mode. "This room contains six works by the esteemed Dutch artist Johannes Vermeer, more than any other museum in the world."

After a polite thank you from Vince, we were alone.

We took a moment to admire the paintings adorning the walls. One of them had a plaque indicating it had been donated by the Covington family.

"Is this why we're getting the royal treatment?" I asked.

Vince put his arm around me. "They donated several other priceless paintings as well, but being a Vermeer fan, this one in particular earned them points with Cromartie. It lets him boast more Vermeers than even the Dutch National Museum."

Two waiters in waistcoats entered with bread, water, wine, and salads.

We took our seats.

Vince raised his glass. "To a wonderful weekend with a lovely lady."

I accepted the compliment, and we clinked glasses.

"Vince?"

He looked up from his salad. "Yes?"

"What is this all about?"

"You need a little cheering up. And that falls under my job description. So here we are."

This man was so over the top.

"You could have just bought me ice cream, and I would have loved it."

I would have been head over heels with a simple date at an ice cream parlor, especially after the flowers.

"Nonsense. You said you wanted to visit, and tonight is your night."

His thoughtfulness brought tears to my eyes.

"What's wrong?"

I dabbed at my eyes with my napkin. "Nothing. You just make me so happy." I sniffed.

"I try."

Those words meant so much. I twisted my silver ring absentmindedly.

"I notice you often touch that ring when you're nervous," he said.

I pulled my hands under the table.

"It's obviously important to you. What does it signify?"

I had to tell him the truth. "My aunt Michelle gave it to me. She called it my strength ring."

He waited quietly for me to continue.

"She was retired Navy, one of the fastest women to be promoted to captain. She told me to always wear it and remember that following rules to the letter made us strong. Nothing less was acceptable."

"Sounds like she cared a lot about you."

"She was wonderful."

I changed the subject to ask how he'd come to be at Covington.

A few minutes later, a giant grin took over his face.

"Close your eyes," he said. After a moment he continued. "Now you can open them."

As I did, I gasped.

He held a small red jewelry box out to me. "For you."

~

VINCENT

SHE GASPED AT THE SIGHT OF THE BOX AND JERKED BACK.

"It's for you," I told her.

"But..."

I put the box down in front of her. "Go ahead," I urged.

She hesitated, wide eyed.

"You know it's rude to refuse a gift."

She moved her hand toward it. "I'm just surprised is all."

"Go ahead; open it."

She did.

"It's beautiful." She removed the emerald necklace from the box. "You shouldn't have. This is too much."

"Let me help." I rose and went behind her to fasten the necklace.

"How can I thank you?"

I returned to my seat, overcame my urge to offer a sophomoric sexual innuendo, and ignored the question.

"When I saw it, I knew it would complement your eyes," I said instead.

And my judgment was vindicated. She wore it beautifully, the emerald a perfect match to her eyes.

"It was supposed to be your graduation gift, but..." I stopped there. We didn't need to rehash the pain of what had transpired.

"You kept it...all this time?" she asked with a trembling lip.

"Well, I couldn't wear it. It's not my style."

"You could have given it to Roxy."

Roxy had been my freshman-year girlfriend at USC. "How do you know about Roxy?" I asked.

An immediate blush rose in her cheeks.

"You were stalking me?"

She looked down. "How's your salad."

"For how long?" I asked, not going for her attempted change of subject.

"I might have asked Serena about you once or twice," she confessed.

I'd obviously hurt her more than I realized if she'd been asking my sister about me.

"It was meant for you, Kitten, and you alone."

She reached across, and I took her hand. "Thank you, Vince. It's lovely."

The waiters returned, calling a halt to the awkwardness. They cleared the salad and brought the main course. Steak for me and salmon for her.

"Is it all you expected? The museum?" I asked as the waiters retreated behind the curtain.

She nodded. "And more. It's magnificent."

As we ate, we talked about the art class in California that had precipitated her desire to visit the museum, and the art history courses she took as electives in college.

Eventually, the waiters cleared our plates and dessert arrived. We were almost to the finale.

"Key lime pie? Again?" she asked.

The smile on her face was the thanks I'd hoped for.

A waiter stood in the corner, waiting for us to finish.

She ate her dessert slowly, savoring each bite—and torturing me as I envisioned her tongue on me instead of the spoon.

I finished mine quickly. The tension of the delay was killing me.

She sucked the last of the pie off her spoon with a seductive smile, and eyes that seemed to share the same hunger for nakedness I had.

She finally put down her spoon. "That was delicious."

I motioned to the waiter, and he pulled the curtain open to reveal the group arrayed in the next room.

Her eyes bulged.

CHAPTER 31

ASHLEY

THE WAITER PULLED OPEN THE CURTAIN, AND MY JAW NEARLY DROPPED TO the floor.

A band?

Vince stood and offered me his hand. "May I have this dance?"

In a daze, I stood, and Vince pulled me to him. The heat of his body against mine jolted me. I'd imagined undressing him bit by bit all throughout dinner. The forced propriety of sitting across the table from him, looking as delectable as he did, had shifted my libido up a gear.

Several of those who'd been waiting on us pulled the table to the side of the room as the band began to play.

"I couldn't get the original Sugarloaf, so this will have to do," Vince said into my ear as we started to sway to the music.

They were playing "Green-Eyed Lady," the song he'd declared to be our song at the dance we'd attended in high school, in homage to my eye color.

We danced as the singer belted out the lyrics.

I wept tears of joy. This was unbelievable. We'd eaten a private meal in the middle of the Met, he'd given me a beautiful necklace he'd kept since high school, and now we were dancing as a band played our song, filling the museum with music. I sniffled.

Vince raised my chin with a finger. "You're crying."

"I'm just so happy; I can't help it."

I put my head back on his chest, and we swayed until the song stopped.

When it did, clapping erupted from behind the remaining curtains. The other patrons of the museum must have liked the impromptu performance.

A string quartet began playing next, classical music and much softer—much more in keeping with the decorum of the museum.

"Sorry, I could only get permission for the one pop song," Vince explained as we continued to sway in each other's arms.

My tears soaked his jacket.

"We can dance as long as you like," he said softly.

I didn't reply, just melted into his arms and took in the evening.

"Would you like to wander the museum until closing?"

"No," I said.

I squeezed him tighter. I wanted to stay in his strong arms, just the two of us—no crowds, no onlookers, just us.

He rubbed my back, igniting sparks with his touch. "What then?"

"I've wanted to rip that gorgeous tux off of you since the moment we sat down."

He lifted me and spun me around, setting me down after two turns. "And I've wanted to rip the slit of that dress right up to your shoulder since we got in the car."

I closed my eyes and pulled myself up for the kiss I'd been waiting for all night—the kiss that topped off the evening of a lifetime.

He didn't disappoint as he deepened our embrace, giving as good as he got. He pulled back and nibbled my lip lightly before his tongue traced my mouth. We traded breath and desire as we pulled each other close, attempting to breach the fabric between us and meld into one being, a couple.

The faint eucalyptus of his hair tickled my nose as he loosened his grip and we swayed again to the sounds of the string instruments.

At first I was self-conscious about the musicians as he grabbed my ass and caressed my breast. But as we traded the taste of the lime-flavored dessert and the smoothness of rich, red wine, I cared less and less. I kept my eyes closed, and we were dancing among the clouds—just me and my man. Time stood still, and all that mattered was the protective warmth he'd enveloped me in.

The music continued, and the scene playing behind my eyelids was that of our kiss that night so long ago.

"We'd better go before I lose control and rip that dress right off you," he breathed.

I nodded and took his hand as he led me out.

The quartet continued playing, and a sea of museumgoers parted, *ooh*ing and *aah*ing as we passed through.

The ride back to the hotel seemed interminable as anticipation built within me. Our suite at the top of the hotel awaited. This had to be what a honeymoon was like.

CHAPTER 32

VINCENT

SHE'D SAID SHE COULDN'T WAIT TO GET ME UNDRESSED, AND I WAS HAVING an equally hard time—literally—keeping from ripping her thin dress to shreds to reach the hot flesh underneath. She was making me crazy. The obvious bounce of her breasts as she walked had driven me to distraction, and the slit in her dress had taunted me each time it revealed *all* of her long leg.

As soon as the door to the room closed, she was yanking at my tie, followed by my cummerbund. Then she stopped and pushed me back. "Page one-twenty-eight."

I worked my cufflinks loose and recalled the page: Juliet on her knees giving Dalton a blowjob. My cock throbbed at the mental image.

Ashley slipped off the dress. "I don't want it to get damaged."

She stepped out of it, the picture of elegant beauty: nothing but a high-waisted thong and black heels.

"No," I said. "Not one-twenty-eight."

That scene was too one-sided, and tonight was for her. I was dying for her mouth on me, but tonight it had to be something for her—something new, something unforgettable.

She cocked her head. "But I want to try."

The meaning almost escaped me, but I caught it just in time to clarify.

"You haven't...?" I didn't finish the sentence.

She cast her gaze down. "No. But I can try."

I closed the distance, tipped up her chin, and said the words I should have said to her many years ago. "Not tonight, and not until you're ready."

"But—"

I stopped her with a finger to her lips. "Page two-oh-two," I told her. "Get on the couch."

For a split second she looked ready to argue, but she seemed to change her mind. She walked to the couch and sat. She leaned over to undo the straps of her heels.

"Keep them on."

She let go of the strap and sat up again.

After freeing the second of the uncooperative cufflinks, I shed my shirt.

∿

ASHLEY

HE'D STUNNED ME BY REFUSING THE ORAL SEX I OFFERED. ACCORDING TO the girls I'd gone to college with, no guy ever refused a BJ—not ever. Then he'd turned the tables and changed to page two-oh-two. I couldn't quite remember what that was. There'd been three scenes involving the couch, or maybe four.

My sex clenched, and I shivered with anticipation as he strode toward me, shirtless. He pulled off his shoes one by one.

The heat between my legs grew unbearable as I yearned for his touch.

He pulled at my panties.

I lifted my ass to free them as he slid them to my ankles and picked up one foot then the other.

He spread my legs and licked his lips as his eyes raked over me.

The lights were still on. Feeling exposed, I tried to close my legs, but he wouldn't let me.

"You're gorgeous, Kitten."

I trembled as I finally remembered page two-oh-two.

He knelt between my legs and pulled me forward, my ass at the very edge of the couch.

I spread my legs wider and pulled my knees up, opening myself fully to him.

He blew on my wet lower lips and then traced a finger up one edge and down the other, avoiding my most sensitive flesh—teasing, tracing with just a feather-light touch.

"Give me a finger," I said, trying to remember Juliet's lines.

I trembled as his finger entered me, hooked, and stroked the tenderness inside of me.

"Deeper," I said.

He complied, keeping with the script.

As he moved his finger slowly in and out, stroking my walls, my anticipation built for what was to come. "Another," I begged, as Juliet had. My God Juliet had gotten it right.

The second finger joined the first, adding pressure.

I closed my eyes and tried to visualize Juliet's words. "Now my clit. I'm ready."

And I was as the heat grew, emanating from my core.

His other hand came to my clit, with surprising pressure, and held there.

"Now circle."

He did.

With the fingers inside me moving slowly, and him circling my little nub, the tingles were building.

"Lighter."

"Harder."

He did as I asked, and I began to understand the appeal of the page with every stroke. Juliet's words didn't matter anymore.

"Faster."

"Back and forth."

I pulled my knees up harder as the tension built in all my muscles, and more and more of my nerves became overloaded.

"Oh fuck. Harder."

"A little higher."

"Shit. Right there."

I let go of my knees and grabbed for his head.

He pulled back. That wasn't in the script. At least not yet.

I grasped my knees again.

"Circle...fuck yes." I could barely hear myself with the blood rushing in my ears.

"Lighter."

My breathing was coming faster every second. "Harder."

"Fuck, yeah. Faster."

"The other direction."

"Oh shit."

I arched my hips up into his pressure.

"Holy fuck."

"More."

He pressed harder, and the tremors started, sparks igniting all my nerve endings.

My walls constricted, and my clit exploded under his touch. I couldn't breathe, and my fingernails dug into my legs. "Holy shit," was all I could manage.

Slowly, the tremors receded, and I relaxed, letting go of my knees.

He pulled out his fingers and pushed his palm against the throbbing of my pussy, rubbing up and down with light pressure on the entire area.

I opened my eyes to the intense hunger in his and the monster smile written across his face. I'd have to remember this page for another day.

He stood and marched to his suitcase, returning with a tie. "Stand up."

I stretched out my hand, and he pulled me to my feet.

He spun me around and the tie covered my eyes.

"Page two-ninety-two?" I asked awkwardly. As tender as my pussy was, I wasn't sure I was ready for the spanking.

He cinched the tie tight and took my hand. "Guess again." He led me slowly forward.

I stepped gingerly, now blind to the room. I drew a blank trying to remember another blindfolded scene.

He lifted my hands, and they met the cold glass of the window.

Now I knew the page. "Three-fourteen."

He didn't answer me. "Stand there," he commanded.

I couldn't figure out if the blindfold made it easier or harder to stand naked in the window of a hotel room for anyone out there to see. Probably harder, as I imagined people on the street below pointing upward, guiding other eyes to take in the naked lady against the window. What if they snapped a picture with their cell phones? The thought chilled me.

I heard the tearing sound of the foil packet behind me.

Vince's hands started at my shoulders and traced my arms out to my hands as his cock settled against my back and the scent of eucalyptus invaded my nostrils. I trembled at the feel of his hot breath on the back of my neck.

His hands held mine against the glass. I flinched as his tongue grazed my earlobe.

"How many people do you imagine are down there watching us? A dozen? Maybe two dozen?" he whispered into my ear.

I cringed in fear. When Juliet had removed the blindfold, she'd found a dozen or more strangers gazing up at her.

"Keep your hands on the glass," he commanded. With his foot he urged mine apart. "Shift back a little."

I did.

Fingers traced a fiery trail down my arms and along my sides to under my ass, where they left me breathless and wanting more. I gasped as a single fingernail scraped from my neck down my spine and back up again. The slow torture continued with barely-there fingertips tracing the insides of my legs from my ankles to my knees and then slowly farther north toward the destination I hoped for.

I spread my legs a bit more, but he stopped short. My pussy throbbed with the need to have him inside me.

"What do you want, Kitten?" His voice rumbled through me, extinguishing my inhibitions.

"You. I want you inside me." My words were only half as frantic as my need.

His cock teased between my thighs as his hands clamped down on my breasts. "First you have to come for the crowd."

A vision of people with their cell phones out flashed again in my brain. The danger only amplified the throbbing of my pulse in my soaked pussy.

His grip on one breast loosened to a light caress as a finger of the other hand slid slowly down my chest, over my bellybutton, and parted my folds to trace around my swollen clit in agonizingly slow circles.

He pushed me up against the glass. "You're going to come for me, Kitten."

The slow torment of his light touch was working its magic.

The glass was cold against one breast, with the other protected by the warmth of his hand.

I jerked as he pulled his finger away from my needy nub and brought it to my nose. The scent of me replaced the faint eucalyptus of him.

His finger pushed against my lips, and I opened for him, tasting myself for the second time.

"That's the taste of desire," he whispered into my ear.

I nodded.

"Imagine what our kiss will be like after I give you a tongue-lashing."

My pussy spasmed at the thought of his face between my legs, his stubble scratching my inner thighs.

His fingers returned to my crotch and the ministrations to my hypersensitive clit became strong and rhythmic.

"Faster," I urged him. "Yeah."

The words spilled out as he pressed me against the glass and continued to boil my blood with delicious torment.

"Oh, fuck…Yeah, more…Harder…Oh, shit."

With every movement, he sent me higher, closer to another, bigger climax.

"They're clapping for you," he groaned.

I didn't hear a thing through the thick glass, with the thrum of my own rapid heartbeat in my ears. Lightning bolts shot through my nerves.

He pinched my nipple. "Come for me, Kitten."

Another few strokes and the explosion came, hurtling me over the edge. My inner walls contracted around emptiness, longing to be filled by him.

He held me up as I wobbled in the high heels.

When I could breathe again, he pulled me back and spread my legs farther.

His tip found my slippery entrance, and he pushed in as I braced against the glass.

I finally got the feeling of fullness I'd longed for.

His grip on my hips tightened as his thrusts became forceful and rapid.

My breasts swung forward and back with the movement.

His fingers tightened as the animal in him claimed me with more intensity.

He found his end with a final push and pulled me into him with a groan that was half roar.

As he held me against him, his cock throbbed inside me before he pulled out. He spun me around so fast I almost tripped. His mouth clamped over mine, and with his scent in my nostrils, his kiss said more than his words ever could. He pulled me close, erasing the space between us. I could feel the pounding of his heart against my breasts.

He broke the kiss. "Welcome to New York, Kitten."

I kissed him again.

He loosened the tie and pulled it off my head.

I blinked at the bright light in the room. As I turned toward the window, I realized there was no crowd. We faced the park, and we were more than forty floors up. At this angle, nobody could see a thing. I slapped his shoulder. "You lied."

He laughed. "I just followed the script."

In the book, Juliet had been naked in a second-story window.

This man had given me an incredible evening in a million ways.

CHAPTER 33

ASHLEY

IT WAS SUNDAY AFTERNOON, AND OUR PLANE LEVELED OFF AT CRUISING altitude on the flight back to Boston.

I rubbed the emerald on the necklace Vince had given me, the necklace he'd kept all these years. The necklace that marked me as his Kitten—a title I cherished.

The weekend had been nonstop fun. After a breakfast of Belgian waffles topped with strawberries and washed down with a mimosa, we'd spent Saturday exploring the Big Apple. We'd taken a rowboat from the Loeb Boathouse onto The Lake in Central Park. He'd taken me on a carriage ride. We'd visited the zoo, walked the stores of Fifth Avenue, and kissed on top of the Empire State Building.

We'd had burgers and fries for lunch at the original Shake Shack and dined for dinner at a rooftop restaurant in the garment district.

Vince crossed his legs, and the sight of his ankle crossed over his knee brought up the question that had been bothering me since Saturday morning. Without thinking, I blurted it out. "Who's Deb?" I'd seen her name tattooed on his ankle and I'd been envious that it hadn't been mine. She must have been important to him.

He arched an eyebrow. "Pardon?"

It was too late to pull the question back. "Who's Deb, the girl's name you have tattooed on your ankle?"

A frown replaced the quizzical look, and his eyes deadened.

Instantly, I regretted being so insecure.

He pulled down his sock. "You mean this?" He pointed to the small black letters: DEB. He took a deep breath. "It's so we never forget her. It's for Deborah Ellen Benson, my cousin. She died when I was nine. She was five years old at the time. We all carry this tattoo, the whole family, so that we never forget her." The gesture was overwhelmingly sweet.

My stomach soured at how inconsiderate I'd been.

He pulled his sock back up and returned to his phone.

I sunk in my seat and stayed quiet, reflecting on how important the bond of family was to all of them. It was a lesson about the Benson's that I wouldn't forget.

Before long, the co-pilot called back to tell us it was time to buckle up for landing.

Now the weekend was over, and it was time to return to the real world—the world where bad guys at Covington's competitor were evidently trying to take Vince down, and I had no idea who the inside accomplice was. For a moment I contemplated whether it was time for me to start carrying my gun again. But I discarded the idea, intent on maintaining my cover.

I contemplated what steps I might take next and came up empty, save waiting for John's lab results on the note and fingerprints I'd mailed him before leaving for the weekend.

The time in New York had let me clear my mind of regrets for not yet turning in the evidence I'd found. After all, I'd become more and more convinced it wasn't evidence in Vince's case, but evidence in the case to be brought against the people trying to ruin him.

We'd both agreed to unplug from email and the internet for the weekend, but Vince was now catching up on his emails on the plane.

He looked up from his phone and smiled. "You seem to be doing better with the flying."

"I am, thanks. The breathing thing helps."

He went back to reading messages on his phone. A moment later he put the phone to his ear.

"Hey, Mason. What's up?... I told you I'd be out of touch for the weekend... And the Strongwood transaction?... How much more time do they want?... Tell them three weeks, then. It's only fair...You handle that one. Okay, yeah, I'll be in tomorrow..."

"I thought you gave them a deadline of this week?" I asked after he hung up.

"I did. But in the end, if both parties aren't happy signing the deal, the hard feelings will come back to cost us in the long run. What's a couple more weeks if it allows them peace of mind?"

As I watched and listened to him, I could sense Vince's innate goodness. He was not the criminal here; I knew that for certain. But now I had to figure out how to prove it before his enemy got the better of him.

Vince looked up again. "What's worrying you, Kitten?"

I loved it every time he called me that. It made me feel like cuddling up next to him and purring.

"I'm not sure what you should do next to find out who wrote that awful note," I said.

He shrugged. "I can worry about that tomorrow."

I nodded. He apparently thought the most important word in his sentence had been *tomorrow*, while I was focused on *worry*.

He had resources to throw at the problem. I was a team of one. I'd gone as far as I could by enlisting John's help on the evidence. I couldn't pull in any more Bureau help. *Dread* might have been an even more appropriate word than *worry*.

THE TOWN CAR PULLED TO THE CURB IN FRONT OF THE SLEEK STEEL-AND-glass building. The green of the Common lay to the left.

I unbuckled my seatbelt, but stayed obediently in my seat while Vince raced around to open my door. I'd made the mistake of not waiting twice in New York and had been properly scolded. If he wanted to spoil me, I was game.

On the curb, Vince handed me my roller bag, while he took the other and the garment bag.

The doorman held the door for us. "Welcome back, Mr. Benson. Did you have a pleasant trip?"

Vince stopped. "Carl, this is Ashley Newton. She is to have full access to the building."

"Very good, sir." The man bowed to me. "Very nice to make your acquaintance, Miss Ashley."

"You too, Carl," I replied as he ushered us through the quiet opulence of the building's lobby.

My ears popped on the way up to the twenty-sixth floor.

Vince unlocked the door, disarmed the security system, and rolled our bags out of the way.

I wasn't prepared for the sight. His place was immense and decorated tastefully with manly, black leather furniture, as well as the requisite monster flat screen on the wall. It was probably big enough that the football players looked almost life size on it. I walked to the full-length windows and admired his uninterrupted view over the Common and the rest of the city to the north and west. The people strolling on the paths of the Common were mere ants from up here.

"Like it?" he asked.

"Love it. You're spoiled. You know that, right?"

"Only because I have you."

"You don't have me," I shot back. Those words had always triggered me.

"I meant have you with me."

I controlled my temper and didn't argue. "I shouldn't have snapped."

His arms wrapped around me from behind and his chin rested on the top of my head. "Sorry. I have to go for a run. Want to come along?"

I curled my arms behind me to pull him tighter. "Nah, you go ahead."

"You'll get to see this view every morning now."

It took me a second to process his roundabout way of asking me to move in. "I can't."

"Sure, you can."

"No, I can't. I work for you. It wouldn't look right at the company."

"I could fire you. I'm always firing my assistants."

"You wouldn't dare."

He let go. "We can discuss this after dinner." He strode off to get changed.

I people-watched out the massive windows, wondering what it would be like to sleep with Vince every night, and wake to this sight every morning.

He returned, looking hot as ever in his running shorts. "Order a pizza in a half hour, and then I'll be back about when it arrives," he suggested. "Wallet's on the counter."

"You got it."

The door closed behind him, and I told Siri to set a timer for twenty minutes. The second door I tried was his office, and I started my search.

The timer went off before I finished. I called in the pizza order for half pepperoni and half deluxe before resuming my search.

Another fifteen minutes and I was confident that I could report there was nothing incriminating in Vince's home office.

Whoever was framing him hadn't planted anything here.

The doorbell surprised me. The pizza delivery was faster here than it was in my neighborhood. I scrambled to get Vince's wallet from the counter and raced to open the door.

The freckle-faced kid handed me the box and held his hand out expectantly.

Setting the warm box on the entryway table, I fumbled with Vince's wallet, opening it upside down. Everything spilled on the floor. I gathered up a few bills to pay the kid, along with a tip.

After the door closed, I knelt and started replacing the contents in the wallet. I picked up a photo and froze.

He had a wallet-size copy of our prom picture. He'd kept it all this time—a picture of us.

As I returned the last credit card, a tear came to my eye. Aside from two family photos of his parents and siblings, our prom picture was the only other one he carried. I put the wallet back on the counter with my heart thumping almost audibly.

He has always cared.

CHAPTER 34

THIS MORNING MARKED THE BEGINNING OF A NEW WEEK. ANOTHER BORING spreadsheet filled my computer screen when Vince left his office for downstairs.

It had been a wonderful weekend, though, topped off by the discovery I'd made in Vince's wallet last night. But I remained determined to not let people at work know about us. I'd won last night's argument about moving in with him. It hadn't been easy to go home to my dreary, empty apartment, but it was the right thing.

With nothing to distract me now, I was anxious to know about the lab results. Unfortunately, John hadn't answered his phone the first time I'd called.

This time was different. "Ashley, good to hear from you. How are things going up in Boston? You surviving without me?"

"Still wishing you hadn't left," I told him.

The bustle of the field office was audible in the background on his end. "Couldn't be helped. I go where they tell me, at least until they say Alaska. I might object to that one."

I got to the point. "Are the results in?"

"The doctor said nothing to worry about," he replied.

Clearly he couldn't speak frankly on his end—a situation I should have expected, but I didn't understand the code.

"Did the test results come in?"

He said something on the side to someone in the office, then returned to the line. "I'm putting the papers in the mail for you, don't worry."

"Can't I get them faster by fax?"

"Not to worry, just routine. And I think we can trust the mail."

It seemed he couldn't have the papers out in the open for others in New Haven to see. That made sense. He'd already gone out on a limb to help me keep this under the radar.

"I'll wait for the mail then," I told him.

"Yeah, they're keeping me busy here. Mostly because they're not as organized as we are."

I heard a complaint come from one of the Connecticut agents in the background. John was keeping the conversation real on his end. They would expect him to rib them if he talked to someone from the Boston office.

"Understood. Take care of yourself."

"You too, and don't neglect your range time. It's embarrassing when I beat you so bad."

I couldn't decipher what he meant by that. He never beat me at the shooting range... But we'd been on the line long enough. We couldn't risk this seeming like anything other than a short check-in.

After hanging up, I contemplated the possible meanings of his final comment, and all I came up with was "be careful." I couldn't carry my weapon on this assignment, and for some reason John's gut was telling him it could be dangerous. He always listened to his gut, and it had never steered him wrong.

Anita passed by me on her way into Vince's empty office.

The staccato sounds of the old IBM Selectric came through the door.

I went to the office door. "Do you need me to type something up?" It was the first time I'd seen anyone except Vince use the old typewriter.

She looked up. "No thanks, dear. Mason needs something typed. I got it." She went back to her work. Her fingers flew over the keys faster than I could have managed without the backspace key my computer afforded me.

Anita finished, and I wondered if her fingerprints would be the ones I'd lifted on the typewriter.

It wasn't long before Vince returned from his simulated run downstairs and closed himself away in his office.

Not long after, reception called up to me. "There are two agents from the FBI who would like to talk to Mr. Benson. The guard downstairs told me."

I froze for a second. It couldn't be. John wouldn't have turned over the memo I sent him—not without at least telling me.

"Just a moment. Let me check with him." I put the phone on hold and let myself into Vince's office.

He looked up and smiled.

I closed the door behind me, unsure how to handle this. "Reception called, and there are two agents from the FBI here to interview you."

"Send them up. I've got time."

I couldn't explain my real fear to him. "I'm not sure that's wise."

"Nonsense. I've got nothing to hide. Send them up, and see if they want coffee." He returned to signing the stack of papers in front of him.

"Just don't say anything to them."

He looked up, quizzically. "What's the problem?"

I had to come up with something fast. "The director of security at Tenerife. That was his advice. '*Remember Martha Stewart, and don't say anything.*' He told me that once."

"Thanks for the advice. I'll be fine."

That's what all the suspects who later got tricked into contradicting themselves said. Then they were charged with lying to the FBI.

There was nothing else I could say without blowing my cover.

"Go now," Vince urged. "Send them up."

I left with a chill and picked up the phone at my desk. "Have them sign in and escort them up," I told reception.

A few minutes later, the elevator dinged, and Randy White—the SAC himself, and Frank, Liz's partner, arrived.

This was totally out of the ordinary. We never sent an agent in anywhere near where we had someone planted undercover.

They introduced themselves to me as if we hadn't met.

I kept my cool. "Just a moment, gentlemen." I almost couldn't handle speaking the word *gentlemen* when referring to the SAC.

I opened the door. "The two agents are here."

CHAPTER 35

VINCENT

ASHLEY BROUGHT IN THE TWO AGENTS. BOTH WORE OFF-THE-RACK SUITS that had seen better days.

The older man introduced them both. He was White, and the other was Dunbar.

I welcomed them and closed the door. "Please, have a seat."

White spoke first. "Thank you for seeing us, Mr. Benson."

"Certainly, Agent White. What can I do for you?"

"Special Agent," he corrected me.

I noted the irritation, but didn't respond.

White motioned to the window. "Very nice view."

"Thank you."

"This is quite an office. Are you in charge of this whole company?"

"No, not at all. I oversee the operations here on the east coast, but the true headquarters is located in Los Angeles. I'm sure you know that."

Dunbar smirked, giving it away. No way had they come in to talk to me without doing research ahead of time.

White's face remained unreadable. "But you're in charge of everything in this building?" he asked.

Ashley's warning came to mind.

"As I told you, I oversee a portion of the company. Now, what can I do for you?"

White scratched his jaw, then pulled a photo out of his jacket pocket and slid it across the desk to me. "Have you ever seen this man?"

The open-ended nature of his question had Ashley's admonition rattling around in my head all over again. "I don't know."

White's eyes narrowed. "You didn't even look at the picture, sir."

"I don't need to look to answer your question. I can't possibly remember everyone I have ever met, any more than you could. You asked if I had ever seen him. There's no way for me to know the answer to that question."

"Don't be smart," White said.

"I gave you a truthful answer. What else would you like to know?"

He picked up the picture. "This is Sonny Alfonso. Have you ever met him?"

"Not that I recall at this moment, but I could be wrong. I meet a lot of people and don't remember them all."

"So that's a no?" White said, trying to put words in my mouth.

I took a calming breath. "That's an I-don't-recall-meeting-him-but-I-could-be-wrong. I've met a lot of people in my life, and I don't remember them all."

Ashley had been right. Their game was to trip me up for some reason, and I had no idea why.

"Let's move on," White said.

So far, Dunbar hadn't spoken a word. He was clearly the junior of the two agents.

"Mr. Alfonso is one of the heads of organized crime in town," White said. "Very high up."

I didn't respond to that statement.

Ashley had mentioned that same name… The *Inquisitor* had been trying to tie me to him. It was a good thing she'd gotten that article killed, or at least delayed.

White shifted in his chair. "If he has contacted you, or were to contact you in the future, you would tell us, right?"

"Is that an official request?" I asked.

"Why wouldn't you want to cooperate with us?" White asked.

"I'm open to contacting you," I said.

White shook his head, probably upset that I'd seen his question for what it was. "We have information that he may be—make that *is*—looking for somebody to front for him."

I could guess where this was leading. "What does *front* mean in this context?"

White answered, "To front for the mob would be something like buying a business, which a company such as yours could do, and then selling an interest to somebody like Mr. Alfonso and his associates without disclosing that fact."

"I don't understand. Why wouldn't he just buy it himself if he wanted it?"

White shook his head like I was an idiot. I was getting to him. "Because there are numerous businesses he wouldn't be allowed to buy into."

"Such as?" I asked.

White huffed. "Such as anything to do with gambling."

"I see." And this confirmed where this was all coming from. Gainsboro had seeded the *Inquisitor* and now the FBI with the notion that I was in bed with organized crime in order to ruin my deal with Semaphore.

Gainsboro was taking playing dirty to a whole new level. They couldn't beat us legitimately, so this was their tactic? Get us kicked out of the bidding and leave the field open to them?

If I didn't do something, Semaphore would be yanked from my grasp, and proving the charges false after the deal had been sealed wouldn't help.

Those fucking Gainsboro assholes. At least the nature of my adversary was clear after this visit. There wasn't much they wouldn't stoop to.

"You're certain Mr. Alfonso hasn't contacted you yet?" White asked.

"I said I'd be open to contacting you if I hear from him in the future."

White fumed at my non-answer, but didn't say anything.

"Is there anything else, agents?" I carefully avoided adding *special*. The only thing special about White was his deviousness.

White shook his head. "No. That about wraps it up for today. Thank you for your time, Mr. Benson."

"My pleasure." I rose and escorted them out to the guard waiting behind Ashley's desk. "These gentlemen are done here," I told the guard.

I ignored Ashley's questioning look and returned to my office.

A minute later, she let herself in and closed the door.

She took the chair across from me. "So?"

"So, two things. First, you were right to give me that advice. The FBI is full of snakes. I don't see how they sleep at night."

Her brow knit.

"They tried several times to get me to agree to ambiguous statements, and to agree to have met, or claim to have never met, that Alfonso guy your friend from the *Inquisitor* was asking about."

"She's not my friend," Ashley corrected me.

"Acquaintance then. That underhanded Jacinda girl."

"What did you say?"

"I didn't agree to anything, and I didn't say anything except that I couldn't possibly know the answer to their open-ended questions. But before they left, they said Alfonso was going to approach me. All in all, I think it was a good meeting."

Ashley cocked her head. "How could that be good?"

"Now it's making sense. I can see what's going on. Gainsboro is behind this whole thing. They planted the same information with the feds as with the *Inquisitor*. They're out to paint me as being in bed with this Alfonso guy to screw the Semaphore deal."

"You think so?"

"The pieces fit. Their next step is probably to get the *Globe* to print an article that quotes anonymous sources within the FBI saying I'm under investigation for ties to the mob. Then they'll peddle that shit at Semaphore."

"Makes sense," she said.

∼

LATER THAT MORNING, I ANSWERED DAD'S CALL.

"Vincent, how is that Semaphore transaction you've been telling me about coming along?"

I'd made the mistake of telling him this was underway, thinking it would earn me points. Instead it had led to him calling me every week for an update. He had become a constant backseat driver to the point of annoyance—not that I could tell him that. And anyway, instead of being a positive thing if I got the deal done, it was starting to look like it could only be a negative if I failed at it.

"Nothing much significant. The other potential buyer has made another counterproposal, and they want us to respond."

"And how do you feel about that?" he asked.

The question was pretty much the same every week.

"We haven't decided how to respond yet."

For a moment he didn't say anything. "Sometimes going slow is the best option," he said. "Seeming too eager can be a detriment at times."

His opinion mirrored Mason's on this.

"That's why we're taking our time," I told him.

"Good boy, Vincent. You know I'm available if you'd like to talk through some of your options."

He couldn't help reinforce that he wasn't sure I could handle this by myself—just as he had done my entire life.

"Thanks, Dad. I appreciate that."

I wasn't about to avail myself of the offer right now. I'd save that for some truly sticky situation he'd appreciate for its difficulty.

I took out my coin and tapped it three times lightly on the desk. "Come in," I said off to the side. "Hey, Dad? I gotta go. Thanks for the call."

We hung up after perfunctory goodbyes.

I turned the coin over and read the inscription for the millionth time. *I have not yet begun to fight.*

Shortly before lunch, Ben, my head of security, called up to see if I was free. He joined me in my office five minutes later.

He closed the door behind him. "I've got some preliminary information for you." He opened a folder and turned it around on the desk for me to read.

"What am I looking at?"

"Remember we said somebody in the company could have planted that malware on your computer?"

"Yeah. But your guy said it was most likely through some email trojan or something."

He took a breath. "That was one theory. But now we know it was done from inside."

"How exactly?"

"Remember I told you we'd disabled it, but we hadn't removed it in case you wanted to use it to send misinformation?"

I nodded.

"Well, it disappeared off your computer. Which means somebody inside put it there, and then they removed it after we found it."

"Any way to tell who?" Mason and I had discussed the possibility of a mole on this floor after the keylogger had been found.

"I've been looking into the most likely candidates upstairs here, and these are the first results." He offered me a spreadsheet.

"You'll have to explain."

He pointed out a series of numbers that ran down the page. "This third column here is the monthly bank balance for Mason's secretary, Anita."

"Assistant," I corrected him.

"Sorry, I'm just a little old-fashioned. Mason's assistant, Anita."

There was a significant jump in the numbers near the end.

He pointed to the jump. "A lot of money came in recently. Unless you've given her a big bonus or something, we don't see anything that explains it."

His implication was ominous, and one I couldn't accept. Anita couldn't be involved.

"What do you mean, you can't explain it?" I asked.

"Exactly that. She didn't transfer any money from her brokerage account or anything like that. She hasn't sold her house, car, or anything else that could account for that amount of money. And it would have to be one hell of a car, anyway."

We hadn't given out bonuses recently, and certainly nothing of that magnitude. "You're implying she's a mole."

He sat back in his chair. "I'm not implying anything. I just bring you the data and let you make your own conclusions. She's come into some money, and I have no obvious way to explain it. That's all I'm saying."

I shook my head. It didn't make any sense. Anita had been with us forever, since even before I started. Liam had told me he'd trust her with his life, if it came to that.

Not implying anything, my ass. Ben was accusing Anita, pure and simple.

"You want me to talk to her?" he asked.

I shook my head. I was certain about that. "Not yet."

If I let Ben come at her, with his lack of tact, we'd be down one very capable assistant in a flash. Anita wasn't the sort to take that kind of accusation in stride. Not any more than I was. It would be the ultimate insult to a long-term employee such as herself.

"Let me handle it," I told him.

He nodded. "A more direct route might be to review the video of your office. We haven't done that yet."

"Let me handle that. I'd rather do that myself." The last thing I needed was one of his guys reviewing footage of Ashley and me doing it over my desk.

"One or two of my guys could help, and it would go quicker."

"I said I'll do it myself."

"Yes, sir. I'll get you the equipment when you're ready. But be warned—it can be quite tedious."

"Got it. Another thing, Ben. I just had a meeting that makes it pretty clear to me that all this links back to the Gainsboro company."

"Anyone in particular there?" he asked.

"I don't have a name yet, but we should be looking for anybody here with links to anybody there as a suspect."

"That's a pretty wide net. I might have to pull in outside help to get it checked out."

"Whatever you need. Just keep it quiet."

"Yes, sir."

He stood and prepared to leave. "Like I said, I'm just giving you the data. It's nothing personal."

After the door closed, I looked down at the open folder on my desk, a folder filled with a nice, smelly turd. It couldn't be Anita.

The people who insisted shit always flowed downhill had never been in my position before. Sometimes the really shitty situations floated up for the boss to take care of.

I closed the folder and placed it in my drawer.

Not today.

CHAPTER 36

ASHLEY

WHEN I GOT HOME FROM WORK ON MONDAY AND CHECKED MY APARTMENT mailbox, there it was. Just as John had promised.

The Express Mail envelope was rolled up and stuffed into my box. It almost didn't fit, and it took some careful pulling to get it out without ripping. My mail lady was the only one I knew who could truly stuff ten pounds of shit into a five-pound bag—or a tiny mailbox, in this case.

I carried the envelope under one arm as I opened the door and went to the kitchen for scissors to open my present. Once I'd unpacked, all the enclosed papers covered my table. A quick perusal showed he'd found nothing useful on the note itself, which had been returned in the plastic evidence bag.

The lack of any of Vince's prints, or even partials, settled it once and for all in my mind. This was a setup. There was no way to load paper into the old typewriter without at least partial prints unless you were wearing gloves while doing it. The case had officially, as far as I was concerned, shifted from determining if Vince was guilty or not into finding who was trying to frame him.

I would have to put it back where I'd found it for now.

Additionally, the fingerprints came back with two hits: Anita and Sophia on the typewriter keys. The one from the blotter was not complete enough for a match.

I'd hoped for something of a home run and had gotten a single at best. Tomorrow I would plan my next step.

I opened my purse to pull out my phone.

There was a note inside: *My place for dinner. Uncle Benny.*

I laughed at his corniness. He'd obviously slipped the note in there while I was away from my desk at some point.

During the Uber ride to Vince's place, I found my mind wandering. I was excited to be working this case to protect Vince now, rather than to convict him. It was all backwards, but felt right. For the longest time, the bullpen group in Chelsea had been my family, but things had changed there. Or maybe something had always been off. Either way, now I was essentially working against them.

In my heart I believed I was serving justice by working on Vince's side, not the Bureau's. The top of my ID read *Federal Bureau of Investigation*, but also *Department of Justice*, and I would be doing a disservice to both if I were the instrument of a frame job.

I couldn't prove it yet, but my gut feeling, and the lack of prints on the paper, was too strong to ignore. The note Staci had gotten was clearly from an adversary. Plus, the way the DOJ had been fed such specifics on the fake contract and I'd been told exactly where and when to find it all pointed to an elaborate setup. Paint Vince as fronting for the Alfonso family, and he was right, Semaphore and their gaming business would be out of his grasp—all so convenient for the competition.

The Uber came to a stop out front, and Carl waved me through as I entered Vince's Tremont building. I punched the button for the twenty-sixth floor and fingered the necklace I was wearing—the one Vince had given me in New York. I'd been doing that a lot.

At the door, I knocked.

Vince opened the door after a short wait. "Kitten, you're late."

He picked me up with a hug that threatened to flatten my breasts and let me down with a quick peck.

A black monster of a dog came up to sniff me. I crouched down to pet her. "Hi there, girl."

"Meet Rufus, my roommate. Call him a girl again, and I can't be responsible for the outcome."

I stood and the dog nudged his head under my hand, demanding more petting. "He's a cutie." After a series of scratches behind the ears, he walked to his master and demanded some more of the same.

"You hear that Rufus, you're cute. He's never been called that before. He scares most people."

" Not me. I love dogs." The aromas of what would undoubtedly be pizza wafted over me. "Pizza again?"

"Alexa, play 'Green-Eyed Lady' by Sugarloaf," he said loudly.

Alexa complied, and the music started.

"May I have this dance?"

I took his hand, and we began to sway. He sang some of the lyrics in my ear as we danced. My heart ached at his corny routine. Even if it was only frozen pizza for dinner, I could really get used to this treatment every time I got home—not that this was my home, but whenever I was with him, it felt like home.

The song ended, and he released me.

Rufus had retired to his bed.

"We need to talk," I told him.

It was time for me to level with him about my job and work openly with him to find out who was attempting to frame him.

He ignored me and continued to the kitchen. "Talk is overrated. First we feast." He opened the oven and surprised me by pulling out two pizza boxes. We weren't having frozen grocery store pizza after all. "We're splurging on Papa Luigi's tonight. I can afford it."

His use of the word *splurge* was odd. He could afford to buy the restaurant a hundred times over if he wanted.

"First I need to tell you something—"

"Second. I told you, first we feast on Papa Luigi's finest." An evil grin overtook his face. "Or I could feast on something even more delicious. You might like that."

His implication had me squeezing my thighs together. "Okay, pizza first, and maybe the other later."

He waggled his eyebrows. "I'm going to hold you to that."

"Have you been drinking?"

He opened the boxes on the counter. "Your choice of pepperoni, Hawaiian, veggie, or combo. We have half a pizza of each." This was way too much for the two of us, but like he'd said, he could afford it.

The pizzas smelled delicious, but I had a more immediate issue.

I followed him into the kitchen and hugged him from behind. "What's with the crazy routine?"

He was charismatic and fun this evening, but not my normal Vince.

He spun around in my arms and took my head in his hands, planting a quick kiss on my forehead. "Today started off so shitty— first the FBI visit, then the update I got from Ben—I decided tonight I was going to be happy no matter what."

"What did Ben have to say?"

"Later. Tonight I'm going to be happy."

I could smell it on his breath. "You have been drinking."

"A little," he admitted. He wiggled away and grabbed plates from the cupboard. "Did you make your choice, Kitten?" He pointed to the pizzas.

I wasn't letting him off so easily. "How many?" I asked.

He held up two fingers.

I cocked my head and fixed him with a stern stare.

He added a third finger. "You need to catch up." He picked up a glass of wine on the counter that I hadn't noticed before.

I relented and took the glass, sipping a bit.

"Well?"

"Pepperoni for me, please. And no jokes about my breath later."

He laughed. "Deal." He served two slices of pepperoni for me and chose Hawaiian for himself.

We set the table and made a game of feeding each other pizza and drinking our wine from interlocked arms. As I caught up to him in the wine department, our laughter filled the room.

It was a side of him I hadn't seen before. I'd seen the serious and businesslike Vince. I'd experienced the threatening Vince that night with the news team. The puppetmaster had reared his head, thinking he could tell me and everyone else what to do. I'd thoroughly enjoyed the romantic Vince he'd shown me in New York. This funny jokester, however, was also a nice addition.

My Vince had a way of transporting me away from the day to day to a special place. I'd never met anybody like him, and as I fingered my necklace one more time, I vowed to never let him go.

After dinner he wanted to watch a movie, and he chose *Top Gun* with Tom Cruise. It was more serious than I would've chosen. I never liked the part where Goose dies in the crash.

"You wanted to talk?" he said during a slow part.

"Another time."

The discussion I'd planned would go better when we weren't drinking, but mostly I didn't want to spoil the mood tonight. He'd had a shitty day, and he deserved a happy evening.

When we reached the singing at the piano scene in the bar, I repeated Meg Ryan's line, "Take me to bed, you big stud, or lose me forever."

I had to say it twice, louder the second time, for Vince to get my drift.

He flicked off the movie, sparing me the sad scene with Goose, and scooped me up from the couch.

He laughed as I repeated the line again, and he rushed me into the bedroom, without bothering with the lights or the dishes.

Our discussion could wait.

Tonight was happy night.

~

VINCENT

I KICKED THE DOOR CLOSED BEHIND ME AND PLOPPED ASHLEY DOWN ON the bed.

She started removing her clothes, and I helped her wiggle out of them as quickly as I could.

I was hard as a rock. She'd been stroking my thigh as we watched the movie, revving my engine all night.

"You have no idea what you do to me, Kitten." I struggled out of the last of my clothes and moved to spread her legs. I was going to feast on her as I'd promised earlier.

211

She resisted, with her legs clamped together. "Hold me first."

I moved up alongside her and pulled her into my side, her head on my shoulder.

"Tell me what you want, Kitten."

She stroked my chest. "I want it to be special tonight."

"It's always special for me with you," I told her. "I'll give you a tongue-lashing you won't forget."

She was silent for a moment, her hand circling my nipple.

"I don't want..." She didn't finish her sentence.

"We can just snuggle then." It would be insanely hard to resist, but for her, I could be gentlemanly. At least I hoped so.

"No," she said slowly. "I want skin."

"You mean no..."

"Yeah, you inside me without a condom." She paused. "I'm on the pill, and I don't have anything."

"I'm clean too. But I might not last very long."

She rose up and straddled me. "Another thing, I want to be on top." She leaned over and playfully licked the tip of my nose.

I could go for that. "It's your night, Kitten." I palmed the weight of her marvelous breasts, soft mounds topped with those responsive pink peaks.

She rubbed her slippery slit over my length, slowing down as her clit ran over my tip. Each trip elicited a moan as she pleasured herself on me.

Her wetness had her gliding back and forth with heavy pressure, trying to milk my length and drawing shudders from me every time she rode over my sensitive tip.

It took all my concentration to resist the urge to lift her up and enter her. I let her guide her hips to her own rhythm while I attended to her breasts, holding their weight and circling her nipples with my thumbs, letting her murmurs be my guide. I looked up into her closed eyes as she vulva-fucked me, coming ever closer to the end of her rope.

She increased her tempo, and her breathing became the ragged little breaths that told me how close she was. Her hand went to mine, squeezing it against the warm softness of her breast.

Without warning, she lifted up, guided my cock with her hand, and slid down on me. She was so wet I slipped in easily, and she took me to the root, lifting up and sliding down first slowly, then more quickly. She arched her back and sat up, bracing her hands on my knees.

The sight of her breasts bouncing every time she came down on me was too much. I closed my eyes and concentrated on holding off long enough to satisfy her. Every stroke made it harder than the last as she lifted up to tease my tip at her entrance and then slid down fast to take my length. Each stroke sent a jolt all the way to my toes.

She reached around to tickle my balls, and they nearly exploded from her touch.

I retaliated by taking a thumb to her clit.

She ground forward and back against the pressure of my thumb as the words spilled out of her between quick breaths.

"Holy shit… Oh God…I'm gonna…come… Oh…my God… Holy crap…I can't."

And with the next rock of her pelvis, I rubbed her clit hard, and she crashed over the edge, tensing, shaking, and clawing my shoulders.

She shuddered and cried out my name—convulsing around me as she rode the wave down with several gyrations forward and back— and then collapsed on top of me, her breasts hot against my chest.

"My God," she said over and over again. "I had no idea."

She rolled off, panting to regain her breath. "Your turn." She put her head on the pillow and poked her butt up. "Ride me, cowboy."

I didn't need any more encouragement. I got behind her and let her position me with her hand before I pushed in—hard.

She moaned. "That all you got?" she asked with a giggle.

I grabbed her hips and dug my fingers in, pulling her to me, seating myself fully, and holding her there.

She wiggled her ass, and I started, pulling out and ramming home —all the way home. She was so fucking wet and so deliciously tight that I couldn't hold back.

"Harder," she urged.

I knew she said it for my sake, not hers, but I gave her harder. The sound of flesh slapping against flesh filled the room as I thrust again and again.

She'd been right, the sensations without the latex were to die for, and in no time, the pressure that had built behind my balls was too much to hold back. The strain finally snapped and I shot my load with a final thrust, tensing up and holding her hips tightly to me, welding my cock inside her. Slowly, the throbbing eased. I pushed her forward onto the bed and lay half off of her, sparing her my weight as I panted against her shoulder.

"That was fucking fantastic," I managed between breaths.

"Yeah," she replied, angling her head enough to give me a kiss.

After a minute I got up to wipe off and returned with a warm, wet washcloth for her.

I curled up behind her, cradling a breast with my hand. Our sweat mingled as I held my Kitten tight. She was mine, and I wasn't letting her go.

Her breaths eventually slowed to the rhythm of sleep.

Content, I soon joined her, my Kitten's warm back against my chest and her coconut scent in my nose.

CHAPTER 37

Vincent

I was busy with the last of our breakfast waffles when Ashley finally emerged from the bedroom.

She was a sight to behold. She'd pulled on one of my button down shirts, but only bothered with the bottom two buttons. Her cleavage taunted me, and I wondered if she'd grabbed panties or not.

"Morning, Kitten. Sleep okay?"

She walked directly to the orange juice I'd placed on the table. "Like a baby." She popped pills in her mouth and took a long slug of the juice.

"Only two, remember? Don't try to go crazy like last time."

"I need four, but for you, I'm keeping it to two."

I turned back to the waffle iron. "I hope you like waffles."

She came over and wrapped her arms around me. Her hot breasts squeezed against my back.

I opened the waffle iron and forked the last sections onto the plate. "Careful there, or you might end up on page one-seventy-eight."

That one was her on the kitchen counter.

She let go. "We don't have time."

She was probably right.

"There's bacon staying warm in the oven," I told her.

She snagged a pot holder and pulled the plate out. "You spoil me."

I carried the waffles to the table. "It's in the job description."

We sat, and her eyes returned my loving feelings.

I moved waffles onto each of our plates.

She cut into one. "Chocolate chip. I should have guessed." She poured maple syrup over it and offered me the bottle.

I took the bottle but set it down without pouring any. "Chocolate makes everything better."

"No syrup?" she asked.

"Don't want it to cover up the taste." I forked a bite.

She took another bite. "You know we can't keep doing this."

"What, breakfast?"

"Me sleeping over during the week. Somebody's going to see us."

"Let them. I'm proud of you."

She put her fork down. "Stop joking around. It's not okay. They may not be judging you, but they sure as hell will be judging me, and I don't want to be seen as the office slut."

This was obviously a bigger concern to her than I'd realized.

"We still on for lunch?"

"Yes, but we have to cool it. No more weeknight sleepovers." She lifted the waffle to her mouth.

This was completely new territory for me, having to negotiate access to my woman. "I don't know if I'm going to last till Friday."

She shrugged, but I wasn't giving up. We were going to come back to this topic and soon.

She devoured breakfast and looked like a chipmunk with her cheeks stuffed full.

"I'll be in later," she said. "I have to go home to change." She took one last bite and rose from the table.

"You could leave some clothes here to make it easier," I offered.

"Stop it. I'm not sleeping over."

I thought it was worth one last try. "I could sleep at your place."

She laughed. "They have a rule against rich people in my neighborhood. And besides, you have to take care of Rufus."

She had a point there. Rufus trotted over at the sound of his name.

Ashley disappeared to get dressed, and I managed to drop a few bites of bacon on the floor for my dog.

∼

AN HOUR OR SO LATER THE AIR SEEMED UNUSUALLY CLEAR AS I LOOKED out my office window toward the north. The Gainsboro building was in that direction, and that's where the enemy was hiding.

Last night with Ashley had certainly lifted my mood after my shitty Monday, but I wasn't about to let this lie.

With some free time this morning, I decided to get busy locating the mole working with Gainsboro. And it had damned well better not turn out to be Anita.

I dialed Ben. "Hey, can you set me up to review that video in my office?" I asked when he answered.

"Sure thing. Give me a few minutes to put it together."

He appeared quickly and soon had the software set up on my computer. After showing me how to navigate the videos, he left me to it.

I told Ashley I didn't want to be disturbed at all this morning, and I soon discovered just how boring it was to go through the video. I started with the most recent date and decided to work backward. I had no idea if that was the smart way to do it, but I had to begin somewhere.

The software only let me speed it up so fast, and that meant it took a long time to go through the workday and even longer to cover the night. I got to the first overnight and almost fell asleep.

I jerked awake when there was a quick movement in the room and the lights came on. It turned out to be the janitor. I slowed it down and watched carefully. I couldn't miss anything.

Ben had been right that this was tedious in the extreme. When I got to a logical stopping point, I checked my watch and realized I was going to be late for lunch.

Ashley was still concerned with appearances, so she and I had agreed to meet, but not to walk out together.

She wasn't at her desk when I opened my door, so I grabbed my coat.

"Anita, I'll be at lunch for a while."
She smiled, nodded, and waved.

~

ASHLEY

I STRODE CONFIDENTLY OUT OF THE DEPARTMENT STORE TOWARD MY LUNCH meeting with Vince. I'd run short of office-appropriate skirts for my work at Covington. I checked my watch and picked up the pace to our rendezvous. We were having sushi today.

My hand went to my ever-present necklace as I thought back to last night and this morning. Nine years ago, as we'd parted without any kind words, I'd longed for an ending like this, but known it couldn't be. Back then I'd been too scared to give him what he wanted, too scared of how it would end.

Today I'd given him my trust without reservation. He'd earned it with every comment, every gesture, and every action. I finally understood the meaning of the word *love*. I would trust him with my heart, for he was my man.

I reached the restaurant a few minutes late. But a quick glance around showed that I'd still beaten Vince. The place was almost completely full, and the normal lunch rush was about to start. I asked for a table for two and was shown to one near the center of the floor.

Vince arrived before they had a chance to bring our tea.
"Sorry I'm late."
"I only just got here myself," I admitted.
He took the seat across the table from me, and I didn't get a chance for a kiss.
"Did I tell you how good you look today?" he asked.
My heart fluttered at the simple words, and heat rose in my cheeks. "Only three times this morning. But don't stop on my account."
His smile grew. "I'll control myself."
The waitress came and took our order.
I wasn't very adventurous, so I stuck to the simple things and

avoided eel or octopus. If I was going to have seafood, it was going to swim, not hang out on the bottom.

Vince chose the octopus, and two kinds of rolls with more things in them than I could keep track of.

"You want to tell me what Ben had to say now?" I asked.

He took a sip of tea before responding. "He thinks it's Anita."

"Anita is what?"

He swirled the tea around in his cup before continuing. "I've had Ben looking into the people upstairs who might have had the access to plant malware on my computer."

"Malware?" I asked.

"Yeah. Ben found a keylogger installed on my computer, and it disappeared a few days later."

"What's a keylogger?" I asked, feigning ignorance and choking back my fear. Stay calm I reminded myself.

"A program that logs what you type and sends it off over the internet to whoever is spying on me."

"That's terrible." I fought back a shiver. What if he found out I was involved? I steadied my breathing. This was the always the trickiest part of being undercover—the moment the subject suspected being under investigation and became paranoid. *Keep it together girl.*

He shook his head. "The kicker is that it appeared and then disappeared, and Ben tells me that means someone in the offices put it there and then deleted it. After looking at everyone on the floor, Anita is his suspect."

"I don't believe that," I said as relief flooded in. At least I hadn't been mentioned as one of those under suspicion, but that could change quickly. "She doesn't seem the type to be a spy." We'd been taught that the worst thing to do was to eagerly agree with someone pointing the finger away from us.

"Me either, but she came into a lot of money recently."

Our waiter interrupted us, delivering the food. At least mine was food; I wasn't prepared to put Vince's octopus in the same category.

With his chopsticks, he held a piece of his octopus with the gross suction cup thingies sticking up. "Did you know an octopus's blood is blue instead of red?"

"That's gross," I told him, making a face. "And another reason not to eat them. They were probably left behind when the Martians built the pyramids."

That got the desired chuckle out of him, just before he grossed me out by biting into the blue-blooded monstrosity.

I looked away to keep from turning green. At least we'd left the keylogger topic.

"It's the copper," he said. "It's copper in their blood to carry the oxygen. Unlike the iron we use, which makes our blood red."

I didn't need the scientific explanation. Being left here by the Martians was good enough for me. I kept my eyes down at my plate to avoid looking at the ugly octopus tentacle staring back at him.

"You sure you won't try it?"

I put my hand in front of my mouth to keep from upchucking. "No thanks," I said, still not looking up.

His phone dinged.

I looked up enough to see that he had taken the entire gross sushi piece and put it in his mouth. At least while he chewed, I wouldn't have to look at it. He checked his phone and a strange look came over his face.

"Something wrong?"

"It's nothing." He put the phone face down on the table and grabbed a piece of one of his rolls.

The phone dinged again with another message. This time he didn't check it. His brow furrowed.

"You sure nothing's wrong?"

"Sure," he said, not meeting my eyes.

The phone dinged again, and his eyes flashed to it.

I'd done enough interrogations to know a lie when I saw one, and this one wasn't hard to spot.

His phone dinged a fourth time. He checked it, put it on the table, and looked around the room, searching. His eyes came to a halt at the far corner, and recognition flashed in his eyes. Not in a good way, near as I could tell.

I turned the phone to face me while his gaze was averted. The text messages were the second thing to make me want to puke.

BARB: Is she why you won't call anymore?

BARB: Are we still on for this Saturday night?

BARB: We could do a threesome

BARB: Does she know you like anal?

His eyes flashed to the phone and his mouth dropped as he realized I'd read the messages.

I got up and threw my napkin on the table. "I've gotta go."

I was out the door five seconds later, gasping for air as I hit the sidewalk. I turned right toward the Covington building before I changed my mind and turned the other way, walking as fast as I could away from his office.

"Ash," he called from behind me.

I didn't stop. I didn't look back. I didn't know a thing about him after all. Barb Saturday night? A threesome? And that other thing?

His footfalls were loud as he ran up behind me and came alongside. "Stop and talk to me," he demanded.

"Nothing to talk about," I said, continuing on.

He kept pace with me without saying anything. Then suddenly, he grabbed my shoulder and turned me toward him.

"You can't just leave."

"Watch me. You can finish lunch with your girlfriend." I started off again down the street.

He jogged ahead and placed himself in my path, forcing me to stop. "She's not my girlfriend," he said firmly.

"So now total strangers are propositioning you for threesomes?"

He put a hand on my shoulder.

I pulled away.

"Her name is Barbara."

"That part I got," I spat.

"We used to see each other."

"She apparently thinks you still are."

"That's a lie. She's in the past."

"How long ago?" I asked. "I thought Staci was your girlfriend."

The look on his face told me I'd hit a home run with that one.

"No... Don't tell me you were seeing them at the same time?"

"I was completely open about it with both of them," he said, shuffling his feet.

"That doesn't make it right. You're a dickhead, you know that?"

"Barb's just a girl," he said, as if that made it okay. "She's just pissed I'm not interested anymore."

"You disgust me."

"I know it looks bad."

"Bad? This isn't in the same universe with bad. Who the hell sees two girls at once? Do you have a sex addiction or something? You need help." I tried to move to the side, but he matched my movement, blocking me still.

"The only thing I need is you. You're my girl."

I clenched my fists. "I need to go. Get out of my way or I'm going to scream my head off."

He moved aside, and I started walking again. I didn't know where I was going, but away was the right direction.

"We need to talk this out," he called.

"We just did," I yelled.

I hadn't missed the words. I'd been demoted from his Kitten to his girl, and it made me feel like shit.

CHAPTER 38

VINCENT

A CAR HONKED.

I jumped back onto the sidewalk.

I'd almost crossed the street in front of a speeding taxi. That could easily be a fatal mistake in this town.

Telling Barb to fuck off and blocking her number didn't go far enough; I needed to square this with Ashley. I needed her to understand. After our argument, I was a wreck.

The whole thing was my fault for not breaking it to her earlier, finding a way to explain what I'd been like before she'd come back into my life. She needed to know how she had changed me for the better—immeasurably better. I'd told her about Staci, but never mentioned Barb.

I made my way back to the Covington building and closed my door. There was nothing to do until she returned and I could talk to her.

The video setup was waiting at my desk, so I went back to it.

To fight the tedium, I ventured out to get myself a cup of coffee-flavored caffeine.

I locked the door behind me upon my return. Without Ashley to guard it, only the lock would give me the privacy I needed for this.

The pick-me-up seemed to be working as I sat back down and started the video rolling again. A lot of routine comings and goings, punctuated by a boring static image of my office, rolled by as my eyelids got heavier.

The knocking at my door woke me, and I jerked up.

The video had switched to nighttime.

Fuck. I'd fallen asleep in spite of the coffee.

The knocking sounded again, more insistent this time and accompanied by Mason's voice.

"I need a few minutes. It's important," he called.

I paused the video, rose from my chair, and walked to the door, rubbing my sore neck. The desk chair was fine for sitting, but it left something to be desired when it came to sleep.

I unlocked the door, and Mason rushed in.

He closed the door behind him. "It's Semaphore. They called. We're out of the running. They've decided to go with Gainsboro."

Double fuck.

"But we still had a week to respond," I said.

"The marketing guy told me—off the record, mind you—that it's because they heard we're being investigated for ties to organized crime, and they won't sully their reputation by talking to us any longer."

"Fucking FBI."

He stepped back. "What the fuck does the FBI have to do with this?"

I went back to my desk. "Have a seat. The FBI was here yesterday."

He took his seat. "Why didn't you tell me?"

"You were out all afternoon."

He shrugged.

"You know the rumors that were being fed to the *Daily Inquisitor*?"

"I thought we got that story squashed."

"Well, Gainsboro obviously peddled the same shit to the FBI, and they were here yesterday asking about it."

"They told you it was Gainsboro? That's great. That at least gives us something to work with to get back into it."

"No, they didn't, and they won't. But that's Gainsboro's play here. They feed rumors to the feds, then leak to Semaphore that the feds have been to talk to us, and we're instantly guilty by innuendo. It clears the field for them, like it just did."

"Those assholes."

His description was milder than my feelings right now. Gainsboro had outmaneuvered us so far.

Mason stood. "I think I can get us one more audience."

"Not yet. Ben and I are working on gathering evidence. When we have something concrete, that's the time to go in and talk to them and get Gainsboro knocked out—not before."

"So, what are you doing?"

"Ben and I are working on it."

His face dropped. He wasn't pleased about being left out of the mole hunt.

"I'll let you know when we have something."

He left without argument, and I relocked the door.

I would have to rewind quite a ways and restart my video search.

I would locate the mole, and Gainsboro was going down.

ASHLEY

AN HOUR OF WALKING LATER, I STILL COULDN'T GET THE TEXT MESSAGES out of my head. He'd been seeing two women at once. Gross. That didn't match the Vince I thought I knew at all. I pulled out my phone and typed a text to him.

ME: Have errands to run won't be back in this afternoon

I hailed an Uber to get me within walking distance of the field office.

Downstairs Joe let me pass without my ID.

Upstairs, the bullpen was oddly empty.

I went to my desk, located the file, sat, and opened it.

Amid the papers and pictures the DOJ had collected, I found it: a picture of Vince at dinner with Barb. The picture was annotated with her name, Barbara DeBecki, and also showed another girl whose name wasn't known. I noted that the second woman was as pretty as Barb, before realizing how fucking jealous my thoughts were. This was completely unprofessional.

I found another photo of him and Barb alone at dinner, interspersed with pictures of him and the woman I now recognized as Staci Baxter.

Banging another girl at the same time as he'd had a *Sports Illustrated* swimsuit model for a girlfriend? He was seriously fucked up. And threesomes?

Liz came around the corner from the bathrooms. "Hey, what are you doing in here?"

"Afternoon off."

"I wish I got afternoons off, or evenings, for that matter."

I controlled my sneer. "It's just today."

My phone vibrated with a text message.

VINCE: Miss you

I ignored the text and the quizzical look I got from Liz.

She lifted a hefty file from her desk. "You can help me with this one in your spare time." She set it in front of me. "I've got three others ahead of it."

I closed the Benson file. I would have complained, except I welcomed something to occupy me other than obsessing over Vince and his women friends. What was I supposed to do with this information?

I took a deep breath and opened the tall file. It was a smuggling case running through Logan Airport. The transfer agent was suspected, but he dealt with multiple local companies, and finding the single end destination here was going to mean going through a ton of paperwork. A mind-numbing ton of paperwork—exactly what would force Vince out of my brain.

Another text arrived.

VINCE: Miss you Kitten

I turned my phone off. I didn't need any more of these messages.

BY THE END OF THE DAY, MANY OF THE AGENTS HAD RETURNED, AND A FEW had left for the day.

Then I found it.

Gainsboro was one of the companies whose paperwork was included as suspect in Liz's smuggling case. This might give me leverage to investigate Vince's enemy.

I closed the file. "Liz, I'll work on this one in my spare time."

"Thanks."

I put the Benson file away, hefted the large smuggling file, and left the building.

I hailed an Uber to get me home.

The traffic was stop and go. I glanced out the window at the bus stop billboard. It advertised an exhibit at the Boston Museum of Fine Arts, and the image brought back memories of my evening at the Met with Vince.

My chest tightened. I closed my eyes and was transported back. I bit my lip. How could I have doubts about the man who had arranged such a magical evening for me? It was so much more than an elegant dinner. It had been special—he'd treated me as special—much more than special. I needed to listen to what he wanted to say about Barbara and whatever his dating life had been before me. I owed him that.

I'd had a completely petty reaction to the text messages. I needed to grow up. My fingernails dug into my leg. I was such an idiot.

CHAPTER 39

VINCENT

THE TEXT ARRIVED BEFORE ONE O'CLOCK.

ASHLEY: Have errands to run won't be back in this afternoon

I called, but she didn't pick up.

I called Ben. "I'm not making any progress on this video here at the office. Can you set me up at the condo so I can go over it in the evenings?"

"Sure, we can do that, or I can have one of the guys screen it for you."

"No thanks. I got this. The condo would be better."

He agreed to bring it over this evening.

I went for a late-afternoon treadmill session downstairs and headed home early.

I hadn't heard from Ashley since the message after lunch, so I sent a text.

ME: Miss you

I checked my phone several times, but there was always the same blank screen. Willing it to show a message from her didn't work.

Ben arrived at my place shortly after I did. He must have instructed the lobby guy at Covington to tell him when I left so he could synchronize his visit. It didn't take him long to set everything up and be on his way. By eight o'clock, I'd gone through several more days of video without finding evidence of the mole removing the malware. But it had to be here, so I kept at it.

After ordering Chinese, I started back on the mind-numbing surveillance video.

The doorbell rang a half hour later.

I paused the video.

The tired-looking delivery guy got a twenty for a tip, which immediately improved his mood.

Opening the paper cartons filled the kitchen with mouth-watering aromas. I dispensed with my usual insistence on eating Chinese with chopsticks and started the video chewing my first forkful of kung pao chicken. The smell of the food got Rufus's attention, and I dropped some chicken on the floor for him before getting back to the video.

I texted Ashley again.

ME: Miss you Kitten

An hour later, I saw a girl enter my office.

My heart raced; I had her.

My first piece of good news.

Mike's assistant, Sophia, was at my desk. I couldn't make out what she did, but she'd definitely been in there alone.

Stopping and reversing, I played it over three times to be sure. She hadn't touched my computer, but she'd been right in front of it.

This wasn't quite good enough—not yet. I noted the time-stamp to be able to get back here.

I started the video again.

Ten minutes later, the doorbell rang.

～

ASHLEY

VINCE OPENED THE DOOR. BLOODSHOT EYES GREETED ME.

I pulled at the hem of my shirt. "I know I'm not supposed to be here."

"Nonsense."

Rufus came out to greet me and sniff my crotch.

I pushed the rude dog's nose aside.

"He has good taste," Vince said, opening the door wider.

I smirked and entered.

Once Vince closed the door, I wrapped my arms around him and buried my face in his shoulder.

His arms enveloped me, and he kissed the top of my head.

I waited for him to say something, but he didn't. We just rocked in each other's arms.

I looked up. "I want to use one of my favors."

He rubbed my back. "Name it."

"I want you to forgive me for acting like a bitch."

He loosened his grip and pulled my chin up with a finger. His eyes held mine with warmth and intensity. "No need. It's my fault. It's... never mind." He kissed my forehead. "Suffice it to say, I was a different person before you came back into my life, and I couldn't be more grateful for the changes you've led me to make. I could never be upset with you, Kitten." He released me.

Rufus sat expectantly in front of us.

Vince pulled a small chew from the bowl on the front table and threw it for him.

The dog chased it and carried the prize back to his bed.

Vince walked toward the kitchen. "Want a cider?"

I followed him. "Sure." I stopped at the table where he had video paused on a laptop. "Going through surveillance?"

"Yes," he called from the refrigerator. He pulled out two bottles and opened them.

"This looks like your office." It could get bad if he had Liz or me on tape.

"It is. Ben just put it in recently. I'm trying to find out who put that malware on my computer."

I steadied myself against the chair. "Find anything yet?" I mentally crossed my fingers that he hadn't found me at his computer deleting Liz's keylogger or rummaging through his office.

He brought the bottles over and handed me one. "Just one thing. I'll show you." He sat down and scrolled to a time-stamp he had written on a pad next to the laptop.

I stood behind him, watching the screen.

This had better not be me.

"Here." He started the video at normal speed. "Sophia went into my office here. She goes to the desk and messes around, but she doesn't touch the computer."

I saw something more than he did. Sophia lifted the blotter and looked underneath. She had checked for the planted memo. Now I had an opening.

He stopped it after she left the room. "So this doesn't say it was her that put on the keylogger, because she didn't touch my computer. But she had no reason to be in my office, so it's suspicious at least. I have a lot more to go through."

I couldn't tell him it proved Sophia was the mole, but it gave me an idea for tomorrow.

I rubbed his shoulders. "You're tight."

"Ooh, that feels good." He stretched.

A fear came over me. "Hey, are we on here?"

"Huh?"

"Page sixty-eight?"

"You want to watch it?"

I slapped his shoulder. "Get real. I just don't want it getting out on the internet."

He laughed. "I was kidding. I already deleted that day. Now, I need to get back to this."

That was the last thing I wanted. "Can't we just relax and watch a movie tonight?" I couldn't have him see me at his computer on that video.

He closed the laptop. "Sure, anything you want." He got up and led me to the couch. "Does the lady have a request?" He picked up the remote and took a seat.

I sat next to him and leaned in to snuggle. "Can we watch *Music and Lyrics* again?"

I'd liked the movie, but mostly I wanted to find a way back into a good place with my man.

"Coming right up." He worked the remote, and the movie began.

After about ten minutes, he asked, "Do you want to know about Barb?"

"No." I sighed.

I'd decided to be an adult about it, and what I didn't know couldn't hurt me, right? What he'd done before was ancient history, water under the bridge and all that. Only a middle-schooler would obsess over it.

His fingers traced lazy circles on my upper arm. Every once in a while, he'd squeeze me tighter for a moment.

I reveled in the safe warmth of his arm around me. It felt so natural to be leaning into him—my warm little cocoon of safety.

When I couldn't hold it in any longer, I asked, "Were you really going to see her Saturday?" Not all my worries had melted away.

His hand moved to scratch my head. "Of course not."

"But she said—"

"She was angry and trying to push your buttons."

I settled in for a second. "And you don't expect me to do a threesome?"

He laughed. "Of course not. I would never share you with anyone else, Kitten."

"And the other?" I couldn't bring myself to say the word *anal*.

"Not unless you're asking me to."

I snorted and shook my head.

There had to be a reason Barb was angry. I dreaded the answer, but it would eat at me if I didn't ask. "Did you care for her?"

He paused the movie and pushed me to sit up. He held my gaze and took my hand. "She was a girl I went out with, but it never progressed to the *friend* part of girlfriend. I'm not seeing her again. You're my woman—end of story. Can we drop her and focus on us?" His eyes conveyed even more conviction than his words.

I closed my eyes and nodded.

He took my face in his hands and pulled me closer for the lightest of kisses. "I told you she didn't matter. I trust you, and you should trust me." He brushed my nose with his.

"I do." I was his Kitten again.

He restarted the movie, I snuggled back into my cozy spot, my worries finally put to rest.

When the movie finished, I was even more teary-eyed than the first time. The hero had written a song just for the girl, and when she heard it, her heart melted. She learned he wasn't guilty of what she had imagined, and they were happy together. Just like me and Vince.

ASHLEY

THE NEXT DAY, VINCE WAS OFF-SITE VISITING A CUSTOMER AND AFTER THAT was scheduled to spend the afternoon with his swim coach, working on his technique for the triathlon.

I needed him here to execute my plan, and I was getting antsy about the timing.

He returned to the office around five.

I closed the door behind me and found him standing by the window, looking out quietly. I rounded the desk to come up behind him.

"What do you see?" I asked.

"It's what I don't see yet: him."

"Who?"

"The asshole that's messing with me. He's out there somewhere."

"You'll figure it out."

He sighed. "Just don't know if it'll be in time."

I turned toward the desk. "So, Sophia was messing around at your desk..."

He turned back toward the desk as well. "But she didn't touch my computer."

I lifted up the blotter. "Didn't she… Oh my God." I lifted the blotter farther, and the planted memo showed itself. "Look."

Vince grabbed the paper before I could stop him. He started reading.

I watched helplessly as he added his fingerprints to the page.

I also grasped the corner of the paper. "What does it say?"

"This is exactly what that FBI ass was asking me about." He gave me the paper.

I took it, adding multiple sets of my prints to the sheet, and read. I couldn't let his prints be the only ones on the paper. I rubbed where I thought he'd grabbed it.

"That fucking bitch." He started for the door.

"Vince. Stop."

He did, and turned to me.

I lifted the corner of the blotter. "Did the video show her placing it here, or just looking?"

"Just lifting the blotter edge," he replied.

"Then you need to go farther back and find when she put it here, or see if there's a second person involved."

His brows knit. "A second?"

"It's possible."

"You're probably right. I'll start tonight."

"Can I help?"

"No. This is something I have to do alone."

CHAPTER 40

VINCENT

I SWATTED THE ANNOYING ALARM AT FIVE O'CLOCK THE NEXT MORNING. Last night I'd gotten tired after a few hours of the video search, and I'd set the alarm to get an early start on finishing today. This would be the day to confront Sophia, and possibly another, if Ashley was right.

After hours of video watching, the doorbell rang with my lunch delivery.

The pizza box warmed my hands as I juggled it and tipped the delivery guy.

Back at the screen, I punched go and pulled a steamy slice from the box.

Oh so good.

I loved the fare at Vitaliano's, but sometimes I needed the simple pleasure of finger food instead of elegant dining. For me it was a bit like getting back to my roots, when our ancestors had huddled around the fire and eaten with their fingers—not that they had Papa Luigi's, of course. But still, it held a visceral appeal for me.

I was focused on the screen when I pulled at the third slice to get it loose. The stringy cheese didn't want to release its grip on the rest of the pizza. Another yank, and instead of coming free, the whole box slid to the edge and over, off the table.

Splat.

Face down.

"Fuck," I yelled at the disobedient box.

Just my fucking luck.

I hadn't let go of the piece I was pulling loose, so I still had that, but the rest of my lunch, and tonight's dinner, was a goner.

I plopped the remaining slice on a napkin and went to retrieve a roll of paper towels from the kitchen.

When I returned Rufus had already nosed at the box and was scarfing down a piece of my intended lunch.

"Get out of there," I yelled as I shooed him away. "You know that's going to make you fart all day."

He didn't care, and I couldn't blame him. Ultimate Pepperoni was the best.

After cleaning up the mess, I returned to the table and my video hunt.

It was still running, and the door had just closed as I sat.

Double fuck.

That was a close one. One second longer cleaning pizza grease off the floor, and I might have missed it entirely.

Someone had just gone in and out of the office on the screen. Turning back the video, I reset it an amount I thought was far enough and watched again.

Sophia.

She entered, went to my desk, and slipped something under the blotter.

I slowed it down and watched two more times.

No doubt about it. I couldn't prove it was the same memo, but she'd definitely put a paper under my blotter.

I noted the time stamp and circled it.

Checking my watch, I dialed Ben.

"What's up, boss?" he asked.

"I found what I needed on the video."

"And who is it?"

"Sophia."

He laughed. "Really? I wouldn't have guessed she'd have the guts for it."

"I need you to put a tail on her night and day. Bug her phone—whatever you can. I need to know who she's working for."

"Sure, boss. Between my people and outside resources I can rustle up, we'll put a tight blanket on her. She won't be able to fart without us knowing."

"Let me know as soon as we find anything."

"You got it."

I finally had a string to pull to unravel the mystery of who was calling the shots.

∾

ASHLEY

MY PHONE BEEPED A REMINDER AT ME.

Shit.

I had a check-in meeting with Liz scheduled, and I didn't feel like it. Besides, John was due back next week, and if I delayed, he would be my contact again. I pulled out my phone and composed a text message to her.

ME: Can't make meeting

I sent it.

Moments later, my phone rang. Checking the screen, I read, *Nurse Parsons*, my coded contact for Liz.

I ducked into the conference room to take the call. I answered the phone. "Yes?"

"Can't cancel. We need to talk," Liz said at a whisper.

This was a complete breach of protocol for the operation. "Why?"

"Big problem," she said softly.

"Explain."

"The op is not what it seems."

I knew the op wasn't what it seemed, but how did she know? More importantly, *what* did she know?

"How so?" I asked.

"Not over the phone."

That couldn't mean anything good.

"I can't make it," I told her.

"Alt three at two."

"Alt two is next on the rotation," I reminded her.

"Alt three, two sharp." She wasn't taking no for an answer.

"Alt three at two," I repeated.

"Be careful…very careful," she said before the line went dead.

Liz wasn't the most experienced agent, but she wasn't one to get rattled easily either, yet that's how her voice sounded today.

My stomach lurched. I shivered and stared at my phone. The call had taken less than thirty seconds, but already it had worsened my mood.

The call everyone dreaded during an undercover assignment was one telling us to get the hell out of Dodge, because our cover was blown and the bad guys could come for us at any moment. This call felt only one notch short of that.

She hadn't told me to abort; that would've been a fake phone call pretending to order pizza with extra anchovies. Telling me there was a problem just opened up nervousness on my end, without any resolution.

She'd insisted on alternate location three, the most desolate and out-of-the-way of our prearranged meeting spots. It was a small, empty warehouse that had given me the creeps when John and I had scoped it out.

Being abandoned, the building didn't have anybody around to observe us, but it also didn't have any utilities. The inside was dank, filthy, and dark, and that was before adding in the rats or the smell from the occasional homeless person using it as his personal outhouse.

I put away my phone, asked Anita to tell Vince I had an errand that could take a while, and left. There was nothing to be done until the meeting, and worrying wasn't going to get me anything more than heartburn.

~

I'D BEEN WALKING IN THE GENERAL DIRECTION OF THE MEETING FOR SOME time now.

Checking my watch, I realized I wasn't going to make it in time on foot, so I pulled out my phone again. I called up the Lyft app and put in an address about ten blocks from the warehouse. Proper protocol wouldn't allow a ride any closer than that. An electronic trail was bad operating procedure.

A few minutes later, a small yellow Hyundai pulled up, and I climbed into the backseat.

The driver tried to engage me in conversation, but I wasn't having any of it.

I wasn't about to break protocol any further or leave any inadvertent evidence about myself behind. Liz had said to be careful, so I would be.

To avoid panicking, I replayed the night at the Met in my head, and my hand went to the necklace again. How many girls got to experience a night like that? The man of their dreams takes them to the biggest museum in the country, arranges a candlelight dinner surrounded by priceless paintings, and then has a rock band serenade her? He'd remembered my favorite dessert, kept a photo of us from high school in his wallet all this time, and presented me with a necklace he'd bought years ago just for me.

Vince was a keeper if ever there was one. He was no longer the boy who'd left me abruptly in high school.

The third time the driver looked back toward me to start a conversation, he rear-ended the Chevy in front of him.

It was only a gentle bump, but I didn't bother telling the fucking idiot it was his fault.

He got out, and a shouting match between the two drivers ensued. Entertaining on any other day, but I was already running late—and so much for remaining inconspicuous.

It took ten minutes of cell phone pictures, pointing, yelling, and more yelling, before my driver slipped the other man some cash and we were on our way again.

Boston drivers.

The ride across the river to the warehouse district continued slowly in traffic, but he finally let me out at my chosen destination.

I punched up the app and gave him a two-star review, with no tip.

I started a fast walk toward the meeting place. Two blocks later, with the building numbers increasing, I realized my mistake. I'd gotten my directions mixed up and started walking the wrong direction.

Reversing course, I hustled as best I could in these shoes. It was already after two o'clock. I needed to know what had Liz so worried. None of this was like her at all.

My phone rang again as I neared the final turn. It was her.

"I'm almost there," I told her.

"Hurry. This will take a while to explain."

Her comment didn't make any sense. If she was out here to have a meeting with me, she could take as much time away from the office as she needed.

"Be there in a minute."

"I'm in the back," she said.

"Got it." I hung up the phone and made a left turn onto the street. The alt three building was just ahead.

A flash of light.

The noise was deafening.

An explosion blew out the front of the warehouse.

The brutal shockwave threw me back against the brick building on my side of the street.

Pain radiated through me as my head hit the wall, and a choking dust cloud rushed to envelop me.

I coughed, fell to the ground, and coughed some more.

The world went dark.

CHAPTER 41

VINCENT

ONCE BACK IN THE OFFICE, I WENT TO DO BATTLE WITH THE EVIL COFFEE machine.

Anita informed me that Ashley had gone to run an errand.

The cup started to fill, and my phone rang with Ashley's smiling face on the screen. It was a cute shot I'd taken of her over dinner.

"Kitten," I said as soon as I answered the call.

"Sir." A woman's voice came through the phone, but it wasn't Ashley. "Do you know an Ashley Newton?"

I felt stupid for the way I'd answered the phone, but I'd never heard a dumber question.

"Yes, who is this?"

"There's been an accident..."

The words stopped my heart. My chest tightened.

"I'm calling from Boston EMS because your number was in her phone as the last call received. Are you a relative, or do you know how I could reach one?"

"Yes, I am," I said without thinking. I couldn't have this woman hang up on me. "What kind of accident? Is she okay? Where is she?"

My mind was going a mile a minute with bad possibilities. I got up and grabbed my coat on the way to the door.

"Slow down, sir, please, and listen. She was near the site of an explosion on Burntwood Avenue. We've just brought her to Memorial Hospital, and she's being admitted now."

"Explosion? I don't understand." I pressed the down button on the elevator.

"Sir, I'm with the ambulance division. I don't know any more than that."

The elevator door opened. "Can I talk to her?" I frantically pushed the lobby button.

"She wasn't conscious when we brought her in, but her vitals are good."

"What's wrong with her?" I asked as the floors dinged by on the downward journey.

"You'll have to discuss that with the hospital staff."

"Thanks," I said, exiting the elevator and sprinting for the street.

I flagged down the first cab I found and told him to hot-foot it to the hospital. In the afternoon traffic, that didn't amount to much faster than if I'd jogged.

The ride to my Kitten was interminable as questions ran through my head. Why would Ashley go anywhere near Burntwood, and why would there be an explosion? And most importantly, how badly was she hurt?

When I reached the hospital, I couldn't get the attention of anybody who knew anything other than that she'd been admitted and was in the hospital computer.

I dialed Ryan Westerly. Ryan worked at Chameleon Therapeutics, one of my neighbor Liam Quigley's personal investments, and from our previous meetings, I knew his position gave him serious pull with this hospital.

"Ryan, I need your help. A friend of mine was in an accident and brought to the hospital, but I can't get answers out of anybody here," I told him after he picked up.

"A friend?"

"My girlfriend, actually."

"Where are you now?" he asked.

"The waiting room in Emergency."

"Vincent, wait there. If somebody doesn't find you in five minutes, call me back."

I thanked him and paced outside the waiting room, unable to sit still.

It took less than two minutes for a doctor to enter the small room and call my name. His name tag read Dr. Kulkarni.

"What's the name of the patient?" Kulkarni asked.

I followed him to the desk. "Ashley Newton."

He double checked the computer. "She regained consciousness here in Radiology, and she's about to be scanned. You can see her after we evaluate the results."

"What results?"

"In head trauma cases like hers where the patient has lost consciousness, a CT scan is called for. Just wait here, and I'll find you when they've completed her scan."

The words *head trauma* and *CT scan* made me shiver.

∾

*A*SHLEY

"ONE, TWO, THREE," THE NURSE SAID AS SHE AND TWO OTHERS SHIFTED ME off the table and onto a rolling hospital bed.

My shoulder hurt with the movement, but not as much as my head.

They placed several blankets over me and pushed me out into and then down the hall.

I focused on the two IV bags suspended on a pole above me. *Drip, drip, drip.* Liz's time was fading away with each drip.

"FBI," I said to the nearest nurse. "You have to call the FBI."

"You have to get better first," he responded. "You can give your statement to the police when you feel better."

They maneuvered me into an elevator, and the door closed.

I squinted to read his nametag. "Nelson, I'm FBI. Call them now, or I'll come back here and shoot you."

243

He laughed. "Miss, you've had a pretty bad bump to the head. Last week we had the pope in here."

His joke garnered laughs from the other two nurses.

The elevator door opened after a moment. I grabbed his arm. The pull of the IV in my wrist hurt like hell.

"I'm not kidding," I hissed.

"Okay, already. I'll get the floor officer to your room right away."

They wheeled me around a corner and into a room.

After a minute of hooking me up to beeping instruments, I was alone, and cold.

But Nelson had gotten the message, and after a moment a Boston PD uniform entered my room.

"I understand you want to make a statement." He flipped open his note pad.

"My name is Ashley Newton. I'm a special agent with the FBI."

He cocked his head. "Sure. You have identification?"

I was wearing a hospital gown under this blanket. "No. Not on me."

"Right," he said as he closed his notebook.

"There was another agent in the building that blew up. You need to call the FBI field office in Chelsea right now."

"I'll talk to my sergeant about it."

I fixed him with my best evil glare. "If you don't call them this moment, so help me God I'll get you charged with a four-oh-seven," I hissed. "Failure to render aid to a federal officer in distress. That's good for ten to twenty. Your choice, officer..." I read his nametag. "Davenport."

The blood drained from his face, and he quickly keyed his radio. "Dispatch, place a call to the FBI field office. We have one of their agents down here at Memorial, a victim in that gas explosion in the warehouse district, and there might be another agent still in the structure."

"Good choice," I told him as he left.

I'd made up the law that he had to help me or go to prison. There was no four-oh-seven, but it seemed like the kind of bluff that would get him off his ass.

Only minutes later, the cop was back at the door with SAC White.

White pressed his finger into Davenport's chest. "And I want a guard on this room twenty-four-seven, is that understood? Nobody comes in except doctors and nurses."

Davenport got back on his radio.

White came in and closed the door.

I lifted up a bit to speak. "Liz?"

"She's downstairs in surgery now. It's serious. That's all we know."

I sighed and relaxed into the mattress. She'd made it out.

"The cops on the scene called us when they found her creds while clearing the building."

I nodded.

"She was lucky," he said. "It looks like she took a cigarette break out back and wasn't inside when it blew."

I'd always been telling her the smokes would kill her, but instead a cigarette had saved her life.

"Gas explosion?" I asked.

"That's for the media. The gas to the building was off. This was a bomb." White paced. "And I'm going to get the bastard, so help me God."

"Who?"

"Benson, of course. Who else would have motive to attack you?" White apparently thought I was the target.

"It couldn't be him."

"Bullshit," he shot back. "Of course it's him. Attempted murder of a federal agent, for God's sake. That bastard is mine."

"I need to see her." It was Vince's voice, outside the room, arguing with the cop.

"You can't. FBI only," the cop yelled.

White opened the door and fell back as Vince shoved his way in.

Davenport grabbed Vince and pulled him back into the hallway.

White rushed out. "You're under arrest, Benson, for assault on a federal officer."

Vince got shoved against the wall, and I heard the click of the cuffs as they went on.

"It's not him," I yelled through the open door.

"Close that door," White ordered the cop, and I couldn't hear any more after that.

I yanked the leads off my chest and finger and rolled off the bed. Pushing through the pain, I dragged the IV pole behind me, opened the door, and yelled after White, who was leading my man away. "It's not him."

"I got this, Newton," White called back.

For the briefest second, I caught the pain in Vince's eyes as he looked back before White shoved him forward again.

The cop blocked my path. He and Nelson, the nurse, directed me back into my room and into bed again.

"You're a pain in the ass. You know that, agent?" Davenport said.

"Special agent," I shot back.

My side and hip hurt from the exertion, but not half as much as the pain of seeing Vince led away in cuffs.

At least Nelson called a female nurse in to reattach the leads to my chest.

CHAPTER 42

Vincent

"*It's not him,*" Ashley had yelled, but the FBI asshole was having none of it.

After listening to a recitation of my rights, I was smart enough to not say a thing.

"FBI only," the cop had said.

"Assault on a federal officer," the FBI agent had said—the same fucker who'd accused me of working with the mob. He'd known Ashley's name, and been in her room.

FBI Agent Ashley Newton? It didn't make sense, but I didn't dare open my mouth.

I sat in the backseat as White and two other angry feds drove me away.

They took me through booking and told me I'd be arraigned on eighteen US code one-eleven, assault on a federal officer. The surprise came when I was informed it was three counts: one for shoving White's dumb ass, and two others.

At least I knew Ashley wasn't hurt that badly. She'd been able to make it to the hallway to yell out my innocence.

I was supposed to get to make a call, but that didn't happen right away.

Eventually, I got the phone call and chose my boss's brother and my neighbor, Liam Quigley. I considered calling in the big guns and dialing my father, but rejected it. This wasn't going to stay hidden from him, but right now I didn't need a lecture.

Liam answered, "Vincent, good to hear from you."

That opinion was about to change.

"Liam, I need your help. I've been arrested and booked, and they won't be letting me out tonight."

He morphed instantly into the get-it-done manager I knew him to be. "Don't say anything to them at all. Not a solitary word. I'll handle all the legal arrangements. Where are they holding you?"

"Suffolk County Jail," I responded.

"On what charge?"

"Assaulting a federal officer. But—"

He cut me off. "Don't say anything over this line, not a word. I'll arrange a lawyer."

"Thanks, Liam."

"It's what we do for family, and with the help your dad gave us, you Bensons are just like family."

I knew what family meant to them, and to us. "About family. Don't tell anyone. I can't have this getting back to my father until I get it straightened out."

"Are you sure? He could—"

"Not a single solitary word."

I hung up and was called in for questioning not long after.

It was that FBI douche White and the other agent who had visited my office, Dunbar.

"Why did you do it?"

"When did you pick the location?"

"When did you meet Ashley Newton?"

"Why did you go to the hospital?"

"How did you know Elizabeth Parsons?"

"Why target those two agents?"

The question about two agents raised a question for me, but I vowed to not say a word and kept my curiosity in check.

"When did you plant the bomb?"

"How did you detonate the bomb?"

"What did you do today?"

"What was your schedule today?"

"When did you get up today?"

"When did you get to work today?"

"When did you leave work today?"

"How long had you known Agent Newton was undercover?"

I controlled my reaction to the gut punch that question delivered. I looked down at the table and asked for water, which they denied. I asked again, churning the question over and over in my head.

How had I been so gullible? Ashley had lied to me. She was working for the FBI and trying to uncover some crime I didn't commit, all while claiming to love me. Mason's distrust of women suddenly looked prophetic. I'd let my cock override my intellect and hadn't questioned her arriving back in my life at the exact same time as that fucking note.

This had to confirm that Gainsboro had fed the FBI made-up dirt on me. That made sense. The bombing was another attempt to frame me. But why? Semaphore was already theirs for the taking.

In the end, the interrogating officers got no information from me, but I got a few tidbits from them.

The other agent at the bombing was named Elizabeth Parsons.

And they'd confirmed that the Ashley I thought I knew now was not the Ashley I'd known back in high school. That sweet girl would never have done this to me. The woman she'd grown into had the morals of a pit viper.

Two guards led me to a holding cell after being told I was a high-priority prisoner. At least that got me my own bunk instead of sharing —who knows what kind of scum was also locked up here tonight.

I lay back on the hard bunk and thought long and hard about the day.

My enemy had tried to do one of two things, I decided. He was trying to frame me for the attack, which was the most likely with what little I knew. Or, he knew how I felt about Ashley and was attacking me by going after her.

That second one hurt the most, because it meant I might be the cause of Ashley and the other agent being hurt. It meant that if I hadn't hired her, none of this would have happened.

In here, I was completely cut off. I couldn't find out how Ashley was doing or demand to know how she rationalized what she'd done to me.

The questions haunted me all night.

Who could be framing me? And how could I have been so gullible with Ashley, the one woman I thought I could trust?

∾

ASHLEY

BY THE TIME DINNER ARRIVED, I'D ALREADY TRIED TO CHECK MYSELF OUT and had been stopped by Officer Davenport at the door.

He seemed to relish the idea of keeping me restricted to my room—payback of sorts.

I finished what little I cared for of the hospital's offerings: meatloaf with the texture of cardboard and a taste to match, with a side of over-done green beans. Naturally, dessert was Jell-O.

The door opened, and SAC White let himself in with a folder and notepad in hand.

"Newton, how are you feeling?"

I doubted he really cared. "Fine. I'm ready to get out of here."

"Yeah. I hate hospitals too."

"Then tell little Napoleon at the door to let me by."

"He's there for your protection."

I noticed his shirtsleeve rolled up and a bandage on his arm. "What happened to you?"

He held up the injured arm. "Argument with a dog." He opened his notepad. "Let's go over a few things."

It was clear he was here for a debriefing rather than to see how I was doing.

"First, how's Liz?" I asked.

His countenance clouded over. "She's alive, thanks to that cigarette break."

That sounded ominous.

Pain shot through my hip as I shifted up in bed.

"The doctors tell me the surgery went well. But…" He hesitated. "They've put her in an induced coma. She has some bleeding and maybe swelling of the brain, and they say that's the best way to safeguard her for now. We'll know more in a few days."

I felt a chill merely thinking about what she was going through.

"Her log shows the meeting was a scheduled check-in. Is that right?"

"Yes."

"Why that location?"

"It was one of the alternates, and Liz picked it."

He knew our procedure was to change up meeting locations. "You didn't pick it?"

"No, she did."

He continued with a series of questions about my and Vince's whereabouts during the day.

I was sick of it. "He doesn't have a motive."

A grin appeared on White's face. "That's where you're wrong, Newton. We executed a search warrant at the office and his residence." He held up his bandaged arm again. "That's where I got this. Damned dog."

"What?" I felt like congratulating Rufus, but held my tongue.

He pulled the evidence bag out of the folder he'd carried in. "We found this. A memo that ties him to Sonny Alfonso—the one you couldn't locate. Two hundred million worth of ties."

I did my best to school my face and not give away the disappointment I felt.

"The DOJ's source was dead on. He had a deal with Alfonso involving a gaming equipment company. This gives him motive. He had to know you were close, and he tried to close the investigation on his terms. And no way are we letting this fucker get away with attacking the Bureau. We'll put him away forever."

I nodded, saying nothing. Answering White's questions had brought the biggest problem into focus for me: only an insider could have known when and where Liz and I were meeting. There was a mole at the Bureau, and a dangerous one. I needed to get the fuck out of here. The regs wouldn't let me work the case, at least not overtly, but I'd damn well work it from the fringes.

CHAPTER 43

ASHLEY

WHITE HAD GONE, AND THEY'D CLEARED THE DELECTABLE DINNER offering, when the room phone next to my bed rang.

I answered it.

"Ashley, I know it's a dumb question, but how are you?" It was my partner, John.

"Okay, considering. I got my bell rung pretty good, but I'll be okay. However, I've got Boston PD posted at my door, and I can't even get to the Coke machine. I'm more worried about Liz."

"She's tough. She'll be okay. She's stable for now."

"How do you know that?" I asked.

"When one of our own is targeted, everybody in the Bureau knows everything."

I guess I shouldn't have been surprised. The only one who wasn't being kept in the loop was me. "I need your help on this. Any way you can get back here?"

"I already requested that, but Randy shot it down."

"That sucks. Well, with or without you, I'm on this as soon as I get out of here."

"You know they won't let you work your own case."

I knew all too well what the regs said, but I was not going to take a simple no.

"And anyway, you may not have much to do," John continued. "The scuttlebutt is they've already collared Benson for this."

"They've got the wrong guy."

"How can you know that?"

"Trust me, I just do. This wasn't him. The story's a lot bigger than it looks."

"Enlighten me."

I delayed for a second, considering my options. I decided I couldn't handle this on my own, and John was probably the one person in the Bureau I could trust to help me. "Do you have some time to talk?"

"For you, I've got all night, partner."

I started with today. "Liz insisted on this meeting. She had something to tell me about the op that had really upset her. She said things weren't at all what they seemed."

"And what does that mean?" he asked.

"Sensitive enough that she refused to discuss it on the phone."

"That's not good."

"It gets more complicated. Before that, White had called me into his office to give me specific instructions on finding a particular one-page document linking Benson and the mob."

"That paper you sent me to have the lab check?"

"The one and only, but there's more."

"Go on," he urged.

"When I met with White, I had just searched the office and found the exact document he was talking about. One problem though, it's a fake. It was planted in the office, and I was sent in to find it with more specific information than we've ever gotten from a source."

"You're sure it was a fake?" It was the obvious question.

"I'm sure," I said. "You saw it—there were no prints on it. How do you load an old-fashioned typewriter without touching the paper, much less sign the damned thing?"

I didn't have enough proof, but I believed Vince, and that made me sure enough.

"Did you tell the SAC you thought it was a fake?" John asked.

I put my career in John's hands with my next statement. "I didn't even tell him I'd found it."

The other end of the line was silent for a few moments as John processed what I'd said. "You better damn well be sure."

"I am," I responded, more with hope than knowledge. "I was sent in there as a tool to frame Vince."

"You know what you're saying?" he asked.

"Yeah. Somebody's dirty. I just have to figure out who."

"And you think Liz figured this out?"

"I don't know, but that's my working theory tonight."

John let out a long breath. "Are you saying the bomb was also an inside job?"

I swallowed hard. "That's what I'm saying. Only somebody with access to Liz's logs could have known the time and location of our meeting."

"And there's no way Benson could have known?"

I felt insulted, but I knew he didn't mean it that way. "*I* didn't even know until just before the meeting. Liz set the location. There was no way for him to know. The only person who knew both the time and location was Liz, or somebody in the office with access to her log file."

Laying out the evidence like this gave me a shiver. Before today, I would have trusted any one of my fellow agents with my life. Now, that wasn't a luxury I could afford.

"Then you better find out what it is Liz found."

"I know. But first I have to get the hell out of here."

"Any candidates come to mind?" he asked.

My answer wasn't going to please him. "The SAC had access to her log—"

He cut me off. "It can't be Randy. He's as straight as they come."

I continued. "He also was in here this evening asking odd questions. And he's the one that arrested Benson this afternoon. Now, how often have you heard of an arrest happening within an hour of the explosion? Before we even have forensics?"

He was silent.

"It's not conclusive, but you have to admit it looks odd," I said.

"Just like you insist it's not Benson, I'm convinced it's not Randy. I know the guy."

"Fair enough. But you're the one who asked if I had a thought."

"Better find another one quick. Accusing the SAC isn't something you can take back," he said. "I'll be up as soon as I can, and we can find the real perp."

I said goodbye, put the phone down, and settled back into my bed. The problem seemed intractable.

When Vince had first shown me a picture of the threatening note Staci got, I'd taken it for a joke, or a prank. The fake memo had upped my impression of his opponent, but today's events showed me I'd still underestimated whoever it was. Someone dangerous was playing for keeps. This was no street punk or pissed-off boyfriend. Bombings were rare—less than one a year on average—so this was a serious player. He was not going to be easy to track down. But the FBI specialized in the difficult.

When I closed my eyes, I couldn't get the vision of Vince hand-cuffed out of my head. What must he think of me? I hoped fervently that he had faith in me, as I had no idea what this must look like to him now.

As I tried to sleep, memories of him kept intruding. He couldn't be behind this; that was the one solid truth my heart knew.

CHAPTER 44

VINCENT

THE NOISE STARTLED ME, AND I JERKED UPRIGHT. I MUST'VE FINALLY
fallen asleep in the cold cell. The guard rapped his baton on the bars
again to rouse me. I went to check my watch, but it wasn't on my
wrist.

"Breakfast time," he said as he slid a tray through the slot.

I stumbled to the bars and grabbed it from him. The oatmeal was
only lukewarm, but that didn't stop me from spooning it down. The
long interrogation last night had meant no dinner. My stomach was
ready for anything, even jail food.

I smeared jam on the two pieces of toast. A carton of orange juice
wet my parched throat, and I followed it with part of the milk. I'd been
afraid to drink from the faucet in the sink last night.

The guard arrived to unlock my cell door before I'd finished the
second piece of toast.

"You've got an appointment," he told me.

I put the breakfast tray aside, and he led me down the hall to an
interview room similar to the one I'd been in last night. This room

smelled of vomit, though. It was empty, save a table and two chairs. I checked to see if one of them had better padding than the other—no such luck. I took a seat and waited.

The door opened and the guard escorted in a suited man with an ID badge hanging around his neck.

I recognized the name as soon as I read it.

"So we meet again, Mr. Benson," he said.

Assistant United States Attorney Kirk Willey was the walking definition of arrogance. He and I had only met once before, and it hadn't been under the best of circumstances. Liam and I had threatened to derail his campaign for attorney general of the Commonwealth—and it had worked.

I didn't stand, and neither of us offered the other a hand.

He took a seat and placed a voice recorder on the table, turning it on. "AUSA Willey interview of suspect Vincent Benson at seven-twenty AM. Please state your name for the record," he said.

"Vincent Benson."

His eyes were cold as ice.

He pulled out a plastic envelope with a piece of paper enclosed and pushed it my way. "Care to explain this?"

I silently read the paper. It was the fake contract Ashley and I had found. It purported to be an agreement between me and Sonny Alfonso arranging to sell him a stake in Semaphore for two hundred million dollars.

Willey smiled as I looked up. "We found this in your office, under the blotter on your desk. I've got you now on racketeering."

I kept quiet.

"Why did you attempt to kill two federal agents yesterday?"

I was done. "I have nothing to say without my lawyer present."

He leaned forward and spoke into the voice recorder. "Interview terminated at the request of the suspect." He clicked off the voice recorder.

I waited for him to say something or leave, but for the longest time he did neither. He just stared at me.

"It was a bad move on your part to threaten me last year."

I didn't respond. He was obviously trying to goad me into saying something.

"You probably thought I'd forget. I don't forget things like that, and I don't forgive. Your money can't save you now. I've got you, and all the years you spend in prison, you're going to regret ever having met me."

I held his stare and returned it in equal measure. One thing my father taught me: never flinch in the face of a bully. And Willey was a skunk in a suit, a bully with a capital B.

He stood to leave, done with me for today, apparently. He knocked on the door for the guard to let him out.

"Good talk," he said as he exited.

It *had* been a good talk. It told me what I needed to know about Gainsboro. They were playing for more than control of Semaphore. They were after me.

Willey departed, and all I had left were questions for Ashley. Why? Why had she lied to me? Why had she worked with them against me?

~

ASHLEY

I woke the next morning still in my hospital bed. I wasn't cuffed to the bed railing, but it felt like it. I hadn't slept well. The triple problem of worrying about Liz and Vince at the same time as figuring out my plan of investigation had kept me up.

A nurse brought breakfast for me.

I shifted up in the bed as she rolled the table over with the tray. I winced at the soreness of my hip and shoulder. At least the pain told me I was alive; that was the good news.

Breakfast looked only slightly more appetizing than dinner last night: oatmeal and apple juice. But even this horrible hospital food was probably a step up from what Vince was enduring this morning.

"Any way I can get eggs and hash browns with this?" I asked.

"This is good for you. I can get you cream of wheat instead, if you like."

I interpreted her comment as a firm no. I likely hadn't been the first to complain about the food.

The doctor came around after I'd finished, and the exam began. The checking of my bandages, the stethoscope to the chest, the pen light in the eyes, and the balance test were followed by his version of twenty questions.

No, I wasn't nauseous. No, I didn't have a headache except when I touched the massive bump on my noggin. No, I wasn't dizzy, no, I didn't have blurry vision, and yes, I remembered the event and every-thing leading up to it clearly.

He said he wanted me to stay another day for observation, gave me a warning to take it easy, and told me to call a nurse if I developed any of the symptoms he'd asked me about.

Nurse Nelson from yesterday showed up five minutes later to check my vitals.

I wasn't staying. "I'm ready to leave. The doc says I'm good to go, but I didn't see my clothes in the closet."

"They took your clothes as evidence," he said.

"Figures."

"I apologize for doubting you yesterday. It's just—"

I raised a hand to cut him off. "No biggie. I get it."

He moved to the door. "Let me get you something to wear."

My clothes were probably a loss anyway, ripped, bloodied, and soiled from the blast.

He returned a few minutes later with blue hospital scrubs and a pair of tennis shoes. "Will a size nine and half work? I borrowed these from Susie."

"Thanks. Close enough." I accepted the shoes and clothes.

He left, giving me privacy to dress.

I winced as I sat to pull on the pair of men's cotton briefs he'd supplied—they were better than nothing—followed by the scrub pants. There wasn't a bra in the pile.

"Back up, sir. Nobody is allowed in this room." Davenport's voice came from outside my door.

"I'm FBI, son. Stand aside before I charge you with obstruction," John's welcome voice sounded from the hallway.

I pulled on the top just before John opened the door.

"Morning, Newton," he announced.

I cinched up the drawstring on the pants and prepared to reclaim my life. "Doc says I'm fine. Let's go."

He closed the door behind him. "First, I know everybody's asking, but how are you?"

"Pretty sore, but good enough to get the hell out of here." I grimaced as I leaned over to pull on the shoes. "Last night you said you weren't coming."

"No, last night I said Randy wouldn't pull me back. But as soon as I told the SAC in New Haven you were my partner, he couldn't release me fast enough. So here I am."

I pulled on the second shoe and tightened it up. "I'm glad you came."

Now it was two of us against the system.

"Have you thought about a plan?" John asked as he opened the door for my escape.

"First stop, my place for some clothes," I told him.

Davenport stopped us. "She can't leave. Orders."

John's hand moved to the butt of his gun. "You're relieved of responsibility for her, son. The FBI has her now."

John didn't lose stare-downs like this, and after a few seconds, the cop relented.

We started down the hallway as the poor officer got on his radio to tell dispatch overwhelming force had arrived to spring me from lockup.

Our first stop was the ICU, where John's badge got us entrance.

Another Boston cop was stationed outside Liz's room. His badge read *O'Mara*.

We introduced ourselves. After hearing John's last name was McNally, the two Irishmen bonded, and we were allowed in to see her.

I moved around the bed and gently took the hand that wasn't hooked to an IV. "Liz, I'm here with John. We're going to find the bastard who did this."

I didn't expect her to respond, but I hoped her subconscious could hear us. A bandage worthy of the movies covered most of her head, and a tube ran from under it to a bloody collection bag hanging below the bed.

We spent a few minutes telling her to be strong, that John and I were on the case, and that the bastard would pay. Then reluctantly, I let go of her hand and we left. As annoying as she had sometimes been, she was a fellow agent above all else, and John was right, an attack on one of us was an attack on all.

"She certainly got hit worse than you," John observed on the way out.

"They told me she only survived because she'd snuck out back for a smoke."

John cocked his head. "And to think I always told her the smokes would kill her."

I nodded. I'd already had the same thought.

Vincent

Liam had arranged for my lawyer.

David Perlman seemed like a nice enough guy when I met him this morning a few minutes before entering the courtroom.

"What is Ashley's condition?" I asked him.

He ignored the question and gave me simple instructions at the door. "The purpose of this hearing is to enter your not-guilty plea and to set bail, nothing more. Don't say anything at all in there, except if the judge asks you if the plea is correct. And if you answer the judge, don't forget to address him as *your honor*. No matter what, don't allow the prosecutor to push your buttons. That can only hurt us with the judge."

I nodded. "Okay."

Liam and Ryan Westerly were both in the public section of the courtroom when Perlman and I entered.

I exchanged nods with them.

At nine o'clock sharp, the court was called into session, and my case was first on the docket.

Perlman slid over the charging paperwork. It said I had assaulted a federal officer during the performance of his duties while investigating a bombing targeting federal agents.

I turned to the second page, which contained pictures of the blast site and the two agents. One was a federal ID picture of Ashley.

The second was Jacinda. She'd been an FBI plant as well, and Ashley had lied to me again about her being only an acquaintance.

Kirk Willey himself was at the prosecutor's table. His summary of the charges against me made me sound worse than Al Capone, and possibly worse than Osama bin Laden. According to him, I'd personally attacked the entire country by conspiring with organized crime, yada yada, yada, racketeering and conspiracy were the charges, along with one of assaulting a federal officer. And he intended to add the attempted murder of two federal agents.

The judge lost patience and cut him off mid-sentence. "We're only here to discuss today's charges. I'm sure you're aware of that, Mr. Willey."

Perlman entered my not-guilty plea and pointed out that I was a respected member of the community with no prior record. He started to go on, but the judge cut him off as well.

"What bail is the government proposing?" the judge asked Willey.

"One hundred million," he said coldly. "The crimes are serious. The defendant is a man of means and poses a significant flight risk."

Perlman objected to the amount, pointing out that there was no evidence tying me to any crime and suggested no bail.

"Bail is set at twenty million," the judge said. He didn't rap the gavel as they did on TV.

I let out the breath I'd been holding. That amount I could handle.

Willey stood. "Your honor, because of the obvious flight risk the defendant poses, we would ask that electronic monitoring be included."

Perlman complained that I wasn't a flight risk in the least, but the judge wasn't swayed.

"Electronic monitoring is ordered. The defendant will be confined to his residence." Then he rapped his gavel. "Next case."

I was led out the way I had come in and returned to the deputies. The whole event was over in minutes.

Once out of the courtroom, Perlman and I were escorted to the small conference room.

"I need to know how Ashley is," I told my lawyer.

Once the door had closed, he opened his mouth.

"Mr. Benson, have a seat. The first rule is we don't talk except in private. Do you understand?"

"Got it." I sat, and so did he.

"Who is Ashley?" he asked.

"Ashley Newton is my girlfriend and was injured in the explosion. She was taken to Memorial yesterday. They arrested me before I could see her."

"You must be confused, Mr. Benson. The only injuries were to two FBI agents."

"That's right, and she was one of them."

His brow creased. "You mean to tell me your girlfriend is one of the FBI agents?"

"I didn't know that until yesterday, but yes. Exactly."

He steepled his hands before going on.

"I'll check in with the hospital, but this presents a problem. You mustn't have any contact with her. She's on the prosecution's team and most certainly a witness. The court won't allow it, and her bosses at the Bureau won't allow her to have contact with a defendant. It's out of the question."

He paused for a moment. "Now, about bail," he said.

"If you call Mason Parker at Covington Industries, he can raise it."

"No need. Mr. Quigley told me last night that anything up to twenty-five million, he would take care of."

With Liam, at least I had one person on my side in this town.

Perlman rose and handed me his card. "We'll talk later. The deputies will take you back to the jail until bail is arranged. And one more thing."

I waited.

"The ankle monitor is not a joke. You mess with it, and bail is revoked. You'll end up back in lockup until the trial. You go outside of the radius you're allowed, and the same thing happens. There are no second chances. None."

~

Ashley

John drove me home to pick up clothes, my weapon, and my credentials.

I added Liz's smuggling case file to the pile I carried out.

"Which safe house you figure is best?" I asked after locking up.

"Neither. If somebody on the inside is involved, those will be compromised. You're going to stay with Ivy."

I'd met his sister once, and the prospect of a day with her didn't excite me. "I'd rather stay with you."

"Too obvious. Don't worry, you two will get along just fine."

"Yeah. She's dangerous, but I'm armed."

He laughed. "She's not that bad."

"I need to call Vince," I blurted.

John pulled the car to the side of the road and stopped. "Vince, huh? I warned you about going under with someone you had a history with. Talking to him is the one thing you can't do. I'll pass a message to him that you're worried and explain that you can't contact him, and that's the best we can do."

On the way to Ivy's, John made several changes of direction and reversals. In the end, we were fairly confident no one was tailing us as he drove south.

"She takes some getting used to," John said.

This was obviously his attempt to prepare me to meet Ivy again.

I'd thought she was pretty out there when I'd met her at John's barbecue, but that was after at least three beers more than she should have had.

She and her boyfriend had been in the pool doing chicken fights with Liz and her boyfriend. And Ivy had had the bright idea to pull at the bow holding Liz's top up. It only took another minute before Liz retaliated and they were both topless. Of course all the guys were having a great time, and I got several invitations to form a team and join the pool shenanigans. But I worked with those guys, and no way was I losing my top.

John called ahead. "Ivy, I need your help. My partner needs a place

to crash for a while… Yeah, we just got her out of the hospital…
Thanks, sis."

After a while, John turned left and pulled up in front of a little
green house.

This was so different from where I lived. A wide, tree-lined street
with plenty of space to park and cute houses with well-kept front
yards—unlike the hardscrabble apartment buildings in my section of
town.

Ivy opened the door as we approached the porch and greeted John
with a hug, followed by me.

"It's going to be nice to have a girl around here to talk to," she
noted as we moved inside with my luggage. One of her arms had an
ivy vine tattooed on it.

"Yeah," I replied, although I felt less than enthusiastic about adding
girl talk to my agenda.

Her tight tank top read *Polite as Fuck* in giant black letters on the
light blue fabric—not something I would be caught wearing.

She saw me staring. "Never mind the shirt; it's work clothes."

"Work?"

"I tend bar, and a few things make for better tips: strong drinks, a
low-cut top, and something that gets them to stare. After you catch
them, they feel obligated to tip well."

This lady had a smart business head on her shoulders.

"Oh, and the third thing, walk with a bounce in your step, if you
know what I mean."

I knew the boob-jiggle walk well.

John shook his head. "And she gave up acting classes to do this."

"It pays better," Ivy countered.

"I'll be on your case, and I'll let you know what we find. Remember, you can only work this from the fringes. Randy won't let you in on
it." John excused himself toward the door. "Keep her safe, Ivy. I have
to get back to work."

"She's the one with the gun," Ivy said.

After John left, Ivy showed me to her spare room. "It's not much."

"It'll be fine, thanks. I don't need much space."

"I need to go to work. You want to come along? We could talk," she
suggested.

"No, thanks. I think I'll rest."

"We can talk when I get back, then."

I wasn't really in the mood. "I might just go to bed early."

She pointed a finger at me. "Look, girl, I read people for a living. You almost got your ass blowed up. You need to talk; I can tell."

"Maybe so," I admitted.

After she left, I dialed my sister. She was the one I needed to talk to. There was no answer.

I was alone.

CHAPTER 45

ASHLEY

THAT AFTERNOON, I LAY ON THE COUCH IN IVY'S HOUSE WILLING THE PAIN in my shoulder to recede—it wasn't working. Thirst forced me to get up to find another bottled water.

My hand went instinctively to the gun on my hip with the sound of a key turning in the deadbolt. I resisted the urge to draw.

Ivy came through the door, shopping bags in her arms. She kicked the door closed behind her.

"I appreciate you being protective of my house, but if you draw your gun on me, we're going to have a problem."

I pulled my hand away. "Sorry, just a habit."

She dropped the subject. "Want to help with dinner?"

"Sure," I said, coming over and taking one of the bags from her. "What's on the menu?"

"You heard of three-alarm chili? Well, tonight were makin' my six-alarm chili. Helps you to forget all your troubles. After a dozen bites, you can't think about anything except dunking your head in a bucket of ice water." She laughed.

It sounded like just the ticket. "Game on, then."

We unloaded the bags together, and she started to grill the ground beef while I chopped celery.

Ivy looked away from the skillet for a moment. "Tell me about it."

"What?"

She waved her spatula in my direction. "Girl, I'm a bartender. You got that face, like you're struggling with a decision and you gotta talk about it."

"Shows, huh? It's my boyfriend." Just saying I had a boyfriend calmed me.

She went back to stirring the meat. "I'm listening."

"Did you hear about the blast out in the warehouse district?"

"John told me about it. He said you were outside, and I'm guessing that's what those are about," she said, pointing to the butterfly bandages on my face. She stopped stirring. "Gas explosion, the news said, but John told me the truth. Oh, and we'll need that red onion chopped up in a sec, to go in with the meat."

"Sure." I put the celery to the side to peel and chop the red onion. "You want the white too?"

"You can do that next. The white goes in with the beans. Only the red one sautés with the meat."

I followed her instructions. "Yeah, it was a bomb, and another agent got hurt. Worse than me."

She turned around. "Like a take-you-out kinda bomb?"

I shrugged. "Liz, that's the other agent, and I were supposed to meet there. I was running late. Otherwise..." I could feel the bile rise in my throat just thinking of what would have happened if my Lyft driver hadn't gotten in that accident. If I ever got that driver again, he was getting a monster tip. Exchanging gunfire was one thing, because you could take cover, you could shoot back, but a bomb, you were helpless, completely at the mercy of the bomber.

"That's serious shit."

I didn't answer. Instead I opened the two cans of white kidney beans she'd put on the counter.

"Do you know who did it?"

I added the cans of beans to the red ones already in the pot. "Not yet. That's the scary part."

She sighed. "So that's why you're hiding out here." She stirred the pan. "And John doesn't know either?"

"Not a clue, at least not yet."

After the beef and onion had browned, she poured them into the pot.

"Now six strips of bacon, if you please."

I located the bacon in the fridge, and the strips sizzled as they hit the hot pan.

"What's this have to do with your boyfriend?" she asked.

Red, green, and yellow peppers were next on the cutting board. "I need to talk to him, but the Bureau won't allow it."

"They can't tell you that shit."

The bacon aroma filling the kitchen had my mouth watering. "They can, and they have. I'm a witness against him in a case we're working."

Ivy pushed the bacon around. "You're in the FBI and you want a criminal as a boyfriend? You got a few screws loose, if you ask me."

I slid the chopped peppers into the pot. "That's the thing; he's being framed."

"One bunch of cilantro as well when you're done with the carrots," she said.

Her chili certainly had a lot more ingredients than mine, which was mostly chicken, tomato sauce, kidney beans, and spices.

"And you can prove that?"

I started on the carrots. "Not yet, and not being able to talk to him makes it harder."

She turned the bacon. "Then talk to him. It's the right thing to do."

"I can't."

"You mean won't," she shot back.

"The rules are pretty clear." I appreciated her argument, but the rules were unambiguous. "Your brother's going to get him a message from me."

After the bacon crisped up, I chopped it while Ivy added so many spices, I couldn't keep track.

When she got to the chili powder, she spooned it rather than shaking it in. This was going to be as hot as advertised. "I say you should still talk to him."

I stirred the concoction while she tasted and added even more spices to the aromatic pot.

"After three bites of this, all your cares will melt away. I guarantee it," she said.

I kept stirring, hoping she was right. I could use a carefree evening. Even the preparation had taken my mind off the soreness of my shoulder and hip. My head only hurt when I touched it, but the bruises constantly reminded me of their presence. I put the wooden spoon down and retrieved some Advil from my purse. It had been four hours, and I was allowed another dose.

"Still hurts?" she asked, spying the pills in my hand.

"Yeah," I admitted.

"Then I've got just the thing for you," she said. She moved quickly to open a cabinet full of liquor. She poured from various bottles before adding ice and handing it to me.

"And this is?" I asked.

"A zombie, pretty much the strongest mixed drink on the menu. Guaranteed to take the edge off." She pulled a beer out of the fridge for herself.

I sipped the drink and could instantly tell she wasn't joking about its potency. I took a slug to swallow my Advil, then sipped some more.

She put a lid on the pot and turned down the stove. "Let's give dinner a while to simmer."

We parked our butts on the couch, and I could feel the drink getting to me, just a little.

"The right thing to do is talk to him," she said, without prompting.

I'd been considering it all day, but recoiled at the implications of breaking this rule. If I got caught, it could be bad for Vince as well. Asshole that he was, White would probably try to add witness tampering to the charges.

"I told you, I can't get approval."

"I didn't say ask. Just do it. Don't tell your boss—what he doesn't know won't hurt him. It's like stopping at a red light in the middle of the night. You go through it when nobody's around. No harm, no foul."

I slurped another sip of the zombie.

She lifted her beer bottle. "Your choice, but I think you sometimes gotta bend the rules to do what's right. And not talking to your man? That's not right. Now you're breaking the girlfriend rules." She knocked back a slug.

I pondered her argument over the remainder of my drink.

"Just do it so you don't get caught," she said.

I didn't know if it was her encouragement, or the effects of the zombie, but I picked up my burner phone and closed myself in her guest room.

Five minutes later, I'd made a call and gotten an agreement to help me with my plan. I returned to the couch.

"Chili's ready, if you're up to the challenge," Ivy called from the kitchen.

I felt the drink's effect as I stood. I brought my glass and deposited it in the sink. "I think I'll stick to beer for the rest of the night."

"Good choice. Two of those will put you on your butt faster than you can spell Massachusetts."

I changed my mind and poured myself a water from the fridge while she ladled the chili into bowls.

She carried them to the table. "First one to finish wins. You up for this?"

"Like I said, game on."

~

VINCENT

IT HAD TAKEN THREE HOURS TO BE ESCORTED FROM THE COUNTY LOCKUP back to my Tremont Street condo with the uncomfortable electronic monitor fastened around my ankle.

Rufus was even more excited than usual to see me and got a quick breakfast.

My condo was now my cage, but at least the fridge held beer.

After a beer, I found my checkbook and a pen. That Willey guy was such an asshole. He'd demanded an ankle monitor like I was a common criminal. I didn't have the federal government behind me, but I did have a checkbook, and he'd pissed me off. A one-million-dollar check made out to his opponent's campaign committee in the election for attorney general was a terrific way to retaliate. Fuck you, Kirk Willey. It might not be the best idea I'd had, but it made me feel better to strike a blow against the arrogant ass.

Let's see how a little payback feels, you asshole.

It felt so good, I decided I might write an additional check to start off each day for a while.

"Rufus, what do you think? Should I write another check every day for a week?"

Rufus lumbered over to me, tail wagging.

"I'll take that as a yes." I threw him a chew.

Rufus's ears perked up when my phone rang. The caller ID showed a blocked number. I ignored it, but it rang again and I answered, ready for another annoying marketing call.

"Mr. Benson, I'm calling for Ashley. If you are not alone, hang up and I'll call back later." The words were ominous.

"I'm alone."

"Please listen. My name is John McNally. I'm Ashley Newton's partner at the Bureau."

"How is she?"

"She'll be fine—a little banged up right now, but nothing that won't heal."

"Thank God. They wouldn't let me see her."

"I know. She wanted to know how you are. The problem is that Bureau regulations will not allow her to have any contact with you until this matter is resolved."

The "matter" was obviously the trumped-up charges the FBI had leveled against me.

"I'm okay." I didn't add how pissed I was that she'd lied to me.

"She and I are going to be working from this end to untangle this mess."

He made it sound like we were mopping up a kitchen spill instead of dealing with potential prison time for crimes I hadn't committed.

"I have to go now. And, another thing…"

"Yeah?"

"We never had this conversation." He hung up.

Rufus looked over at me.

"Sorry, boy. I'm not allowed to take you for a walk." It sucked that I couldn't even go across the street with my dog.

I sat down to wallow a bit in my feelings of betrayal. I'd so wanted to believe Ashley was the one, but she'd proved I didn't know her after all. I'd trusted her, I'd cared, I'd thought she cared, but she'd lied to me and been a part of the setup the whole time. None of it made any sense.

I kicked the other chair.

Fuck.

How could I have been so blind?

I retrieved my phone, wandered out to the patio, closed the door, and dialed Ben.

"How you doin', boss?" Ben asked.

"I've been better. What do we have on Sophia so far?"

"Nothing yet."

It was time to let the dogs loose. "We can't afford to wait any longer. I want you to interview her. Scare the living crap out of her. Tell her we've got her on tape and get a confession. That's what I need. And I want it right away, before this thing gets any more out of hand."

"No problem, between me and Mickie, we got scary down to an art," he said.

Mickie was three hundred pounds minimum, and with the tats that showed above his collar, he would be scary reciting a nursery rhyme.

"I want to know who put her up to it," I added. "Most of all, I want proof that the memo's a fake, a plant."

"Got it. I'll call you when it's done."

"Thanks, Ben."

I hung up, wishing I could be a fly on the wall when he and Mickie confronted her.

I wandered the rooftop patio, circling the perimeter like a caged animal.

Rufus gave up after a few laps and lay down, watching me wear out my shoes.

How I could have been so stupid as to believe Ashley cared after all these years. She hadn't tried a single time to contact me since that day we'd parted ways—not even a Christmas card, just complete radio silence. That wasn't the behavior of a woman who'd been pining over me for nine years.

I'd bypassed my own procedures, hiring her without a background check. Her beautiful green eyes had short-circuited my brain and blinded me to the fact that after nine long years, I couldn't possibly know who she'd grown up to be.

The next minute, the thought of those gorgeous eyes and the way the necklace I'd given her matched them brought me back to our weekend in the Big Apple. Nothing had ever brought me more joy than the feel of her in my arms and the look on her face as we danced to our song in the museum. It had been the first weekend since I started at Covington that I hadn't done one iota of work. And I hadn't even wanted to while I was by her side.

She'd looked equally happy. How could that have been an act? Was anyone that good an actress? I could normally spot a bullshitter in seconds, and I'd gotten none of the warning signs with her, not a one. Every feeling of love I gave her, she returned in kind. Her eyes couldn't lie that well. I couldn't lie that well—I'd fallen for her, and she for me.

My feelings ping-ponged from one extreme to the other every few laps of my personal prison exercise yard. The only truth that remained was that she'd lied to me, and since I hadn't detected it, I had no idea how I could trust anything she said in the future. She'd been working against me, hadn't she? For the very FBI that was complicit in this scheme of Gainsboro's to take me down.

As evening came, I went inside and powered on the TV. Scrolling through the options, I decided to watch her favorite, *Castle*.

I was less than ten minutes in when the doorbell rang.

Opening the door, I found Amy, Liam's wife. She held a package.

I opened the door wider. "Amy, come on in. How are you?"

She entered and didn't utter a word until I'd closed the door. "Just fine, Vincent, thank you," she said, putting a finger to her lips. "I'd love a glass of water and some fresh air." She pointed at the door leading to my patio overlooking the Common.

"Sure, one glass of water coming up. Still or sparkling?"

"Sparkling, if you have it."

I poured us each a glass of Pellegrino.

She opened the door to the patio, and I followed, closing the door behind us. She accepted the glass, but didn't speak until we reached the edge, overlooking Tremont Street below. "This is for you, from Ashley," she said in hushed tones.

I took the package she offered, unclear about her odd statement.

"How is she?" I asked.

I couldn't trust Ashley, but I could still care about her.

"Okay. A bump on the head and scratches and bruises. Mostly she's scared for you and also herself after the bombing, but she can tell you that." She tapped the padded envelope. "That's what this is for."

I tore open the package and carefully removed a flip phone, a charger, and a slip of paper with a phone number on it.

A smile came to my lips. "A Batphone?"

Amy put a warm hand on mine. "She said not to answer it in the condo, or when anyone else is around."

"Got it. No eavesdroppers." I hadn't considered that they might be bugging my condo, but it was the government, and there wasn't much I would put past the fucking FBI at this point.

"She said she'll call when she can and that it might not be right away." She took a swig of her water and leaned over the railing. "Also, Liam said to remind you that of course whatever help we can provide, we will."

"Thanks. You've been a great help already."

She appraised me with caring eyes. "I can't imagine how hard it is."

I shook my head. "I'll survive." I decided against telling her anything about the Gainsboro asshole after me.

Amy left after finishing her water, and I was alone again.

Even if Ashley called, how could she explain herself?

After pulling another water from the fridge, I opened my wallet, took out the photo from behind my license, and asked out loud how she could have done this to me. The photo landed on the kitchen counter.

I knew Ashley was all right, and for the moment, that's what mattered. I shifted my focus from her to my foe. I needed to locate the mole.

I put the water to my lips and tried to piece together all that I knew about the problem.

~

LATER IN THE EVENING, I CLOSED THE DOOR TO THE GUEST ROOM AND picked up one of my burners. I called the number of the phone Amy had told me she'd bought for him.

"How are you?" Vince asked.

Just the sound of his voice eased my pain.

"I'll heal, but it's you I'm worried about."

"How is Elizabeth?"

His mention of Liz surprised me, though it probably shouldn't have. "She's not out of the woods yet, but we think she'll be okay."

"That's good. I didn't do this. I want you to know that."

How could he think I suspected him? "Of course not. I know that."

He took a long breath. "Ashley, how could you?"

His question hit hard. It was so open-ended, and his reversion to my name was a bad sign.

I only had one place to begin. "It started as my job."

"Your job is to lie to people and pretend to care about them?"

"I wasn't pretending. I love you, Vince."

It was the first time I'd uttered the words to him, but they were true, if only he could believe me.

"Sure. I can't believe a single thing out of your mouth. Everything you told me about yourself was a lie. Your entire job is lying."

I pleaded with him, "I'm serious, Vince."

"Serious and truthful are two different things. You should learn that."

"But I mean it."

"Just like when you told me Jacinda was an acquaintance?"

His accusation stopped me cold. I'd been caught in another lie.

"Goodbye, Ashley. At least I can be honest when I say I'm glad you're okay."

"But…"

He had already hung up.

I redialed.

He didn't answer, and he didn't pick up when I tried again either.

I turned off the phone.

CHAPTER 46

ASHLEY

THE NEXT MORNING, I WOKE TO THE QUACKING OF MY PHONE'S ALARM.

Stretching the directions on Advil usage and adding a bottle of beer had allowed some sleep, but my Vince problem kept intruding.

My biggest failure was that I hadn't leveled with Vince on my terms, when I could have explained how I was bending the rules to help him, not hurt him. I'd meant to tell him at dinner, then at lunch.

If only I had.

How could I repair his trust in me? Only one possible path remained: find his enemy. It damned well wasn't Sophia. This was beyond her. She was a pawn doing someone else's bidding.

And I had a second task as well. I had to find whoever had attacked Liz and me, because it damned well wasn't Vince. Liz had wanted to warn me about something, and I had to find out what.

After a sponge bath and dry shampoo, I ventured out to find Ivy cooking a delicious-smelling breakfast.

"Sleep okay?" she asked as she turned. Her shirt today read *Drink the Fuck Up*, probably another crowd pleaser at work.

"A little. Thanks." I put a pod in the coffee maker and pressed the button.

"Did you call him?"

I nodded.

"And?"

"It didn't go well. He's mad I lied to him."

"Wouldn't you be if the roles were reversed?"

"I guess."

She pulled out a frying pan. "We got sausage and eggs, or we have leftover chili, if you want that."

I opted for eggs.

"Chicken," she chided me.

She'd won the chili contest last night by a mile.

After breakfast, John arrived right on time and drove me to get my car after I insisted I was well enough to drive myself to work.

I didn't dare tell him I'd ignored his advice and called Vince. It risked putting him in danger as an accessory. After I started my car, he followed me all the way to Quincy.

I stopped off downstairs at logistics to get a new smartphone to replace the one White had locked away as evidence—no telling when I would get that back.

Upstairs, the bullpen seemed familiar, yet oddly foreign. I'd only set foot in the field office twice since this episode had started, and somehow the Covington offices seemed more like home to me.

It took almost an hour for the well-wishers to disperse after I finished assuring everyone I was ready to get back to work. It was Liz we all needed to worry about. I called the hospital, reached the ICU desk, and after getting the initial runaround, asked to talk to Officer O'Mara. He quickly told the nurses to add me to the list of people they could release details to. Before me, the list had only included the SAC and Liz's partner, Frank.

The update itself was anticlimactic: no change. But that was a good thing, and the tube in her skull continued to drain properly, keeping the pressure at bay. The nurse told me that was the doctor's chief concern.

I thanked her and promised to call in regularly.

White appeared mid-morning, bitching about having to drive

downtown first thing to meet with the DOJ at the courthouse. The man hated rush-hour traffic.

"Newton, my office," he said with his usual charm.

I followed him and shut the door before taking a seat.

"Shouldn't you still be in the hospital?" he asked.

I sat up. I wasn't going to let him intimidate me. "I'm a little sore, but I'm ready for duty. And I owe it to Liz to find out who did this."

He waved his hand. "You're a victim. You can't be involved." He'd clearly shut the door on any way for me to join the investigation. "Besides, you know the drill. You're on a desk until the Bureau doc clears you for field duty."

"I could help Frank with Liz's workload while she's still laid up."

"Yeah, whatever. That probably makes sense."

He didn't realize he'd just given me the opening to work the case from the inside. Hopefully I could locate what it was Liz had wanted to tell me.

"Yes, sir. I'll book an appointment with the doc."

"Besides, we need you to help nail this Benson bastard. Like I said before, this is a top priority, so what do you have on him that we can add to the file?"

"I can't think of anything right now."

"Does he beat his wife?"

"He's not married," I said flatly.

"Well then, does he beat his girlfriend? Take some time and write down what you know. You've been there a while. There's gotta be some dirt you've seen or heard. The lawyers will want whatever you've got. These scumbags always have skeletons hiding somewhere."

"I understand."

I knew what he wanted, but I didn't like the way it smelled. This is not what we did.

He turned to look at his computer monitor, his habit for nonverbally telling us the meeting was over.

I rose.

"Newton," he said, before I escaped.

"Yes, sir?"

"Dirt on this guy, that's what we need."

"Understood." I closed the door behind me, locking the pig in his pen.

The exercise was obviously biased. Thinking back, I couldn't come up with a single other case where the request had been made, an order given to find dirt on a suspect unrelated to the crime we were referring for prosecution. That practice had gone out with J. Edgar Hoover.

This officially stinks.

WHEN I CHECKED IN WITH FRANK, LIZ'S PARTNER, I HELD UP THE smuggling case file I'd brought from home. "Mind if I work on this at Liz's desk?"

"Be my guest."

It took a few minutes to organize a bit of open space in the heap of papers Liz called her desk. I opened the folder and went through the motions, reviewing what had already been checked on and figuring out what was left to do. She'd been right that this case was a lot of boring paperwork.

I kept busy until lunchtime, when pretty much the entire gang decided to head out for pizza.

"You coming, Newton?" Frank asked.

I patted my stomach. "No, thanks. Something they gave me at the hospital seems to have interfered with my digestion. Next time, though."

He didn't argue, probably happy to not sit next to somebody farting all afternoon.

I took my mug to the coffee room, filled it, and returned, double checking that our floor of the office was empty for a while.

One by one, I opened the drawers to Liz's desk and started my search. It wasn't likely that I would find anything, but I had to be methodical about this. I wouldn't get very many opportunities to rummage through her desk. In the bottom drawer, I found three envelopes. They were addressed to the Inspector General—none sealed.

The only other thing of interest I found was her handheld voice recorder.

I checked it for recent recordings and found only two. After listening to them both, I deemed them unrelated and put the recorder back where I'd found it. My watch told me I still had plenty of time before the group returned, but the hairs on the back of my neck were standing up with an uneasy feeling. Closing the center drawer, I had the odd feeling I'd missed something obvious.

I reopened the drawer and reviewed the items one by one. That's when I realized the silver pen was not what it seemed to be. Liz had been into buying Bond-like gadgets off the internet, and this was a pen with a built-in voice recorder she'd shown me once. I placed it in my purse to check later. I'd have to research how to access it on the internet back at Ivy's.

I turned on her computer, which is when I hit the roadblock. I knew Liz had started with her badge number as her password, but when I tried that, it didn't work. Now it was going to be a matter of guessing.

I tried the standard things like her birthday, her sister's name, her favorite rock band.

I tried a few more combinations, and to my surprise, 'Garfield' opened the computer. Who names a cat Garfield anyway? A quick review of the file structure didn't show anything that leaped out at me. I started a search for files that had been created or modified in the last few days.

The sound of the elevator door opening almost tripped my heart. I killed the search window, started the shut down, and turned off the monitor. I was back to reviewing the paperwork on Liz's boring smuggling case by the time they rounded the corner into the bullpen.

It was two agents I didn't recognize.

"Where is everybody?" the tall one asked.

"They went out to get pizza."

"Pizza sounds good," the short one said.

Based on their accents, they must've been on loan from the New York office.

"Any idea where they went?" the tall one asked.

"They didn't say exactly, but Pizza Hut is the usual destination." I tried not to sound as nervous as I felt.

"Sounds like a good plan to me," the short one said. "You want us to bring anything back?"

I touched my stomach again. "No thanks. Stomach issues today."

After dropping off backpacks in the conference room they disappeared around the corner, and after a moment I heard the sound of the elevator door closing.

I was alone again.

It took another minute before my heartbeat returned to normal. Trying to go through Liz's things while people were at lunch wasn't a winning plan. Coming back late at night after everybody had gone made a lot more sense. Checking her computer was not going to be a five-minute task.

I resigned myself to spending the afternoon working through Liz's boring folder of paperwork. The idea of making an appointment with the Bureau doctor was looking better by the minute. I looked up the number and called. A time slot was available tomorrow morning, and I took it.

After a half hour I couldn't keep my curiosity at bay and looked inside the first of the three mysterious envelopes addressed to the Inspector General. It was a sexual harassment complaint against the SAC from before he was promoted—the weekend in New Hampshire. The other two were similar, but with different events and later dates.

Now I saw the connection: Instead of offering herself to White to get the good assignments and preference for the California promotion, Liz had been holding this over him.

The envelopes went back in the drawer, and I sat back. I didn't know whether to be proud of Liz for resisting him, or pissed that she hadn't filed them, because White deserved to be investigated. I settled on both.

By the end of the day, I hadn't found anything that gave me a hint of what Liz had wanted to talk about, unless it was the three envelopes.

John had been out in the field all day with Frank on the bombing, and he hadn't returned by the time I was ready to call it quits.

CHAPTER 47

ASHLEY

I OPENED THE DOOR TO IVY'S HOUSE AND WAS ONCE AGAIN GREETED WITH delicious aromas emanating from the kitchen. "Smells wonderful. What's cooking?"

"Chicken scaloppini with hot dogs on the side."

It was the wackiest menu I'd ever heard of. "Hot dogs? What's with that?"

"I figured since you're flunking girlfriend one-oh-one, we should go back to basics and practice sucking the wiener."

I laughed. "I don't need a lesson, thank you very much."

Maybe I did, but I planned on having my man teach me. I dumped my purse on the front table and headed to the kitchen. I didn't see a hot dog anywhere.

"Ha ha."

"Just thought I'd offer, if you need a few pointers."

I ignored her and went to the guest room to change. Was I really flunking as a girlfriend? The thought hurt. I was protecting him.

When I returned, Ivy was serving dinner. That's when I noticed the small letters on her tank top that I'd missed earlier. It read *Learn speed-reading, dumbshit. You're staring too long.*

As we ate, she asked how work had gone, and I had to explain how boring my paperwork day had been. I didn't recount the scary episode of almost getting caught searching Liz's desk. My poking around needed to stay between John and me.

Ivy seemed actually interested in my musings and asked probing questions for an outsider to our investigations. It was no wonder she earned good tips as a bartender; she had a knack for making people feel listened to.

Mentally I shifted Ivy from the weird-keep-at-a-distance column to the interesting-friend column. Being sassy was just her style. Her poking at me about my relationship with Vince had been her way of helping, while keeping it light. I had to remember that through the ages, barkeeps had been the first psychologists, parceling out advice over mugs of ale or shots of whiskey. She would make a fun drinking buddy when I had the time.

"I make a wicked martini," she offered.

"Not tonight, thanks." I had to keep a clear head for work tonight.

"A zombie, then?"

I shook my head. "Double no on the zombie."

"Lightweight," she said. After a moment she added, "Go ahead, make the call."

"What?" I asked feigning ignorance.

"Your boyfriend, of course. I know you're dying to talk to him. At least I would be if I was in your position."

I leveled with her. "He won't talk to me. Because I lied to him."

"He wanted to know if you were okay?"

"Sure, but—"

"No buts. That's a man who still cares for you deep down. Sure he's pissed and he's hurt. But that's not a man who hates you."

I thought through her logic, and liked it. "Thanks."

"But you still got a ton of groveling to do, girl. And that's something you gotta do in person."

That deflated me, but a spark of hope was better than none at all.

We ate for a few minutes, and Ivy suddenly asked, "When are you going to sneak over there and see him?"

I didn't know how to respond. "I can't," I said. "The rules don't allow it."

"I say your rules suck," she said between bites.

"I agree, but that doesn't change 'em."

She took another gulp of beer. "You suck at the girlfriend thing."

"He won't even take my calls." My words were more polite than my attitude. If I hadn't been a guest here, I would have told her to fuck off.

She pointed her fork at me. "No offense, but if he were my boyfriend, I'd be there to support him, no matter what. But that's just me, what do I know?"

Her words slammed into me. How was I being a bad girlfriend by protecting him from another possible criminal charge? I stuffed a forkful of chicken in my mouth to keep from saying anything I would regret.

The more I thought through her words, the worse I felt. I was caught between two impossible choices, and she was right. I didn't know how to do this girlfriend thing. I had to figure out how to regain his trust.

"You said he was training for a triathlon?" she asked, changing the subject.

I nodded with my mouth full, and mumbled, "Mm-hmm."

She lifted a folded shirt from the chair next to her and handed it to me. "For when you decide to go over."

I put down my fork and unfolded the tank top. It read *I don't do triathlons. I do a triathlete.* I laughed. "I like it."

"For when you go over," she repeated.

She'd said *when*, and not *if*.

After dinner, it took me a few minutes of internet searching to find the online user manual for Liz's audio recording pen. I took off the cap to locate the micro-USB connector to download it.

Before I could hook it up, my phone rang. The number was the Covington offices.

"Hello?"

"Agent Newton, this is Ben Murdoch, head of security at Covington. Are you alone, and do you have a moment?"

I was intrigued. "Sure, Ben. What can I do for you?"

"Agent Newton—"

"Ashley, please."

"Ashley, I have some information I think you need to hear right away."

That got my attention. Murdoch hadn't seemed like the excitable type.

"What kind of information?" I asked.

"Information that proves my boss was set up, and by whom."

"I can put you in touch with my partner who's on the case."

"Ashley, it has to be you. The boss said not to trust anybody but you with this."

My heart leaped at his words. "He said that?"

"Exactly."

Vince told him he trusted me?

"How is he?"

"Worried—for himself and for you."

Ivy had been right in her assessment after all.

I told Ben where and when I wanted to meet.

A LITTLE WHILE LATER, I SAT ON THE BENCH AT THE EDGE OF THE RED-brick circular walkway surrounding the Parkman Bandstand, with the closed Earl of Sandwich sub shop to my left and the tennis courts behind me. The area was quite open, with yards of empty grass in all directions. There was no way for anyone to get close enough to hear without me seeing them. I didn't care about being seen with Ben Murdoch; I merely needed the conversation to be private, and this was much better than trying hushed tones over the table of a diner.

Ben approached from around the far side of the bandstand. He'd obviously had training, judging by the way he surveyed the area as he came.

I didn't stand to shake his hand.

He took a seat beside me. He handed me a voice recorder with earbuds. "I think you'll find this very interesting."

I put the earbuds in and started the playback.

The voice was Sophia's, by my estimation, and it was laced with fear.

I stopped it. "You edited this."

"We also have a full recording of the session. This one is just her confession."

He didn't say it, but I was guessing the other tape contained a fair amount of coercion or threats based on the sobbing I'd heard.

I restarted the recording.

"Sophia, did you type this memo?" Ben asked.

A sob, followed by, "Yes, I did."

"Did Mr. Benson ask you to type this?" Ben asked.

"No, sir."

"Who asked you to type this?"

Sophia's answer. "Mr. Paisley."

"And did Mr. Paisley give you the wording?"

"Like I said, yes,"

"And did Mr. Benson sign this?" Ben asked.

Another sob. "No, I copied it."

"Copied what?"

"I copied his signature. I have it on lots of papers. I practiced it."

"And what did you do with the paper after you signed it?"

"I put it in Mr. Benson's office under the blotter."

"Why?" Ben asked.

"That's where Mr. Paisley told me to put it."

"When?"

"The middle of last week."

"So this contract was dictated by Mr. Paisley and signed by you and placed by you in Mr. Benson's office, is that correct?"

Another sob. "Yes. I told you. Yes. Can I go now?"

The recording stopped there.

"Can I keep this?" I asked him.

He nodded. "I've got a copy."

Of course he did; he was a professional. I'd never checked, but he'd probably been government trained.

I pulled out the earbuds and handed them back to him before slipping the recorder itself into my jacket pocket.

"I don't get it. Why?" I asked.

He smiled. "We got that, too. I just didn't think it was necessary on the confession. It's on the second file."

I waited for the explanation.

"Her sister was in a jam with the law. Paisley said he could get her off if Sophia did this favor for him. And I guess he has the pull he claimed, because the charges against her sister were dropped this morning."

"And what does this Paisley get out of this? Why does he have a beef with Vince, I mean Mr. Benson?"

Ben chuckled. "Simple greed. He works for Gainsboro."

So Vince's first instinct had been right after all. Covington's competitor, Gainsboro, had been behind this the whole time.

"I'm going to need to talk to her," I told him.

Actually John would need to talk to her, but I didn't need to go into that with Ben.

He pulled a piece of paper out of his pocket and handed it to me. "I figured that. Here's her home address, and you know where to find her at work."

I opened the paper, looked at it, and pocketed it as well.

"I'll be on my way, if you don't have anything else, Ashley," he said.

"This is good. Thank you for this."

"Anything to help Mr. Benson," he said as he stood. "Have a nice evening."

He turned to walk back the way he'd come.

"Oh, and Ben? Tell him I'm sorry about all this."

He nodded and left.

We were almost there. I wrapped my hand around the recorder with the key to releasing Vince from the nightmare that held him right now. This could all be wrapped up in a day or two.

John would need to bring Sophia in for a proper interview and a signed confession. It shouldn't be too hard with this recording.

My task would be to get to Paisley, and I recalled seeing his name on some of the paperwork I had from Liz's smuggling case. Interviewing him tomorrow would be my task.

I'd ask him if he knew Sophia, and if he denied it, I'd have him. He wouldn't know we had Sophia's confession yet, and once he'd made a false statement, the trap would spring shut. Proving that Gainsboro was behind this would be good enough to clear Vince, at least of the racketeering charge. And there was no way they had any evidence tying him to the bomb.

Ben had disappeared around the other side of the bandstand.

I got up to leave and turned down the red-brick path.

Ivy's words haunted me as I strode back to my car. *"You're failing girlfriend one-oh-one."*

CHAPTER 48

ASHLEY

I KNOCKED ON THE LARGE, SOLID DOOR.

Nothing.

I rang the bell.

The door opened.

Vince.

I tried to read his expression—a mixture of surprise and, could it be, happiness? His visage faded to stern.

"You shouldn't be here."

He was right; he was always right.

"I don't care. I've been breaking a lot of rules recently, and we need to talk."

He blocked the doorway, clad in jeans and a USC T-shirt instead of the suit he always wore to work. "You need to go."

I pushed aside the hurt of his words. "Not until we talk."

He moved to let me in. "And then you go."

I passed through the doorway.

He pulled away when I moved to put an arm around him.

I followed him toward the kitchen. "Do you have anything to

drink?"

He opened the large refrigerator door, pulled out a hard cider, and offered it to me.

"Thanks."

He removed a cider for himself as well.

"You converted to cider now?"

He took a sip. "No. I got them for you."

I smiled. "Thank you."

"Should we talk outside?" he asked, cocking his head toward the door leading to his rooftop patio.

I'd learned from John that there wasn't surveillance on his condo. "No. Inside's fine."

As I turned, I noticed the old, worn photo on the counter.

It was our prom picture. The one I'd found in his wallet. I'd been worried he'd moved on to greener pastures, easier girls, and forgotten about me.

I averted my gaze before he caught me staring, and wandered toward the full-length windows overlooking the Common and the city beyond. He'd brought me here after our New York weekend only a few days ago. I hadn't taken in the full grandeur of his place that night.

"Paisley's out there somewhere."

Vince joined me by the wall of windows. "I don't want to talk about him."

I winced when he touched my left shoulder. "Ow."

He yanked his hand back. "Sorry."

I turned to him. "I'm a little sore from the blast."

"Tell me what happened. I was worried about you," he said as he moved away from the window.

I followed and took a seat on the couch. "First I want to explain."

Instead of sitting with me as I'd expected, he sat in the old leather wingback chair.

"You should have told me who you worked for," he said curtly.

"I couldn't."

"Yes, you could."

"No, I couldn't. That's the job."

"So I was just a job?"

I huffed. "Stop it. You know better than that." I took a breath and lowered my voice. "I meant to tell you after things had progressed between us, but I didn't get the chance."

"You could have refused the job," he shot back.

"No, I couldn't. And if I had, you'd be in even worse shape now."

"Bull."

I sat up. "You owe me another favor."

"I said that when I thought I could trust you."

"Are you going back on your word?"

That stopped him. "No. Of course not."

"You need to know the whole story, and I just want you to listen to me. Can you do that?"

He nodded. "I guess."

"I've been trying to find out who did this to you."

"I should have shredded that letter when you found it."

"What happened to listening to the whole story?" I reminded him.

He shrugged.

I pulled out my phone. "Look at this." I pulled up the memo photo and handed it to him.

He looked at it briefly. "So?"

"Look at the date on the snapshot. I found this eight days ago. I didn't turn it in to the FBI like I was supposed to. Instead I sent it out to a friend for analysis to prove you didn't write it."

He cast me a wary glance before checking the phone again. "If you knew it was planted, why am I in this mess?"

I moved closer to him. "I have to have evidence. I tried, but I couldn't identify who wrote it. I put my job on the line for you by not turning it in when I found it. If any other agent had been assigned to this case, it'd be game over for you right now. And if the Bureau finds out I held that back, I could get fired."

His eyes softened. "I didn't know that."

I shifted forward on the couch. "I believe in you, Vince. I know it's a forgery, but we have to prove that."

"Since when do I have to prove I'm innocent? What about Sophia's confession?"

"It's part of the solution, but not good enough on its own. You and Ben don't understand how the system works."

"If a confession that the evidence was planted isn't enough, I don't care for your system."

I straightened up. "I get that you're pissed, but the justice system is what I know. I've had to work really hard to get where I am, and I'm damned proud of it. I carry a gun every day and face real bad guys. You need to trust me on how to handle this."

He waited for me to continue.

"Look, the cards have been stacked against you from the beginning. Paisley planned this really well. He had Sophia plant that contract, and he fed information to the DOJ that got them to assign us to investigate you. After I was in place, I was given very specific instructions about how to find that memo. We only caught Sophia because I didn't turn it in. What we need now is to have my partner, John, get a signed confession from Sophia. The recording won't cut it. Then I'm going to pay Paisley a visit. If it goes as I expect, he'll deny knowing Sophia. That should get us the leverage we need. Lying to the FBI is a serious crime."

Vince moved to the couch and put his arm around me.

"I'm sorry I doubted you," he said softly.

I wrapped my arms around him, and we hugged each other tightly. "I have to go."

He took me into one of his intense kisses, the kisses that drowned out the sound of the outside world and all my fears.

He nibbled my earlobe and whispered, "You should stay."

"I can't. Tomorrow is too important."

After another intense kiss meant to change my mind, I pushed away and stood. "With John's help, we should be in a better position by tomorrow night. Now I really have to go."

WHEN I GOT BACK TO IVY'S, THE RECORDING PEN STILL SAT NEXT TO MY laptop. Curiosity beat out my desire for sleep.

Three minutes later, I had it downloaded and was listening to Liz and White discussing her progress on two cases she'd been assigned. The kicker came a few minutes later.

"What makes the Benson case so hot?" Liz asked.

White answered. "I got no fucking idea, but AUSA Willey is all over my ass. If Newton fucks this up, he's going to be royally pissed, and my neck will be on the chopping block."

After that, the rest of the conversation was mundane, and then the recording stopped. A moment later I replayed it to confirm one more thing: In private, Liz wasn't calling him Randy. She was sticking to *sir*. Interesting.

CHAPTER 49

ASHLEY

THE NEXT MORNING, WITH BEN'S VOICE RECORDER SAFELY IN MY HAND, I rode the elevator up to our floor in the FBI field office. It felt good to have a weapon on my hip again—the hip that didn't hurt. I found John upstairs at his desk, and I nodded to have him follow me into the conference room.

He closed the door behind us. "What's up?"

I played the confession from the voice recorder.

He waited until it was over before speaking. "Where'd this come from?"

"The security guy at Covington got this out of a girl that works upstairs. Her name is Sophia Nazarian."

"But how did you get it?" he asked.

"Vince found her on the video surveillance of his office."

He stopped me. "Then why didn't he tell us so we could check it out?"

"Because he thinks somebody here is out to get him, that's why."

"That's bullshit."

"You tell him that. When he found the footage that showed her planting the evidence, he had his security guy interrogate her."

John shook his head. "And he gave it to you, right? You know this isn't how we're supposed to be doing this. You can't be handling evidence on this case."

"How could I know he was gonna give it to me?" I handed him the recorder. "Now you need to bring her in and make it legit. Get her to sign a statement. Tell them Benson called you last night and turned this over to you."

He sighed. "Name and address?"

I fished the piece of paper from my pocket and handed it over. "Just keep my name out of it."

John shook his head. "This better not blow up in my face."

"Right," I agreed.

"Who's this Paisley character, anyway, and how is he tied to this?"

"That's what I'm going to go find out."

"You can't interview him about the Benson case."

I nodded. "I'm not going to. He's involved in one of Liz's cases that I'm working. I just might happen to ask him if he knows who Sophia Nazarian is, that's all. Her name is on one of Liz's papers. He'll deny it, and then when you get her signed statement, we got him. Perfectly neat and by the book."

"This *has* to be by the book," he cautioned me.

I nodded again, but John was still shaking his head as we left the conference room.

I sat at Liz's desk and gathered up the papers I needed for the interview with Paisley. Before I left, I took a pen in my left hand and scribbled Sophia Nazarian at the bottom of one of the sheets. Writing with the wrong hand was a lot harder than it looked. Satisfied that it didn't look anything like my normal handwriting, I put it in the middle of the stack and closed the folder.

I called the hospital to check on Liz again. The nurses knew me by now and were chattier than the first time I'd called. Liz was doing well, in their opinion. The pressure inside her skull was controlled, she didn't have a fever, and the doctors were saying encouraging things— all good news.

A background search on Thomas Paisley didn't show anything out

of the ordinary: VP of software engineering with a degree from Berke-
ley. Multiple years at some southern California software companies,
and hired at Gainsboro a few months ago. Nothing criminal to suggest
this was a pattern with him.

After gathering my files, I told Frank where I was going and
escaped without running into the SAC.

~

VINCENT

THE BATPHONE RANG IN THE LIVING ROOM AT LUNCHTIME. I RUSHED TO
answer it.

"We got him. I got Paisley," Ashley said in an excited voice.

"He confessed?"

"No way. He denied knowing the name Sophia Nazarian, and I
have him on tape. My partner should be getting Sophia's statement
right about now. That will be the nail in his coffin. We'll be able to play
the two against each other to get him. And regardless, Sophia's admis-
sion that she planted the memo is going to get you off the hook on the
racketeering charge."

I soaked in her words. "That's terrific."

"I'll call you later. Right now I have to get this back to the office."

"Miss you, Kitten," I said as we ended the call.

After I put the phone back on the coffee table, I took my coffee out
on the patio and surveyed the scene: people walking the Common, free
to go wherever they pleased. Soon I'd be joining them, thanks to
Ashley. Once we signed the paperwork on Semaphore, and Gainsboro
was officially beaten, this would all be over. Paisley and Sophia would
get whatever the penalty was for planting evidence like that, and they
wouldn't be a threat any longer.

I sat back in the lounge chair, and the sun warmed my face,
improving my mood even more.

It's about fucking time.

CHAPTER 50

ASHLEY

LETTING VINCE KNOW HE WAS SOON GOING TO BE IN THE CLEAR HAD
lightened my mood. This didn't solve finding who had attacked Liz
and me, but one problem down, and now on to the next.

I finished my Whopper and started the recording one more time
with an earbud in one ear. I could hear the hitch in his breathing when
we came to the sensitive part.

"This document is authentic as well," Paisley said.

My voice followed. "Do you recognize the name written there on
the bottom? Sophia Nazarian?"

"No, I don't. Should I?" was his clear response.

Gotcha.

I had him on a ten-oh-four violation at least, lying to the FBI. Along
with Sophia's confession, it would provide the leverage to get them
both.

I took the last onion ring in my mouth and rewound the recording
to listen to it again.

I smiled as I left the Burger King, vanilla shake in hand.

An elderly man recoiled from the door at the sight of the gun on my hip.

I was used to it. Something about a woman strapped with a weapon seemed odd to many men.

"Government agent," I said as I held the door open for him.

He passed through. "Thank you."

While I drove back to the Chelsea field office, I realized it wasn't just the Paisley recording that had lifted my mood, it was last night as well. Ivy had been right about me failing as a girlfriend, and I'd underestimated how important that was. Going to see Vince had been a violation of all the rules, but it had been the right thing to do.

Rounding the corner into the bullpen, I caught sight of John, and he nodded toward the conference room.

I put my files down and joined him there.

John's expression telegraphed bad news. "We're fucked. She skipped town," he said.

My heart sank. "Sophia?"

"She and her sister boarded a flight at Logan this morning."

Shit.

They were probably on their way back home to Armenia, out of our reach.

"What did you get out of Paisley?" he asked.

"Nothing. He denied knowing her." That would have been more than enough with Sophia's signed confession, but without it, my recording was useless. I paced the small room, racking my brain for a next step. "Maybe I can find a financial trail that links them."

"Not likely," John said. "The recording said dropping the sister's charge was the payoff."

I started pacing again, trying for another angle.

"I know this is important to you," John said. "But I have to get back on the bombing. Forensics came back and matched the explosive to that Russian mob car bomb we had last year. They're sure it's the same bomb maker, Yuri Meledev."

We had worked the case with ATF and nabbed Yuri and the stash of bombs he'd been about to sell last year. Things had just taken a twist.

"What do you think that means?" I asked.

"No idea. Larry and I are going to roust Yuri in lockup and see what he knows. In the meantime, the forensics guys are chasing down the extra bombs to verify the detonation mechanism. Our evidence room says Boston PD has them, and they say ATF has them, and ATF is pointing at us. A regular circle jerk. Somebody has to have them."

I shook my head and went back to Liz's desk. I was looking through the smuggling file when the SAC burst out of his office.

"Newton, in here now," he yelled.

I put the file down and followed him into the glass-enclosed pigpen.

He held out his hand. "Your badge and your gun," he demanded.

My chest tightened. "What?" I squeaked.

"Now, Newton. You violated Bureau policy and my direct orders. You interviewed a man today, scrounging around for information on the Benson case."

How could he possibly know?

"But, sir…"

His hand stayed out, demanding my weapon and badge. "Now."

If he were a cartoon, steam would have been coming out of his ears.

I handed him my credentials, pulled my weapon from my hip, released the magazine, ejected the chambered round, and examined it to be sure the chamber was empty. Then I placed the gun, bullet, and mag on his desk. I could barely breathe.

"Newton, you're suspended. And if I get my way, terminated. Now get the hell out of my sight and out of my building."

There was no point in arguing; the sentence had been handed down. I was temporarily—and maybe permanently—out of the Bureau.

All eyes were on me as I left the stinky office with my heart pounding. They'd obviously seen and heard it all.

My knees were weak as I shuffled to Liz's desk to collect my things.

They could all see what had happened through the glass, and probably heard it as well.

I was no longer one of them. I was persona non grata. I might as well have had a red letter painted on my forehead.

As special agents, we were a tight-knit family. Now out of that circle, I was a nobody.

In my current mood, I didn't give a shit about the Bureau rules on contacting Vince; I needed him. Even worse, I had to tell him the evidence we thought we'd had an hour ago had gone up in a puff of smoke.

But first, I turned my car toward the hospital to check in on Liz. At least unconscious, she wouldn't reject me.

How had everything turned so utterly to shit?

How can I explain this to Vince?

I dialed his number. He needed to hear the bad news right away, and from me.

~

Vince

I was out on the patio with Rufus when the Batphone rang for the second time today. I rushed inside. By now they probably had Sophia's signed confession, and I could start counting down the hours until this whole thing was over.

"Hi, Kitten. Such a treat to hear your sexy voice again."

She sobbed. "It's not good news, Vince."

"Tell me. What's wrong?"

She sobbed again, and the background noise told me she was driving. "Sophia's gone, left town. And my boss suspended me."

"What? Why? That's not right."

She took a loud breath. "He found out I interviewed Paisley somehow."

I leaned against the couch to steady myself. The world was collapsing around us. "Where are you now?"

"On the way to the hospital. I need to visit Liz."

I ran a hand through my hair. "Okay. Come over when you're done, Kitten. I'm here for you."

"Vince, I'm so sorry. I let you down."

"Stop that talk. No, you didn't. This is Sophia's fault, and Paisley's fault, not yours. Come home after your visit."

She sniffed. "I will. I love you."

"Love you too. Drive safe."

After hanging up, I was ready to kill that fucking Paisley guy, whoever he was.

I grabbed the nearest thing, the TV remote, and heaved it blindly against the wall. It hit the picture, the glass shattered, and the picture fell to the floor.

Rufus escaped out the open door to the patio.

"Come back here," I yelled after him. "It's not you."

He didn't believe me.

I went to the liquor cabinet and pulled out my best bottle of Macallan. I poured a hefty glass and put it to my lips.

Ashley would be on her way soon.

I didn't drink it. I poured it down the sink.

She needed me, and I wouldn't be drunk when she came.

My phone rang with my sister Serena's name on the screen. "Hi there," I answered with as much cheer as I could.

"Why the hell didn't you call to tell me you got arrested?" she screamed. "Dad is going to be—"

"You can't tell Dad." I said emphatically. "I'll do that once I have it all figured out."

"Hey, Vincent," her boyfriend Duke Hawk said over the line.

"Hi, Duke." I liked him he was a former SEAL, a great guy, and had saved Serena when she had been kidnapped in LA. That had been a nerve-racking time.

"You said you need to figure shit out," he said. "We have great investigators in Hawk Security and we can have a team on a plane tonight—anything you need."

"I appreciate it. Maybe later." Dad had lots of tentacles in LA and bringing in the Hawk team would certainly get back to him.

After assuring them that I had it under control, I ended the call.

I paced between the patio and the great room, looking out the window and over the edge of the railing at all the free people outside. I needed to hold Ashley and apologize for getting her involved in this. If I hadn't hired her, none of this would have happened to her.

Finally Rufus felt safe enough to follow me again.

My regular phone rang. This time it was Perlman, my lawyer, who wanted to visit.

I wasn't in the mood, but since he was already downstairs, there wasn't any way to put it off.

When I opened the door, he had what amounted to a broad smile for him. "I have some good news, Mr. Benson."

"I sure could use some about now."

Rufus approached.

"Oh, my." Perlman backed away.

"Don't worry; he's harmless," I assured him.

He came in tentatively, walking around Rufus, and I offered him a seat at the dining table.

We sat, and he opened his worn leather briefcase. It seemed an odd truism that the successful lawyers relished carrying old, worn briefcases, whereas the young, unaccomplished ones carried shiny, new bags.

"I—we—have received an offer from the other side."

The other side seemed to be a polite way of not referring to them as *prosecutors*, which in this case meant *persecutors*.

"Already?"

"Yes, we're quite lucky in that regard. It often takes much longer for them to consider things."

That sounded ominous.

"I'm listening."

He pulled out a two-page document and began to review the details with me.

Nausea rolled over me at the mention of jail.

"Only three months. That's quite generous," he said.

Three months was ninety days longer than it should've been, in my book. I hadn't done anything wrong. Not a single damned thing. It was the Gainsboro creep Paisley who should be going to jail.

"Let me go over it again to make sure it's clear," Perlman said.

I nodded and listened as he explained each of the points in detail a second time.

"You should think this over carefully, Mr. Benson, before responding. Talk with your family."

That last part I didn't relish.

I rose. "I will."

He left me the papers and gathered up his briefcase.

"However, the clock is ticking," he added as I walked him to the door. "We don't have forever."

"I'll get back to you," I told him as I let him out of the condo.

The door closed behind him, and I was alone again with Rufus, and a decision to make.

Trapped.

CHAPTER 51

*A*SHLEY

OFFICER O'MARA LET ME PASS. LIZ LOOKED VERY MUCH AS SHE HAD
yesterday—peaceful, despite the beeping of the hospital equipment
around her.

I'd checked in with the nurses at the desk on the way in, and they'd
assured me she was doing better. The volume of excess cerebrospinal
fluid was down considerably. They said that was a good sign.

Rounding the bed, I sat beside her and took her hand. "Well, it
looks like you're gonna beat me out on that California promotion. I got
myself suspended today."

She would normally have laughed at me.

"John and the guys are working hard to run down who did this to
you. All we know so far is the explosive was the same as the others
made by that guy Yuri we collared last year. So the thinking is, he
must've sold one of his bombs before we got to him."

For the longest time I'd been wrong about Liz. I'd thought she was
sleeping with White to get better assignments and evaluations. Instead,
she'd held the threat of those envelopes over him. And, she'd been
trying to warn me about something when she ended up here in the

process. As much as she'd annoyed me at times, we were sisters in the same FBI family, and we had to stick together. She'd had my back, and now I had to have hers.

I squeezed her hand, hoping for a responsive squeeze back, but I didn't get one. A tear clouded my eye.

"I wish you had given me a clue—a clue about what you wanted to talk about that day. It would really help our search."

Her hand closed imperceptibly around mine.

Or had I just imagined it? Was she trying to communicate?

"Is it somebody in our office?" I asked.

I waited carefully and watched. There wasn't any response from her hand or any indication in her eyelids that she could hear me. I'd just imagined it.

I stroked her hand. "I'll be by again tomorrow. You can count on it, because I have lots of time on my hands now. A suspension will do that." I tried to laugh but couldn't.

One of the nurses came in, checked the monitors, and felt Liz's skin on her arm, her leg, and her cheek. "I think she needs another blanket."

"I think I felt her squeeze my hand," I told the nurse.

She smiled at me. "That's not possible, dear." She opened the closet door and retrieved a blanket that she spread over Liz.

On the floor of the closet lay a clear plastic bag with bloody clothes inside.

I pointed to the bag. "Are those hers?"

She turned to look. "Yes. They were cut off of her down in the OR, so the police missed them when they were picking everything up. I've been meaning to call."

"I'll take them in," I told her.

After she left the room, I pulled out the bag and searched through it.

In the pocket of the pants I found something—house keys...and...

A thumb drive.

I pocketed the little treasure. "Thank you, Liz. I hope this is it."

I might finally have a clue.

VINCENT

PLEAD GUILTY TO SOMETHING I DIDN'T DO AND SPEND THREE MONTHS IN jail. Perlman thought the deal was a sweet one I should jump at, but I'd learned long ago to sleep on big decisions.

Between Ashley's call and Perlman's visit, this was shaping up to be one super shitty day. And it would only be worse once I told my Kitten what was on the table.

I paced back and forth.

Jail time. Had it really come to that?

They'd planted the memo.

I had proof, but it wouldn't be admissible in court. They'd claim I'd paid an actress, anybody, to record the confession, and that I'd paid Sophia to disappear.

The Semaphore purchase was hosed no matter what. And my job back at Benson? Fat chance of that. I was either the admitted felon or the one everybody knew was guilty but had been rich enough to get off. Either way, I was screwed. No amount of money could rehabilitate a ruined reputation.

And Ashley sticking with me while I fought this was sure to ruin any future law enforcement career for her. Hanging out with even an accused felon would be poisonous to her ambitions.

I made another circuit out to the fresh air of the patio and back to the couch with Rufus following.

The picture on the floor taunted me—broken, just like my future.

I picked it up off the floor to rehang. At least I could fix one thing. I pulled the remaining shards of glass carefully out of the frame. The painting itself was unhurt, just without the protective glass. I gently hung it back on the wall, finding it even more impressive now that it was naked to the room.

The picture was a special gift from Dad: an oil copy of Richard Willis' painting of the battle off Flamborough Head in the Revolutionary War. It had been one of Dad's prized possessions, and he'd sent it with me when I moved out here. It depicted the battle between the Bon Homme Richard and HMS Serapis—the battle that had made John Paul Jones the hero of the American Navy.

The painting went along with the John Paul Jones coin Dad had given me. He'd said there was a lot I could learn from studying John Paul Jones. Some Christians approached a decision with the saying "What would Jesus do?" But a naval captain was expected to approach his decisions with "What would John Paul Jones do?"

"Surrender? I have not yet begun to fight," Jones had said more than two hundred years ago.

That paperwork Perlman had brought me was asking me to surrender.

FUCK THAT.

I wasn't Navy, but I was damned well going to fight this fucking battle to the end.

Fuck you, Paisley. Fuck you, Willey.

Before Ashley arrived, I needed to make the one call I dreaded most.

I dialed.

"Hi, Vincent. It's good to hear your voice," my father said across the wires.

"You too." I swallowed hard. "I need help."

"Okay."

"I assume you've heard about the situation out here." Calling it a *situation* sounded better than my problem, better than my arrest.

"Yes, I have."

I felt the urge to clear up one thing. "I didn't do it." He needed to know—to hear it from me.

"You don't need to tell me that. I know you didn't. You couldn't. You forget I know you."

I wanted to thank him for the confidence, but didn't. "I need to know what to do."

"You just did it, Vincent," he replied.

I had missed something. "What?"

"You needed to ask for help. That's all. It's your Achilles heel. You take on too much alone. You need to use the resources around you. John Paul Jones didn't defeat the Serapis alone; he needed his whole crew to accomplish that."

I realized this was another of Dad's John Paul Jones teaching moments.

"I'm in China today, and it will take me a couple shakes to get back," he continued. "Call Dennis, if you think he can help, but I'd start with your Boston neighbor, Liam Quigley. Those Covington boys know a thing or two about fighting problems, and their uncle can be quite resourceful as well. But first, do you know who's behind these shenanigans?"

"I'm pretty sure it's a guy at our competitor, Gainsboro, and maybe a federal prosecutor out here named Willey."

He took a loud breath. "A federal prosecutor? You sure know how to pick your enemies. Well, start playing offense. Take the fight to them, I say. Damned lawyers are all pussies anyway."

"That's what I intend to do."

"I'll back you one hundred percent in any way I can."

"Thanks, Dad."

"You don't need to thank me. It's what family does."

I nodded. That was one truth every member of our family knew. "I remember."

"Well, don't waste time on the phone with me. Make a plan and kick those sons-of-bitches so hard they know never to mess with a Benson again."

I laughed. "I will, Dad. I will."

Those fuckers. Paisley wasn't going to know what hit him.

I hung up and closed my eyes to think for a few minutes.

In order for Paisley to be able to promise to get Sophia's sister's charges dropped—and then deliver—someone in the prosecutor's office had to be involved.

"You're going to wish you'd never met me," Willey had said.

It could be him, or it could be someone else in the office. If I went after the wrong target, I'd be kicking a hornet's nest.

This was suddenly more complicated than it had seemed a minute ago.

It was time for all hands on deck. I located my phone and dialed Liam.

CHAPTER 52

VINCENT

WHEN I OPENED THE DOOR, ASHLEY RUSHED IN TO HUG ME.

After yesterday, I was careful about returning the embrace. Those bruises on her side and shoulder still looked awful.

She broke the hug, but looked up at me with a smile a mile wide—not what I expected from a woman who'd just been suspended.

"I might have something," she said in a giddy tone.

She held up a thumb drive.

"What? What is it?"

"I need to use your computer. The agents missed this. It was in her pocket, Liz's pocket."

I pointed down the hall. "The laptop's in the office."

She rushed off in that direction.

I followed her and typed in the password when the machine booted up.

She inserted the thumb drive, and surprise came across her face when the directory window opened.

"These are keylogger files," she told me, pointing at the screen.

I didn't understand the significance of her statement. "And?"

The doorbell rang.

I started toward the door. "We have dinner guests coming over."

"I'll be there in a minute. I have to check these first," she said.

I closed the door to the office to give her some privacy. She was obviously on a mission.

I opened the condo door to find Liam and his wife.

"Dinner is here," Amy said as she strolled in with two bags that smelled scrumptious.

I gave her a peck on the cheek as she passed.

Liam shook my hand. "We're here to help."

"After dinner," Amy corrected him. "We don't want this to get cold."

"Give me minute to pry Ashley away from the computer," I told them.

Amy began unpacking the dinner she'd brought.

I found Ashley still glued to the computer screen.

"I'm almost there," she told me.

"You can get back to this after dinner."

"Give me five or ten minutes; that's all I need, I swear."

I returned to my guests, without Ashley. "She's found something she needs a few minutes to analyze."

"Does it have to do with this whole problem?" Liam asked.

I pulled the plates down from the cupboard. "She seems to think so."

"Then this will keep," Amy said.

I opened the wine fridge. "White or red?"

"White," Amy answered. "Red sometimes gives me headaches."

Liam shrugged his acceptance.

I retrieved a nice bottle of pinot grigio and poured four glasses, handing two to my guests.

"Tell me about this plea offer you got today," Liam said.

I explained the offer fully, and he had several questions about sentencing guidelines for the individual charges.

"You've got 'em on the ropes, if you ask me," he said after I finished. "There's no way they'd offer something like that this early unless there's time pressure for some reason, or they don't have anything and they want you to cave before going to trial. No way."

I knew they didn't have anything real, just the fake memo, but it was comforting to hear his analysis of the situation.

The office door opened, and Ashley emerged carrying a few sheets of paper with a Cheshire Cat grin on her face.

"Liam and Amy, I'd like to introduce Ashley Newton."

Ashley exchanged greetings with Amy first.

Then Liam took Ashley's hand. "Ashley, that is such a beautiful name, from the old English words for *ash* and *meadow*, I believe. I like it —a beautiful name for a beautiful lady."

My woman beamed with pride at the compliment.

"Ashley, why don't you and I gather up the food while the men set the table," Amy suggested.

Liam and I did as instructed, and in no time we were seated with veal parmigiana, chicken piccata, fettuccine marinara, and garlic bread to fill our plates.

We'd started to serve ourselves when Liam said, "Why don't you start at the beginning and tell us—"

His wife interrupted him. "First, Ashley, how are you feeling? That explosion must have been an awful experience."

Ashley moved her hand to the bump on her head. "I'm still a little sore, but that'll pass. My friend Liz—she was the other agent at the scene—she got the worst of it. She's still in the ICU."

"We hope she gets better soon," Liam added.

Ashley nodded. "Thank you. She's getting better day by day. She's tough. She'll make it."

I cut into the veal on my plate.

Ashley held up the papers she'd brought out from the office. "Want to guess what I found?"

I waited, unwilling to play a guessing game tonight.

Ashley handed me the papers. "Sneaky Liz had a keylogger on the AUSA's computer. And guess who told Paisley what the memo should say and where to hide it?"

"Willey?" I asked.

Ashley nodded enthusiastically. "And, I think Willey is behind this—"

"Stop," Liam interrupted. "Would that be Kirk Willey and Thomas G. Paisley?"

"Tom Paisley," Ashley answered. "Don't know about the middle initial."

Liam shook his head. "Those fuckers. Kirk Willey is Monica Paisley's brother. She's the wacko that's doing prison time for attacking my sister, and Thomas Paisley is her husband, Willey's brother-in-law. I thought he was still in California." The hatred in his face was obvious.

Amy leaned over to rub her husband's shoulder.

"Well, that explains a lot," Ashley said. "Vince thought Willey might be involved, but we couldn't see a connection."

"I told you it was him," I added.

Liam raised his glass. "Here's to bringing down the Willey family… again."

The rest of us joined the toast.

Liam put his glass down. "If we're going to stick it to those two, I can't wait to hear the plan."

"That's where I need some help. I don't really have a plan yet," I admitted.

Over the next two hours, the four of us devised what I thought was a workable approach.

"Will your partner help out with this, or are we on our own?" I asked Ashley.

"I'll have to check. But either way, this will only work if we move on it tomorrow," she responded.

CHAPTER 53

ASHLEY

JOHN HAD AGREED TO HELP, AND THE NEXT MORNING HE PULLED A HALF dozen encrypted radios from the field office. An urgent operation with Boston PD, he'd told them.

Ivy and I were in the middle of the Common, ready to make the call. For once she wasn't wearing a shirt with some outrageous saying printed on it.

Liam and Amy were fifty yards to the north on a bench.

Vince and John were atop his condo with binoculars, waiting on the call.

"They got his phone," John said over the radio. That was something we'd needed to go right. John had promised Petra and Vanda to get the latest charges dropped against their brother Dorek if they lifted Paisley's phone off him this morning.

I turned the radio volume down. We were ready to drop the hook in the water.

"Okay, you're up. You ready for this?" I asked Ivy.

"Yup."

Ivy dialed the phone and held it so we could both listen.

"Willey here," came the answer from the other end.

"Mr. Willey, this is Sophia Nazarian."

He paused before answering. "You must have the wrong number."

"Mr. Willey, I have to get out of town after what I did for you and Mr. Paisley."

"I don't know who you are or what you're talking about," Willey said.

"The paper I put in Mr. Benson's office for you. They know it was me, and I have to leave and go back to Armenia. It's not safe here."

"I don't see what I can do for you."

He'd stopped insisting he didn't know who she was. His answers so far meant we'd guessed right that he didn't know Sophia's voice, and this was going to work.

"The security man from the company, Mr. Murdoch, he has a video of me putting the paper under the blotter in the office."

We'd put the mention of the exact placement of the memo in the office into Ivy's script to convince him she was Sophia. That fact would be in the file he had on the case, and only Sophia and the agents involved should have known it.

"I still don't see what that has to do with me."

Ivy gave him the punch line. "I need money for me and my sister to go back home."

"Your sister got out of jail; that should be good enough."

We had his attention.

"He said he was going to call the FBI. I can't go to jail. We need money to go home to Armenia. We need five thousand dollars."

We'd picked an amount he should be able to get quickly.

"I'm not a goddamned travel agency." Now he was riled.

"Today," she added. "I don't have anywhere to go that they won't find me."

"I'll need time to get the money, and I have a conference at the courthouse at one this afternoon. I'll call you after that."

"Okay," Ivy said and hung up the phone.

I turned up the radio volume again. "The fish took the bait. We land him this afternoon. We're done till after lunch. Amy, he has a court appointment at one, so you can stake out the courthouse then and let us know when he leaves."

"I'll be there," Amy said over the radio.

"In the meantime, we can all do lunch up here," Vince's voice added.

I checked my pocket to confirm I had Nancy Sanchez's card for later.

A*SHLEY*

AFTER LUNCH, AMY LEFT FOR THE COURTHOUSE.

John called the Sheriff's office to tell them he'd be taking Vince for questioning for a while, so Vince would be off his electronic tether and could join us.

And then we waited.

The call came around two.

Ivy picked up the burner phone I'd given her and answered. "Hello?"

I huddled next to her to listen.

The others were quiet.

"I've got the money," Willey said.

I gave the group a thumbs up.

"Good. Meet me by the bandstand on the Common in an hour," Ivy told him.

His response was cold. "No, I set the place. 401 Morninglight Ave. in an hour."

I shook my head at Ivy. We needed the meet to be in the open.

"No, the Common. I don't know where that is."

"Google it," he said, and hung up.

I double checked that the call had terminated before talking. "He moved it to 401 Morninglight." I didn't recognize the street name.

John was the first to speak. "That's an industrial area halfway to Roxbury. I don't like it. The meeting needs to be in the open so we can see Ivy."

"I'll be fine," Ivy assured him. "Besides, I didn't have a choice. This

Sophia girl has to be scared and desperate. It would be out of character for her to refuse."

I put a hand on Ivy's shoulder. "I'll go in the building with her and be able to be closer than if we were on the Common. We don't have a choice."

John shook his head. "I still don't like changing the plan."

Vince spoke into his radio. "Amy, has he left yet?"

"Not yet," she replied.

"The meeting spot's changed to farther out of town. He should take Harrison or Albany over the Turnpike. If you can follow him to there, we'll pick up the tail on the south side."

"No problem," she said.

I pulled my backup weapon, ejected the magazine, and verified the load before slamming it home again. "Ivy and I better leave now so we can get the cameras set up."

"Take care of my sister," John said.

I patted my holster and nodded.

The guys gathered up their things, and we all left the condo.

IVY AND I ARRIVED AT THE LOCATION PLENTY EARLY, AND I PARKED IN THE back behind the cinderblock-enclosed dumpster. Just before we arrived, Amy had announced that Willey was on the move.

It was a smaller building adjacent to a larger industrial building. The door in the front was oddly unlocked.

Going inside, the putrid smell of disuse permeated the air. The light switch inside the door was unresponsive, but enough light filtered in through the dirty upper windows in back to allow the filming we needed to do.

Ivy coughed. "This place stinks."

I turned on my cell phone's light. "Careful where you step. The homeless sometimes take a crap in empty buildings like this."

Ivy stopped in her tracks. "Eww." She switched on her phone's light before proceeding.

A few crates and cardboard boxes near the back wall were the only contents of the room. I went to the back door, unlocked the deadbolt, and ventured outside into the clearer air and bright afternoon light. After retrieving the camera gear from the trunk, I returned to the dim interior.

Ivy leaned against one of the crates, scrolling through her phone and muttering about how disgusting the place smelled.

After surveying the space, it was clear concealment would be an issue. I picked up a small cardboard box. The dust I shook off it floated in the air, lit by the sunlight coming in the windows above and behind us. Folding the top panels inward, I placed it on its side in the front left corner, with the camera hidden inside facing the center of the room.

Another cloud of dust rose as I prepared a box for the second camera, which I placed on one of the crates facing the door. I walked from the door to the crates and assured myself that the shadows of the boxes' interior kept the cameras hidden. I started both cameras.

"Remember your lines?" I asked Ivy.

"Sure do."

"And remember to get the money from him."

"Duh," she replied.

I cringed. "Sorry. It's just that things can be missed when you get nervous."

"I handle drunk bikers for a living. A paper-pushing lawyer will be no problem."

I realized I didn't appreciate the occasional difficulty of her chosen profession.

The radio calls told us Amy had stopped following, and the guys were now tailing Willey here.

I didn't relish kneeling behind the crates any longer than I had to. "Let us know when he's close," I told the guys.

"Roger that," Vince said.

"Now we wait," I told Ivy.

She continued scrolling through her phone.

～

VINCENT

. . .

AMY HAD RADIOED THAT WILLEY WAS ON THE WAY IN HIS BRIGHT RED Maserati.

We waited in my Escalade on the south side of the Turnpike.

"He's on Harrison now," Amy said over the walkie-talkie.

I repositioned the car one block up to be ready to turn right on Harrison to follow him.

"He's about to go over the Pike. I'm turning off now," Amy announced.

John started counting down. "Ten, nine, eight..." Just after he reached one, the metallic red sports car passed across the intersection. "Give him space... Now."

I pulled away from the curb and turned right to follow him. From our perch in the tall SUV, picking out the bright red car among the string of dull whites, tans, blues, and blacks was easy.

"This distance is good. Don't get any closer," John said.

The Maserati crossed an intersection on the yellow, and we got stopped.

I thrummed my fingers on the wheel with impatience.

"Don't worry. We know where he's going," John assured me.

Two streets later, we stopped four cars behind him at another light.

I wiped my sweaty palms on my pants. We were about to nab my nemesis in the act of paying off the girl he thought had planted evidence for him. I should have been giddy at the prospect. I didn't have a specific fear, but something about this bugged me. It was probably that it had been so long in coming.

A few blocks later, he turned, and we followed him.

"With less traffic here, you want to fall back and give him more space."

I slowed as John suggested. We would be there soon, and this nightmare would be over.

Two blocks from the destination, Willey suddenly pulled to the side and stopped.

"Pull over," John said abruptly.

I stopped by the curb and checked my watch—five minutes to the meeting time. "What's he doing?"

"I don't know." John keyed the radio. "The target has stopped and parked two blocks short."

"Roger," Ashley replied.

~

*A*SHLEY

"R*OGER*," I *SAID*. I *CHECKED THE TIME: FIVE MINUTES BEFORE THE HOUR.*

"Why would he stop?" Ivy asked when I finished talking into the radio.

"No idea."

The phone in Ivy's pocket rang.

I stood up. "Answer it. Maybe we're about to find out. Remember, you're scared."

"Hello?" Ivy said tentatively as she accepted the call.

"Are you there yet?" Willey asked.

The tone of his voice raised the hairs on the back of my neck. I grabbed Ivy's shoulder and shook my head vigorously, mouthing the word *no*.

"Not quite," she said.

"How much longer?" he asked.

Ivy looked to me for guidance.

I held up two fingers.

"Two minutes or so," Ivy answered.

"Good. I'll be there right at three," he said, and the call ended.

I quashed the temptation to check with John to see if he'd made a move yet.

"Not much longer now." I got down behind the crates.

Ivy paced back and forth. "I hate people who are late."

I didn't tell her I had a hundred other reasons to hate this guy.

I checked my watch again. One minute before three.

~

*V*INCENT

.   .   .

WE WAITED FOR SEVERAL AGONIZING MINUTES.

"Maybe he wants to walk the rest of the way," I offered.

"Or he wants to be late. Either way, we wait."

The top of the red car was visible, but other parked cars blocked our view of the interior.

Willey didn't get out of the car, and he didn't drive the rest of the distance.

I checked my watch again. Two minutes past three.

He was now late.

A FLASH.

The shockwave of the explosion shook the car.

Debris and a dust cloud spewed from the building two blocks ahead.

"Ivy," John yelled into the radio. "Ashley."

I yanked the car into drive and floored it.

CHAPTER 54

Vincent

I ROARED PAST WILLEY'S CAR AND THROUGH THE NEXT INTERSECTION without even bothering to slow down.

"We're okay. Get the bastard," Ashley yelled over the radio.

I hit the brakes hard and spun the car around in the wide street.

Willey was pulling slowly away from the curb.

"Don't let him get away. He'll outrun this tank," John yelled.

Willey turned in the middle of the street to head back the other direction.

I floored the big V-8 and aimed for the shiny red target. "Brace yourself."

Willey's car spewed smoke from the rear tires.

Metal and glass crunched as we rammed the rear quarter of his car and spun him around.

The airbag exploded in my face and dazed me, and I fought to punch it down and open the door.

John was already out the other side with his gun drawn. "Show me your hands," he yelled. "Show me your hands."

The tank had done its job. The rear of Willey's Italian speedster was twisted and crumpled metal and rubber. It had been no match for the three tons of American steel I drove.

Willey struggled to get out of his car.

"You're under arrest, asshole. Interlace your fingers. You know the drill."

"I'm a US attorney; you can't arrest me," Willey hissed.

John kicked the back of Willey's knee. The man's legs folded, and in seconds John had him facedown on the ground and cuffed.

"Save it for the judge."

Willey stopped struggling.

The smell of gasoline filled the air. I turned to find gas streaming from the rear of the crumpled red car.

"It's going to blow," I warned John, pointing to the growing puddle of gas.

John pulled Willey roughly to his feet. "Get this piece of shit to the sidewalk."

I grabbed Willey and yanked his ass toward the curb as instructed. All I needed was one excuse to kick this asshole into the next county.

John did the unthinkable: he rushed toward the car that was about to go up in flames.

I pulled myself and Willey behind a parked car.

Ashley

My knees had hurt from the cement floor. I had checked my watch incessantly while we waited for Willey.

When it was one minute past three, I'd put it together. John said Willey had parked, and his voice had been tinged with annoyance when Ivy told him we weren't in the building yet.

I'd jumped up and grabbed Ivy. "Out. Get out now."

"Why?" she'd complained as I'd pulled her through the back door.

I'd hustled us into the cinderblock dumpster enclosure and pushed her to the ground just in time.

The explosion threw me against the wall, on my good side, and my head hit the cinderblock. Glass and bits of building had rained down on us amid the suffocating dust cloud.

My ears rang, and the dust had made it impossible to see.

That fucker Willey had been behind the explosion that put Liz in the hospital.

Ivy coughed from the dust.

I'd pulled my shirt up to my mouth to breathe through and yelled into the radio, "We're okay. Get the bastard."

As the dust started to clear, I still couldn't hear, but I pulled Ivy to her feet, and we started around the building.

Reaching the street, I keyed the radio again. "Did you get him?"

A fireball erupted several blocks to our left.

Ivy took off in that direction. "John," she yelled.

I hobbled after her, unable to keep up with my injured leg. My head hurt, and my hand came back bloody after I felt my hair.

When I made it to the scene, both cars were engulfed in flames. Ivy was hugging John on the far sidewalk, and Vince had Willey on his knees—at just the right height for me to kick his teeth in.

John was on the phone, and sirens wailed in the distance.

Vince grabbed me into a tight hug as I reached him. "I was so scared you were in there."

I didn't care about the hurt of his squeeze; I hugged him back with all my might.

"I figured it out just in time."

John held up a controller from a radio-control car. "Look what I found in this dirtbag's car."

Willey sneered.

"Ashley pulled me out just before the bomb," Ivy told her brother.

John nodded his appreciation to me. "Thanks."

"I should have figured it out sooner," I told him.

In retrospect, it was so obvious. The Russian bombs that had gone missing from evidence used the same radio-controlled car detonation mechanism the Marathon bombers had employed. That meant the radio-control transmitter had to be within a few blocks to set off the bomb. That's why Willey had stopped where he did, and why he'd wanted to know when we would be in the building.

Vince released me. "You're bleeding." Alarm clouded his voice.

"Good," Willey said.

I kicked his leg.

He screamed.

"Oops."

If his head had been on the ground, that would have been my target.

"You have the right to remain silent," John began reciting Willey's Miranda rights.

Willey didn't say anything. He was a smart enough lawyer to clam up at this point.

Two fire trucks were the first to arrive. One stopped to work on the car fire. The other proceeded to the explosion site.

Vince called one of the firemen over to look at my head wound.

I felt woozy and sat on the curb.

Vince joined me.

The fireman looked at my head and radioed for an ambulance pickup.

Boston PD rolled up just after that and argued with John for a moment about jurisdiction. But John's charge of attempted murder of a federal officer trumped anything they could come up with.

Willey was going to get a taste of the other side of the bars.

After they loaded me into the ambulance, I blew Vince a kiss.

"Love you, Kitten," he called as they shut me in.

I pulled the business card from my pocket and dialed Nancy Sanchez.

CHAPTER 55

ASHLEY

THE ROOM WAS BRIGHT, AND THE BEEPING OF THE HOSPITAL MONITORS WAS annoying.

My head sported a second bump to match the original one on the other side, as well as bruising on my right side to go with the purple marks healing on my left.

Vince pulled his chair next to mine and took my hand—about the only part of me that didn't hurt.

It had been two days since Willey's arrest.

The charges against Vince had been dropped the same day. One inquisitive call to Willey's boss, the US Attorney, from Nancy Sanchez at Channel 8 had done the trick. News coverage of the details was the last thing the government wanted. Nancy hadn't wanted to sit on her scoop, but she seemed to understand how much cooperating could pay off for her career in the end.

I'd been carefully examined after the second bump to my head but cleared to leave yesterday. Vince and I now sat in Liz's room, waiting for her to wake up.

The tube in her head had been removed, and they had stopped

administering the barbiturates that had kept her unconscious. The doctor expected her to wake up any time this morning and allowed us to stay, with the proviso that we have the nurse call him as soon as she woke.

Liz's eyes fluttered and then opened into slits.

"Hi, sleepyhead," I said softly, taking her hand and squeezing it.

"What happened?"

I took a breath. "A guy tried to kill us both with a bomb."

"Is that why I feel like I'm gonna throw up?"

I pressed the nurse call button.

"A bomb?" she asked. "Is that why you look like shit?" She laughed weakly and winced.

The nurse arrived, pulled her phone, and summoned the doctor.

"AUSA Willey planted a bomb at the alt-three meeting place," I told her.

"Fucker. I was going to tell you he was a problem. I found—"

"I know. I found the thumb drive."

The doctor walked in and asked us to leave.

"No, I want them to stay," Liz objected.

The doctor relented and started his exam. It was similar to what I had gotten twice now, but longer and more thorough.

"You seem to be in fine shape," the doctor told Liz as he moved to leave.

"Then why do I feel like crap?"

He stopped. "I meant mentally. You have two cracked ribs, and the deep bruising will also take time to heal. We'd like to get you up and walking right away, though. I'll send a nurse in to assist you."

"Make sure he's a cute one," she countered.

The old Liz was back.

"And I need a smoke."

The doctor crossed his arms. "Absolutely not."

After the doctor left, Vince offered Liz a paper bag. "Nicotine patches."

I'd mentioned Liz's habit, and he'd come prepared.

"Thanks," she said, accepting the bag. "Maybe we could go out for dinner after all this."

I couldn't believe Liz was making such a brazen play for my man.

"Sorry, Jacinda," he said, putting his arm around me. "I'm taken."

And I wasn't giving him up.

I planted a kiss on my man hot enough that even Liz blushed.

"By the way, those envelopes you forgot to mail? I put the postage on them and sent them to the IG's office."

Her mouth gaped open. "You what?"

I met her stare. "It was the right thing to do, and you know it."

Her frown indicated her preference would have been to keep holding them over the SAC.

"You think he's a pig, and I agree. He needed to be turned in."

She shrugged. "Yeah."

Changing the subject, I pulled out my phone. "I've got someone who wants to talk to you," I told her.

"Huh?"

I hit the special speed dial I'd programmed.

She cocked her head "Who?"

I held up a finger to hold her off.

"Director Kelly's line," the person on the phone answered.

"She's awake," I told the FBI director's assistant.

"Just one moment," she said.

I handed the phone to Liz.

"Who is it?" she asked.

"The director."

"Fuck no," she protested. "Oh no, not you, sir," Liz said into the phone. "Sorry, that was somebody else here trying to poke me with a needle…"

When the director finished wishing Liz a speedy recovery, I took back the phone and made sure the call had been ended before I spoke.

"We nailed AUSA Willey, and he's being held on attempted murder and conspiracy. That gives the director quite a bit of leverage on his boss, so you and I get postings wherever we want."

Director Kelly had been rumored to be on thin ice with the Attorney General, but our arrest had changed the power dynamic in DC in favor of the Bureau. We were now on the director's Christmas card list.

"We?"

"I told him it was your intel that allowed us to trap him."

"What does *trap him* mean?"

"I'll let John fill you in later. My part in the thing only amounted to getting my ass blown up for the second time."

Her face clouded over with concern. "You didn't tell the director about the…" She glanced nervously toward Vince. "You know what?"

"I had to. But for the official report, you overheard a conversation outside his office. That software is something we'll never talk about again."

Relief washed over her face.

"He also told me to warn you that if you mention a word about this, or ever do it again, he will personally see to it that you are collecting your social security behind bars."

She shivered visibly.

"Do you understand?" I asked.

Liz made a zipping-her-lips-shut motion. "Got it. I've got no idea what you're talking about."

Her nurse reappeared. "Time for you to take a few laps up and down the hall, young lady."

Vince stood, and I followed.

"You'll get the rest of the details later," I told her. "Until then, best not to talk about this."

The nurse started unhooking Liz from the monitors.

"Thanks, Ashley," Liz said with more conviction than I'd ever heard from her.

EPILOGUE

"THE BEST AND MOST BEAUTIFUL THINGS IN THIS WORLD CANNOT BE SEEN OR EVEN HEARD, BUT MUST BE FELT WITH THE HEART." – HELEN KELLER

ASHLEY

I WOKE EARLY AND LISTENED TO MY MAN SNORING LIGHTLY BEHIND ME.

Vince did that sometimes when he lay on his back, which was one of the reasons I enjoyed spooning so much.

Today was the big day. We'd spent a week preparing for this afternoon's barbecue, and Vince tried not to show it, but he was nervous.

His father was coming out to join us.

My attempts at getting Vince to even acknowledge his nervousness, much less talk about it, had been an exercise in futility. It wasn't up for discussion.

Still, I had an idea to help him relax.

I reached over to the nightstand and brought the lube under my pillow. I started without him. With my legs spread, my finger slid through my curly hair to part my slit and circle and rub my most sensitive flesh. I rubbed myself slowly then faster, all the while imagining Vince's fingers doing the work—teasing, darting, pressing, and tweaking. It didn't take long to have my engine humming and my juices flowing.

I slipped my head under the covers to execute my plan.

A gentle lick to the tip of his cock, and I got his attention.

"Morning, Kitten," he said groggily from above the covers.

The skin of his engorged shaft felt silky smooth under my finger-tips. It gave a slight jump with my every touch. I positioned my mouth above his tip and licked it with every jump upward. The magazines were right, and his hardness proved it—a man's testosterone level was highest in the morning.

One hand found my scalp and started the fingernail massage I loved.

"Keep that up," I urged him.

The other hand cupped my breast to begin the massage that turned him on as much as it did me.

I'd learned that the feel of my breasts in his hands was something he couldn't get enough of. When we watched TV or a movie on the couch, his hand would automatically take up gentle bra duty.

I cupped his balls and pulled lightly, then teased his tip with my tongue.

His fingers knotted in my hair—a warning to be careful.

I eased up, rolling his balls lightly with my fingers and taking the crown of his cock in my mouth. The exquisite moan I elicited as I worked my tongue over and around him was music to my ears. I gave him a playful rasp of my teeth.

"Careful there," he warned me.

I might be a beginner at this, but his moans, and watching the tension of his legs and abs, had proven a good guide to what turned him on.

He tried, but I shifted position so he couldn't reach my soaked lady bits. This morning was my turn to call the shots.

"What's your pleasure, Kitten?"

I paused for a moment, tracing the sensitive underside of his cock with my tongue. "Page two-twelve."

"You dirty vixen, you." He threw off the covers.

Quickly I straddled him. Reaching down to guide him inside me, I couldn't help but gasp as he filled me to the brim. Every time with Vince was a rapturous new experience. His cock never disappointed.

His legs tensed, and his breath faltered as I started to rock back and forth. His hand held my hips firmly down against him. Then he brought his thumb to my clit, and every push forward sent electric jolts up my spine.

On the page I'd chosen, he wasn't allowed to touch my breasts— torture for both of us. I followed the script by grinding into him and his thumb, quickly finding my rhythm. Every rocking motion forward pushed my tiny nub into him and sent arrows of heat racing through me. Every movement back pushed me farther up the hill of building pleasure as the tension within me grew nearly intolerable in no time.

He cheated by pulling my neck down and my breasts to meet his chest.

My nipples scraped across his skin. I rocked into his thumb again as my orgasm erupted. I screamed out my pleasure as the fireworks played against my closed eyelids, and I fisted the sheets. My toes curled, and the shaking took over as my body clenched around him.

Vince pulled me close and I melted onto his chest, breathless and spent. I shifted my legs down to his.

In a simple move he rolled us over, pulled out, and straddled me.

I found the lube under the pillow and filled my palm. The cold gel quickly heated as I stroked his length with slippery hands. A double-handed motion, running my slippery fingers up and over the tip and down again, had him shaking as he held back.

His breathing became labored.

I started slow, then quickened the pace. I loosened my grip on the down stroke and tightened on the pull upward.

His hands went to my breasts as they always did, and his eyes slammed shut. In no time, first his legs then his torso tensed. Finally the guttural groan of his orgasm came as the spurt landed on my chest. It was followed by another and another of the sticky liquid as my man marked me as his.

The contented smile on his face as he tried to catch his breath was the reward I needed this morning.

"You dirty vixen, you," he repeated.

I'd chosen this scene just for him. "Relaxed now?"

"You have no idea." He got up and brought me a washcloth to clean up, but the warm, wet cloth did nothing to wipe away the warmth I'd felt as his seed covered my heart.

~

VINCE WAS OUT ON THE PATIO GRILLING THE BURGERS AND DOGS. HE wanted this to be a version of the family barbecue we'd missed when I'd been in the hospital after the second bomb blast. Simple, with burgers and hot dogs, was the order of the day.

The doorbell rang for the tenth time, and I opened it.

"Ash." Rosemary stood in front of me.

She rushed in, and we hugged for what seemed like an eternity.

"How'd you get here?" I asked when she released me. "I thought you were still in the bush."

"*Was* is the operative word. Didn't Vince tell you?"

So *she* was the surprise Vince had hinted at.

"No, that rat didn't." I looked through the open door, confused. "Where's Jeremy?"

"He's out in the bush again," she said.

"Is there something you want to tell me?"

"He promised it would be over by now, but he can't give it up. And I can't keep going weeks without a shower, so here I am. I hear this state needs nurses."

I gave her a comforting hug. "I'm sorry."

"I'm not. It's good to be back to civilization."

I ushered her out back, and we made a round of introductions.

Vince's father, Lloyd, was in some debate with the FBI crowd I'd invited.

Anita joined them. Vince had been relieved to find out that Ben's suspicions of Anita had been unfounded. The extra money she'd come into had been a small inheritance from an uncle in Australia who'd passed away.

John was throwing back a beer with Vince.

Those two had become fast friends when we learned it was John's note to Staci that had gotten Vince concerned enough to put in the video surveillance that eventually led us to Paisley and Willey. Staci Baxter, it turned out, was John's cousin, and he'd felt he had to warn her when he saw her picture in the file the DOJ sent over.

"And Paisley folded like a wet noodle when we started listing the charges," John told us. "Turns out the whole scheme had been concocted by Willey to enable Gainsboro to buy Semaphore. And you'll never guess why."

Neither of us ventured a guess.

"For Paisley to be able to rig the voting machine software to ensure Willey won the election for attorney general."

Vince's face screwed into a sneer. "That slimy fucker. I hope he gets a million years."

John nodded. "With the extra bomb we found in his garage, it's a pretty sure thing the sentence will be stiff."

Willey was as low as they came.

When John wandered off, I gave Vince a nice, hard spank on the butt.

"Hey, what's that for?" he complained.

I elbowed him. "You didn't tell me you were bringing Rosemary out here."

"What kind of surprise would it have been if I told you? I thought you'd like to see her."

"But you didn't give me any warning to find her a place to stay."

He spanked me back, but not as hard as I'd gotten him.

"Fine sister you are. I invited her to stay with us for a while."

Once again, Vince surprised me with his generosity.

When I went back inside, Rose was talking with a group from Covington.

I joined Liam, Amy, Lloyd, Liam's uncle Garth, Liz, and John at the dining room table.

I pulled Liz aside. "I like your hair, by the way."

She'd come today as a honey blonde, and I hadn't been the first one to comment on it.

She smiled and played with the ends of her locks. "Thanks. Do you think I'll fit in now?"

"Sure. They'll love you."

Liz had taken the director up on his offer and had selected Los Angeles as her new posting.

She winked. "I know why you're staying. And I don't blame you."

I'd decided to remain in Boston for now and see how things worked out with Vince.

White had resigned after being called down to the Inspector General's office in DC, and John had just been announced as the new SAC in Boston. Things in our office would be looking up.

I located Vince and headed his direction.

He was turning the last of the burgers on the grill and talking with his father when I walked up.

"You sure about that?" Lloyd asked Vince.

Vince smiled at me. "Absolutely. Thanks for the offer, Dad, but I'm happy right here."

Lloyd stepped back from the smoke of the grill. "I thought it was what you wanted."

"So did I," Vince replied. His arm encircled me. "But things have changed."

"Let me know if you reconsider."

After his father left, I had to ask, "What was that about?"

"He offered me the job of running Benson Corp. back in LA."

"But haven't you been working toward that? Isn't that why Semaphore was so important?"

He took my face in his hands. "Not nearly as important as what I have here with you." His words made my heart melt and my head spin. "I love you, Kitten."

"Hey, are they done yet?" Mason complained from behind Vince.

"Take over for me." Vince handed him the spatula and focused his attention on me. "What's your favorite restaurant in Hawaii?"

I struggled to get my voice back. "Duke's."

He laughed. "Serena would be tickled pink that you picked a restaurant named after her boyfriend."

"It is not, silly."

"We'll have dinner there tomorrow. We fly out in the morning."

"I can't—"

"You have the week off," he informed me.

"No, I don't."

He gave me a sweet kiss on the forehead. "Yes, you do. It's all arranged."

~

*A*SHLEY

. . .

I CLOSED MY EYES, LISTENING TO THE RHYTHMIC SOUND OF THE SURF. WE'D had to leave early to make it to Honolulu with the sun still shining, given the six-hour time difference. I hadn't been thrilled about waking up before dawn, but Vince had insisted.

I'd taken a quick nap after we arrived, and Vince had chosen a walk.

Now the sun was low over the ocean as I leaned on the lanai railing. Warm trade winds rustled the fronds of the palm trees lining the beach. Beyond them lay dozens of pink umbrellas on Waikiki Beach in front of the historic Royal Hawaiian hotel.

When I tore myself away and opened my suitcase to unpack, I found books inside. I held them up. "Look what I found."

Vince chuckled from the mahogany dining table of the Ali'i suite he'd booked for us. "Vacation reading."

He'd packed two copies of a new book: *Seducing the Bazillionaire*.

"We can read to each other."

I didn't complain. We were going to have some exciting new pages to quote.

"Ready?" he asked.

I turned to see my man smiling in my direction. He closed the laptop in front of him.

"Sure, whenever you are."

I still couldn't believe my life. Vince had given up his dream of running his father's company to stay in Boston with me, and he'd asked me to move in with him.

Duke's Waikiki had been my favorite restaurant the one time I'd been lucky enough to come to the fiftieth state before. It was named after Hawaii's hero, Duke Kahanamoku.

We walked in past the posters and articles devoted to Duke. Descended from Hawaiian royalty, he'd won multiple Olympic medals in swimming and water polo across a staggering twenty-year span, but was even better known for bringing the Hawaiian sport of surfing to the mainland United States. A sportsman and goodwill ambassador for Hawaii, Duke had been loved on the islands, and a statue of him welcomed tourists to Waikiki.

After a whispered conversation between the hostess and Vince, accompanied by a bill pressed to her hand, we were led to a table by the railing. We had a clear view over the bar deck to the beach and ocean beyond. A band played on the deck below us.

After perusing the menu, Vince went for the sesame-ginger ono, and after waffling, I chose the macadamia-and-herb-crusted mahi-mahi.

The view and the meal brought me back to the second happiest time of my life, the week I'd spent here on the beach and in the warm Pacific waters.

"Tell me about it," Vince urged.

"What?"

"You're thinking back to the time you were here before." He pulled my hand to his lips and kissed it. "Aren't you?"

"Guilty as charged. It was summer like this, and my aunt Michelle brought the three of us here: Louise, Rose, and me. That week of walking, sunshine, and swimming will always define this place for me." It had been my third happiest time, after the night I'd danced away with Vince in high school and the night he'd arranged at the Met.

"You can always make new memories here."

Those entrancing dimples made another appearance to go with his heartfelt smile.

"I guess." It was hard to see how anything could compare to that week with my family.

The sun threw gorgeous yellow, pink, and orange hues on the clouds as sunset approached.

A little while later, our dinner had been cleared, and I enjoyed the colorful sky with my second blue Hawaii drink.

Vince raised his coconut mojito to my glass. "To making memories."

"I can drink to that." My bruises had healed, and I was looking forward to basting myself with sunscreen and laying by the pool.

"I'm ordering dessert," he announced.

I'd already told him I was stuffed. "I'll pass." I held up my tall blue glass of liquid happiness. "I'm drinking my dessert."

The band playing on the lower deck started a new song "Sweet Home Alabama," and the crowd sang along.

Vince waved over our waitress.

The girl looked on expectantly while Vince perused the dessert menu one last time. "I'd like the hula pie, and the lady would like the ke komo lima chocolate cake."

"No, nothing for me," I objected.

"Yes, you will," Vince insisted with a firm glare.

Then the waitress got in the middle of it. "I think you'll really like the cake," she told me. "It's to die for."

I gave up and rolled my eyes. "Okay."

He could order it, but I didn't have to eat it.

The sunset colors burst against the horizon as dessert arrived— Vince's a monster piece of hula pie large enough to feed a soccer team, and mine in a pink cardboard box.

He dug into his dessert, with a watchful eye on me.

I set mine to the side. "Perfect. It's already in a box. I'll take it back to the room for tomorrow."

"At least try a little of the frosting," Vince encouraged. "It's chocolate. You can tell me if I made a mistake getting this hula pie instead." Vince raised his hand high and waved down to the band.

They interrupted their song. "By special request," came over the speakers, and they started our song, "Green-eyed Lady."

"You didn't?" I accused.

"It's amazing what a hundred dollar tip can get you." He pushed the box toward me. "Just a taste."

A photographer who had been wandering the floor stood nearby and aimed his camera in our direction.

I ignored him and opened the box.

I gasped.

It was gorgeous.

The photographer's camera flashed.

"Ashley Lindsay Newton, will you marry me?" Vince asked, loud enough for the neighboring tables to hear.

The photographer's flash went off again.

The nearby guests were staring.

I stood to round the table, and Vince did the same. I wrapped my arms around him, and his mouth clamped over mine as he squeezed the breath out of me. The kiss he devoured me with claimed me as his Kitten, and soon to be his wife.

"The question demands an answer," he said as he pulled away. The area had gone quiet as the surrounding diners looked on.

"Hell yes," I answered.

He lifted me off my feet and swung me around with the crowd clapping and the camera flashing. When he let me down, we retook our seats.

The crowd went back to their meals, and I pulled the sparkling diamond ring from the cake and licked the frosting off. "Ke komo lima?"

"Hawaiian for engagement ring."

The gorgeous ring fit on my finger tightly enough to not slip off. The day I'd dreamed of since I was a little girl had come, and in a totally surprising way.

Vince's eyes conveyed the warm love I'd felt flowing through his touch as he'd held my hand on the walk here.

"Do you like it?" he asked.

"I love it. I love everything you give me." He'd given me his heart, and now offered me his name, and I couldn't wish for anything more.

The camera flashed one more time. "A photographer?" I asked.

"I'm going to add one of tonight to my wallet."

I smiled as I remembered the picture he'd carried with him all these years.

Tomorrow was a new day, and I gazed into the loving eyes of the man who was my future.

Bending and breaking a few rules had made my dreams come true.

Vince had been right; a new memory would now define this place for me: ke komo lima chocolate cake at sunset across from my man.

THE END

THE FOLLOWING PAGES CONTAIN A SNEAK PEEK AT THE NEXT BOOK IN THE series: **The Driven Billionaire.**

Available on Amazon HERE.

SNEAK PEEK: THE DRIVEN BILLIONAIRE

CHAPTER 1

BRITTNEY

I WAS FIVE MINUTES LATE AFTER INTENTIONALLY PARKING THREE BLOCKS away, behind the restaurant.

Benji knew I liked this place, and I couldn't have him cruise by and see my car outside.

This was the only night of the week I didn't work and could fit in a date. I passed my date for the evening, Jeffrey's, BMW out front and hurried up the walk to the Tres Pinos entrance. He'd suggested this place after our first date last week over coffee, and I didn't want to jinx anything by objecting to his choice, so I told him I'd love to try it. The food here was great, and the prices were reasonable.

Jeffrey smiled from beside the ficus tree as I pulled open the door. He kindly didn't check his watch. "I was hoping I didn't get the time wrong."

I smiled. His button down shirt and blazer were more formal than average for this area, but I put that down to him working in marketing.

"No. I'm just running late. Traffic on Pico."

His hand at my waist guided me to the hostess station where he whispered something to the cute young thing.

Cute Young Thing beamed a smile back. She showed us to one of the primo tables by the front window. "Will this one do?"

Jeffrey nodded. *"Perfecto, señorita."* He slipped a bill into her hand and pulled out a chair for me.

"Hablas español, Jeffrey?" I asked after the hostess left.

"No. You just heard it all, if you don't count asking for a Dos Equis. I had Spanish in middle school, but these days I couldn't even ask where the bathroom is."

"Dónde está el baño," I told him.

"I'll take your word for it." He arched an eyebrow. "And what did I do wrong to be demoted to Jeffrey?"

His correction caught me off guard. "Sorry, Jeff. Nothing at all."

His smile told me he was letting me off easy.

It had only been a week, but I shouldn't have made such an obvious mistake. Benji's harassment was screwing with my concentration.

So far I was finding Jeff's modesty refreshing after all the braggarts I'd met on the SuperSingles dating site—not that I'd had many dates. Somehow dating seemed to bring out the need to show off in men, which often translated into exaggerating everything in their lives. I was over having men try to impress me with the car they drove, their expensive tastes in wine, or the latest concert tickets they'd snagged.

Jeff had showed up in a BMW, a million steps above the Accord I drove, but at least it was only a three series instead of one of the more expensive models. And, he hadn't mentioned it once on our previous coffee date—ten points for him.

Our waitress arrived with chips and salsa, both medium and hot. They didn't serve mild here.

Eager to get past my embarrassment, I ordered a margarita on the rocks, no salt. I couldn't tell if Jeff was following my lead, or we merely like the same adult beverage when he ordered the same.

"So what do you think's good here?" he asked ladling the milder of the two salsas onto his chip.

I chose the hotter salsa. "Pretty much everything."

"So you've been here?"

I maneuvered to escape my mistake. "No. But my friend Lillian eats here all the time, and she raves about it." That was a close one.

He switched to the hot salsa for his next chip. "I'm liking the looks of the burritos. What about you?"

I perused the menu slowly before answering. "I think I'll try the fajitas." That was my go-to order here when I didn't feel like an enchilada.

"Then maybe I'll try that too."

I inquired about his work, and he started to tell me about his recent customer visits. At least he got to talk to his customers.

"I guess your clients don't talk much," he noted.

I laughed. "The jabs and scrapes of my instruments against their teeth keep their responses to mumbles when they aren't shrinking away from the pain."

I didn't drill teeth, but patients still cowered at the sight of curettes, scrapers, scalers, and probes. If a root canal was on someone's most-hated list, a visit to my chair was not far behind. Nobody ever moved a dental appointment up because they were looking forward to the experience.

He grimaced. "Ouch." A bit of sweat appeared on his forehead after another chip with the hot salsa. The hot stuff here was scorching hot.

I took pity on him and switched to the milder salsa.

The waitress interrupted us to take our orders, and once again I went first. Jeff copied my order of fajitas, even down to choosing chicken and no sour cream.

I raised my margarita. "I'm used to it. Nobody puts a visit to get their teeth cleaned at the top of their wish list."

He joined me with a sip of his drink, and his next chip went into the mild salsa.

"My dentist only works four days a week. Does that mean you get a lot of time off as a hygienist?"

"More than you might think. My dentist has us all under twenty hours so she doesn't have to provide benefits."

He grimaced in sympathy. "That's not fair."

"Fair isn't in Dr. Call's vocabulary. It is what it is."

Jeff finished the chip he was chewing. "Can you fill in with another dentist when she won't give you work?"

"I wish, but she keeps moving our days around, so that won't work."

"That's tough."

I smiled. Jeff was the first of my dates to understand the unfairness of the way she treated us. "I fill in my other hours tending bar."

"Very ambitious of you."

I smiled and sucked down more of my margarita. "A girl does what she has to do to make ends meet."

"That must keep you pretty busy."

"Busy girl, that's me. What about you? I hear startup hours can also be on the brutal side."

He was detailing his most recent few days when our food arrived.

As always, the fajitas were served still sizzling on hot cast-iron plates.

Mine was as tasty as always, and Jeff seemed impressed with his.

"You said you had a sister?" he asked.

I had to finish chewing before I could answer. "And a twin brother, Doug. Samantha is two years younger and getting her MBA at Wharton. Doug is in the Marines."

Just then my heart skipped a beat as I caught sight of Benji's purple Charger driving by.

Benji's taste in colors sucked, and it made his car impossible to miss.

I crossed mental fingers that he wasn't prowling for me.

Jeff's brow creased. "Something wrong."

I willed a fake smile onto my face. "Oh no," I lied. "Just trying to remember when her tuition is due." Picking up my drink, I tried to be casual about looking out the window in the direction Benji had disappeared.

"You're paying? That's an expensive school, I imagine."

I knew that better than anyone. Putting my younger sister through school had fallen to me and Doug, and he couldn't help much with his meager salary. Providing for Sam's education kept my bank balance hovering near zero, and sometimes below, even with all the overtime I pulled down at the Pink Pig.

"My mom passed away two years ago," I told him. My father's departure years before didn't warrant a mention. "It's my responsibility now to get her through school."

There were months I wouldn't have been able to feed myself if it weren't for credit cards.

"She's a grown-up. She should take care of herself," he remarked.

That was a common feeling, I'd learned.

"It's not how I was raised. The older ones look out for the younger ones."

He nodded and smiled without offering an opinion on my version of family values.

I scooped veggies and chicken inside a tortilla and asked about his family.

That successfully steered the conversation away from my plight, and had me longing for the simple situation he enjoyed.

All through dinner I kept a cautious eye out the window for Benji—without any sightings.

I finished the last of my fajitas, save the green bell peppers I never ate.

Jeff checked his watch again—the third time in the last few minutes.

This dinner was coming to a close soon. If the third date didn't improve from this, there likely wouldn't be a fourth.

I wasn't heartbroken about it. Jeff seemed nice, stable, almost normal—unlikely to be an axe murderer—but there was no spark. He was stable, but as exciting as cream of wheat. I was almost nodding off listening to his description of his sister's latest venture—she was the Waikiki hamburger queen—when I caught it.

Jeff lived with his parents. At least he probably didn't live in the basement, almost no houses in California had basements.

Five minutes later, we'd both declined our waitress's dessert query, and I followed him out the front door into the warm evening air.

Jeff stopped at his car and unlocked it with his key fob. "Next week, would you prefer sushi, or perhaps a movie instead?" The marketing guy was on his game. His question presumed a third date.

I considered my choices.

"Hey, get away from my girl." The yell came from down the side-walk as Benji approached at a fast clip.

He'd been behind the hedge, probably for a long time. Sneaking around was his style.

Jeff backed up, looked first at Benji, then at me. Fear marked his face.

Benji's version of crazy could do that.

"Get out of here, Benji, and leave us alone," I yelled. I put my hand in my purse, feeling for my pepper spray, just in case.

Jeff disappeared around his car and climbed in. He didn't have any interest an altercation with my crazy ex.

My heart was galloping a mile a minute, but I stood my ground and pulled out my phone.

Jeff burned rubber pulling away from the curb, with Benji giving him the finger as he did.

"Benji, get the fuck out of here before I call the cops," I yelled.

He stopped.

I pulled out my phone.

An older couple that had just come out of the restaurant retreated back inside.

"You can't go out with him," Benji yelled.

The guy didn't get it we were not an item, and weren't ever going to be again. Not ever.

I lifted my phone with my finger poised over the emergency button. "I'm calling the cops in three… two… one."

Benji turned and ran back the way he'd come.

As soon as he turned the corner, I left in the opposite direction, working to get my breathing back under control.

I couldn't take this shit.

My ex-boyfriend was getting crazier every time.

ZACHARY

A SALTY BEAD OF SWEAT TRICKLED INTO MY EYE. WIPING IT AWAY WITH MY gloved hand made it worse when a fleck of sawdust joined it.

"Shit."

Standing up and removing the glove, I blinked like crazy and coaxed the irritating particle out of the corner of my eye with a fingernail.

With two operative eyes again, I located the last cold can of ginger ale, popped it open, and took a few long, stinging gulps. I reversed the towel that had covered it to find a clean section. I wiped my brow and surveyed the dusty room.

After two evenings of work, I was only a quarter done with this room. I refolded the rag dirty side out.

What idiot would glue crappy fake laminate like this over the marvelous oak flooring the house was built with? And a second layer glued down without removing the first was double sacrilege against this fine old mansion.

It would take a lot of work, but I could already envision walking on the warm golden strips of oak, dotted with tasteful area rugs, instead of the half-plastic crap the last two owners had glued down.

I gulped down the rest of the can before tossing it in the corner garbage bag and knelt down with my pry bar to attack the offending laminate again.

Three small sections later, the music started up next door.

Fucking punks.

I rose, brushed a layer of dust from my jeans, and walked back to the kitchen—the only semi-clean room downstairs during this project of mine.

I wiped down my hair and torso with a clean towel and pulled on a T-shirt. The snub-nose pistol went into my waistband at the small of my back, and I grabbed a flashlight from the counter.

Neighborhood kids had taken to using the abandoned house next door as their occasional nighttime party spot, and I was sick of it.

Twice I'd tried calling the cops. But the cops rolled up an hour later, turned on their flashing lights, and the kids dispersed out the back, only to return a few days later. The officers viewed scaring them off as the easy way to deal with it, and they never attempted to catch any of the buggers.

Moonlight lit the way as I moved toward the back porch door I knew to be open. One of the delinquents had broken the lock on the door knob and removed the deadbolt for easy access. Tomorrow I'd replace the missing deadbolt and put an end to their parties.

ERIN SWANN

God-awful rap music blared out of an open window. How they could even call that music was beyond me.

The back door was ajar. The squeak of its rusty hinges as I entered was drowned out by the cacophony coming from the boom-box toward the front.

I passed through the old dining room to the front parlor. The kids had laid down their cell phones with the lights pointing to the ceiling for illumination. They were so busy dancing, none of them noticed me as I approached.

A solid kick of my work boot, and the plastic boom-box went quiet as it shattered against the wall. Simultaneous protests from the three couples replaced the music.

The tallest of the boys started toward me. "What the fuck, asshole?"

I pointed the pistol.

The click as I cocked the hammer was loud in the instantly quiet room "What did you call me?"

The boy backed up and the front of his jeans went dark with piss. "I didn't mean…"

The others grouped together and backed toward the wall. Piss Boy didn't have any rescuers in this group.

"I catch you creeps in here again, and there'll be hell to pay. Do you understand me?"

Piss Boy nodded and backed toward the others.

One of the others stooped to pick up a phone.

"Leave it," I yelled.

The girl dropped the phone.

I rounded the room toward the door. "All your phones on the floor. Now. Get over there." I motioned toward the corner with the gun.

The group shuffled toward the corner.

I counted and only saw five phones. "I said all the phones." I waved the gun at the group.

A girl in the back slid the missing phone to the middle of the room.

"Listen carefully. This is how this is going to go. You can come to my house next door at dinner time tomorrow…" I pointed toward my house. "…with a letter of apology, and I'll give you back your phones. Do you understand?"

The group nodded, even Piss Boy.

I unlocked the deadbolt of the front door and backed away from it. "Now out." I raised the pistol toward the ceiling and fired.

The loud report of the gun reverberated in the room as Piss Boy made it to the door first with the rest of the pack only seconds behind.

It was only a starter pistol loaded with blanks, but it got the point across. Piss Boy and his crew wouldn't be back.

I locked the front door after them, gathered up the phones, and exited through the back. Tomorrow when they came back to retrieve their phones, they'd get a reminder not to come back in a language they'd understand.

Back inside my house, I locked my doors, set the alarm, and placed my starter pistol back in the drawer.

If I knew teenagers, the word would spread, keeping them from destroying the majestic house next door any further.

Fucking juvenile delinquents.

CHAPTER 2

BRITTNEY

I TURNED INTO MY ASSIGNED PARKING SPACE BETWEEN THE TWO PICKUPS, and noticed it just in time. I hit the brakes. I got out and pocketed the nail—placed conveniently on end where my tires normally rolled—before getting back in to finish parking.

Fucking Benji.

He'd told me two weeks ago, "*What if you get a flat tire? You'll need me then.*"

This was the third time I'd found a nail or a screw in my parking spot since.

Safely upstairs in my apartment, I locked the door behind me. The gray envelope on the table taunted me to open it.

I resisted.

Saving me from my envelope dilemma, my phone rang, with my sister Samantha's pretty face on the screen.

"How'd your date go, Brit?" she asked immediately.

I winced as the scene with Benji replayed in my head. "Okay," I said. Technically, the date had been okay; it was the ending that got all fucked up.

"Tell me about him. I think Jeffrey is an okay name, but not a leader."

She thought a lot of names were cool, as if you could judge a guy's character by what his parents had named him when he was mere hours old. Although, she'd thought Derrick was a creepy name, and her theory had borne out, and same with Norman before him.

But after watching Hitchcock's *Psycho*, I should have known better than to go out with anyone named Norman.

"We went to Tres Pinos," I told her, as I sank into the couch.

"I bet he had the fajitas and a margarita on the rocks," she guessed.

"What makes you say that?"

She laughed. "Simple. Jeffrey is a follower name. Like I said, not a leader, and you always get a margarita on the rocks and the chicken fajitas." She knew me too well.

"Sam, that was just a lucky guess."

"Was not. Bet it ended without a kiss. Jeffreys move slow." She had guessed right again, but not for the reason she thought. "Well, was I right?"

"No kiss," I confirmed.

"I knew it. Boring, huh? Brit, you deserve better. You deserve hot. You deserve tall, dark, and studly."

"He was okay."

"But no third date, right?"

She had no idea how right she was about that.

"I'm pretty sure that's not happening."

"I hear it in your voice. Spill, big sister. What happened?"

I sighed, caught again. I swear my sister must have hidden a webcam in my apartment last time she was here. "Nothing. I just don't think he'll be calling again."

"Stop holding out."

"It was Benji. He accosted us outside the restaurant."

She gasped. "Worse than last time?"

"Yeah, a little."

I underplayed how I'd felt for my sister's benefit. She needed to concentrate on school instead of worrying about the drama in my life.

"That idiot's a dozen crayons short of a box. You better get a gun."

"That's one thing I'm not doing."

"He's dangerous, if you ask me," she retorted.

"He's got no balls. I know how to handle him. He'll get over it sooner or later."

My words were more confident than my feelings.

"He doesn't need balls to be dangerous. He can poison your cat, or burn down your house without having the guts to face you."

"I don't have a cat."

"Very funny, Brit. You know what I mean. Benjamin is a back-stabber's name. Better be careful, sis."

"He'll get tired of it sooner or later."

So far all my predictions of that had been premature. Sooner wasn't looking likely.

"You know Gram's house is empty, and it's half yours now."

Our grandmother had passed on last year and left Doug the lake cabin and my sister and me her house in west LA. The thought of living there would be tempting if she hadn't died in the house.

I dodged the suggestion. "Dealing with ghosts is not on my agenda."

"The house is just waiting for you. And you could save on rent." Her mention of rent brought my gaze back to the gray envelope.

I'd never shared with her how hard it was keeping my nose above water financially with her tuition. If I could handle it another two semesters, she'd be done and launched into a career with loads of potential. She deserved that.

"I like it better up here."

"Right. Well, just keep the house in mind and don't turn your back on Benji. I don't trust him."

She had warned me against Benji from day one. I wished I'd listened to her.

But move back to LA? I didn't intend to ever go back.

I changed the subject. "What classes are you signing up for?"

As she started to talk I glanced across the room. The clock I kept on the counter was facing the kitchen instead of toward me on the couch. I couldn't remember turning it.

After ten minutes discussing her upcoming semester and another ten on her non-existent dating life, we hung up.

I got up and repositioned the errant clock, and settled in for a little television.

CHAPTER 3

Zachary

Tuesday morning, I took a deep breath as the red digits increased one by one, with a ding at each floor. The elevator doors opened on the top floor of Benson Corp: Galactic HQ, where my father reigned supreme over all he surveyed.

I turned right toward marketing.

My ever-cheery assistant, Abby, was at her desk ahead of me as always.

"Good morning, Mr. Benson. Make much progress last night?"

Abby understood my passion to get my old house restored to its former glory. There was something majestic about an old Victorian like this—the craftsmanship of the woodwork and the unique personality of each design. They'd been built in a time before cookie-cutter designs and mass production became popular. They were built lovingly by hand and exuded a warmth missing in the square McMansions of today.

"Slow and steady. Still arguing with the laminate those two idiots had laid down. Any emergencies this morning?"

"Just the usual."

"Let me guess. Stanton from the London office?"

He needed something pretty much every morning, and the issues were almost always minor. He had the mistaken impression that phone time with me, just because my last name was Benson, would accelerate his career. He didn't get how Dad operated.

"One point for you. And your father wants to see you."

I schooled my face to not show the irritation I felt, but the cock of her eyebrow revealed I'd been unsuccessful. Abby knew how much I enjoyed my father's interruptions.

Not.

Yesterday's breeze had cleared out the smog, and I took a moment to enjoy the view of the Pacific Ocean out my office window.

"Anything special?" I asked Abby as I picked her coffee cup up off the desk and headed to the break room with mine in the other hand.

"The usual will be fine, thanks." She enjoyed a mocha with non-dairy creamer most mornings. On occasion, she'd change it up and ask for decaf.

My first and only argument with Abby had been my insistence that it wasn't in her job description to get me coffee the way she had for Walt before me. Walt was old school in that respect.

I'd insisted on changing that dynamic, and it was my routine to make and bring coffee for each of us—black for me and mocha for Abby. It seemed like the civilized thing, and Abby wasn't wrong when she suggested I did it to be different. Different was good.

After a sip of the hot brew, I took off my coat and settled in behind my desk for the inevitably boring call with Stanton. I opened my cell phone to the timer screen and hit the speed dial on my desk phone to Stanton's London office number. Dad insisted we use the landlines when communicating between offices to avoid interception of calls.

Stanton picked up after a few rings, and I started the timer on my cell. He wanted to review some customer quotes that he'd emailed.

I pulled the messages up, and we went through them one at a time. Predictably, half of them were within his pricing authority and didn't require a call to get my authorization.

We finished the last one with two minutes to spare on my timer. I'd warned him often enough to keep the calls below fifteen minutes so I had time to call the Rome office before they went home for the day.

After a short call to Lucio in Rome, it was time to see the old man. I gathered a notepad and made my way to Dad's office on the other end of the floor.

My father was on the phone, but he waved me in as he finished up his call. "Zachary, how are ya this morning?"

"No complaints."

"Great. I wanted to congratulate you on the Swankstead deal. That's another first-rate piece of business."

"Thanks, Dad, but it was mostly Franciscovich."

Swankstead had taken a month and seven trips to their headquarters to put together, but hundred-million-dollar equipment sales didn't happen overnight. Franciscovich, the sales guy, had done most of the legwork.

"He'll get a fat commission check for this one. But either way, you handled that admirably."

I nodded.

"So well, in fact, that I think you're ready for your next challenge."

I had no idea what he meant, but I didn't like the sound of it. "I don't need a new challenge."

"Nonsense, Zachary. A position is opening up in finance at the London office.

"London?"

"Sure. It's a great little town."

Only Dad could call London a *little town*.

"I'm fine here," I told him.

"You'll have to get used to warm beer, and don't eat the mushy peas. Those mushy peas are awful."

Apparently, he'd already decided I was moving. All that remained in his mind was to set the date.

"I'll think about it," I told him.

"I think you could learn what you need to in less than three years there."

He evidently hadn't heard me.

"I said I'll think about it."

My words finally registered, and the effect wasn't pretty. His brow furrowed and his eyes bored into me.

I returned his glare in equal measure.

"Think about it?" he asked.

This conversation was reminiscent of the one we'd had three years ago when I'd agreed to take my current marketing position at the company. That time I'd folded quickly and agreed to do as he suggested.

He meant well. He was doing his best to train me, and all of us, for the futures he envisioned for us. But his and my vision had never been properly aligned.

"But," he started.

"Like I said, I'll think about it."

I was not going to allow myself to be railroaded this time.

"Okay. You think about it. Review it with Harold in finance. He has all the particulars."

"I will," I said as I stood.

I'd won this round, but his meaning was clear. The conversation hadn't come to the conclusion he intended, which meant we weren't done—not by a long shot. He wasn't going to make this easy for me. He never did.

I turned to leave.

"Congratulations again on Swankstead. I mean that."

"Thanks, Dad," I replied as I departed his office.

London?

CHAPTER 4

Brittney

I HADN'T SLEPT WELL, WORRYING ABOUT SAM'S BENJI WARNINGS. IT WAS the first time she'd been so adamant that she thought he was dangerous.

I'd written him off as obsessive, but last night's encounter had been worse than anything yet. Sooner or later, he'd get tired of chasing after me. He had to. Didn't he?

My ponytail didn't look quite right on the first try, so I redid it. Dr. Call was picky about her hygienists' appearance.

I opened the door and saw it immediately. The chill went all the way to my toes.

SLUT in big red letters, spray-painted on my apartment door.

Fucking Benji had gone too far—way too far.

I looked both ways down the hall before closing the door behind me and locking the deadbolt.

The nasty word was also painted on the wall next to my door, with the drips from the letters making it look like the word was bleeding.

Mrs. Butterman exited her unit. Her mouth gaped, and she shook her head before scurrying for the stairs.

I waited a moment before following.

~

MY FIRST PATIENT WAS MR. SNODDER. HIS CHART SAID HE HADN'T BEEN IN since last year, and the tartar he'd accumulated took especially long to clean off.

"I can tell you haven't been flossing as often as you should," I told him.

"Probably right."

"And, you really should have a cleaning every six months," I encouraged him.

"I come in as often as I can afford it," he said.

Dr. Call came in shortly after and told him the same things, and got the same responses.

"Your insurance covers it," she told him.

"Really?" he said, faking surprise.

A visit to our office was just something he wanted to avoid.

The rest of my appointments for the morning were pretty ordinary. I put my fingers and instruments in patient's mouths, and tried to avoid getting bitten. I was used to it, staring down at teeth, bleeding gums, and dealing with the occasional dose of bad breath. It wasn't glamorous, but the pay was good on an hourly basis. If I could get more hours, I'd be in better shape, but with Dr. Call, that wasn't likely.

I was in the middle of my last patient before my lunch break when I heard him.

"I'm here to take Brittney to lunch." It was Benji's loud voice coming from reception.

"You need to leave, sir," Rosa at the front desk told him.

"No. I'm not leaving without Brittney," Benji said even louder.

Dr. Call came to my station. "You need to take care of this."

I got up and excused myself from my patient.

"Benji, you need to leave," I told him as I reached reception.

"Not without you."

Rosa rolled her eyes.

The two patients in the waiting area looked on apprehensively.

"I'm not going to lunch with you."

Benji kicked the reception partition. "Yes, you are," he said angrily.

One of the waiting patients got up and left.

"Call 9-1-1," Dr. Call said from behind me.

Rosa dialed.

I pointed to the door. "Get out of here, now."

He didn't move, but the remaining patient did.

Dr. Call followed him. "Mr. Carson, don't go."

It was a standoff for ten or so seconds until the wail of a police siren sounded outside and Benji bolted for the door.

Dr. Call poked her head in the door from outside and motioned for me to join her.

Once I'd stepped outside, she said, "Brittney, it's not acceptable for your boyfriend to impact the practice and scare patients, not to mention the rest of us."

"He's not my boyfriend," I explained.

Her countenance didn't soften. "I'm canceling your shifts for now."

My stomach clenched. "But..."

"Collect your things, and call me when you have your situation sorted out."

"Now?" This couldn't be happening.

"Right now."

The police cruiser pulled up in front, and Dr. Call went to talk to them while I walked back inside, stunned.

As I left, Dr. Call whispered to Rosa, who gave me the side eye.

The police car was gone, and my life was a shambles. The gray envelope with Samantha's tuition bill loomed as an even bigger problem than it had been yesterday.

I drove back to my apartment in a funk. I'd have to start checking with other dentists for a hygienist opening right away.

Maybe I could explain that I needed more days than Dr. Call was willing to schedule me, but that was tenuous. If they called her, the truth would sink me.

Benji had fucked my life big time.

I must have looked odd to the other drivers on the road. I spent the drive home yelling at the windshield, telling Benji to fuck off a hundred times.

Upstairs, the paint had been removed from the door, and the wall had been repainted, with a wet paint sign taped up.

I let myself in and collapsed on the couch.

I'd barely caught my breath before the knock sounded on the door.

I braced myself for a confrontation with Benji through the closed door. It would be just his style to show up now to apologize and ask to be forgiven.

Fat chance.

The view through the peephole, though, showed Mrs. Honeycutt, the manager's wife.

I opened the door. "I'm sorry about Benji," I started.

She forced a folded up paper my direction. "And I'm sorry about this. But we run a, quiet, respectable complex here."

I opened the paper.

THREE DAY NOTICE TO QUIT.

"But, I can't possibly find a place—"

"Three days. You can call later about where to send your deposit, if any is left," she said before she turned and walked away.

I couldn't breathe as I closed the door and let the ugly paper fall to the floor.

The first tears rolled down my cheek.

A knot of dread formed in my stomach.

Find a place to live and a new job at the same time?

How?

What would I tell Samantha?

This was impossible.

I had to pull myself together. I tore open the gray envelope from the Wharton School of Business and took in the total. It didn't include books, and it was way too big for me to handle now.

I logged onto my bank account. The meager total almost made me sick.

I could ask for extra shifts at the Pink Pig, but the number still was still insurmountable. And even if I could find a place in three days, Sam's tuition, first, last, and a security deposit was a bridge too far anywhere in this part of the state.

"You know Gram's house is empty, and it's half yours now," Samantha had said.

But when I'd left, I'd told myself I would never go back to LA.

Now it was either that, or call Sam and tell her she couldn't finish her degree this year.

Getting help from Doug was out of the question. We'd talked last week, and he'd already maxed out his credit card sending me what he could. Deployed as a Marine, he had no options for a side job, so that was out.

I pulled a pen from my purse and started working numbers. If I got my job back at the Rusty Bucket in LA, and also managed to get a few shifts as a hygienist down there, it could work.

And, moving would provide a workable explanation for leaving Dr. Call's practice. Dr. Fosback might even have some open shifts. He'd take me back in a minute; I was sure of it.

LA was looking more and more like the solution to my and Sam's money problems.

My phone said two in the afternoon. I pulled up Dr. Fosback's number and dialed.

Fifteen minutes later, I fist-pumped the air as I hung up. I had a verbal offer of eighteen hours a week in his practice.

I could do this. I had to do this.

Clothes started going into garbage bags as fast as I could fill them. In an hour, my car was filled to the brim with bags of clothes, the contents of my bathroom, and some food. It didn't all fit, so I left some winter things in the closet.

I put my key under the mat and pointed my car south on the freeway. My legs were jittery as I dialed my bartending buddy Lillian.

"Hey, what's up?" she answered.

"Lil, I've gotta leave town. You can have my shifts, if you want them."

"Sure, I could use the hours. How long will you be gone?"

I spit out the truth. "A long time."

"Why?"

I ignored the question for the moment. "I'll call Tony and tell him I can't come back, but I'm also calling about my place. You were interested in my couch last time you were over."

"Yeah."

"The key's under the mat. Take the couch and any of the other furniture you want. Could you do me a big favor and box up and send me the clothes that are left in the closet? But you gotta do it in the next two days, and you can't tell anyone where I went."

"Brittney, what's going on?"

"I'm getting kicked out of my apartment because of Benji, so I'm getting as far away as I can. And I don't want him finding me."

"I'm sorry about the apartment. Randy and I'll go over tomorrow and get your stuff."

"Thanks, Lil."

"Are you sure you're doing the right thing? I mean, just up and leaving?"

"It's the only thing I *can* do."

"What about a restraining order or something?"

She meant well, bringing up alternatives.

"That would cost money, and I don't think it would work with him. He's just crazy." I was too embarrassed to admit I'd also lost my job with Dr. Call because of him. "Where are you going?"

I kept my answer vague. "LA."

"Call when you get settled and let me know you're okay."

"I will, and thanks," I answered.

A bit later, I turned onto route 152 toward Interstate 5, which would get me into the LA basin in six hours, give or take.

Heading south on the interstate, I couldn't get past the feeling that I'd forgotten something. When I finally figured it out, it was too late to turn around.

I redialed Lillian and asked her to add the contents of my desk to the care package she was sending me.

CHAPTER 5

ZACHARY

ALL DAY AT WORK, I'D ONLY WANTED TO GET BACK TO MY PROJECT.

This restoration kept me grounded. I was expending real sweat, creating something that would last. Working with Dad, nothing lasted. Each price negotiation gave way to the next, and would be forgotten a week later. No PR plan had any lasting impact. I couldn't point to a single thing I'd done in the last year at Benson Corp.—nothing that was visible this year. Nothing I'd accomplished withstood the tyranny of time.

I wanted something solid, something lasting, that I could point to and say I fucking *did* that. I fucking *made* that.

"Fuck," I hissed as the section of floor I pried up splintered and a piece hit me on the forehead. My safety glasses protected my eyes, and at least my glove came back without blood on it as I wiped my brow. Even more care was required on this section with particularly difficult glue holding the stupid laminate to the beautiful oak strips below.

A glint of light caught my eye from next door. After a look out the window showed the neighboring house still shrouded in darkness, I refocused on the flooring.

A minute later I saw it again, upstairs this time.

Those good-for-nothing kids were back. Four of them had come by with apology letters to retrieve their phones earlier this evening—the three girls and one of the boys. The girls had come by in a group, likely too scared to approach the crazy man alone.

I stretched my legs after getting up, and unclipped my knee pads. With my flashlight, I went out my back door and slid sideways through the hole in the fence and up to the back door of the house next to mine.

There wasn't any music tonight to mask my approach, so I climbed the stairs slowly. This might have been avoided if I'd stopped at Home Depot after work to get a new deadbolt for the door as I'd originally planned. Unfortunately, my father's words had rattled around in my head all day crowding out my rational plans. In short, I'd forgotten.

I'd also neglected to put fresh batteries in the flashlight, and it was almost useless, emitting only a dim yellow glow.

The back door to the abandoned house opened with a squeak. I paused. Footfalls came from the second floor. Walking softly, I made my way to the stairs and started up.

"I warned you," I called.

The sound of scurrying came from above, but no voice accompanied it.

If this was Piss Boy again, I was going to drop-kick him across the street.

I reached the top of the stairs and stepped over a garbage bag on the landing.

I turned right down the hallway, and it happened.

The kid came from behind a door, kicked me in the shins, and sprayed me with pepper spray. My lips burned and my nose stung, but the safety glasses I still wore protected my eyes. The flashlight dropped as I grabbed my injured leg.

He came at me again.

I grabbed his hand and twisted it, wrenching the can loose from his grasp. I pointed it back at my attacker, giving him a long spray in his face.

He fell back, hands to his face, and let out blood-curdling scream.

A woman's scream.

I picked up the flashlight. It was a woman all right, and not one of those teenagers.

She moaned and writhed on the floor.

I pulled her up. "Get the fuck out before I call the cops."

My lungs burned from the acrid mist. I pulled her toward the cleaner air of the stairway.

"*You* get the fuck out. This is my house." The voice was oddly familiar. She moaned and rubbed at her closed eyes.

"Brittney?" I asked incredulously.

It was Brittney Spear, a vision from my past.

THE DRIVEN BILLIONAIRE IS AVAILABLE ON AMAZON.COM.

Made in the USA
Columbia, SC
08 April 2025

56396310R00204